UNTAMED DELIGHTS

Also by Suzanne Wright

From Rags

The Dark in You Series

Burn

Blaze

The Deep in Your Veins Series

Here Be Sexist Vampires

The Bite That Binds

Taste of Torment

Consumed

Fractured

The Phoenix Pack Series

Feral Sins

Wicked Cravings

Carnal Secrets

Dark Instincts

Savage Urges

Fierce Obsessions

Wild Hunger

The Mercury Pack Series

Spiral of Need

Force of Temptation

Lure of Oblivion

Echoes of Fire

UNTAMED DELIGHTS

THE
PHOENIX PACK
SERIES

SUZANNE
WRIGHT

This is a work of fiction. Names, characters, organizations, places, events, and incidents are either products of the author's imagination or are used fictitiously.

Published by Montlake Romance, Seattle

www.apub.com

ISBN-13: 9781542009683
ISBN-10: 1542009685

Cover design by Erin Dameron-Hill

Printed in the United States of America

For everyone who has supported this series—whether by reading, reviewing, or recommending the books to others. I adore you all.

CHAPTER ONE

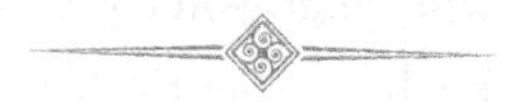

She could just see the headline now . . . WOMAN ARRESTED AFTER STABBING BROTHER TO DEATH WITH PITCHFORK.

Cursing under her breath, Mila Devereaux tossed her lip gloss on the dresser and sank into her seat. In the well-lit mirror of the chic greenroom backstage, she could see that her eyes were hard, her mouth had flattened, and her cheeks were flushed. It wasn't the first time that Alex had put that sour look on her face.

Grip tightening on her cell phone, she asked, "How can *nobody* know where he is, Mom?"

Fond of roaming, Alex often dropped off the radar for months while he went traveling, so it was no big deal that he wasn't answering his phone or checking his messages. But there was usually *somebody* who had, at the very least, a vague idea of where he could be. Not this time, which was bad because Mila had a couple of questions for him. Like why would a bunch of brutes wait for her outside her apartment building, convinced that Alex was her roommate, and demand to see him?

"I do not know," replied Valentina in her thick Russian accent. "But I do not think he is the on run. He would not have left if he thought humans would bring trouble to your door."

Mila had to agree with that. Alex was as protective of her as she was of him, despite their trying to kill each other more than once as kids. And no, she wasn't kidding.

"What exactly did those men say to you?"

"Not much. Just that Alex had pissed off someone who he never should have fucked with." Mila rubbed at her forehead. "Why couldn't you have given me a *nice* brother? One who doesn't piss off thugs, gamble like it's his job, or blab his sister's secrets?" If you couldn't trust your twin with a secret, who could you trust?

"Alex did not want to tell me about your plans to move to Russia," said Valentina. "He fought the truth serum hard. You would have been proud."

Mila pinched the bridge of her nose. "You know, Mom, I'm sure there's a law somewhere against giving your children truth serum."

"Bah," Valentina scoffed. "My mother gave it to me and your uncles all the time when we were younger—it did us no harm. It is useful when dealing with wolverines. They lie with skill."

The latter was true. Although Mila and Alex were twins, they weren't the same breed of shifter. She was a pallas cat like their father; he was a wolverine like their mother. Pallas cats were vicious, unpredictable, and carried bags of attitude. But compared to wolverines, they were positively saintly.

Wolverines were adept thieves, natural-born liars, considered gambling a hobby, and would brawl with their own mother just because. Fearless and cunning, they were also well known for their berserk rages and win-or-die mentality. That meant they'd attack anything, never back down, and wouldn't stop fighting until someone was dead. Hence the all-important rule for dealing with wolverines: don't deal with wolverines.

"You should have told me about these plans yourself, Mila," Valentina admonished. "I knew you and Alex were keeping something from me, but I had not imagined this. It hurts my heart to know you are in such pain that you would leave your home."

Mila swallowed. "I dealt with my pain, but my cat can't deal with hers."

"Well, of course you dealt with it. You are not only a Devereaux, you have Ivanov blood—that makes you strong. Tough. But pallas cats do not forgive easily—your feline needs more time. Come to me tonight. I will cook. We will talk."

"Can't. I'm working at the club tonight." Turning away from the mirror, Mila allowed her eyes to drift across the framed and hung portraits and posters of various artists and bands who'd performed at the shifter club in which she sat. Located underground, the Velvet Lounge looked more like a large train tunnel with its red brick walls. It belonged to the Mercury Pack, with which Mila's Alpha had formed an alliance after fighting alongside them to defend a mutual friend. Madisyn Drake had been a lone pallas cat shifter until she mated a rather ruthless Mercury Pack enforcer.

Mila had been visiting her maternal family in Russia at the time, so she hadn't been part of the battle. Which was a shame, really, because she did love a good fight.

Mila didn't need to work at the club, considering she had a job at a barbershop. But she loved to perform, always had.

"Then come see me tomorrow," Valentina urged. "I understand why you have not told Joel the truth, but he has right to know and decide for himself if—"

"No," Mila clipped. "He's happy. I won't do anything to change that." Joel was a great guy. Smart. Strong. Reliable.

He was also Mila's true mate.

She'd known it the second she'd inhaled his scent when her cousin Adele first brought him to meet their pride a year ago. Every shifter dreamed of that moment when they found their true mate. Mila had envisioned several different scenarios, but never one in which he was partially imprinted on another female.

Every vision she'd ever had of her future with her true mate died right there on the spot. Just evaporated like smoke. Seeing him so devoted to Adele, something in Mila simply . . . went. And, God, she'd hated him.

He hadn't sensed that they were mates—most likely because he'd been partially imprinted on Adele at the time. Thankfully, Adele had joined his Canadian pride, which meant that Mila hadn't been forced to watch the couple grow closer and closer until, finally, their bond formed fully.

It had also given Mila the space to come to terms with the fact that she'd never have her true mate. It had been a lot like grieving. He wasn't dead, but Mila had had to mourn what she'd never have. So there had been shock. Anger. Numbness. Depression. And, eventually, acceptance. The hate had fizzled away, because she couldn't truly begrudge him his happiness.

Her cat, however, still struggled to find peace. The way the feline saw it, their mate had chosen another female over them. It was the ultimate betrayal. He hadn't sensed they were mates, true, but her cat—too elemental in her way of thinking—didn't believe that excused any of his actions. And when he and Adele transferred to Mila's pride a month ago, her cat lost her mind. The feline didn't want this male who had betrayed her, but neither did she want to see him with another.

What made it harder was that Joel sought Mila out. Liked to talk to her. Liked to hear her thoughts on things.

Of course, he didn't know *why* he was subconsciously driven to seek Mila out, and she had no intention of telling him and fucking with his head. Still, even though she'd made her peace with the situation, it wasn't easy to see him committed to another female. And she knew she'd find it hard to watch him and Adele start a family—something the couple were eager to do.

"Choosing you over Adele would save him pain in long run," said Valentina. "She is weak. You know how I despise weakness."

Mila sighed. "Adele is sweet and kind."

"Yes, weak."

"Well, Joel loves her." There would be no point in Mila trying to win him anyway. For one thing, her cat would *never* accept him. For another, Mila couldn't take him as her mate. Not after seeing how crazy he was about Adele. Not after knowing he'd already formed a bond with someone else. If he were to leave Adele for her, Mila would feel second best, and the true-mate bond wouldn't feel as special as it should.

While in Russia, Mila's cat had been calmer. More relaxed. Probably because there was nothing there that reminded her of Joel. So when Mila's uncle had suggested that she pack up her shit and move to Russia, it hadn't sounded like a bad idea. The more she'd thought about it, the more attractive it had become, despite her uncle hoping she'd agree to an arranged mating with the wolverine he'd introduced her to—something Mila hadn't yet shared with anyone but Alex.

Maksim was actually a nice guy, and she was open to getting to know him better and seeing what came of it. In Russia, she'd be far away from Joel and Adele, which could help Mila's cat find the peace that had so far eluded her.

"I still think you should tell him truth," stated Valentina. "It is not fair that you carry this secret. It weighs heavily on you."

Mila hadn't told anyone except Alex and her parents about Joel being her true mate. It was times like this that she wished she'd kept it to herself. "Mom, please let it go."

"I just don't want you to hurt and—" Valentina broke off at the sound of a loud bang followed by a riotous laugh. "James, quiet. I am on the phone!" she yelled at her mate, imperious.

"Is that Skeletor?" he asked, and Mila could hear the smile in his voice.

Valentina gasped in outrage. "I have told you a thousand times, James Devereaux, you cannot call my mother 'Skeletor'!"

"She looks like a starved rat," he said. "And I've heard her called worse. That man-slave she calls a mate actually refers to her as 'that bloodsucking Rasputinette.'"

Valentina spat a stream of Russian curses at her mate, who just laughed.

Mila's lips twitched. Considering both sides of Mila's family "dabbled" in organized crime, you'd think that her extended maternal and paternal relatives would get along pretty well. Not at all. Oh, they did business with each other. But her mother's family had never quite forgiven Valentina's mate for having the gall to be American. The situation was made worse when James refused to move to Russia. And when the Ivanov wolverines had visited his home for the very first time only to find he didn't stock vodka in his cupboards, they'd declared him a psychopath.

There was a light knock on the door of the greenroom. "Mom," said Mila. "I have to go."

"But we must talk—"

"Not now, okay? We'll talk tomorrow, I promise. Tell Dad I said hi." Mila hung up the phone and then called out, "Come in!"

Harley, the club's manager, breezed inside the room. "Hey, I came to see if you were ready."

Looking at Mila closely, Harley tilted her head. "You okay? You look . . . off balance."

"It's just nerves. I love performing, but I'm always nervous until the moment I walk onstage."

"Hmm. Well, get your ass in gear, because you're up next."

For the first time that day, Mila's smile was genuine. "I'm ready."

Reading the sheet of paper, Madisyn chuckled. "Well, Dominic, I shouldn't be surprised, but I am." Placing it on the bar, she slid it toward him. "Did it work?"

"The fuckers are gone now, so, yeah," Dominic replied.

A group of overzealous religious wackos had gathered near the club, preaching the evils of shifters, calling them demons, and damning them all to hell. Dominic had gone to Harley's office, printed off a bunch of "Make a Deal with the Devil" contracts, and stood outside the club offering a dollar to anyone who'd sign one. The religious group had eventually stomped away, utterly furious.

Dante, his Beta, crumpled up the contract as he spoke to Madisyn. "You should have seen how many women joined the line to sign this shit." He threw an amused glance at Dominic. "You didn't have to kiss all of them."

Taking a swig from his beer bottle, Dominic shrugged. "It would have been rude not to." He took a moment to glance around. He liked the Velvet Lounge. Unlike most clubs, it was classy and had a bluesy feel. Even when the place was packed, it wasn't too hectic, and the air didn't feel too hot and stuffy—

"Okay, what did you do this time?"

Dominic turned . . . only to find his Alpha standing there with his arms folded across his chest and his mouth set in a white slash. Not fond of clubbing, Trey didn't go to the Velvet Lounge often. But his mate, Taryn, had accompanied some of their female pack mates to the club, so Trey had insisted on coming along to "keep an eye on things." He hadn't exactly looked happy before he headed to the restroom. Now he looked even more vexed.

"Emmet Pierson," Trey tossed out.

Dominic pursed his lips. "Is that name supposed to mean something to me?" Because it didn't. He shot a questioning look at Dante, who shook his head to indicate that he didn't recognize the name either.

"I checked my cell phone when I was in the restroom," said Trey. "Pierson called me and left a message, requesting a meeting with me. He asked for you to be there. Said the matter was important, and that it concerned you. So who is he, and what did you do?"

"I haven't got a clue who he is, and I don't know why he'd want to speak to me." Leaning against the bar, Dominic took another swig of his beer. "As for the 'What did you do this time?' question, you'll need to be more specific."

Wiping down the bar with a cloth, Madisyn snickered. "It can't be something bad. Dominic always manages to charm his way out of trouble. It's a twisted sort of charm, but it works for him."

Dominic flashed the barmaid a smile. "Aw, thanks, Mads. You know, that dress is very becoming on you. If I were on you, I'd be coming too."

She rolled her eyes. "See? Twisted."

Dante shook his head. "Dom, you can't keep using cheesy lines on people's mates and expect not to get shot one day. Seriously, you flirt with death far too often."

Dominic's brow furrowed. "Is it my fault that none of you have a sense of humor?"

The Beta exhaled in exasperation and then turned to Trey. "Back to Pierson—can't you ask Rhett to do a background search on him?"

"I called him after I heard the message. Rhett didn't have enough time to give me anything other than the basics." Trey's gaze sliced back to Dominic. "Emmet Pierson is a fifty-nine-year-old human attorney. He's married to a human woman, Corrinne Pierson, and they have one child. Their daughter, Rosemary, is a twenty-eight-year-old shop assistant who's recently divorced."

The latter details tickled Dominic's memory. "Oh."

Trey's eyes sharpened. "So you know the daughter?"

"Vaguely," said Dominic.

"Meaning you slept with her?"

"Only once. I met her at a bar, went home with her, but I didn't spend the night." Dominic never spent the night at a woman's house.

"When was this?"

Dominic blew out a breath. "About two weeks ago."

"Any idea what he could want?"

"Not a clue."

Madisyn braced her elbows on the bar. "Did your night with Rosemary go badly?"

Affronted, Dominic straightened. "My nights never end badly."

She rolled her eyes again. "I'm not implying that she didn't thoroughly enjoy herself. I mean, was she upset that you didn't stay the night or something?"

Dominic thought about it for a moment. "I didn't get that impression from her."

Dante looked at Trey. "How did Emmet sound? Pissed? Upset?"

"Perfectly civil," said Trey. "There was no undercurrent of anger. I'll call him tomorrow morning and arrange a meeting. The sooner we find out what this is all about, the better."

A curvy blonde appeared and set a tray of empty glasses on the bar. "Hey, guys."

Dominic smiled at the waitress. "Charlene. Looking pretty as always." The fox shifter had been a friend of his for years, and he'd helped her get the job here.

"I do, don't I?" She tilted her head. "What brings you here tonight? You don't come often."

"I'm here on bodyguard duty." He gestured at the bunch of females from his pack who were breaking out all kinds of moves on the dance floor. They paused as the DJ made an announcement over the speaker, and then the whole crowd was cheering.

Perfect, soulful notes danced through the air, snaring Dominic's total attention. Damn, nothing about that voice would bring a person peace. No, it would bring thoughts of satin sheets and soft skin. That voice was pure sex. Raw, rich, and scratchy with a suppressed power.

He glanced at the stage, seeking the source of the sound. No lie, his heart jumped when he found it. With her hauntingly beautiful blue eyes, full red mouth, olive complexion, and the riot of glossy corkscrew curls that were such a deep brown they were almost black, the female made him think of a painting he'd once seen of a gypsy fortune-teller. Her dark eyeliner and heavy eyeshadow only made her look that much more mysterious, exotic, and elusive.

Soft and supple with legs up to her shoulders, she moved with a sensual, catlike grace as she glided across the stage like a wisp of air. She wasn't his type. Too thin. Too fine boned. Almost fragile looking. But he had to admit there was something very bewitching about her. And when she sang . . . fuck, those dark, velvety, breathy vocals seemed to sink into his bones and thicken his blood.

And now he was rock hard.

"Who's that?" he asked Charlene.

The fox's smile faltered. "Her name is Mila Devereaux."

"Devereaux?" He knew that name. He looked at Madisyn. "Is she part of Vinnie's pride?" At Madisyn's nod, he pursed his lips. Hmm. That meant Mila was likely a pallas cat. Interesting.

Most would have been put off by that. Cute, cranky, and crazy, pallas cat shifters had quite a reputation. Their inner felines looked like overstuffed plush toys. All you wanted to do was pick them up and give them a cuddle. That would be a bad move—especially since they were highly antisocial and somewhat unstable. When they attacked, they became a demented creature straight out of the bowels of hell.

One thing that could be said for them was that they didn't start trouble. But they would always end it, and that ending was never good for their foe. Those snuggly little suckers would bite off your hand and eat it while looking you dead in the eye.

"She has a really distinctive voice," Dominic added. "How long has she been performing here?" He hadn't seen her before.

"Not long," replied Charlene. "So anyway . . ." The fox chattered on and on, and Dominic nodded in the appropriate places, but his attention was on Mila. She absolutely fucking owned that stage, and his wolf found her rather entrancing.

"You're not listening to me, are you?" Charlene sighed.

Dominic blinked. "Sure I am. I'm just enjoying the show."

She rolled her eyes. "Yeah, right." Her brow furrowed. "She's not your usual type."

True. Curvy Charlene was more his type—which was why they'd had a fling many, many years ago. "Doesn't mean I'm not still appreciating the view."

At that moment, the song tapered off, and the crowd once more went wild. Mila launched right into another song—this one more upbeat, which had people going crazy on the dance floor.

Charlene swiped the tray off the bar. "Got more glasses to collect. See you guys later."

"Later," said Dominic. He glanced at Madisyn. "Is Mila mated?"

Dante sighed heavily. "You have a group of females sitting at your table, waiting for you to get your ass back over there."

Yeah, well, none of them really appealed to Dominic. No matter what others thought, he wouldn't fuck anything that moved.

"Aren't you tired of flings and one-night stands?" asked Dante. "Honestly?"

Tired? A little. Dominic had perfected the art of seduction long ago. It was like a dance, in some sense. But for a while now he'd become bored with the steps. Bored of the song. Bored of how easy it all was. But he had no wish to dive into a relationship, which meant keeping things shallow and simple.

As Dominic didn't like "talks," he asked airily, "Why would I be?"

The Beta's mouth thinned. "You know, I once thought something serious might come of you and Charlene."

Dominic's brows drew together. "Why?"

"Because you kept her around for longer than a month."

That hadn't been out of some deep interest in the fox. Back then, Charlene had been much like him—in no rush to mate and happy to stick with flings. Later, that had changed for her, and she was now fully imprinted on a lion shifter who Dominic kind of liked. Dominic, however, hadn't changed.

"By behaving like a player, you're cheapening yourself."

Dominic shot his Beta a glare. Okay, Dominic might *come across* as a player, but . . . "I'm not some asshole who treats women like they're sex objects or something."

"No, you're not," Dante conceded. "You show a girl a good time. You treat her with respect, you don't play games, and you don't lead her on. Which is probably why I've yet to hear any female talk smack about you. But you don't give them even a little bit of *you.* You just give them the *illusion* that they know you."

"Illusion?"

Trey nodded. "On the surface, you're social and open, so no one expects you to have secrets. But you're not really such a simple creature, and you have more boundaries than most."

"If growing old alone will make you happy, keep going as you are," said Dante. "But if it won't, get your shit together."

Dominic bristled. "You talk like I'm a middle-aged guy clinging to his freedom."

"I just don't want you to *become* that guy," said Dante. "But you're on that path."

Dominic snorted. "You're only on my ass because I'm the last unattached adult male in the pack. Just because the rest of you are mated doesn't mean it's wrong that I'm not. And just because all of you are happy in your mating doesn't mean that being single makes me *un*happy."

"But that's the thing, Dom. I don't think you are happy. I don't think you've been happy in a long time. And I don't like it."

"Happiness isn't always linked to whether or not you're in a relationship." Mating bonds could be a blessing, but they could also be a trap. Dominic's parents had been trapped in a broken relationship, and his mother had been so desperate to escape that she'd walked out, condemning her own mate in the process. So yeah, the need to find his true mate had never nagged at Dominic. Even his wolf was in no rush to find her.

Dominic wasn't stupid. He knew there was every chance he'd be as happy with his true mate as his pack mates were with theirs. But he also knew that he'd be a difficult partner. He'd find it hard to open up and bare his soul. He'd struggle to fully commit to something that he knew there would be no going back from . . . especially when it would make him feel suffocated and trapped.

With shallow relationships, there was no need to open up. But when it came to mating bonds, you had to give it everything you were. Dominic wasn't sure he was ready for that. And if he couldn't be sure that he was someone a female could fully trust, rely on, and care for, he had no business asking anything more from her than what he could give in return.

Dante lifted his hands, palms out. "All right, I'll back off. But just keep in mind what I said, okay?"

Dominic made a noncommittal sound, and Dante rolled his eyes. Just then, Mila drew out her final note and the crowd went wild again, clapping and hooting. More than happy to distract himself from thoughts of his parents, Dominic turned his attention back to her.

Nursing his beer, he watched as she thanked her audience and then stalked off the stage, ass swaying provocatively. An ass he wouldn't mind getting a firm grip on.

Moments later, she slipped through the door that led backstage and sort of . . . flowed toward the bar, as light and fluid as music. People waved at her and shouted out compliments, but she didn't break stride as she cast them each a smile. He got the sense that she didn't relish the attention but didn't find it uncomfortable either.

Reaching the bar, she slipped onto a stool. "Water, please, Mads."

Damn if that sultry voice didn't slide down Dominic's spine. His pack mate, Frankie, spoke in a low-pitched, smoky rasp, but Mila's voice was a scratchy, gravelly, *dirty* kind of smoky that was almost hypnotic and made a man think of sin.

"You were great up there," Madisyn told her as she handed her a bottle. "But then, you always are."

"We should do a duet," said Mila. "Don't even lie and say you can't sing for shit. I know you can."

The barmaid shook her head madly. "That would gain me attention. Attention leads to 'fuss.' You know I loathe 'fuss.'"

With a snicker, Mila unscrewed the cap from her bottle and took a swig. "Needed that."

As if feeling Dominic's gaze, Mila looked at him. Her direct stare was like a punch to the gut. There were shadows in those eyes. A soul-deep loneliness he could relate to. But there was also pure iron. Whatever had put those shadows in her eyes wouldn't break her.

Another female might have, at the very least, nodded at him in greeting. Not this female. She didn't smile. Didn't frown. Didn't even change expression. There was no feminine appreciation in her eyes at all. Then, her voice dry as a bone, she said, "No sense in staring. You can't afford me." She looked away, dismissing him.

Dominic smiled.

Damn, the wolf was just . . . delicious. A salivating, tantalizing signature dish dusted with hotness, laced with sheer masculinity, covered in self-assurance, and topped with a sprinkle of raw charisma. Mila couldn't help wanting to savor every bite.

She'd never spoken to him before, but Mila had seen him from afar plenty of times at the bars and nightclubs she frequented. She'd always referred to him as "GQ" in her head. Dangerously compelling and loaded with sexual energy, he was an expert at making girls part with their panties. Everything about him—his killer smile, his perfectly sculpted body, and his smooth-as-honey voice—made you think of sex.

Any female with a pulse would want to spear her fingers through that short blond hair that made Mila think of spun gold. Any female would imagine licking the taut, tanned skin that covered all that hard, honed muscle. His powder-blue eyes were as clear as water and held a hint of infectious mischief, but there was also an almost imperceptible glimmer of shrewdness. She'd bet the guy was nowhere near as harmless as he liked to appear.

Mila had always admired the personal power he wielded. The moment he walked into a room—moving with the swaggering, confident gait of someone who knew his own appeal and would make no bones about exploiting it—people looked at him. Watched him. It wasn't just his model looks. It was how he moved. Fluidly. Deliberately. At perfect ease with himself. Like everything was natural and effortless.

He never had to work the room. No, he just found himself a seat, and people flocked to him like bees to honey. A master at social Tae Kwon Do, he initiated conversation with total ease and seemed to both enliven and draw energy from the crowd.

Everyone loved him. Both men and women flirted shamelessly with him, and he took it all in stride. But even as he chatted and laughed, he was always alert and vigilant; his gaze often swept his surroundings, processing every little detail.

She had no idea why said gaze had landed on her. She'd seen the type of girl he went for—curvy, blonde, sultry. Mila was none of those things. Well, *something* had caught his roaming eye. Oh God, she hadn't smudged her mascara, had she? Probably. It was a little habit of hers. No doubt he'd found something much more interesting to look at by now.

She snuck a quick glance at him from the corner of her eye. Shit, he was still staring right at her. No, he was *eye-fucking her.* Mila's heart slammed against her ribs. Just like that, she felt awkward. She wasn't good at flirting. It felt too much like a game, and she hated games. Mila wasn't a girl who flicked her hair, licked her lips, or gave off other sexy "I'm up for it" cues. She was too straightforward for all that.

Fuck, shit, fuck, what should she do? Well, she wouldn't look at him again—that was for sure. She'd just look straight ahead. She'd ignore him. He probably wasn't watching her anymore anyway. Right? There was no harm in just checking, though, and—

Shit, he was still looking at her. He probably thought she was going to do what other females did and fall all over him. Well, she wasn't. Nuh-uh. She wasn't even going to look at him again. Not even once.

Or maybe she could try eye-fucking him back? You know, for practice. And experimental purposes. Or something. No, it was best not to attempt it—she'd get it wrong for sure. She'd just come across as creepy and weird and then need to triple-blink with the pressure.

It would be better to go home and play with her vibrator. Because although Mila was just as susceptible to him as other females, she had no interest in a fling. Her ex was a lot like GQ in that he used sex as an escape and was interested only in one-sided relationships. She'd bet that, like Grant, GQ could suavely talk his way out of your life just as fast and as smoothly as he'd talked himself into it . . . somehow leaving you feeling good about yourself even as he ended what little you had together.

These people were sheer fucking magic. They were also hard to be with. The fact that they were always surrounded by others meant that you were constantly vying for their attention. Women would flock to and flirt with them right in front of you, act as if you weren't even there. Mila had learned fast that guys like GQ weren't for her.

That didn't stop her heart from beating a little faster as he sidled up to her, his mouth curving into a slow, lazy smile. And now he was eye-fucking her again. She didn't look away this time. No, she forced herself to face him, determined to play it cool. But her blood heated as his hooded, brooding eyes blatantly raked over her from head to toe.

Sexual energy hummed in the air, stirring her hormones and whipping them into a frenzy. And his darkly delicious scent of amber, rum, and caramelized sugar only made her hungrier.

His eyes came back to hers, glittering with something dark and hot that made her pulse skitter and her cat snap to attention. The air thickened. Charged. Crackled. And little sparks of electricity whispered across Mila's flesh, making it prickle. Fuck, the guy was beyond potent.

His eyes dropped to her mouth, which was now bone dry. As he stared at it hungrily, his tongue briefly flicked out to touch his lower lip. Her pussy quivered. *Quivered.* Shit, how did he *do* that?

This male was dangerous. Far too tempting. Far too compelling. A distinct threat to the composure of all womankind. But she'd be damned if she'd let him see what he did to her. No, she was absolutely determined to stay strong under the weight of all that sex appeal. Luckily, she'd always been good at feigning disinterest in things or people.

"Madisyn tells me you're one of Vinnie's cats," said GQ, his voice so silky smooth it gave her goose bumps. "I'm Dominic. And you are . . . ?"

The name suited him, she thought. "Mila."

He tilted his head. "Why are you looking so down, Mila? Let me guess—it hurt when you fell from heaven, right?"

"No. But hauling my ass out of hell was a bastard of a climb."

Chuckling, he cast her bottle of water a quick look. "Let me buy you a real drink."

"I'd prefer to just have the cash."

Dominic's brows lifted, his eyes twinkling. "Would you now?"

"Yeah, these are hard times we live in."

"True." Dominic tipped his chin at the mountain of muscle behind him, although he kept his eyes on her. "See my pack mate over there? He wants to know if you think I'm hot."

"Why? Does he have his eye on you and consider me competition?"

Dominic's smile widened. "Yeah. He and I are both gay. Think you can convert me?"

She snorted and then turned to Madisyn. "Is he always like this?"

With a regretful sigh, Madisyn nodded. "Yeah."

Dominic edged closer, his eyes dropping to her enticing mouth again. Lush and bow-shaped, it was straight out of every X-rated fantasy he'd ever had. Up close, he could see that although Mila was slim, she wasn't all skin and bones as he'd first thought. No, she had delicate curves in all the right places, and damn if he didn't want to get a better look at them.

He itched to touch her flawless olive skin and see if it was as petal-soft as it looked. Maybe even take a bite. His wolf liked that idea, wanted to leave a mark or two on her flesh—not out of possessiveness but to get her attention. She had such an aloof "I could give few fucks" way about her that his wolf felt overlooked. Especially now as she chatted with Madisyn, like Dominic wasn't even there. Which, perversely, made him smile.

She laughed at something the barmaid said, and Jesus, the smoky sound was like fingers curling around his cock. He'd been rock hard since she'd started singing onstage, and his dick showed no sign of standing down. A greedy ache to possess her had him in a tight grip, and it was made worse by the electric energy she gave off that fluttered across his nape. And God, her scent . . . *Frosted berries, rosewood, and sweet honey.* Yeah, he wanted more of that. His wolf wanted to lap it up.

The odd "note" to her scent told Dominic that her parents weren't the same breed of shifter. When different breeds conceived a child, said child would be the breed of one of their parents. But just as they would have the *physical* characteristics of both parents, they would carry a hint of both breeds in their scent. He could smell the pallas cat in her, but he couldn't quite make out what the extra "note" to that smell was. "Which one is the pallas cat—your mother or your father?"

Mila blinked at him, surprised. "My dad."

"What's your mom?"

"A wolverine."

His brows flew up again. "Your mother is a wolverine? Oh, Mila, you just get more and more interesting. Can you introduce me to her? I've never met a wolverine."

Mila could only stare at him. The guy *wanted* to meet a wolverine? Most breeds of shifter pointedly avoided them. "I'm beginning to think you're not quite sane."

"Admittedly, you're not the only person who feels that way. Does that mean you won't go home with me?"

"Is there much point? I doubt it would be easy for two people to fit in a cardboard box."

He laughed. "Mila, you're a tough audience." Damn, he *really* liked this cat. Liked her sharp wit, dry humor, and aura of electricity. Liked her quiet confidence—it was in her easy smile, her unapologetically direct stare, and the self-assured way she carried herself.

Her feline air of indifference was like a challenge, and he just wanted to find some way to crack that poker face. But she wasn't giving him any openings. She practically batted away his pickup lines. Dismissed his flirtatiousness. Snorted at his attempts to charm her.

He knew she was attracted to him—he could see it, sense it—but she didn't appear interested in acting on it. She wasn't playing coy or hard to get. Wasn't testing him or attempting to take control of the situation by leading their dance; he knew those games and could spot them easily.

He had the clear sense that she was simply very selective in her choice of sexual partners and, for whatever reason, he didn't meet her standards. Yeah, *that* poked at his ego. It also made him determined to meet this challenge she presented.

Fighting the urge to tug on one of those unruly curls and then watch it spring back into place, Dominic said, "Come on, you're not going to make me go home all alone, are you? That's mean. Or maybe you're just nervous. What is it, are you a virgin?"

She frowned. "No."

"Prove it."

Oh, this guy is pure trouble, Mila thought. Especially since he was stirring the interest of her moody cat—not just sexually, but because the cat sensed there were many facets to this male, and she couldn't quite understand why he was hiding them. Yeah, Mila herself got the feeling that he wasn't quite the shameless, shallow flirt he came across as to others.

When he stepped farther into Mila's personal space, his eyes fixing on her mouth yet again, she knew it was time to go. Bottle of water in hand, Mila slid off the stool and said to Madisyn, "Good luck protecting this one from himself."

Dominic pushed away from the bar. "You really won't take me with you? Come on, if you don't enjoy yourself, well, you've only wasted five hours of your life. Eight if you wanna include foreplay."

Mila snorted. "Sorry, GQ, you're not my type."

"GQ?" he echoed. "Why am I not your type?" Dominic was pretty sure no one had ever said that to him before.

"Because I like men. You're just a little boy." Mila patted him on the head. "A little boy who comes across as a deceptively harmless flirt so that people label you a player, which makes them think they have you all figured out. But I'll bet very few people really know you, and I'm sure that suits you just fine."

A wide smile curved his mouth. "Damn, Mila, where have you been all my life?"

"Exactly where I'll be during the rest of your days on this earth, sweetie—in your most imaginative dreams." With that, she turned and walked away.

Trey sidled up to him, oozing amusement. "Crashed and *burned*."

"Oh, I like her." Dante chuckled. "I really, really like her."

"I think I love her," said Dominic.

Madisyn snickered. "Give it up, Dom. She's not a female you'll be able to charm into bed."

He frowned. "Why not?"

"Because she'll want a person with a little more substance. You *have* substance. You just prefer to keep it hidden." Madisyn gestured at the rest of the club. "Turn your attention elsewhere. God knows, there are plenty of welcoming smiles being directed your way. That group of girls is *still* waiting at your table."

But Dominic didn't want any of those females. He wanted the little cat who'd done what no other female had ever done—called him on his shit.

CHAPTER TWO

As Emmet Pierson sat hemming and hawing at the menu the next afternoon, Dominic exchanged an impatient look with Trey. The human had chosen the restaurant as a meeting place, and it was fairly busy. Servers walked back and forth carrying steaming trays of food to the many booths and tables. It served everything from simple burgers to ethnic-inspired dishes. Music played softly in the background, combining with the sounds of voices murmuring, food sizzling, and silverware clinking. The cool air wafting from the vents eased the warmth coming from the low-hanging lights.

Going by the brittle smile the waitress shot him, Emmet was a regular there and not well liked. Dominic wondered if he was someone who complained a lot or who skimped on the tip.

Dominic sipped his coffee and then set it on the coaster. The human was the only one at the table ordering food. Any other time, the scents of grilled meat, spices, and fragrant steam would have made Dominic's stomach rumble. But he, Trey, Taryn, and Dante had eaten well before they came.

After *finally* placing his order, Emmet raised a brow at them. "Are you sure you don't wish to order anything?"

"No, thanks," said Taryn while the others shook their heads.

Emmet snapped the menu shut and handed it to the waitress, who then walked off. He adjusted his tie, his eyes on Dominic. "I believe you know my daughter, Rosemary."

"Vaguely," Dominic allowed.

"Vaguely," Emmet echoed, his lips thinning. "She may have mentioned to you that she was married until last year. Her husband of nine years divorced her when she was unable to conceive a child. Bastard," he added under his breath.

Rosemary had briefly mentioned the divorce, but she hadn't gone into any detail. "I'm sorry to hear that."

"We have shifter blood in the family. My great-great-grandmother was half shifter. None of her children had an inner animal, nor did any descendants from the following generations. We don't have enhanced strength or accelerated healing either. Rosemary, however, has always believed that she possesses an inner wolf. As a child, she would say that it was 'sleeping.' I thought it was a child's imagination. But she still swears she can feel it inside her. Swears that she feels its presence, though it remains asleep."

Trey's brow furrowed. "And it's never once woken?"

"No." Emmet unrolled his pristine white napkin, took out the silverware, and examined it. Apparently unsatisfied, he began to wipe his fork with the napkin. "From what I understand of shifters, they are only able to produce children with whomever they form a mating bond."

"That's true," Trey granted.

"Which means it could very well explain why she wasn't able to have children with her husband," said Emmet. "As a shifter, she requires a mate."

Lips pursed, Trey shook his head. "I doubt that's the issue here. Her shifter blood is simply far too diluted for that to be a factor."

"But she has an inner wolf." Emmet shifted his gaze to Dominic, and his perceptive eyes narrowed. "You don't believe that, do you?"

No, Dominic didn't. "If she had a wolf, I would have sensed her. My wolf would have sensed her." Plus, the woman smelled purely human.

Emmet's jaw hardened. "As Rosemary said, the animal is sleeping. 'Latent,' I believe you call such a thing."

"'Latent' is when the animal hasn't surfaced," said Taryn. "It isn't asleep, though. It's very much alert; it's a big presence within the person."

Impatience flitted across Emmet's expression as he looked at the Alpha female. "Perhaps that's the case in some situations, like with *yours*, but not in this one."

Trey stiffened. "And what is it exactly that you know about my mate?"

"It's not uncommon knowledge that she was a latent shifter until you mated with her. That brought out the wolf." Emmet looked at Dominic. "I want you to do the same for Rosemary."

Dominic did a slow blink. "Say again?" He *had* to have misheard the guy.

"If you mate with her, you can bring out her wolf. Allow her to have children." Like it was really that simple. "You had a relationship with her until recently, so I'm sure it wouldn't be a chore for you to simply bite her."

Relationship? Dominic straightened in his chair, unable to believe he was truly fucking hearing this. "I don't know what your daughter told you—"

"She told me everything. How you met at a supermarket, how you swept her off her feet, how loving and attentive you were, how you spent most nights at her apartment and spoke of moving her onto your territory. I don't know what led to the argument you had, she wouldn't speak of it. But these things can be worked out."

What the fuck? Dominic's wolf growled, enraged that the female had falsely alleged that she had some sort of claim to him. "You're far off base here, Pierson," Dominic told him, keeping his tone carefully controlled. Still, his voice deepened in anger. "I was not in a relationship with your daughter. Far from it, in fact. Regardless, mating with someone isn't simply a case of biting them."

Emmet waved that away. "I've read up on shifters, I know how it works. You bite the female to make your claim on her. That mark makes her your mate. A bond then forms between you. A bond that gives the human added strength, accelerated healing, and enables her to have children. And you *were*, in fact, in a relationship with her; she told me all about it.

"If you don't think the mating will work in the long run, fine, end it at some point. But at least keep her as your mate until she becomes pregnant and her wolf has surfaced. She'll have no issue with you having contact with the child."

Dominic could only stare at the human. The guy was either fucking deluded, like his daughter, or he was vastly uneducated on the ways of shifters.

Taryn sighed. "There's a great deal of misinformation out there about mating bonds, Mr. Pierson, and—"

"You cannot claim that you weren't latent," clipped Emmet.

Trey bristled. "As a matter of fact, we can claim whatever the fuck we want—we don't owe you any explanation about anything. But yes, it's common knowledge that my mate was latent until we mated. However, I've yet to hear of another latent shifter whose animal surfaced upon mating."

"That doesn't mean it won't happen for my daughter," said Emmet, not in the least bit deterred.

"A bite won't cause a mating bond to form," Dante told the human. "It doesn't work that way. It certainly wouldn't grant your daughter added strength or any other shifter abilities. And even if Dominic did mate with your daughter, it wouldn't be something either of them could walk away from once she had what she wanted."

Emmet scoffed. "No one truly believes that mating bonds are mystical connections or that their mates are predestined."

"Surely you heard stories about the bond your great-great-grandmother shared with her mate," said Dominic.

"She was a kooky woman who was also convinced that the wind spoke to her." Emmet shook his head, incredulous. "If you wanted to get out of a mating, you could. Anyone could."

Oh, you *could* walk away, but not without facing potentially dire consequences. Keeping a distance from your true mate could lead to one or both individuals turning rogue. When Dominic's mother left, his father's wolf had not only turned rogue, he'd also killed three people before the Alpha and Beta of Dominic's old pack managed to take the wolf down.

Lincoln hadn't deserved that ending to his life. He hadn't been evil, hadn't even known what he was doing. And it just went to show that the mating bond wasn't always the pretty, shiny thing it was perceived to be.

Dominic lifted his chin. "I can't give you or your daughter what she wants."

"Maybe this will change your mind." Emmet fished something out of his pocket and then slid it across the table. A check for $50,000. No one touched it. "All I'm asking you to do is temporarily take Rosemary as your mate. Once her animal has surfaced and she's pregnant, you can walk away from the relationship."

Dominic had to clamp his jaw shut to bite back a curse. The human was just not fucking listening.

Emmet's gaze cut to Trey. "I'm a good ally to have. That's what shifters like, isn't it? Allies. It can be very beneficial to have good human connections. I can give you those." He looked at Dominic, clearly expecting him to agree.

Dominic didn't. "If Rosemary really has an inner animal, it's possible that she has a true mate waiting for her. I wish her good luck in finding him. That male is not me. She and I were *not* in a relationship. We met at a bar, we had a one-night stand, and I left before morning—that's it. There was nothing more to it than that, which she knows perfectly well." No, it wasn't nice to tell this guy that he'd had a one-night stand with his daughter, but this human wasn't getting the message.

Flushing, Emmet placed his hands flat on the table. "As I said, I'm a good ally to have. I can also make a very bad enemy."

Trey gave him a shark's grin. "You can't make a worse enemy than I can."

Emmet's eyes flickered. "Don't be so sure of that. You have a son. Is there anything you wouldn't do to secure his happiness? Could you really sit by and watch him suffer?" He banged his fist on the table. "Dammit, you didn't see how Rosemary fell apart after her ex-husband left her. He tossed her aside like she was *nothing*. Ever since she was a child, all she ever wanted was a child of her own."

Pierson looked at Dominic. "You say you can't force her wolf to surface. Fine. But you can at least give her that sense of worth back that her ex-husband took from her. I'm offering you fifty thousand dollars. All you have to do is bite her, claim her as yours, and then impregnate her—all of which you could probably do in one evening."

"I'm sorry for what your daughter went through," Taryn said to him. "I truly am. And I can understand that you love her and just want to make everything better for her. But we've explained to you that what you're asking for can't be done. Mating bonds are complex things that cannot be forced, bought, or simply *willed* into existence. If you don't believe us on that, talk to other shifters. Offer the same deal to them. They'll tell you the same thing."

"She doesn't want other shifters, she wants your pack mate. She loves him." Emmet looked at Dominic. "Not that you deserve her, considering you won't even admit to having had a relationship with her."

"There was no relationship," Dominic told him as he and his pack mates got to their feet. "And there never will be. Take my Alpha female's advice—consult other shifters and offer that check to them. You'll soon come to realize that you're asking for something I can't give her."

With that, the four wolves stalked out of the restaurant and headed to the pack's vehicle.

Riding shotgun, Dominic rubbed at his nape. "I did not see that coming."

"Rosemary never hinted at you mating with her?" Trey asked him from the rear seat, his arm draped around Taryn.

"No." Dominic clicked on his seat belt. "She said she was divorced, that the guy was a complete asshole, and that she envied shifters for having predestined mates. She didn't mention that she believed she had an inner animal."

"Because she was sure you'd know that to be untrue." Dante switched on the ignition and reversed out of the parking space. "I'm guessing she thought Daddy could get her what she wanted. Money talks in the world of humans. In our world? Not so much."

"Although I feel bad that she can't have kids, I also want to wring her neck for feeding her father all those lies," said Taryn. "She clearly lives in a fantasy world. Be careful, Dominic. People like that don't give up easily. They can cling to their beliefs for a long time. She apparently sees you as the answer to all her problems."

Driving out of the lot, Dante sighed at him. "Don't you know better than to sleep with unhinged humans, Dom?"

"Hey, she didn't let her crazy flag fly when I was around her," Dominic defended himself. "She seemed normal enough."

"See, this is what happens when you skip the getting-to-know-the-girl phase—you miss learning she's a living, breathing shit-storm heading your way." Dante met Trey's eyes in the rearview mirror. "Do you think her father will try to cause problems for the pack?"

"I doubt it," replied Trey. "He probably threatened us because he was pissed. Besides, I don't see what kind of trouble Pierson could cause us anyway. He's probably still hoping that Dominic will change his mind. Whatever the case, it's possible that Dominic hasn't seen the last of Rosemary. She won't like that she didn't get what she wanted."

Dominic snickered. "Well, she'll just have to deal with it."

Shoving her pasta around the lunch container with her fork, Mila sighed. She'd known that her parents wouldn't take the whole "arranged mating" thing well. Known they wouldn't want her to take a mate who'd only looked her way because he wanted an alliance with the Ivanov wolverines. Known they'd hate that mating Maksim would mean her staying permanently in Russia. Although she'd been braced for their disappointment, the weight of it still hurt.

Her mother was *beyond* furious. Her mouth tight, Valentina was sharply striding around the barbershop's break room cleaning in fast-forward—wiping coffee grounds from the counter, cleaning mug rings from the table, tidying the newspapers, washing cups, and even wiping the screen of the wall-mounted TV.

"I can't believe I'm hearing this," said James, sitting on the couch with his elbows braced on his thighs and his hand clenched around a porcelain mug. "You're the last person I ever thought would enter into an arranged mating."

"It sounds cold, I know, but I like the guy, Dad." Mila leaned back in the plastic chair. "It's not official yet. I haven't allowed Maksim to lay any claim on me—not even a temporary one. We'll get to know each other better when I return to Russia. I'm not rushing into anything—I *can't* rush, since the visa application process takes time. It's not like I'm leaving next week or anything."

"Arranged matings can be disastrous if the couple never imprints on each other."

"Which is why I won't go through with the mating ceremony unless we imprint. If it doesn't happen, I'll walk away. But there are many instances where such matings *do* go well."

"Oh, couples can grow to care for each other, sure, and the bonds they form can be strong. But not always strong enough that their happiness is long lasting."

"What about my grandparents?" she challenged, referring to Valentina's parents. "They entered into an arranged mating, and they're happy."

James flicked his hand. "Skeletor and her man-slave don't count."

"Why not?"

"Because they're both highly dysfunctional."

Considering her grandfather did odd shit like pretend to be agoraphobic so that her grandmother wouldn't make him go shopping, Mila couldn't argue with that. She dumped her fork in the plastic tub, and her mother instantly snatched it up, along with James's cup. "Mom, sit down, I'll clean them." But Valentina went ahead and did it herself as if Mila hadn't spoken. Wiping her hands on a napkin, Mila turned back to her father. "I'm sorry that this isn't a decision you can support or respect, I truly am, but—"

"I *want* to support you," he said. "I just can't support you shortchanging yourself. Just because you can't be with your true mate doesn't mean that an arranged mating is your only option. It doesn't mean you can't find real happiness with someone else."

"I know that. But who says I can't find it with Maksim?"

"That is not your father's point." Valentina dried her hands on a dish towel and tossed it aside. "You can do better than an arranged mating, Mila."

"It was more like your brothers did a little matchmaking than it was a business transaction," said Mila.

"But your mating the Alpha's son would solidify an alliance; that makes it business." Valentina pointed at her. "You deserve better. You can do better. You have a life here, Mila."

"I enjoy my jobs, but they're not jobs I can't do elsewhere." She'd miss this place, though. She'd worked at Blade and Spice Barbershop since she was a teenager. She loved it here. Loved its rustic charm and relaxed atmosphere. Loved that each day was different and that she could help others feel their best. Offering cuts, shaves, facials, and other services, it was a popular place.

The barbershop belonged to her uncle Vinnie, just as all the other nearby businesses did. Unlike most species of shifter, pallas cats kept the existence of their breed secret from humans and didn't claim territories. They did, however, often group together for protection. The pride owned every store on both sides of the street—some they used themselves; others Vinnie rented out.

Her pride mates didn't work in every store, though. Humans ran the bookstore, and a shifter-witch hybrid ran the herbalist store. The pride hired humans and even lone shifters.

Vinnie also owned two nearby apartment buildings, where many members of the pride lived. The cats working and living so close together was similar to a pack hanging out on its territory. The pride might not have claimed the land and segregated themselves from the public, but they liked to stay near each other.

"What about us?" demanded Valentina, returning dishware to cupboards. "You would leave us—your own parents?"

Ah, here came the emotional blackmail. Her mother could wield it like a pro. "You've been globe-trotters ever since I turned eighteen. If I leave here, I'll still see you about as much as I do now."

"What about your brother? He is your *twin*. You cannot leave your twin."

"Alex is always roaming, and he goes to Russia a lot."

"And what about your friends? Hmm?"

"If they're real friends, they'll get off their asses and come visit me."

With a little growl, Valentina mule-kicked a cupboard door, slamming it shut. "I blame Adele and Joel for this. I will make them pay."

Mila held up a calming hand. "I don't begrudge them what they have, nor do I resent them for what they're building. But my cat does, and I don't know how to help her." Even hearing Joel's name was enough to make her cat curl back her upper lip.

James scrubbed a hand down his face. "I can understand why you'd want to put space between you and them if your cat's struggling so much. But moving to Russia? That's a hell of a distance."

"Like I told you, it'll depend on how things go between me and Maksim," Mila reminded him. "He seems like a nice guy. You'd like him."

James snorted. "No, I won't. Not if he takes my baby girl from me."

Valentina planted her hands on her hips. "And if things do not work out between you and this Maksim, you will come home. Yes?"

"If my cat manages to work through her shit, yeah." But Mila didn't see that happening in a hurry.

"Honey," began James, his voice gentle, "it's unlikely that she'll ever forgive Joel."

"I know." Mila swallowed. "But if she found happiness with someone else, she might be able to look at Joel without wanting to slit him from throat to sternum."

James winced. "That bad, huh?"

Mila nodded. "That bad."

A stream of Russian curses flew out of Valentina's mouth, her voice so loud that it bounced off the walls of the small room. "*He* should be the one to leave. Not you."

"Joel hasn't done anything wrong," said Mila.

Valentina's nostrils flared. "But he was not born in this pride. You were."

"So was Adele," Mila pointed out. "She has just as much of a right to be here as I do."

"Bah," scoffed Valentina. "She is too weak to be pallas cat. Sweet. Delicate. Needy. Eager to please. Your kind are fierce and strong. She is like lost puppy."

In some ways, yeah, she was. Mila's cat thought of the other female as weak too. But. "She's Joel's choice."

"Then he is stupid and does not deserve my girl." Eyes shiny, Valentina turned away and shut a drawer so hard the cutlery rattled.

As her mother worked to close the crooked drawer that seemed determined to remain open, Mila said, "Watch that drawer, Mom. It's stuck and—" But it shut easily for her mother, as if it didn't dare risk her wrath.

"Mila, your client's here!" Archie, the senior barber and manager, yelled from the shop floor.

Standing, Mila straightened her shirt, relieved to escape the break room and the conversation. "I have to go now. My break's over, and it's Archie's turn to take his."

"We are not done, Mila. You will come have dinner with me and your father tonight so that we can talk more," Valentina declared. "I will make Chocolate Spartak Cake."

Mila's mouth curved slightly. "I'll be there."

With a gentle smile, James squeezed Mila's hand. "See you later, sweetheart. Love you."

"Love ya too." Walking out of the break room and into the barbershop, she gave her parents one last wave as they left.

Archie stood at the counter operating the antique brass cash register as his freshly groomed client chatted away to him. The other barber, Evander—who was Archie's son—was getting shaving products together while his client relaxed in a chair with a steaming cloth over his face.

The individual stations each featured a padded swivel chair, a large framed mirror, and a small shelf on which lay combs, shears, scissors, and other tools. Additional glass shelves were stacked with shaving creams, rolled-up towels, gels, waxes, and other products. Framed vintage photos of old barbershops hung on the brick walls, along with a "Don't worry, it'll grow back eventually" sign. At the center of the back wall, just above the door that led to the break room, was a black decal of the business logo.

Mila crossed to her station and caught the eye of the male in the waiting area. He was sitting on the black leather couch with a little boy on his lap. The bobcat shifter, Dean, and his nephew, Finley, were fairly new clients of hers. "Hi," she greeted simply.

Dean stood with a smile. "Hey," he said. "Finley needs another trim, as you can see."

Mila looked at the little boy. "Ready?"

As usual, Finley wrapped his arms around Dean's leg. The kid never liked getting his hair cut.

"I saved some strawberry lollipops for you," said Mila. Finley's head snapped up, eyes wide with interest, and she smiled.

CHAPTER THREE

Standing outside the barbershop, Dominic watched through the large glass window as Mila settled a little boy at her station. Thanks to Harley, he'd learned where the pallas cat worked. He'd planned to give it a few days before paying her a surprise visit, but the conversation he'd had earlier with Emmet Pierson had pissed him off. Not just because Rosemary had told so many lies or because her father refused to consider that he was wrong, but because Dominic prided himself on being good at reading people. He hadn't seen that streak of crazy in Rosemary. Or was it cunning? He wasn't sure.

He couldn't quite shake off the anger. He needed a distraction. Needed to let all that shit just fall away. And he had the feeling that a little banter with this particular feline might just lift his mood.

He recognized the other two barbers as members of her pride. Both Archie and Evander had been present not only at the battle on Mercury Pack territory but also at Madisyn and Bracken's mating ceremony. The two male pallas cats had briefly mentioned the barbershop to him, but they hadn't spoken of Mila.

Dominic pushed open the front door and stepped inside. The oak flooring creaked slightly beneath his feet. With the subtle scents of citrus, leather, and spice, the place smelled clean and masculine.

When Mila met his gaze and he felt her attention settle over him, a savage sexual need twisted his stomach. It was all he could do not to close the distance between them and indulge in a thorough taste of her. His wolf perked up, intrigued by this feline.

Evander looked up from where he was shaving a client and tipped his chin at Dominic. "Hey, Lothario. How are things?"

Mouth twitching, Dominic said, "Good. Very, very good." Planting his feet, he smiled at Mila. "Hello again."

Her eyes narrowed slightly. "Something I can do for you?"

Shit, that smoky voice was like a ghostly finger trailing down his cock. "Sorry to bug you, Mila—I'm lost. Can you give me directions to your place?"

She rolled her eyes while the others chuckled.

Dominic took a step toward her. "I was driving past here, and it occurred to me that it's been a while since I had a haircut. Imagine my surprise when I saw that you work here."

"Surprise," she echoed, her voice heavy with skepticism. "Right."

"So can you fit me in? I just need a trim."

Her eyes flicked to the waiting area. "Sure. Take a seat."

Well, *that* surprised him. He'd expected her to claim to be too busy or to send him to either Evander or Archie. Apparently, Mila was made of sterner stuff.

Sinking into the leather sofa, Dominic plucked a newspaper off the table. He didn't read it, though. Didn't even look at it. His attention was on Mila as she talked with the boy in her chair while she worked. Those slender, capable hands were deft yet precise. She moved with efficiency and confidence, and he could tell that she'd been doing this job for some time. He could just imagine those hands touching him, stroking him, and wrapping around his cock.

While not bubbly or animated, she radiated positive energy. The flow of it was subtle yet constant, and it made her exude a sense of calm that put people at ease—just as it did the boy in her chair. Even with that air of mystery she carried, there was just something very steady about her, especially with that touch of unflappable cool—like a jungle animal that knew it had no natural predators.

He noticed that the male with the little kid watched her just as closely, but there was no lust in his eyes. No fascination or curiosity. But there was a glint of . . . something. Nothing sexual, though, which meant Dominic didn't have to warn him off or—

The boy's toy car fell to the hardwood floor. As Mila gracefully bent to pick it up, Dominic's cock jerked at the sight of her heart-shaped ass encased in those flattering black pants. And when she stood upright, flicking that riot of curls out of her face, he damn near crossed to her and sank his hands into them.

Mila figured she should have known better than to think he'd back off. Guys like GQ didn't take rejection well, did they? Still, she'd never have expected him to seek her out. Try his luck again at the club maybe, but not turn up here.

She didn't like that he'd come. And yet she did. While she didn't have time for the kind of games that such guys liked to play, it nonetheless felt good to have a diversion from the other shit going on in her life. And he was a very pretty diversion.

The moment their eyes had locked, her pulse had skittered, her stomach had done a little flip, and her whole body had come alive. Like she'd stuck her fingers in an electric socket. Then his mouth had curved in mischief, and that sexy-as-hell smile had made her nipples tighten.

Her cat had done a long, languid stretch as she came to full alertness. The feline was wary of who she allowed into her world, and she sensed that this walking enigma was trying to shove his way into it. The cat hadn't yet decided whether she liked his perseverance or not, although his attention did stroke the pride that Joel had wounded in choosing another female over her.

Mila could feel Dominic's gaze on her. He wasn't simply ogling her, he was watching her carefully. Studying her. Probably looking for a damn weakness so he could barge his way past her defenses and get that bout of sex he was seeking just to satisfy his ego. Sigh.

Done with her young client, she led him and his uncle to the cashier's desk. "I'd say your nephew was very well behaved."

"He was," agreed Dean, handing over cash. "He's always fine once he sits in the chair, so I don't know why he fusses."

Mila offered Finley two of his favorite lollipops. "There you go."

"Say thank you to Mila," said Dean.

Gratefully taking the candy, Finley gave her a shy smile. "Thank you."

"Take care, Mila." Dean flicked Dominic a curious look on the way out, but the wolf paid him zero attention.

Once she'd cleaned her station, she gestured at the chair. "Ready when you are, GQ."

Muscles bunching and rippling, he stalked toward her with a predatory purpose that sent a delicious little shiver down her spine. Warmth bloomed low in her stomach because *damn* if he wasn't twelve levels of pure deliciousness.

She kept her smile professional and friendly, ensuring she looked unaffected by the visceral force of sexual chemistry that had snapped the air taut and sent her nerves haywire. And now he was looming over her, giving off all kinds of pheromones and generally muddling her thoughts.

"Want coffee or anything?" she asked.

"I'm good, thanks."

That liquid-sex voice slid over her skin like caressing fingers. As he sank into the padded chair, his brooding eyes met hers in the large mirror, and the heat there made her stomach clench.

It wasn't the first time that a good-looking guy had sat in her chair. Hell, there had been plenty over the years. They'd smiled and flirted and stirred her hormones, but none had ever rattled her. *This* one did, though. He made her feel . . . hunted.

She clipped a cape around him and then covered his nape with a neck strip. His hair was classically styled—short at the back and sides while the slightly longer hair on top was upright and swept ever so slightly to the left. She sifted her fingers through the silky strands, a little annoyed that such a simple thing made her nerve endings tingle. "It could do with a trim."

"Which is why I'm here."

She snorted. He was there because she'd turned him down, and his ego couldn't quite handle it, but whatever. "Hmm."

As she used the clippers to trim the back and sides of his head, Dominic asked, "How long have you worked here?"

"My lawyer told me I don't have to answer that question," she said, deadpan.

Dominic's mouth twitched as amusement trickled through him, soothing the jagged edges of his mood. Yeah, this was just what he needed. Even his wolf began to relax, steadied by her sense of calm.

Dominic's gut clenched as her tongue peeked out just enough to touch her lower lip. He couldn't help picturing that tongue lapping at the head of his cock. "I heard your pride mates are big on supporting each other's businesses and that very few of you work for outsiders. Is that why you work here and not at a salon somewhere?"

"No, I work here because it has great substance abuse coverage. Plus, having a job keeps the parole officer off my back."

Dominic smiled. Anyone else might have thought the witty responses were her way of being friendly, but it was her way of avoiding answering personal questions. He recognized the little trick because he'd used it himself plenty of times. "You weren't part of the battle on

Mercury Pack territory." He'd have remembered her. Remembered that voice.

"No, I was out of the country at the time."

"Where?"

Eyes lit with mock paranoia briefly flicked left then right. "Why, what did you hear?"

"Sources say you were at the Playboy Mansion."

She snickered. "I was in Russia visiting family."

"The wolverine side?"

"Yes." Mila said her goodbyes to Evander's client as the jaguar shifter left. Then, putting down the shears, she lifted a spray bottle and spritzed water on the uncut strands on the top of Dominic's head. "Stop staring at my mouth."

"But it's *right there.* And it looks so lonely. Does it want to meet mine?"

"Not in this lifetime."

Chuckling, Dominic watched as she pinched his hair between her fingers and held it straight while snipping at the ends in short spurts. He let himself relax, listening to the snip of scissors, the low music, and her shoes clicking along the hardwood floor. "How long have you been singing at clubs?"

"A while."

Dominic's cock twitched as her tongue again peeked out to lightly touch her lower lip. He was gonna end up biting that delectable mouth if she kept that up. "Not big on giving real answers, are you?"

"Ask me an interesting question, and I'll give you a proper answer."

"All right. Are you dating anyone?"

Her brows drew together. "That's not an interesting question."

"I find this topic very interesting."

"No, 'interesting' is that the fifty-star American flag was designed by a high school junior for a class project—and his teacher gave him a B minus."

Dominic felt his brows lift. “Where did you hear that?”

“My earlier client mentioned it. He’s a schoolteacher.”

He blinked in surprise as she twirled his chair so that he was facing her. As she snipped at the front of his hair, he took her scent inside him. Fuck, she smelled good. Really good. It was an honest-to-God struggle not to grab those hips and drag her onto his lap. “What time do you finish work?”

Sighing at the sensual invitation in his tone, Mila twisted his chair so that he was facing the mirror again. “I’m not going to sleep with you.”

“But I want you to be the one who takes my virginity.”

Mila tried not to chuckle, and she completely failed. God, she should have sent him to Evander or Archie. Cutting Joel’s hair was hard, although that was mostly because her cat just wanted to rake his face. Cutting Dominic’s hair was equally challenging. He was just so intent on her, as if nothing else existed. He watched every move she made and paid attention on a level that was beyond intense. No one had ever focused so fully on her before—it was both flattering and unnerving. Her cat rather liked it.

Someone so easygoing shouldn’t have such a tremendously forceful personality, but he did. He was just so . . . *there.* Had such a strong presence—the kind that commanded attention.

Dominic wasn’t someone who would ever fade into the background. She really wished he would. Because right then, the air between them was so sexually charged, it was almost stifling. His blatantly lethal sensuality beat at her composure, and it was a sheer wonder that her hands didn’t shake.

“We’d have fun, Mila.”

“We should stick to being strangers with sexual tension,” she said, focusing on the line where the clipper cut met the scissor cut, blending that border by combing sections of his hair upward and snipping off any ends that poked out of the fine-tooth comb. "Since I doubt you're short of offers from women, it shouldn't bother you."

"I'm finding that it does."

She rolled her eyes. "That's just because I turned you down. I'm guessing that doesn't happen a lot."

"No, it doesn't."

Conceited bastard. "I'll bet you're one of those guys who gives his cock a name."

"I call mine 'the truth.'"

"The truth?"

"Because women can't handle it."

She couldn't help smiling. "God, you're weird." Putting down the scissors, she combed out the lingering hair clippings. He vetoed styling products, so she spritzed his hair one last time and then styled it how he liked it. "Almost done." Removing the attachment from the clippers, she then trimmed his neck and sideburns. She took a moment to review her work and, satisfied that she hadn't missed any spots, used a hair dryer and small brush to sweep away hair clippings from his neck.

Grabbing the handheld mirror, she held it at the back of his head so that he could see its reflection in the large mirror he was still facing. "Happy?"

"Always." Genuinely impressed, Dominic decided there and then that no other barber would touch his hair. Unless she barred him from the shop for harassing her, which was quite likely to happen.

She whipped off his cape. "Let me just sweep these bits of hair out of the way before you stand up or they'll stick to the soles of your shoes."

It hadn't been a request, and Dominic had to admit that he liked that assertive note in her voice. Although she was very calm, there was something fierce about her. Something wild that told him she'd never be tamed, never bend to anyone's will, never tolerate any bullshit or be pushed into doing anything she wasn't 100 percent interested in doing.

This female knew what she wanted and would settle for nothing less. He respected that.

He would bet that every single one of his pack mates would tell him he was wasting his time here. They'd tell him to walk away and forget about her. The thing was . . . he couldn't. It wasn't merely the thrill of the chase. No, she drew him. Made his wolf crave her attention. No female had ever done that before.

At the counter, he paid for the haircut and pulled a lollipop out of the sweet jar. "You didn't tell me what time you finish work today."

"And I'm not going to."

He tilted his head. "What is it? You like to be the one who does the asking? Okay then, make my day, Mila. Ask me out."

"All right. Get out."

He laughed. "At least let me tell you your future before I go." Grabbing a pen from the counter, he quickly scribbled his cell number on the palm of her hand. "Your future is clear."

Stifling a smile, she narrowed her eyes. "You're a ballsy motherfucker."

"And you're the first thing that's truly interested me and my wolf in a long, long time."

Taken aback, Mila didn't know what to say. It hadn't been a playful comment. He looked so serious. She wouldn't have thought he did "serious."

Just as Mila pulled her hand from his, the door opened. Her frown melted away as Ingrid Devereaux, her grandmother, walked inside. As usual, she was clad in vintage clothes with her hair styled in an old-fashioned updo. She was also adorned in antique jewelry that was similar to those she sold at the antique store directly across the road. Ingrid managed the shop, overlooking the fact that Vinnie often smuggled money via said antiques.

"Hi, Grams," greeted Mila.

"Hello, doll." Ingrid's face split into a wide smile as she spotted the wolf. "Dominic!"

"Mrs. D." Grinning, he straightened. "How was heaven when you left it?"

Blushing, Ingrid flicked a hand at him. "Always the charmer."

His eyes briefly dropped to Ingrid's burgundy blouse. "That color looks good on you."

It did, actually, but her grandmother would surely snort at that corny . . . Oh my God, Ingrid was lapping this up!

Smoothing a hand down her blouse, Ingrid asked, "You think so?"

He nodded. "Oh yeah. You're totally working it."

Giggling like a teenager, she lightly touched his arm. "Aw, thanks, sweetie." Ingrid blew a kiss at Mila and gave her a look that said they'd talk in a moment. She then headed over to Evander, who was cleaning his station.

Mila lifted a brow at Dominic. "You're flirting with my grandmother? Really?"

"You don't have to be jealous, Mila," he said. "The only girl I want is standing right in front of me. Frowning."

"Yeah, well, I'm unavailable."

His eyes narrowed. "So you *are* dating someone?"

"No, but I'm entering into an arranged mating."

He stilled, his face hardening in a way that made her cat go on full alert. "An arranged mating? When's the big day?"

"It's not official yet, so there's no set date, but it's likely to happen."

The tension left him, and his mouth curved. "Not official yet, huh? Well, arrangements like those fall through all the time, you know."

She cursed, realizing she'd just stupidly presented herself as even *more* of a challenge than before. God, she was such an idiot. "You should drop this, GQ."

"Maybe. But we both know I won't." He skimmed his fingertip down the side of her face. "Be sure to call me, Mila." After saying a quick goodbye to Evander and Ingrid, he breezed out of the shop.

Evander started toward her. "Well, well, well. Lothario has set his sights on Mila."

Ingrid hurried over, her heels click-clacking on the floor, eyes sparkling. "What did he write on your hand? Evander said he scribbled something on your palm."

"It's nothing," said Mila, hoping they'd drop the subject.

Ingrid grabbed Mila's hand. "Ooh, is that his cell number? I saw him here while I was across the street, and I figured he'd be flirting with you. I met him at Madisyn's mating ceremony—that boy could charm the birds out of the trees with just a smile." Ingrid cocked her head. "But I must say, you don't look charmed."

"Well, I'm not." For the most part.

Evander's brows lowered. "You're not gonna call him?"

"No," replied Mila.

Ingrid gaped. "Why not? He's gorgeous and charming, and you're both single."

"Grams, you do realize that he only wants a quick fumble in the dark with me, right?"

Ingrid lifted her shoulders. "And whatever's wrong with a fumble? Really, doll, I don't see why there has to be anything *quick* about it."

Mila held up a hand. "I don't feel like being another notch on GQ's bedpost. That's all I'd be to him. I don't think he's quite the player he pretends to be, but I know he wouldn't want more than sex. You're my grandmother. Shouldn't you be offended on my behalf?"

"Would you *want* more than sex with him?"

"No."

"Then I don't see the problem."

"Neither do I," Evander chipped in.

Mila lifted her hands. "And I'm done with this conversation."

"What conversation?" asked Archie as he came strolling out of the break room.

Leaving the three of them to gossip like little old women, Mila tidied her station.

Archie didn't push her in Dominic's direction; he simply reminded her of something he'd been telling her for years: "Dominant male wolves are more trouble than they're worth."

Ingrid waved that away. "You say that about every species other than pallas cats."

"Doesn't mean I'm wrong," said Archie.

Ingrid shot him an exasperated look. "Well, I have to get back to the store." She said her goodbyes, pausing to whisper in Mila's ear, "Life's for living, doll. Now you call that boy, and let him help you live it."

Mila just smiled. "Take care, Grams." Her smile faltered when none other than Joel and Adele walked in just as Ingrid was leaving. *Shit.* Mila's cat stood with a hiss, hackles raised, fangs bared.

As Adele and Ingrid paused to chat, Joel headed straight to Mila. Like Dominic, he was tall and had quite the smile. His shoulders were a little broader, though, and his skin didn't have GQ's sexy tan or . . . Why was she comparing them? Ugh.

"Hey, stranger," said Joel, grinning. "Haven't seen you in at least a week. I came to pick up Adele from work, so I thought I'd pop in and say hi."

One thing Mila was grateful for was that Joel, unlike most of the pride, didn't work on this street. If he had, he'd have probably popped in quite regularly. Adele worked at the pawn shop a few stores down from the barbershop, but she rarely visited. It also helped that they lived in their own house as opposed to Mila's apartment building where many of the pride resided.

He spared Adele a brief glance, noting she was still engaged in conversation with Ingrid, and then turned back to Mila. "Notice the flowers?" he whispered.

Yeah, Mila had seen the huge beautiful bouquet that Adele was carrying.

His voice still low, he continued, "I went on a night out with the guys and didn't get back until five the next morning, even though I told her I'd be home no later than midnight. She was pissed." His brows dipped. "If I'm honest, she was *beyond* pissed—to the point of overreacting. Seriously, you'd have thought I spent the night at a strip club or something."

Mila frowned. "I don't think I've ever seen Adele anything but happy."

"Well, she doesn't hold on to her mad for long, but she sure can yell. She's had a real bug up her ass lately. The slightest thing sets her off. If it wasn't for the fact that I didn't scent pregnancy on her, I'd have wondered if she were pregnant." He shrugged, his smile returning. "Luckily, she's a sucker for roses—they always get me out of trouble."

Mila forced a smile. He often confided in her about his relationship with Adele, and such conversations were never fun.

"Do you think maybe you could talk to her and check that she's okay?" asked Joel. "There's something she's not telling me, and I'm worried about her."

Oh fuck, he couldn't ask this of her. "Adele and I aren't close, Joel. If she has some kind of issue, I'm not someone she's likely to share it with. I'm sure she'll tell you when she's ready."

His shoulders lowered. "Yeah, you're right. I shouldn't ask you to get involved, I'm sorry. Like I said, I'm just worried about—" He frowned, his gaze locking on her hand as she lifted it to push her curls away from her face. "What's this?" He grabbed her hand, his jaw hardening. "You wrote a guy's number on your palm? Wait, this isn't your handwriting." Joel's nostrils flared. "Who was he?"

Pulling her hand back, Mila shrugged nonchalantly. "A client. His name is Dominic Something."

"What is he? Human? Cat?"

She sighed. "He's a Phoenix Pack wolf. An enforcer."

Recognition flashed across his face, and Joel folded his arms. "Dominic . . . Yeah, I remember him from the battle. You don't want to get involved with that wolf, Mila. He reminds me a lot of your ex, Grant. The ultimate ladies' man. You can do better. And let's face it, the Phoenix Pack aren't the kind of shifters *anyone* should get too closely acquainted with. Their Alpha male's wolf turns feral during battle, and his mate's just plain crazy."

"We're pallas cats, Joel—we're really in no position to judge others on their level of craziness."

"So you're gonna call this Dominic guy?"

She could tell he wasn't keen on the idea, but it wasn't jealousy—just a protectiveness that someone would feel for a close friend. "No, I'm not."

He exhaled heavily. "Good. It would be just like dating Grant again, so you already know exactly how it'll turn out—like shit."

Just then, Adele came toward them, her smile bright. The pretty blue-eyed blonde really had that girl-next-door look going on. "Hi, Mila, how are you?"

"Great, thanks. You?" Fuck, this was hard.

"Never better." She linked her arm through Joel's. "We're just going to grab some Chinese on the way home. Say hi to your parents for me."

"Will do." Her cat hissed and spat right up until the couple finally left the shop. Yeah, Russia and Maksim were looking better by the minute.

CHAPTER FOUR

Curled up on an armchair, Makenna sighed at her mate as she placed her mug on the small table beside her. "I'm just saying, it's bad luck to cut your nails on a Friday." She held up her hands in a gesture of innocence. "I don't make up the rules of the universe. I'm just the messenger."

A muscle in Ryan's cheek ticked, and his hand clenched tightly around the TV remote. "But it's *not* a rule of the universe. It's a ridiculous superstition."

"I don't know why you have to say 'superstition' like it's a dirty word."

"I don't know why you can't just be normal and accept that they're bullshit."

"You know what I just heard? 'Blah, blah, blah, blah, I'm a shithead.'"

Gently patting the back of the swaddled baby sleeping against his chest, Dominic watched the couple argue. Makenna was wildly superstitious, whereas her mate was all about logic and reason, so the two often argued over such things. Since Ryan was ordinarily quite stoic and mostly communicated with grunts, it was always fun to watch the enforcer lose it with his mate. She was literally the only person who could wrench such a reaction out of him.

The other pack members scattered around the living area were also enjoying the show. In fact, Roni and Marcus—a mated couple who acted as enforcers for both the Phoenix Pack and the Mercury Pack—had even switched their attention from the movie they had been watching to the other couple, observing the argument while sharing a bag of strawberry licorice.

Like the other rooms within the large multifloored cave dwelling, the living area was all modern furnishings and woodsy colors. Decorative swirls were carved into the main light-cream sandstone wall of the room, complementing the rustic fireplace. The large sectional sofas and plush armchairs were all angled toward the state-of-the-art audiovisual system.

"I've never even heard of that dumb superstition before," Ryan went on. "It wouldn't surprise me if you made it up to irritate me."

Makenna's eyes widened. "I didn't. There's even a rhyme about it."

"You say that as if the rhyme gives it credibility. There's also a rhyme about Humpty Dumpty. *He* was fictional too."

"Actually," Roni cut in, "there are some who believe that Humpty Dumpty was King Richard III of England, who was defeated in the 1400s despite how big and tough his armies were. And there are others who think Humpty Dumpty was actually a cannon that was placed on a city wall but later fell to the ground."

Makenna smirked at Ryan. "Don't know everything, do you, White Fang?"

"There is no such thing as bad luck," he maintained.

"You're tempting fate again." Makenna pointed at the coffee table. "Knock—"

"Do *not* tell me to knock on wood."

"Fine. Tempt fate. See if I care." Makenna picked up her e-reader and returned to her book, dismissing him. Ryan honestly looked close to leaping off his chair and snatching the e-reader right out of her hand.

Dominic exchanged an amused look with his Beta female, Jaime, who was sprawled beside him on the reclining end of the sofa. As her mouth opened wide in yet another jaw-popping yawn, he said, "You look zonked."

"Sleepless nights will do that to a girl," she muttered, adjusting the soft blanket that was tucked around her legs.

"Why don't you go rest in your room while the baby's sleeping?" Makenna suggested.

Jaime gave a tired shake of her head. "I'll stay."

"He'll be fine," Dominic assured her.

"I know, I just . . ." Jaime lowered her voice, as if confessing a shameful secret. "I don't want to leave him. Clingy, aren't I?"

"I'd say it's normal," Makenna consoled.

Jaime gently skimmed the baby's cheek with her fingertip. "I can't believe how easily he falls asleep for you," she said to Dominic.

"What can I say? I'm his favorite uncle," said Dominic. "I'm still surprised you called him Hendrix."

Jaime frowned. "And what's wrong with that name?"

"Nothing," said Dominic. "It suits the little guy. I just wouldn't have expected Dante to go for something unusual. Also, he was set on Daniel."

"Hendrix doesn't look like a Daniel."

In agreement with that, Dominic nuzzled Hendrix's downy head. He was so small and cute, and he smelled so fresh and sweet.

"You know, Dom, this is the most laid-back I've seen you in days," Jaime observed. "You've been a little moody lately. Seemed kind of distracted."

"It wouldn't have something to do with a certain pallas cat called Mila, would it?" asked Trey. Well, it was more of a taunt than a question.

Marcus chuckled. "I really wish I'd been there to see her blow you off."

"Oh yeah, I heard about that from Madisyn," said Makenna, her mouth quirking. As the barmaid's best friend, she'd gotten an earful.

Trey balanced his coffee cup on the arm of his chair, his eyes on Dominic. "I got a call from Vinnie. He said Ingrid mentioned something about you turning up at the barbershop where Mila works and giving her your cell number."

"Really?" Marcus lifted a brow at Dominic. "Has she called you?"

Dominic narrowed his eyes at the other enforcer. "Since when do you care about my sex life?"

Marcus chuckled again. "I'll take that as a no."

"Madisyn *did* tell you that Mila's not someone you'll be able to charm into bed," Trey reminded him. "I asked Vinnie if he was going to warn you away from Mila. He laughed and said he wouldn't need to—said she'd see right through your shit."

Dismissing his pack mates with a Ryan-like grunt, Dominic nuzzled Hendrix again. It was true that Dominic had been moody and distracted recently. Six days. It had been six days since he'd last seen Mila. She hadn't called. Had he expected her to? No. She seemed determined to resist him, and it was clear that she was stubborn as hell. It shouldn't bother him so damn much, but it did—hence the moodiness.

Generally, Dominic didn't "think" about women. Didn't wonder what they were up to or where they were or who they were with. But Mila popped into his head several times a day. Hell, he'd even dreamed about her. Dreamed he was fucking her mouth, her sleek curls bunched in his hands.

She'd be singing at the Velvet Lounge tonight, and he fully intended to be there. He liked being around her. She amused him. Intrigued him. Teased him. Wasn't easily impressed or charmed, which meant he had to work for her attention. Her eyes lit up when he amused her, which he liked, but she hadn't fallen at his feet. Didn't flirt or encourage him. She was just . . . refreshing.

Trey's cell began to ring, and Hendrix fussed a little but thankfully didn't wake.

"Hey," Trey greeted the caller.

Thanks to his shifter-enhanced hearing, Dominic recognized the voice on the other end of the line as Gabe, Jaime's brother, but he couldn't quite make out the words.

Trey's face hardened. Without ending the call, he spoke to Dominic. "You have a visitor, but I'm not so sure you're going to like who it is."

"Emmet Pierson?" Dominic had expected as much.

"No. *Rosemary* Pierson."

Dominic swore under his breath.

Roni licked her front teeth. "That bitch is either ballsy or stupid."

"I'm leaning toward crazy," said Trey. His gaze slid back to Dominic. "If you're willing to hear what she has to say, I'll ask Gabe to tell her to wait outside the gate."

"I'll speak to her," Dominic told him, carefully handing Hendrix back to Jaime.

"Want company?" Marcus asked him.

Standing, Dominic shook his head. This was his mess. "I'll deal with her."

He stalked through the network of sandstone tunnels, exited the main door, and descended the steps that were carved into the cliff face. The ancient cave dwelling was situated deep in their territory, surrounded by forests and mountains. It had been increasingly modernized over the years and comfortably housed all twenty-seven members of his pack.

The breeze kept him cool as he jogged through the maze of wild shrubs and weathered trees, alarming the small animals who then fled into the underbrush. The sounds of birds chirping, wings fluttering, and branches creaking were as comforting as the scents of pine, wildflowers, and sun-warmed earth. But none eased his irritation.

Arriving at the security shack, he nodded at Gabe and asked, "Has she given you any trouble?"

"No, she politely asked for you," said Gabe. "When I said you'd be down shortly, she didn't complain that I wouldn't let her through, but she didn't look happy about it."

Crossing to the wrought iron gates, Dominic opened one just enough to slip through and then stalked to the driver's side of the Volvo. His wolf snapped his teeth as Rosemary lowered her window, her smile both shy and uncertain.

With her sleek blonde hair, hourglass figure, and gorgeous long legs, she'd easily caught Dominic's eye. He'd made it clear when they met that he wasn't looking for anything other than a one-night stand, and she'd been fine with it. Or, at least, she'd *seemed* fine with it. Dominic was learning that Rosemary was very good at acting.

"Hi." She glanced at the gate. "Can we talk? Please?"

She was high if she thought he'd ever permit her on his territory. He planted his feet and folded his arms. "You have two minutes, so make them count."

She winced. "I can see that you're upset. I'm sorry if my father—"

"This isn't about your father. This is about you. You lied to him. You spun him a tale about us being in a relationship."

"I didn't tell him it was a one-night stand for two reasons. One, he would have been disappointed in me. Two, he might have tried to twist it into you using me. He can be vindictive at times, and I didn't want him causing problems for your pack."

"Why was I even a topic of conversation between you two?"

"I mentioned to him that I thought mating a shifter could be what my wolf and I need. He agreed with me, and he asked if I knew any shifters. I told him about you, but I didn't think he'd go to you and make that offer. I swear, I didn't."

She could "swear" all she wanted—Dominic wasn't buying it. He cocked his head. "You really think you have an animal inside you?"

"I know I do, Dominic." Rosemary put a fist to her chest. "I *feel* her. She's sleeping, but she's there. If I mated another shifter, if she had a mate of her own, I think she'd wake for him and his animal."

Dominic shook his head, sure to the bone that she was wrong. Maybe it was a fantasy she'd concocted as a child because it comforted her, just as a kid might invent an imaginary friend. But it was pretty fucking warped that Rosemary hadn't let that fantasy go. "Like I told your father, if you had an animal inside you, I'd sense her. My wolf would sense her. There's nothing there, Rosemary. I'm sorry, but it's the truth."

Her eyes hardened. "Like I said, *she's sleeping.*"

"I'd still sense her."

"You're wrong." Rosemary's hands clenched so tightly around the steering wheel that her knuckles went white. "All I need is to mate with a shifter. She'll surface to be with his animal. She will." The feverish glint in her eyes told him there'd be no convincing her to even consider that she could be mistaken.

He backed up a few steps. "If you want to believe that, fine, but keep me out of it."

"Dominic, wait. Look, I know you don't want to be mated—"

Bristling, he stilled. "You don't know anything about what I want."

She scoffed. "Come on, Dominic, you go through women like they're a dying breed. People are often judged for wanting to be single, but if that makes them happy, it should be fine."

It was an argument that he himself had made many times to others who'd criticized his lifestyle. And yet, when he heard it from Rosemary, it sounded weak.

"If you want to be forever single, that's your choice. But surely you want kids, Dominic. Surely you want a child you can love and teach and share your wolf with. Surely *he* wants it."

It really wasn't until Rosemary put the idea in his head that Dominic realized how much he did want kids. He'd never thought about it before, mostly because he was all about the "now" and wasn't someone who thought too much about what the future held.

"I can give you exactly what you want—you can have a child without being in a relationship. If you mate with me, we can end it as soon as I'm pregnant. You can resume living a single life, if that's what you want. This would work for both of us, Dominic."

His wolf jerked back at the thought of having anything more to do with this female, let alone having a pup with her. "I don't know what you think you know about mating bonds, but I'm guessing you're as ignorant as your father. The bonds don't form just because you want them to."

"But I—"

"There have to be emotions like respect and trust between the pair. There can't be secrets, fears, or barriers. You have to be completely bare to the other person. And you sure as shit can't just walk away from a bond if it does form." Not without grave consequences that could ruin several lives. "So no, this won't work for either of us."

Her lips thinned. "We might not love each other *now*, but that doesn't mean we *can't* feel that way. We just need to take the time to get to know—"

"What we need is to go our separate ways." Done wasting his time on this shit, Dominic turned his back on her and headed for the gate. "There are other shifters, Rosemary. Talk to them, make your offer to them." They'd tell her the same thing, and then maybe she'd realize she was pissing in the wind.

"You don't want to walk away from me, Dominic."

Slipping through the gate, he glanced back at her. "Oh?"

She licked her lips. "I didn't want to tell you this because I was worried you'd freak out. When I'm around you, I swear I feel my wolf starting to stir. Not awaken, exactly. But . . . it's like you disturb her sleep. As if you make that sleep lighter. It could be that we're true mates."

His gaze flicked upward, and he almost laughed at the sheer ridiculousness of that statement. "Go home, Rosemary."

"You know it, too, Dominic. I *know* you do—you gave off all the signals of a male who's found his mate," she said, her words coming sharp and fast. "You may not want a mating bond, but what about your wolf? Wouldn't he like the gift of finding his mate? Don't you see, Dominic? We could all get what we want out of this. It's the perfect solution!"

Locking the gate, Dominic firmly stated, "We're not true mates, Rosemary."

"But my wolf—"

"Doesn't exist. Even if she did, it doesn't change that this situation will not work for *me.* Like I said to you earlier, you don't know a damn thing about what I want. You just think you do." With that, he stalked off.

"It doesn't surprise me that you'd walk away from this!" she yelled. "It just proves I was right, that you don't want attachments!"

Ignoring her, Dominic spoke to Gabe. "If she comes back, send her away."

Gabe nodded. "Got it."

Hoping to walk off his anger in the woods, Dominic didn't hurry back to the caves. *"Signals,"* she'd said. He hadn't given her any fucking signals. He hadn't led her on by word or deed. Hadn't done anything that would give her the false impression that he was looking for something serious.

She was wrong in thinking he didn't want a serious relationship *eventually.* He'd come across countless females in his time who'd claimed they "knew" why he didn't commit, who'd been so certain that they'd seen through him. They'd tossed out all kinds of theories—he feared commitment, he was pining for someone he couldn't have, he'd become relationship-shy after a woman he'd loved had betrayed him.

They'd all been wrong.

It had long ago become instinct for Dominic to keep a large part of himself separate from others. His parents lost their first son, Tobias, when the kid was ten. His mother, Allegra, had crashed the family car after falling asleep at the wheel, and the brother he'd never known was killed. She'd never stopped hating herself for it. Grief had begun to drive his parents apart, so they'd had Dominic to "fix" their relationship, to "heal" them and bring them back together.

The problem was that they'd never been able to fully *see* Dominic. They'd always compared him to Tobias. Always marveled over their similarities and frowned at their differences.

In many ways, Tobias had been held up to him as a measuring stick. No matter what he'd done, Dominic could never quite meet their expectations. And when someone didn't see you, when they'd twinned your identity up with someone else's and made you feel both unknown and unwanted, the world could be a very lonely place.

As an adult, Dominic could see that his parents had held back from him out of fear that they'd lose him just as they'd lost Tobias—they hadn't wanted to feel that same level of pain again. But as a child, Dominic hadn't seen it that way. He'd felt unimportant, unloved, and not good enough. Felt like he didn't belong.

He'd not only maintained an emotional distance from his parents, he'd also developed a habit of keeping that same distance from others. He'd subconsciously hidden his pain and anger as well as his true self, only giving people small glimpses of the real Dominic. It was something he hadn't really noticed until the day his mother left when he was just thirteen—deserting both him and his father—and Dominic hadn't felt more than a twinge of hurt.

His own mother had *abandoned* him, but he hadn't felt the expected level of betrayal and pain. As if the true impact of her actions just hadn't been able to touch him. He'd realized then just how much he'd withdrawn from others. Realized that he'd built a metaphorical shell around himself.

He'd met many people who were hard and rough on the outside while hiding a soft center. Dominic might not have a *hard* outer layer, but he was still surrounded by a protective shell. There couldn't be walls like that between mates. Both needed to be open to the other, and that left them incredibly vulnerable.

Allegra had known that separating herself from her mate, Lincoln, could lead to one of them turning rogue. She'd known that the rogue wolf would then be killed, and that the likelihood of the other surviving the breaking of the mating bond was slim. Allegra hadn't cared about any of that. Hadn't cared that Dominic would be left alone.

He had no idea where she'd gone or what had happened to her, although he believed she was likely dead. His old Alpha, Rick—who was Trey's father—had survived after his mate had turned rogue, but Dominic suspected that was because Rick and Louisa hadn't been *true* mates.

Dominic had never tried to find out what had happened to Allegra. He honestly didn't care. Louisa had left her mate, knowing what fate could lie ahead for her, but she'd done it to be with her son; she'd done it to start a new pack with Trey after Rick had banished him. Allegra, on the other hand, had completely deserted her family. If she was alive, she'd know that Lincoln was dead, and she'd know that Dominic was alone . . . but she'd never come back for him.

If Allegra and Lincoln had been a human couple, they could have divorced and started fresh. True-mate bonds didn't allow for things like that, and they sure didn't guarantee the happiness that most people assumed they did.

Dante was right; Dominic wasn't truly *happy.* But he still enjoyed his life. He didn't yet feel the need to find his mate and, despite what Rosemary claimed, he never gave off any signals that implied differently.

Except with Mila, he thought. He'd never pursued anyone before, and such a thing could certainly be misconstrued. But he'd been completely honest with her from the start; he'd been clear that he just wanted a bit of fun.

Still, it would be wise to ease up on her, but Dominic knew that he wouldn't. And he realized that part of the attraction for him was that there was no risk of emotional entanglements with Mila. No expectations. No complications. No chance of her wanting more, and then finding him lacking. Intent on an arranged mating, Mila wouldn't want anything from him. She'd insist on distance and boundaries. It would just be sex. Rough. Hard. Raw.

Ignoring the odd sensation that he felt in his gut whenever he thought of her bound to some asshole—and yeah, Dominic had simply decided that the guy was an asshole based on nothing—he quickened his pace. He needed to get ready for his trip to the Velvet Lounge tonight.

CHAPTER FIVE

Mic in hand, Mila let the lyrics and raw emotion pour out of her and into the song. Harley perfectly complemented the dance tune as she played her electric violin, and the DJ hyped up the cheering crowd with his own mic. There was so much energy in the club, it was crazy. Performing was a rush for Mila. An intoxicating, unparalleled high that made her feel alive and free . . . taking her up and up and up.

Her cat loved experiencing that rush. Loved the feel of so much adrenaline pumping through her.

Onstage, Mila could forget everything else. Could shed her frustration with her pride for having spent the past six days trying to convince her not to mate with Maksim. Could shed her anger with Joel for going ape-shit on her earlier when she refused to budge on moving to Russia. Could even shed her irritation at the bitches who were trying to edge their way into the VIP area where Dominic was sitting.

He hadn't bothered her once since that day at the barbershop, so he'd obviously accepted that she had no interest in starting anything with him. Yeah, all right, a very illogical part of her was disappointed by that. But it was for the best.

She was surprised to see him back at the club, since Harley had told her that he wasn't a regular there. When Mila had first spotted him sitting at the table with a few Mercury Pack members, her heart had slammed against her rib cage. Knowing better than to make eye contact and get ensnared by one of his "I am *so* going to fuck you" looks, she kept her gaze on the people crowding the dance floor.

As she reached the instrumental portion of the song, Mila moved aside while Harley did a solo. Like the audience, Mila clapped and cheered for the insanely talented margay shifter.

Whipping out her phone, Mila put her back to the crowd as she took selfies and even recorded a little video of them all bobbing, singing, dancing, and hooting. That only made them go wilder. And then, once again, she was pouring herself into the song.

Dominic could only stare at Mila, sincerely blown away by how much raw natural talent she possessed. Her smoky, scratchy voice was filled with soul and power. Her joy and exhilaration bled out into the crowd, which was loving her performance because *she* was loving it.

A siren. She was a fucking siren. Engaging and entrancing the crowd so effortlessly. All those snarls, twangs, and gritty vocals went straight to his cock.

There was so much passion in her, she was unbelievably compelling and made him feel . . . greedy. At that moment, he wanted to own all that passion. Wanted it for himself. Wanted *her* for himself. And that thought made him straighten in his seat, double-blinking, because there had never been a single time in his life when he'd felt remotely possessive of a woman.

He barely knew Mila. Hadn't even touched her. And yet, there was something about her that pulled him in. It was because she was real, he realized as he watched her perform onstage—no alter ego, no fake stage persona. She was authentic. Didn't put on a show or wear a mask. She was true to who she was whether she was cutting hair, singing onstage, or merely sitting at a bar.

Many people wore masks, even if it was only for the workplace or for dealing with strangers—it was human nature, really, to wrap your sense of self in protective layers. If people hurt or rejected the mask, it wasn't so personal; it lessened the pain. But Mila was just . . . Mila. And he suspected that was part of where her steadiness came from. Only someone who was truly genuine could have that degree of inner balance.

His wolf was just as captivated by her performance. Was just as hungry to touch and take.

A hand snatched his empty beer bottle from the table. "Want another?" Charlene asked.

"No, thanks, I'm driving," he told her.

Everyone clapped as the song ended. Mila gave a brief shout-out to Harley and the DJ before thanking the crowd and wishing them a good night. Dominic watched her disappear off the stage and then waited impatiently for her to walk out of the door that . . . and there she was. Instead of walking to the bar, she turned the corner that led to the restrooms.

Dominic stood as he spoke to Jesse. "I'll be back soon."

Jesse sighed, casting a brief glance in the direction that Mila had headed. "You're wasting your time with that one. I'm sure a woman being uninterested is something of a novel concept for you, though," he teased, his mouth quirking.

"I don't think you should take her rejection personally, Dominic," said Charlene. "I've seen plenty of guys come on to Mila. She's not mean about it, but she shoots them down."

Dominic's wolf growled, not liking the idea of her being hounded by other males. "I won't be long."

Charlene frowned. "But—"

Ignoring her, Dominic left the VIP area and began winding his way through the cluster of tables. Some of the females tried catching his attention, but he simply said his hellos and never broke stride as he shouldered his way through the throngs of people and finally turned into the long corridor.

There was a line near the entrance to the women's restroom, so he waited near the exit, his hip propped against the wall. It wasn't long before Mila came strolling out the door. Seeing him, she came to a sharp stop and sighed, rubbing her temple as if weary. It was probably odd that that made him smile.

Dominic let his gaze rake over her. "Me. You. Handcuffs. A paddle. Any questions?"

"Yes, why haven't you been committed to a mental health facility?"

He put a hand to his chest. "That hurts."

"Not as much as our weird-ass conversations do."

Chuckling, he pushed off the wall and crossed the space to her. "As it happens, my Alpha *is* considering having me committed. Especially since I keep claiming my watch is magic. But it really is."

She gave him a droll look. "Is that so?"

"Oh yeah." He glanced at his watch. "According to this, you're not wearing underwear."

Her brows drew together. "Actually, I am."

"Really? Hmm." Frowning, he tapped the watch. "Must be an hour fast."

She shook her head, lips twitching. "Unreal."

Dominic boldly stepped into her personal space and cupped her hip. Her pupils swallowed the color of her eyes, and a flush built on her cheeks. "You didn't call me," he said softly.

"No, I didn't."

"Why not?" He traced the hollow of her hip bone with the pad of his thumb. "You want me. Maybe even as much as I want you."

"I didn't say I wasn't attracted to you. Just that I wasn't going to sleep with you."

"Who said anything about sleeping?"

Mila almost shivered as that soft, silken whisper feathered over her skin and promised a sexual satisfaction she'd yet to experience. She was so susceptible to him, it wasn't even funny. Blindsided by sexual chemistry, her hormones were in a frenzy and her skin was all tingly.

Her cat was . . . well, not *pleased* to see him. She was never happy to see *anyone*. But the feline didn't find him quite as annoying as she found most people. She liked his strength, boldness, and determination. Even liked his playful streak, despite not being particularly playful herself.

Feigning indifference—or at least giving it her best shot—Mila sighed. "Don't you think this is a little sad? You're a grown man so bad at handling rejection that you absolutely *have* to seduce the girl just to reaffirm your sense of manliness."

"It *would* be sad if you were right. I won't deny that your unequivocal no pressed a button for me. But that wouldn't have been enough to maintain my interest in you if there hadn't been other things at play. I could list all those things, but you'll just accuse me of feeding you shit to flatter my way into your panties."

"I don't wear panties, I wear thongs."

He swallowed. "And now I know there is a God."

Mila smiled before she could stop herself. "You're insane."

A group of girls stumbled out of the restroom, almost going ass over tit. Before they could bump into Mila, Dominic smoothly pulled her into the little alcove branching off the corridor. He gently straightened one of her curls and then let it go, smiling as it bounced back into shape. "I've been wanting to do that since I first saw you on that stage. I like watching you sing."

Her brow creased. "Don't you mean *hearing* me sing?"

"No, although I do love your voice. It's all sex and sin and soul. I swear, you could sing the alphabet and my cock would get hard just listening to you. But I also love watching you perform. You get this intensity about you, like you're crackling with energy. Your eyes gleam, your face gets all flushed, and your body oozes sex. And it makes me wonder if you look like that when you come."

It wasn't until her back hit the wall that Mila even realized he'd been slowly and expertly herding her backward. "Smoothly done, GQ. Now step aside."

Instead, he caught her earlobe between his teeth. "Shall I tell you what I want to do to you?" He breathed her in, filling his lungs with her. "I want to taste and nip that very bitable mouth. Want you naked beneath me so I can play with those pretty breasts and suck on those nipples. Want to spread your thighs and eat your pussy until you come all over my mouth. And then . . . *then* I'll fuck you. There'll be nothing slow or easy about it. I'll fuck you hard and deep." He slid his hand from her hip to her lower stomach, splaying his fingers wide as he added, "So fucking deep you'll feel me right here. And you'll come screaming."

Mila silently moaned. The bastard really needed to stop talking. The air was thick with a sexual tension that purred against her skin.

Telling herself that he'd probably given that exact speech to dozens of different women, she lifted her chin. "Look, beneath all the weirdness, you seem like a nice guy. But I've told you before, I like men, not little boys. You want sex at its most basic, where there are no ties involved. That's fine, but I want more than that. Which is why I'll soon be moving to Russia."

Dominic went completely still. "Moving to Russia?"

"For the arranged mating, remember?" Mila's last word came out a little breathy, because he'd crowded her even more against the wall. Their bodies were pressed so close that Mila could feel his cock throbbing against her clit even through their clothes. Jesus, that was quite a lot of heat he was packing. Her cat unsheathed her claws, ready to rake at his face if he made a wrong move.

"You said it wasn't official."

"It's not."

Dominic's eyes narrowed. "You're immigrating to Russia, leaving your pride and family and friends . . . even though it's not official?"

She shrugged. "I need a change of scenery."

"There's more to this." Dominic sensed she was leaving out some details. "What are you determined to get away from?" He traced the line of her jaw with his fingertip, fighting to keep his anger in check—yeah, he did know it was an illogical anger. "You're not a runner. No, you'd stay and look your problems right in the eye. For you to move to another country, it must be something big. Something bad." The same something that was responsible for the shadows in her eyes, maybe. "Tell me what it is, Mila."

Her eyes flared. "How about instead I buy you a glass of mind your own goddamn business?"

Sensing she was ready to push him away, he softly said, "All right, easy. If you truly don't want this, I'll back off and leave you alone. But I want a kiss first." He brushed his nose against hers. "I want just one taste of you, Mila. No harm in that, right?" He ground his cock against her clit, delighting in her little throaty moan. "Just one taste. Let me have it."

In the grip of a hissing, spitting, clawing need, Mila swiped her tongue along her lower lip. "Just one," she said. He slowly dipped his head, lowering his mouth to hers. And the tension between them just . . . exploded.

He took her mouth like he owned it, lashing her tongue with his. Mila moaned, gripping his shoulders. The kiss was hard. Hungry. Carnal. Red-hot waves of need coursed through her blood and twisted her insides.

Greedy for more, she curved her body into his and ground against his cock. He growled into her mouth, kissing her harder and deeper, as he shoved his hand under her tank top and closed it around her breast.

Mila dug her nails into his shoulders, holding on as he devastated her senses. If this was going to happen just once, she might as well enjoy it.

Dominic bunched his free hand in those curls, groaning at the silky feel of them. He was now officially obsessed with her mouth—it was soft and hot and tasted so fucking good. He squeezed her breast, barely refraining from clawing off her bra and sucking on the taut nipple that was digging into his palm. He settled for giving it a light pinch, swallowing her thick, needy moan.

This thing between them was no case of simple lust. It was a vicious, wicked hunger that stole every sane thought from his brain. He could feel the heat of her pussy against his dick, and it was driving him out of his mind. All he could think of doing was freeing his cock, slamming it deep inside her body, and fucking her so raw she'd never forget it.

Sifting her fingers through his hair, Mila tried taking over the kiss. The bastard didn't let her. With a possessive snarl, he curled his hand around her throat. Mila tensed, and her cat bucked at the dominant hold. But all thoughts of resistance drained from Mila's body when his mouth latched on to her pulse and he sucked hard. Her soft, raspy moan was laced with the intense desperation that was heating her blood.

"I hope you make that noise when I'm in you."

As his words penetrated her dazed brain, Mila frowned. "You said—"

"That I'd back off if you truly don't want this," he finished, lifting his head. "But you do. I felt it."

She glared at him, chest heaving at the raw need carved into his face. "You're a tricky motherfucker."

"Just think about this, Mila. Soon, you're going to be in a whole other country, part of a whole other pride—or whatever type of shifter group your soon-to-be mate belongs to—and you'll be bound to someone you obviously don't care for. At least enjoy what time you have here."

"What, you offering me one last night of fun before I enter into a mating? Yeah, I've heard you're good at those," she said a little bitterly. "Also heard you often bring a friend to play. Does that mean you're going to invite another guy to fuck—" She cut off as he gripped her chin.

"There won't be a threesome," Dominic growled as a dark, unfamiliar emotion flared inside him. "There'll only be you and me. I won't share you."

"You can't share what you don't have."

"Oh, I will have you, Mila." He nipped her lower lip. "Be honest. It's not that I want sex with no ties that bothers you. It's that you think you'd be nothing more than a faceless fuck. You're wrong in thinking that, Mila. No woman has ever been a faceless fuck to me. Just because I didn't offer any of them a relationship doesn't mean I didn't see them as people; it doesn't mean I didn't respect them."

"I don't—"

"There are many reasons why I want you—none of which I'll say aloud because, as I said before, you'll only think I'm feeding you compliments to weaken your resolve. But I will say this: no one has ever done what you did tonight."

She swallowed. "What's that?"

"Made me feel possessive." Dominic swooped down and took her mouth again, letting her taste that possessiveness. He consumed her with a hunger that demanded to be sated, and he knew there'd be no ignoring it. He sucked on her lower lip, barely resisting the urge to give it a sharp bite. "Come with me."

She shook her head. "You may have been lying when you said 'one taste,' but I wasn't." She shoved him back a step, satisfied by the surprise on his face. Yeah, people tended to underestimate her physical strength. Slipping from between him and the wall, she jabbed a finger at him. "You need to do us both a favor and let this go now. I'm not looking for one last crazy night before I commit."

His legs ate up the space between them yet again. "What *are* you looking for, Mila?" he asked, his voice soft but serious. "Because no matter what you say, I genuinely don't think it's an arranged mating."

Mila fisted her hands. "Just keep your distance, GQ."

He looked about to argue with her, but then one of the club's waitresses called out his name. Mila used the distraction to her advantage and headed straight to the greenroom on shaky legs. Inside, she shoved on her jacket so roughly, she almost knocked over the freestanding lamp. All the while, she muttered about how Archie was right—dominant male wolves were more trouble than they were worth.

Hearing the greenroom door close behind her, Mila rolled her eyes. Fucking GQ just *had* to follow—

"Don't move."

Mila froze. That wasn't GQ's voice. No, it was a woman's voice. Unfamiliar. Cold. Despite the warning, Mila would have whirled on the spot if it hadn't been for the snick of a gun. Her cat shot to her feet with a feral hiss, eager to strike at the intruder.

"Oh, this was almost too easy," said the stranger. "Cat shifters are supposed to be tough to sneak up on."

"I heard you. I just figured you were someone else." Thanks to Dominic, she'd been both frazzled and distracted. She took in a long breath and smelled . . . *jackal.* She'd never liked those little bastards.

Looking into the glass of a framed wall poster, Mila caught the reflection of the woman behind her. Average height. Curvy. Red hair. Pale skin. Gray-blue eyes. Holding a whopper of a freaking handgun with a silencer attached to the barrel—a gun that was *pointed right at the back of Mila's head.*

Her heart jumped just as her inner cat hissed again and lunged for freedom, wanting at the bitch. And Mila had no doubt that her cat could take their foe on. The jackal was right to use a gun and attack from a distance. Mila's kind didn't fight fair or easy, and their inner felines were positively merciless. They might be only slightly bigger than a domestic house cat, but they were also, pound for pound, one of the strongest breeds of shifter. And they always went for the face.

"You're a cool one," the jackal observed.

"What do you want?" asked Mila, her voice flat even as adrenaline spiked through her, preparing her, sharpening her already-acute senses.

"Nothing. I'm merely here to collect—"

Mila grabbed the freestanding lamp and swung it as she whirled. The metal base hit the jackal's arm so hard that little reverberations scuttled up the bone of Mila's arm. *Fucking ow.* The gun dropped to the hardwood floor with a clang.

Before the jackal could make a dive for the weapon, Mila slammed the base of the lamp into the bitch's chest, sending her staggering backward. Then, wicked fast, Mila shifted.

Absolutely furious, the little cat flew out of the pile of clothes and wrapped herself around the jackal's head. Snarling and hissing, the cat shredded her face with razor-sharp fangs and claws. Tasted blood. Growled in satisfaction. Welcomed the rush of adrenaline, intent on exacting vengeance.

The jackal's cries of anger and pain were muffled by the cat's thick fur. No one would be coming to help the intruder. No one would interfere.

The jackal shook her head as she stumbled around the room, unable to see. She pulled hard on the cat's body. The cat didn't release her. No. She dug her fangs and claws deeper, refusing to give up her prize. Refusing to show pity.

The jackal retaliated fast and hard. Delivered harsh blows to the cat's head, sides, and spine. Clawed at the cat's face, legs, and flanks.

The cat ignored the pain. The scent of her own blood mixed with the smells of the jackal's blood and fear, and that only drove the cat wilder. She tore more strips out of the female's face. Sliced into the lips, eyelids, and forehead. Bit into the nose and sides of the face. Mercilessly mauled as much skin and muscle as she could reach.

Even through the sound of blood thrashing in her ears, the cat heard the satisfying sounds of the jackal's screams, the tearing of flesh, and the—

Something hard and heavy slammed into the cat's head. Glass shattered. Water doused her fur.

Hurting and slightly dazed, the cat loosened her hold on the female. The jackal took advantage and dug her claws deep into the cat's flanks as she finally ripped the cat away from her face. Screeching, the jackal slung the little cat across the room.

The feline flipped in midair and landed on her feet near the dresser, panting and growling. Ready and raring to pounce once more.

The female growled back at her, eyes blazing with fury as she moved toward the gun. "You crazy fucking—"

The cat launched herself at the female again.

Having finally shaken off Charlene—who was somewhat pissed by his insistence that she stop interfering—Dominic headed straight for the greenroom to track down Mila. He shoved open the door . . . just in time to see a silvery blur of motion spring through the air and latch on to a woman's head. It was Mila's cat, he quickly realized. She savagely clawed at the woman's face and ripped at her scalp. *What the fuck happened here?*

Gaping in shock, Dominic watched as the woman—blinded by all that fur and no doubt disorientated by the cat's weight—staggered all over the place, punching and slapping and clawing at her attacker. The cat ignored her. She had a death grip on that woman, and she wasn't letting go. No. Snarling, the feline just kept on ravaging her enemy with her sharp claws and fangs.

The scents of blood, fury, fear, and jackal slammed into his system, and Dominic's shock was quickly replaced by the same rage that made his wolf let out a guttural roar. It didn't matter that the cat was dominating the fight, Dominic still wanted to slap the little bitch that had dared harm her. That had *bloodied* her.

Mila wouldn't have started the fight—her kind followed the principle of "live and let live." No, the redhead had to have brought the fight to her. He felt some grim satisfaction in knowing that the jackal was no doubt sorely regretting it.

He wanted to intervene and help the cat, but, well, she didn't need it. And it would have been suicidal to get between two fighting female shifters anyway. They'd just as easily turn on you, offended by your belief that they required any aid.

Unable to do anything other than stand there and offer the cat his silent support, Dominic ground his teeth. The patches of blood matting the cat's fur worried him, especially because he had no idea how much of that blood was hers or how serious her injuries were.

He whipped out his cell phone and dialed the number of the Mercury Pack's Beta female. Ally was working the bar tonight, and as a Seer, she could heal physical wounds.

She answered on the fourth ring, but he didn't bother with greetings. "Ally, I need you in the greenroom." He ended the call just as fast and pocketed his phone, wanting to keep his hands free in case the little cat needed him. Right then, she still didn't seem to require help. It was kind of surreal to see a creature so small and fluffy acting like . . . well, like *that*.

He noticed the gun and swore. He picked it up, and yeah, it smelled of the jackal. Rage blew through him yet again, and he took a carefully controlled breath.

Did it surprise him that Mila obviously hadn't let the weapon stop her from defending herself? No. Just like it didn't surprise him that she'd obviously caught the jackal off guard. He'd learned a lot about Mila's kind from Madisyn. There was no warning with a pallas cat. No posturing or hissing. They just struck—no care for whether they were facing someone who was stronger, bigger, armed, or even part of a group. Nope, they straight up wouldn't give a shit.

He heard footsteps just before Ally, Jesse, and Harley came skidding into the room.

"Dear God," said Ally, wincing at the noise level. He didn't blame her. As the cat thrashed, bit, hissed, and snarled, the jackal screamed and cursed and condemned it to hell. "I heard all the hissing and yelling in the background when you called," Ally went on, "so I brought Jesse and Harley, figuring something bad was going down."

"What led to the fight?" asked Jesse.

Dominic shrugged, hating the feeling of helplessness that came from being forced to watch while Mila's cat was hurt. "Haven't got a clue. I also don't understand why the jackal hasn't shifted. It could be that she's latent, or it could be that she's hoping to retrieve this to end the fight." He showed them the gun. "Any of you recognize her?"

Harley blew out a breath. "Kind of hard to say, since I can't see her face. But I don't recognize her scent."

"Neither do I," said Jesse, looking just as eager to intervene as Dominic was.

"She came to the bar earlier and ordered a martini," said Ally. "At least, I *think* it was her."

The cat let out a little yelp, and Dominic spat a curse. He took another steadying breath, reminding himself that, with their thick hides and overabundance of fur, her kind were hard to hurt.

"I don't like that Mila's in pain right now," said Ally. "But I have to be honest, I just love watching pallas cats fight. Even while scratching and biting like a critter of pure horror, they're still somehow immensely cute."

Jesse grimaced. "They're odd-looking creatures that—"

They all jerked back as the jackal tripped, fell, and bashed the back of her head on the glass coffee table. Her arms slipped to the floor as her body went limp. Dominic could hear her heartbeat, so he knew she was simply out cold.

Sides heaving, the little cat detached herself from the jackal and backed away, her teeth bared. Eyes still locked on her enemy, she pitched forward and swiped at the female again and again. Made a series of rumbly sounds, as if trying to provoke the jackal, but the woman didn't stir.

Blood matted the cat's coat, and Dominic thought he could make out some welts, scratches, and puncture wounds—with all that thick fur, he just couldn't be sure. There was blood near the black stripes on her cheeks and over the little dark spots on her forehead, and he wondered if the jackal had clawed at the cat's face to make her let go.

Wanting the feline healed, Dominic cast a brief glance at Ally. "Maybe you—"

The cat's attention snapped his way. Ears flat, she curled her upper lip, baring long, bloodstained fangs. Green eyes—their pupils round rather than vertical—glared at Dominic with an unblinking, crazed stare. And, honest to God, his fingers itched for holy water. *Shit.*

CHAPTER SIX

Hey there," said Dominic, his voice low and gentle.

She let out a long, fierce, pissed-the-fuck-off hiss. And he got the feeling that the cat wasn't just upset by the attack. She was angry at having her fun disturbed. He'd seen the same expression on his Alpha female's face when he'd interrupted her downtime. Taryn was batshit crazy as well.

He made no move toward the cat, knowing it would be suicidal. He needed to lure her to him. "All of you step back," he told the others. "I need plenty of space around me or she's not likely to approach." As the others backed away, Dominic crouched onto his haunches and tapped the floor. "Come on over here."

Fangs bared, the cat let out a doglike bark. It was a definite "fuck you."

"I know you're upset, and you have every right to be, but I just want to check your wounds," he said, relying on Mila to communicate what he wanted to the feline, since the animal wouldn't understand his words.

The cat kept on glaring at him, thumping the floor with her dark-ringed, black-tipped bushy tail. Yeah, apparently, she was totally unmoved.

"She's your prize, I get it. I don't want it. I just want to make sure you're fine." Dominic lay on his side, hoping the relaxed pose might reassure her somehow. "Mila, help me calm your cat. The jackal's going to wake soon. If you want to talk to her, you need to be back in your human form."

The cat cocked her head and chuffed, and he got the feeling she was communicating with Mila.

He tapped the floor again with his fingertips. "Come on, come over here," he softly coaxed. "I won't hurt you. You'd scratch out my eyes if I did anyway, right? Come on. Let me make sure you're okay. Ally can heal those wounds, and the pain will vanish like magic. Wouldn't that be nice?"

Again, she just stared at him, but her tail was no longer thumping the floor.

"Maybe I'm messed up, but even though you're covered in blood, I think you're way too cute right now."

The cat's eyes narrowed, and her face scrunched up into *the* crankiest expression he'd ever seen. The rage was gone. In its place was utter exasperation. Apparently, Mila had interpreted his compliment to her and the cat merely found it pathetic.

After one last warning hiss at the still-unconscious jackal, the cat regally padded her way to Dominic, annoyance in every step. With all that fur, she shouldn't look so graceful, but she did.

"Good girl." Keeping his touch light, he stroked her thick, lush coat as he whispered nonsense to her. Surprisingly soft, her rich gray fur had white tips, as if dusted with frost.

Not doubting for a single second that she'd tear a strip off his face if he made any wrong moves, Dominic kept his touch as gentle as his voice. Her eyes drifted shut as he scratched behind one of her small tufty ears. The cream fur inside them matched the patches on her chin, throat, and underparts.

Purring, she looked up at him through round eyes that were accentuated by the concentric white and black rims surrounding them. The storm had left her gaze.

"Come back, Mila," he whispered.

The cat rumbled a put-out sound. Bones snapped and popped as she shifted. And then Mila was crouched in front of him, panting.

She sighed. "Well, GQ, you somehow charmed my very antisocial cat. It's official. You have special powers."

Sitting upright, Dominic caught her nape and gave her a quick kiss before she could get to her feet. "She charmed me right back." As Harley stepped forward, holding Mila's clothes, Dominic snatched the jacket and wrapped it around Mila. Yeah, shifters were used to nakedness and Jesse was happily mated, but Dominic still didn't want the other male to get a look at her body. He frowned at the wounds on her face. "That bitch got you good right above your eye."

Ally approached. "I can fix that."

Mila stood, grinding her teeth against the pain as her movements pulled on her many rake wounds. She held still as Ally very simply laid a hand on her cheek. Healing warmth radiated through Mila, thick and soothing, and chased away the pain. When the Seer lowered her hand, Mila blew out a breath. "Thanks."

"How are you feeling?" asked Harley, passing Mila the rest of her clothes.

"Fine, albeit pissed with that bitch on the floor."

"There's no ID on her," said Jesse, bending over the body.

"Watch her for me while I just go wash and dress," Mila said to no one in particular. In the small attached bathroom, she quickly showered and then pulled on her underwear, tank top, and jeans. When she walked back into the greenroom with her jacket in hand, she saw that the jackal—her clothes and face bloody and shredded—was wide awake. Her inner cat hissed and swiped out her paw, claws unsheathed.

"I have to question your IQ," Harley said to the redhead. "Mila's kind are one of the most vicious breeds of shifter. Seriously, didn't anyone ever tell you not to fuck with a pallas cat?"

The jackal didn't respond to Harley. No, her attention was on the male wolf who was staring at her with a promise of death in his eyes.

It was . . . strange. If asked, Mila would have replied that, yes, she knew exactly how Dominic would react in a situation like this. Knew he would stand aside, let the situation play out, and leave the weight of it to another enforcer or shifter of a higher rank—not out of fear or an inability to deal with the situation, but because Dominic was all about "fun." People who lived for fun tended to leave the serious stuff to others, just as serious people didn't often go in search of fun—it was only natural.

But there was Dominic, crouched in front of the jackal, his expression remote and unreadable. He didn't look tense. Wasn't rigid with repressed anger. He seemed as steady and in control as always, but there was none of his usual impishness there. No emotion at all.

His dominance was usually so subtle, but not right then. It pulsed around him like a living thing; his power and intensity had never been more evident. That laser-sharp focus of his was locked on the jackal—and not in a way that could melt a girl's bones and fire her need for him. No, it was in a way that could make someone's fight-or-flight instinct kick in *fast.*

Right then, Mila didn't feel like she was looking at the person who'd been pursuing her for the past week. *This* guy had a coldness to him. He was cunning, hard to faze, unforgiving. And she knew instinctively that he would kill without blinking.

Mila had always suspected that Dominic deliberately came across as relatively harmless so that people underestimated him. But, yeah, she hadn't expected to find this kind of darkness when he peeled back the layers.

"I'm going to ask you this once," Dominic said to the jackal, his voice low. Even. Calm. It was a tone that said he had no wish to harm her . . . but he would. And he wouldn't feel much of anything when he did. "Just once. And if you're smart, you'll answer my question. And you'll answer it honestly. If you don't, you'll find out how a Phoenix Pack interrogation goes."

The jackal winced, and Mila didn't blame her. The pack's Beta male, Dante, was well known for being a master interrogator who never failed to get answers, no matter what it took to get them.

"*That's* assuming you survive the trip to my territory," Dominic added. "I have a feeling that Mila is eager to pop your head like a zit. I find the idea intriguing. So tell me: Why did you come at Mila?"

The redhead swallowed. "It wasn't personal."

Dominic's brows slowly lifted. "It wasn't personal?"

"I just came to collect on the bounty." Her eyes cut to Mila's, who must have betrayed her surprise, because the jackal smiled. "You don't know you have a price on your head? Oh, that's just"—her smile faltered at Dominic's growl—"unfortunate," she finished lamely.

Mila took two steps toward her, and the jackal tensed. "Who put the bounty on my head?"

"*That* I don't know," said the jackal.

"You don't know?"

"The website protects the anonymity of whoever requests the hit."

Dominic and Jesse exchanged a look that made Mila tense. "What?" she asked them. "What am I missing?"

"Let's just say we're familiar with this website," Dominic told her.

"So the jackal's telling the truth?"

"We have a way of finding out for sure." Dominic looked back at Jesse. "Make the call."

Jesse headed to the corner of the room, his phone to his ear. A few minutes later, the enforcer turned back to them, his expression grim.

"It's true?" Mila prompted.

Jesse nodded. "It's true. Your name is on that website."

As all eyes turned to her, Mila ground her teeth. She didn't know who'd put the bounty on her head, but she could guess whose fault it was that the bounty was there. "I'll kill him. I swear, I'll kill him. For real this time."

"Who?" demanded Dominic.

"My brother."

Sitting on the sofa with Dominic on her left and her father on her right, Mila rubbed at her forehead. Having a horde of shifters in her living room, all vibrating with rage, was never fun. Her parents, Vinnie, and his sons had all hit the roof on hearing what had happened in the greenroom. But they'd fallen quiet when Dominic and Jesse moved on to the subject of the website.

Her pride mates listened intently. They were all still and watchful, except for Valentina, who was doing more frenzied cleaning—sweeping the hardwood floor, dusting the shelves and mantel, wiping down the black tempered-glass coffee table, and even watering plants.

Dominic had insisted on driving Mila home in his SUV, and she'd been unable to disagree that it made good sense. People hoping to collect on the bounty would be watching out for her car, not his. No one would have expected her to leave the Velvet Lounge with him, and they wouldn't have spotted her through the darkened windows of his SUV.

She'd thought he'd simply drop her off outside her building and then head home—this wasn't his problem. Jesse could easily explain the website to her pride mates, and, well, Dominic had always struck her as someone who avoided getting involved in other people's problems. Apparently, she was wrong.

It was hard not to look at him a little differently now that she knew just how much darkness lived behind the flirtatious perv mask. There'd been a large dose of fearlessness there too. He'd had no compunction about trying to lure a pissed-off pallas cat to him. Had easily sprawled on his side, putting himself at a disadvantage. Hadn't hesitated to stroke the cat when she came to him. That was ballsy.

Just when Mila thought she had him figured out, he did something unexpected.

Her cat approved of his fearlessness and strength. Even liked the dangerous vibe he insisted on dialing down. Well, the bloodthirsty little thing would.

Finally, both Dominic and Jesse fell silent. No one spoke as everyone took a moment to fully digest what they'd heard.

"Let me get this straight," Vinnie finally said, propped on a tall stool he'd taken from the breakfast bar. "There's a website that lists people or groups of shifters that have bounties on their heads; anyone can collect on the bounties, providing they can give proof that the deed was done; but it's not possible for us to identify whoever took out the hit because the admin of the website withholds the personal details of all 'clients'?"

Dominic pursed his lips. "Yeah, that's about it."

"If this website has existed for years, how has it never been taken down?" asked James.

"People have been working on it for a long time," replied Jesse, sprawled on an armchair. "It's not as simple as tracking IP addresses. The site has numerous 'trip wires' that insert viruses into any computer trying to hack its way in. Also, those wires continuously change, much like a moving labyrinth—something my Alpha's contact hasn't seen before or since. The people working to smash through the protective measures of the website believe they're finally close to identifying its creator. The problem is that it's part of the Dark Web. That means it's not accessible to regular users in the first place, and then the admin has added extra layers of cutting-edge defense and obfuscation on top of that."

Vinnie's frown deepened. "How have I never heard of this website?"

"A lot of people haven't," said Dominic. "If someone hadn't issued bounties on both my pack and the Mercury Pack through the website, I doubt we'd have heard of this hit list either."

Valentina tapped her foot. "Those thugs who turned up outside our building, Mila . . . They warned you that you would regret not cooperating, yes?"

Mila rubbed at her nape. "Yep."

"Whoever sent them must have put a high price on her head, hoping it would flush Alex out," said Tate, Vinnie's Beta and his eldest son. Like his brother, Tate was powerful and dominant enough to run his own pride. Thankfully, more than one natural-born alpha could exist within a pallas cat pride, or both Tate and Luke would have had to leave.

Vinnie nodded, his jaw tight. "I agree. It's a high bounty, which means people who wouldn't normally bother our kind might be willing to risk it."

"We need to find Alex and ask him who he pissed off," said Tate. "Until we know who they are, we can't deal with them ourselves."

"It makes sense that he'd disappear off the face of the earth at a time when someone's got it in for him," Jesse commented. "He's probably lying low, waiting for the trouble to blow over."

"Alex wouldn't hide or run," said Mila. "He definitely wouldn't leave others to deal with any fallout. It's not uncommon for him to go off the radar when he's roaming. It's a wolverine thing."

"Any chance he's with your family, Valentina?" asked Luke, who was Head Enforcer.

Valentina shook her head. "I checked. No one has heard from him."

"I'm surprised he's even allowed in Russia after what happened," said Luke. "Isn't Interpol still pissed at him for leveling the police headquarters?"

It was Mila who answered. "Yeah, but they're too scared of my uncles to refuse them anything, let alone access to their nephew." Only Alex could escape a locked cell, free the other prisoners so they'd serve as a distraction, then use a few simple household products to create an explosion before breaking out. To be fair, the charges against him had been utterly false.

"We'll find him." Vinnie looked at Mila. "In the meantime, you'll need to be careful. You'll be safe enough while around these parts. The entire pride will have eyes on your surroundings."

"She'll also be protected while at the club," Jesse vowed. "My mate is infuriated by what happened tonight. She considers Mila a friend, not just an employee. We'll ensure she's safe while there, although I will note that she doesn't need our protection in a confrontation."

Vinnie nodded. "Yes, but assassins don't normally get close to their targets. They usually use firearms and shoot from a distance." His brows drew together. "I'm surprised the jackal didn't."

"She said she liked to get up close and personal with her 'marks,'" Mila told him. "I'll be careful, and I'll make it as hard as I can for anyone to get to me. Hopefully we find Alex soon, because identifying the asshole who put out the hit is our best chance at making all this end."

They talked for a few more minutes, and then everyone began to disperse until there was only GQ and her parents. Mila was just about to send him on his way when her mother moved to stand in front of him, her hands on her hips.

"Tell me, wolf," said Valentina. "How is it you know my Mila so well that you would go into her dressing room without knocking first?"

He stared up at Valentina for a good few seconds and then gave a fast shake of his head. "I'm sorry, what did you say? Every time you speak, I get so caught up in your accent that I don't really process the words."

Her mother's mouth kicked up into a tiny reluctant smile. It had to be a trick of the light or something, Mila thought, because Valentina Devereaux rarely smiled.

James leaned into Mila and whispered, "Oh, this one's good."

Her frown back in place, Valentina looked Dominic up and down. "You say you coaxed her cat to you. That makes you either bold or stupid. Which is it?"

"She was bleeding a lot," said Dominic, seeming to sober at the memory. "I needed to be sure she was okay."

"Bold it is," Valentina decided, and Mila could see that her parents now instantly liked him for his answer. "Good. Stupid is weak. I *despise* weakness."

"I'm guessing you're the wolf who wrote his number on Mila's hand," James said to him. "Evander only referred to you as 'Lothario.'"

Dominic nodded. "Yes, sir, that was me."

Mila's brows lifted. *Sir?*

"And did she call you?" James asked.

Dominic let out a sigh that was heavy with disappointment. "No, sir, she did not."

Again with the *sir.* Mila rolled her eyes.

"And yet, here you are." Valentina pursed her lips. "It is good you are as stubborn as she is."

Dominic smiled. "I like that she's strong-willed, Mrs. Devereaux."

"Is that so?" Valentina lifted a brow. "What else do you like about our Mila?"

Okay, enough was enough. "Mom—"

James raised a hand. "Don't interrupt the wolf, sweetheart, this is getting interesting."

"I like that she's genuine and confident," Dominic went on. "I like that she knows her own self-worth and fully respects herself. I like that she'll call people on their bullshit—me included—and I like the way she absolutely owns a stage whenever she walks on it. And, although it might be considered odd, I like that her cat is undeniably vicious when she needs to be."

Mila wasn't gonna lie, her belly fluttered a little at that declaration. The bastard was good with words. Her feline sure did like the latter comment.

Her mother watched him for a moment, her face unreadable, and then gave a short nod. "You may call me Valentina. This is James, Mila's father."

Mila's mouth thinned as her father actually shook GQ's hand with a freaking smile. Hell, they might as well have said, "Welcome to the family."

Mila stood. "All right, I think we're all done here. I need to make some calls and redouble my efforts to get ahold of Alex. GQ, I'm sure I'll see you at the club sometime. Mom, Dad—before you demand it of me, yes, I promise to be careful when I'm out and about. If you hear from Alex, please call me right away; I'll do the same for you." She gestured at the front door, hoping they'd all file out. They didn't. Hell, they didn't even move.

"You should come for dinner at our home sometime," Valentina said to Dominic. It wasn't so much an invitation as an instruction.

His smile wide, he nodded. "It will be my pleasure."

"Come along, James, we have calls to make." She cupped Mila's chin. "Be extra vigilant, Mila."

Standing, James pressed a kiss to Mila's temple. "Stay safe, sweetheart. I'll see you soon." Her parents then said their goodbyes to Dominic and left.

Pushing off the sofa, GQ turned to her. "I like them."

Mila sighed. "Why are you still here?"

Honestly, Dominic was hesitant to leave her. Not that he intended to stay the night—that would break one of his personal rules. But walking out wouldn't be easy. He knew she could take care of herself just fine. Knew her apartment building had such top-notch security that it would be next to impossible for intruders to penetrate it. Really, she probably couldn't be in a safer place than she was at that moment.

But that didn't stop him or his wolf from worrying. The female had a fucking bounty on her head. Dominic just kept thinking about how differently tonight could have gone if her cat wasn't, well, a total badass.

He glanced around. "I like your apartment. It's . . . warm. Airy." Best of all, it smelled of her. His wolf had grown very partial to that delectable scent.

"You're not staying here, if that's where this is going."

"But it's cold outside."

She rolled her eyes. "You'll survive."

He began to advance on her, gratified at the sound of her pulse spiking. "All right, I'll go now." Although he wanted to know more about her move to Russia, he could see that this wasn't the time to talk about it. She was tired, and she'd had a shock tonight. It could wait until tomorrow. "I want another taste of that mouth before I go. Are you gonna give me that?"

She lifted her chin. "No."

"Hmm. Then it looks like I'll just have to take it." He gripped her chin and closed his mouth over hers, sinking his tongue inside. He wanted to linger. Explore. Savor. But he also wanted to keep his eyes in their sockets, so he pulled back before she clawed at him for the bold move.

Cheeks flushed, she glared at him. "You need to stop doing that."

What he needed was to get her naked and shove his cock deep inside her. "It's your fault for tasting so good." Releasing her, he stepped back. "Call me if you need anything."

She frowned. "Like what?"

He could see it was a genuine question . . . as if she couldn't even begin to imagine why she'd turn to another for help. "A massage. Kiss. Bed fun. A seat."

"A seat?"

He gestured at his face. "I can assure you, it'll be very pleasurable to sit on."

Unable to stifle a smile, she pointed at the door. "Out. Just get out."

"Fine," he said, backing up. "But be sure to get your rest and take your vitamins, Mila, because you'll soon be spending all night beneath me getting—"

"Out."

He chuckled. "Lock up after me." She slammed the door shut behind him. That only made him laugh harder.

CHAPTER SEVEN

The next morning, Dominic caught his Alphas on their way to breakfast. Standing in one of the compound's many tunnels, he gave them a rundown of Mila's situation. As Dante and Jaime were passing—and fighting over which of them got to hold Hendrix—they heard a little of the conversation and nosily came closer, wanting to hear more.

Rubbing his jaw, Trey exhaled heavily. "I had hoped that the website would be crushed *way* before now."

"I spoke with Shaya earlier," said Dominic. "Nick told her that Donovan's super close to cracking through the anonymity network. Then he'll not only have the name of the creator of the website, he'll also have the identities of all those who've put out the hits."

"With any luck, Mila's brother will reappear before then." Taryn bit her bottom lip. "It's weird that no one has been able to get in touch with him. Do you think something might have happened to him?"

"Mila said this kind of thing's not unusual for Alex," Dominic told her. "He's a wolverine—they're notorious for roaming. He doesn't use his phone or the internet while on his travels."

Jaime's brows flew up. "He's a wolverine? Seriously? That's awesome. I find them *fascinating*."

Cradling their son, Dante frowned at his mate. "Fascinating? What is wrong with you?"

"I think we've been over that already," said Jaime. "Several times, even."

Taryn took a step toward Dominic. "So . . . you seem to like this Mila a lot. I've heard her sing—and, hell, she's amazing—but I've never spoken to her. Tell me about her."

So he did, but it wasn't long before he cut himself off and frowned at his Alpha female. "Why are you smiling at me like that?"

"You *like* her like her," said Taryn, beaming.

He shrugged, nonchalant. "She's a likable person."

"You should bring her here," Jaime told him, eyes bright. "We'll be nice, I promise."

"You know you can't rely on your twisted charms with this one, right?" Taryn patted his arm. "I'm sure you've been full of compliments, but—considering your reputation—she knows you're good with pretty words. She's not going to be wowed by them. You'll need to give her something you haven't given others. Something that shows it's different with her."

"No, I don't," said Dominic. "You're reading more into this than you need to."

Dante sighed. "So even though you clearly like her, you still want nothing more than a fling?"

A muscle in Dominic's cheek ticked. "She's entering into an arranged mating soon."

Taryn's mouth fell open. "No way."

"Yes." Dominic couldn't quite understand it—Mila could do so much better than that. "She'll be living in Russia."

Jaime exchanged a look with Taryn and then declared, "Well, I for one think you should spend with her what time she has left as a single woman."

Taryn raised a hand. "I second that."

"Right now, I'm more worried about the assassin situation than I am about her moving to Russia," said Dominic.

"The Olympus Pride is strong, and they rally around each other," Trey reminded him. "Mila will be well protected."

Dominic knew that. Still, he'd thought about trying to talk her into staying on his territory, where it would be next to impossible for a hit man to get to her. He'd practiced the conversation over and over in his mind, thought about what ways to broach the idea with her, but he always hit a wall. Mila would never hide—especially when it wouldn't solve the problem. The bounty would still be there, and anyone hoping to collect on it could hurt her pride mates to flush her out . . . just as she suspected someone was threatening *her* life in order to flush her brother out.

Hearing his cell phone ring, Dominic fished it out of his pocket. Not recognizing the number on the screen, he felt his brow furrow. Nonetheless, he answered, "Hello?" The voice on the other end of the line made him smile.

"You seem a little distracted today."

Shutting the cash register, Mila blinked at Dean. "I'm good. Just a little tired. How's Finley?"

Dean's mouth curled. "Aside from having a bump on his head after he tried and failed to ride his cousin while said cousin was in their bobcat form, he's fine. Hey, I went to the Velvet Lounge last night. I hadn't been to the club before, so I had no idea you performed there. You have an amazing voice."

"Well, thanks."

"My girlfriend's a big fan of music, which is why she's constantly dragging me to karaoke bars. She loves your voice. In fact, I think she now has a crush on you."

Mila chuckled, at a loss. "I don't really have a response for that."

"I'm not sure I would either, in your shoes. Take care, Mila."

Remaining at the desk, Mila merely waved. For the millionth time, she gave the view outside a quick once-over. There were no suspicious-looking characters lurking around that she could see. But then, an assassin would strive *not* to look suspicious, wouldn't they?

Really, she didn't need to worry. Tate, Luke, and the pride's enforcers were spread across the street, surreptitiously keeping a close eye on things while appearing otherwise occupied—relaxing on benches, painting shop doors, cleaning store windows, hanging near the mechanic shop under the guise of waiting for their cars to be fixed. She'd know something was wrong the moment they sprang into action.

Of course, any assassin who came along would no doubt spot Tate, Luke, and the enforcers. But that was the point. Vinnie wanted it to be clear that this would be no easy job. The only reason the cats weren't out-and-out patrolling the streets was that it would attract the attention of humans.

The best time for anyone to attack Mila would be while she was far from her pride, which was exactly why she didn't intend on going far. Why make it easy for the people wanting to collect on the bounty? No one with any sense would strike at her while close to so many pallas cats. Then again, no one with any sense would fuck with a pallas cat pride *at all*, so anyone who came at her had to be a total fruitcake.

Mila quickly tidied her station and then announced to the other barbers, "I'm taking a quick coffee break before my next client arrives." Which wouldn't be for another fifteen minutes.

Archie looked away from his client long enough to give her a brief nod. "Make me one, would you?"

"And me," said Evander, cleaning his shears. "Black. No sugar."

She sighed at him. "I don't think I've ever met anyone else who doesn't always take their coffee the exact same way." Evander changed it up all the time. Earlier, he'd had it extra milky.

Evander shrugged. "I like variety."

"Or maybe you've just never tasted the perfect cup of coffee," she suggested. "When you do, there'll be no going back; no changing it around."

He grunted. "If finding perfection means I'll no longer enjoy variety, I'm not interested."

Her nose wrinkled. "Did you just fart?"

He didn't even look up from his shears. "No, sweetheart, I blew you a kiss with my ass."

She snickered. He'd sounded perfectly serious. Always did. Evander wasn't a joker. Didn't people-please or even *try* to flirt. To be fair, he didn't have to. He possessed a sexy sort of arrogance that reeled females in. His imperious frown somehow made him hotter. She'd crushed on him a little when she was younger, but it faded fast—they just didn't gel *that way.* Still, she could appreciate the pretty picture he made.

Hearing the door open behind her, Mila glanced over her shoulder. And her stomach rolled as in walked yet *another* male who easily drew women to his side. Each step fluid and deliberate, GQ sauntered toward her, his eyes so fiercely intent on her that a rush of sexual energy swept across her skin and heated her blood. Her cat lifted her head, watching him carefully.

Dominic shot her one of his panty-dropping smiles. "Ah, Mila, light of my life."

She sighed, going for annoyed when in truth she was anything but. She liked his company, even though he could be super weird when he chose to be. "What do you want now?"

His brow furrowed slightly. "Didn't you hear? I'm the new milkman. Want it in the front or the back?"

Struggling not to join the others in laughing, Mila shook her head. "It's official—you're whacked."

Evander tipped his chin at him in greeting. "You're early."

Mila frowned. "Early?"

"My appointment's not until five thirty," Dominic told her, eyes dancing with mischief. And then she understood.

"You're my next appointment, aren't you?" she grumbled. Evander must have penciled him in on her behalf, the bastard. "Well, you'll just have to wait; I'm on my coffee break."

Dominic followed her down a narrow hallway and then turned into the break room. "Coffee sounds good."

Making a beeline for the kitchenette, she quickly prepped the coffee machine, switched it on, and then started pulling mugs out of the cupboard. "Who brought my car back?" She'd noticed it parked in the lot outside her apartment building when she began her short walk to work this morning. *Exceedingly* short walk, considering she lived on the same street as the barbershop.

"I did last night," said Dominic. "My pack mate, Trick, drove me to the club and then followed me to your building."

"Ballsy of you to drive the car of someone who has a bounty on her head." She had to give him credit for that. Would even have thanked him if his arms hadn't snaked around her as he pressed his front against her back, catching her off guard. Then his mouth was trailing along her neck, lightly nipping and licking and bringing her nerve endings to life.

She slapped the hand that began roaming south. "Enough." He splayed his hand on her lower stomach, one fingertip excruciatingly close to her clit. A wicked need thickened her blood, tightened her nipples, and sent her pulse racing. Her body responded to him far too eagerly and intensely for Mila's liking.

His mouth grazed her ear. "I dreamed about you last night. Dreamed I was deep inside you."

The finger directly above her clit doodled a little circle that massaged and stretched the skin just enough to tug at the hood of her clit—fuck, that felt good.

"You were so fucking slick and hot. Tighter than anything I've ever felt. I woke up just before you came for me."

She swallowed. "Really turning up the intensity dial, aren't you?" When he channeled it just right, his innate charm could probably reduce any poor girl to a puddle of want. She opted not to tell him about her own dirty little dream—a dream during which he'd sent her body into total meltdown. She had the feeling he'd be able to do exactly that in real life. "I told you last night to let this go."

Sharp teeth raked over her neck. "You knew I wouldn't."

Refusing to let him unravel her control, she very casually poured coffee into four mugs. "You're only torturing yourself, GQ."

"You're right on that one," he said, surprising her. "There's really no point in me pushing for sex." Keeping one arm around her, he moved to prop his hip against the counter. "My cock . . . well, it died. Is it okay if I bury it in your pussy?" He smiled at her exasperated look. "Or you could try giving it some mouth-to-mouth. Hey, it might rise from the dead—you never know."

She handed him a steaming mug. "You have serious issues."

"Not something I haven't heard before."

After giving Archie and Evander their coffees, she settled on one of the plastic chairs in the break room with her own cup in hand.

Dominic grabbed the neighboring chair and angled it so that his front would face her side and he could bracket her chair with his spread thighs. He wanted to look at her. Wanted to watch the emotions flit across her face, see her eyes light with amusement, and get a flash of her dimple whenever her mouth curved.

Resting one arm over the back of her chair, he sipped at his coffee. "I noticed a lot of your pride mates are hanging around, keeping an eye on things. No sign of any bounty hunters?"

"All's been quiet on the Western Front so far."

"Good. You had any luck getting ahold of your brother?"

Her lips thinned. "No. And no one seems to have even the slightest idea where he could be. Let's move on to a subject that doesn't make my cat want to rip someone's arm off."

"All right." He tapped his fingers on the back of her chair. "You finish work at six?"

"Yes, but—"

"Good. We can go straight to dinner from here."

She sighed tiredly. "Even if I wanted to go out with you—which I don't—I couldn't. I'm eating at my parents' house tonight."

"I know. I was invited."

"My mom only said you should go for dinner 'sometime.'"

"Last night, yeah. But when she called me this morning, she said I should be there tonight at six." Dominic took a sip of his coffee as he watched her digest that. He almost laughed at the sour look on her face. "Don't ask me to cancel on them, Mila. It would be rude."

Mila ground her teeth. Oh no, this wasn't good. Valentina didn't invite just *anyone* to dinner. She preferred for meals to be family occasions. For her to invite an outsider, there had to be a purpose behind it. And Mila knew just what it was. "That woman is unbelievable. And my father is no doubt in on it."

"In on what?"

"They're using you, hoping they can push us together and it will keep me from moving to Russia."

Yeah, Dominic had figured as much. "I can't blame them for doing whatever they think it will take to keep you here." And honestly, he didn't want her cheating herself out of a real mating any more than her parents did.

Not that he could be the devoted mate that her parents wanted Mila to have, but he was pretty sure they knew that. They probably just wanted someone to get rid of those shadows in her eyes and make her have some fun, hoping it would be in some way healing for her. Before she could start ranting, he stood. "You got a restroom here?"

Her teeth grinding, she gestured at the hallway. "Second door on your left."

"Thanks, baby." After setting his mug on the table, he disappeared into the hall.

Huffing at his absentminded use of the endearment—and pretty damn annoyed that it had made her stomach flutter—Mila fisted her hand. It was literally seconds later that Joel entered the break room, looking sheepish. Her cat stood with a hiss, slicing out her claws.

"Hi," he said simply.

She summoned a smile for him, but it was somewhat strained. "Hi."

Joel took a deep breath. "Look, I'm sorry I lost it on you yesterday when you told me about the arranged mating. I shouldn't have yelled. I'm your friend; friends are supposed to support each other. I just . . . well, I want you to have a real mating. Plus, the other barbers don't cut my hair right, and there'll be no one to talk to about *Game of Thrones* if you're all the way in Russia."

"We can talk on the phone."

"You don't even know this Maksim guy, Mila. How can you be so sure about someone who's practically a stranger to you?"

She lifted a brow. "Didn't you just say friends are supposed to support friends? You're heading into 'you're making a mistake' territory again."

He cursed. "I'm sorry, I just don't get it. I feel like there's something I'm missing. Something you're not telling me."

"You're missing that I'm a big girl who can make her own decisions."

He exhaled heavily, and seconds of silence ticked by. "This is really what you want?"

"It's really what I want." More specifically, it was what she needed to do.

He sighed. "I can't honestly say that I'm behind you one hundred percent. I want you to stay, and I don't think you're making a move that's best for you. But I won't give you any more grief about it. Just . . . *please* be open to changing your mind."

"Glad to hear there'll be no more lectures."

He moved forward as if to join her at the table, but he stilled when Dominic stepped into the room. The two males eyed each other, one predator studying another. GQ gave him a casual nod and then strode purposely toward her. He returned to his seat and assumed the same exact body position as before, settling into her personal space as if he had every right. His closeness eased her cat ever so slightly, to Mila's surprise.

The males then went back to eyeing each other. The tension ratcheted up until testosterone practically swamped the air.

Joel glared at him. "I remember you. It's Dominic, right? Yeah, I heard plenty of stories about you from females too. They all said the same thing."

Dominic picked up his mug. "It's true—my dick really is that huge."

Mila snorted a laugh, and her coffee went down the wrong tube. *Motherfucker.* Coughing so hard her eyes teared up, she couldn't quite catch her breath.

"You're all right, just swallow it down." Dominic rubbed her nape. "That's it, breathe through your nose, relax your jaw. Just swallow a little more."

Oh, the bastard. Once she'd finally composed herself, she wiped at the tears in her eyes. "Sorry about that."

Joel cleared his throat. "Anyway, Mila, I'm cooking dinner tonight for Adele and her parents. Fancy joining us?"

"Already made plans to have dinner with my parents, but thanks."

"No problem. I wouldn't miss your mom's cooking either. I'm guessing she's making beef Stroganoff, since it's your favorite."

She got the feeling he threw that little fact in as a "Ha, I know her better than you" statement for GQ's benefit. Her cat didn't like the sly dig. "Probably."

Tugging on one of her curls, Dominic said, "Beef Stroganoff is sautéed beef in sauce, right?"

"Yep."

"Then why did your mom ask if I like sour cream?"

"She adds *smetana*, which is sour cream."

Joel tensed. "You're taking him as your guest?"

"Valentina invited me," Dominic told him, although his eyes were on Mila's hair as he playfully plucked at her curls.

Joel's eyes went diamond hard. "I see. Mila, can we talk in private for a minute?"

Dominic lifted a daring brow. "What, you can't talk smack about me while I'm right here? Because we both know that's what you're about to do."

Joel inclined his head. "Fine. Like I said, I've heard a lot about you. I don't want my friend being used by yet another player. She had enough of that shit from her ex."

"Commendable of you. But Mila's no pushover. She doesn't need anyone acting as a voice for her. If she wants me to leave, I'll leave."

Mila snorted. "No, you won't."

Dominic's mouth curved. "No, but it sounded good, didn't it?"

"It did." She looked up at Joel. "Thanks for the concern, but it's not needed."

"If you really think that, you haven't learned your lesson from Grant," Joel clipped.

Her cat snarled and lashed out with her claws. The way the feline saw it, Joel had relinquished his rights to her; he had no business interfering in her life. But Mila saw his interference for what it was—a subconscious drive to shield her, one that his instincts wouldn't allow him to ignore. His intention wasn't to hurt her. "You're back to lecturing me again."

His mouth tightened. "I just wish you were as protective of yourself as the people who care for you are." With that parting shot, he left.

Mila sighed, and her cat's hackles lowered. She needed to start locking the freaking break room door. Feeling Dominic's eyes on her, she stood. "Come on, let's get you sorted." Soon enough, she had him caped and reclining in her chair with a warm, moist towel over his face.

As she browsed the shaving products on the shelves, Evander sidled up to her and asked, "Have you taken Lothario up on his offer of 'fun' yet?"

"I heard that," said Dominic, his words muffled by the towel.

Mila tossed Evander a glare. "I told you, I'm not interested in being another notch on his bedpost."

"I heard that too," Dominic muttered.

"Well, we weren't whispering." Mila swiped off the towel, ignoring his chuckle, and patted his face and neck dry. As she applied a light coating of preshave oil, a low, contented growl rumbled out of him. Her cat kind of liked it.

"You smell good," he said, his voice pitched low.

"Thanks, I do try."

He chuckled. "Do you and Joel have some kind of history?"

At the mere mention of him, her cat's mood plummeted. "No. He's just a friend."

"He's very possessive of you."

"Protective," she corrected, grabbing a tub of shaving cream. "He's mated—you must have sensed it."

"I did. That doesn't mean he can't still have lingering feelings for someone he was once involved with."

"There has never been anything between me and Joel other than friendship."

Dominic watched her closely as she used a little shaving brush to apply the cream. She was telling the truth. And yet she wasn't. He didn't quite get it. Wondered if maybe she'd once tried to push for more than friendship with Joel before he mated and then had gotten her heart broken. "Your cat doesn't like having him around. I sensed her tension. Did he hurt you somehow? Reject you?"

She gave him a curious look. "I never had you down as nosy."

He shrugged. "What can I say? You intrigue me."

"Hmm. Right. I want to leave the shaving cream on for at least a minute."

Before she could walk off and busy herself elsewhere to escape the conversation, he grabbed her hand. "Fine. I'll drop the Joel thing. Besides, I have a question: Should we take a bottle of wine or something with us to dinner tonight?"

Her brows snapped together. "You can't be serious about going."

"I was invited."

"Only because my parents plan to use you in their little bid to keep me here."

"Your mother promised me Prague Cake, Mila. Now it's true that I don't know what that is, but you can't go wrong with cake in my experience. I'm not about to miss out on it just because I make you nervous."

She pulled her hand from his and planted it on her hip. "You do not make me nervous. You make me want to slap you."

Wrestling back a smile, Dominic said, "Hey, it's okay. You make me nervous too. That's why I get so shy around you. When you look at me all predatorily like that, it makes me feel like a baby gazelle about to get devoured by a lioness."

She crossed her eyes. "I don't know whether to laugh or finally give you that slap."

"As long as I'm deep inside you while you're slapping me around, I don't mind. It'll make it feel all forbidden and wrong."

She scrubbed a hand down her face, determined not to laugh. "We are not having sex, and you are not coming with me tonight."

"Oh, I'll be coming with you in multiple ways," he said with a wicked smile. "You know, I've never done dinner with the parents before."

"We're not a couple."

"No, but if you go along with it instead of fighting me on going to dinner, they'll think we just might become a couple. If, however, you don't turn up with me at your side . . . well, they could try their hands at matching you up with other males instead."

Fuck, he was right, Mila thought. Her parents could be relentless at times. Nothing stopped them once they got an idea in their heads. "Hmm. I suppose you *are* the lesser evil."

He smiled. "I knew you liked me."

"Unless you want to donate blood, be still." She rinsed the blade under hot water before taking that first swipe. It glided smoothly and effortlessly across his face and neck with each pass. Once she'd finished, she rinsed him off, applied some aftershave balm to his slightly damp skin, and then patted him dry with a towel. "There."

He glided his hand over his now butter-smooth skin. "Nicely done."

After he'd paid and left a far-too-generous tip, she said, "I just have a couple of things to do, and then we can go."

He gave her a pointed look. "Ten minutes, Mila. My face is leaving in ten minutes—be on it."

"*Oh my God.* Do you ever stop?"

"Being what? Charming? Funny? Irresistible?"

"Bizarre? Warped? Disturbed?"

"Hey, now, there's no need to get mean."

She stalked off, shaking her head. "Hopeless. You're totally hopeless."

CHAPTER EIGHT

Mila had no idea how he did it. Really. It was like he had some magical power that enabled him to enchant people or something. Valentina liked very few people, but she quickly developed a fondness for Dominic—it was apparent in the way she kept refilling his plate and regaling him with stories of her childhood.

Even James clearly liked him, and James didn't like *any* male who had designs on his only daughter. The three were chatting like they were lifelong friends, and Mila knew that Dominic would be invited to eat at this table again and again—even though her parents' matchmaking efforts would lead to nothing.

She supposed that part of why people quickly warmed to him was that he was super good at keeping the conversation light and easy. No invasive questions, no deep talk, no tricky topics like politics. He just joked and flattered and charmed, putting people at ease. It wasn't an act, though. He wasn't playing a part. He was quite simply easy to be around. But he also wasn't being *totally* himself.

Draping an arm over the back of her chair, Dominic absentmindedly traced little circles on her shoulder. Which was bold, really, considering her parents were *right there.* He didn't dial down his behavior around them. He still invaded Mila's personal space. Still touched her how and when he felt like it. Still hit her with cheesy lines, although they thankfully weren't *dirty.* Not that her parents would care if they were dirty—they found him hilarious.

She should push him away, but he was right that it would be simpler to let her parents believe their little plot was working. Also, she liked it when he touched her. Liked that it eased her cat, who was currently quite relaxed, enjoying the light atmosphere. The feline liked GQ a lot too—mostly because he made Mila smile.

Putting down her cutlery, Valentina took a sip of her wine. "You have spoken much about your pack," she said to Dominic. "But not of your family."

Pausing in doodling patterns on Mila's shoulder, Dominic shrugged. "My pack are my family."

"I heard it was once part of"—Valentina clicked her fingers a few times—"the Bjorn Pack. It split at one point, yes?"

"That's right," confirmed Dominic.

"Did your family leave with you when it split?" asked James, forking some beef.

Dominic drummed his fingers on the table. "No. My parents were dead by then. There was only my aunt and uncle, and they chose to stay behind."

Valentina lowered her glass, sobering. "I am sorry to hear they have passed."

"No siblings?" James asked him.

"One," said Dominic, his voice a little stilted. "He died before I was born."

Mila's eyes fell closed, stomach twisting. "Shit."

Dominic nodded. "Yeah."

Valentina rubbed his arm. "What happened to the boy?" Yeah, the woman was *that* comfortable around GQ, she felt no compunction about laying a question like that on him. But before Mila could tell him he didn't need to answer, he began to speak.

"My mother fell asleep at the wheel and crashed into a truck. She and my father survived. Tobias didn't."

Valentina's face went soft with sympathy. "Did she blame herself?"

Dominic looked at Mila, and she sensed he was thinking of lying or, at the very least, only giving half an answer. Finally, he turned back to Valentina and said, "I don't know. I haven't seen her in a long time, although I figure she's dead."

James blinked. "You're not sure?"

"She walked off when I was a teenager," Dominic explained. "My dad turned rogue and was killed. She never came back, and I'm assuming she didn't survive the breaking of their mating bond. But I don't know for certain."

Valentina once more patted his arm. "As you said, you have your pack. They are your true family."

His mouth curved ever so slightly. "Yes, they are."

A little while later, after they'd eaten her mother's Prague Cake—which was made with Viennese chocolate and absolutely *to die for*—Mila and Dominic were ready to leave. As he and James laughed about something or other, Valentina took Mila by the shoulders and led her to the front door.

"So much sadness in that boy," said Valentina. "He keeps it locked up tight. Buried so deep it cannot hurt him." She gave Mila's shoulders a little squeeze and then kissed her cheek. "My Mila will be good for him."

She sighed. "Mom—"

"Go on now." Valentina practically shoved her out the door. Then she was pulling Dominic into her arms, holding him like he was a long-lost son while James smiled at the sight. Mila was pretty sure her parents liked GQ more than they liked her.

Huffing to herself, she headed down the stairs to the floor below and her own apartment. There were fifteen floors, and Mila lived on the seventh.

Unlocking her front door, she was conscious that Dominic was right behind her. Really, she shouldn't have let him in; she should have insisted he go home. Instead, she not only invited him in, she got him a beer. He just had this way of making her forget all the other shit going on in her life. She needed that.

He took a quick swig of his beer. "Tell me more about this move to Russia. Make me understand why it's so important that you leave."

Okay, this wasn't making her forget the other shit going on in her life. Not at all. "I've put a lot of thought into this, Dominic. A lot. It's what I want."

"Are you certain about that?" he asked, his tone neutral. "Moving to Russia is a big step. It's one thing to stay somewhere for a few weeks on vacation; it's another to *live* there."

"I've been going to Russia at least four times a year since I was a kid. I know I'll be happy there." She leaned against the counter. "This will be a good thing for me, Dominic. Really. It's for the best."

"You have a mate somewhere out there who's waiting for you, Mila," he said gently. "Can you so easily give up on finding him?" There was no judgment in his voice.

Mila's hands fisted. "He's not waiting for me."

"And how could you know that?"

She didn't want to answer, and it made her think of that moment in her parents' apartment when he'd looked at her, unsure of how to respond to Valentina's question. He could have given a half-assed answer, but he hadn't. He'd been honest. Mila lifted her chin. "Because I already found him. He's committed to someone else."

Dominic stilled. "How committed?"

"He imprinted on her."

Head tilted, Dominic took a few steps toward her. "How can you know for sure he was meant for you if he's imprinted on someone else? His bond with his chosen mate should have blocked the frequency of the true-mate bond."

"We met before he fully imprinted on her. I sensed we were mates; he didn't."

"And you didn't tell him?"

She shook her head. "He's happy. I don't want to mess with that. Plus, I couldn't take him as my mate after seeing him bonded with another. And then there's the fact that my cat loathes him."

Dominic's eyes widened a little at that. "Loathes him?"

"It shouldn't be possible to hate your true mate, should it? But she does. And I can't blame her for that. The way she sees it, he's the other half of her soul so he should have chosen her. She feels betrayed. Rejected."

Pausing, Mila took a long breath. "At first, I hated him too. It wasn't real, though. More of a self-defense mechanism—if I hated him, I wouldn't want him. But the emotion had no real substance, so it faded over time. He hasn't done anything wrong. Lots of shifters imprint. Hell, I'm planning on doing the same thing. The female he chose makes him happy, so he decided to bond with her—who could blame him for that?"

Dominic sighed, thinking she had a better attitude toward the situation than most would have. So much about her made sense now, and he could even see why she'd want to hurry into an arranged mating. Discovering her true mate would never be hers had to have left her feeling empty. She was looking to fill the void and, although she might not realize it, didn't feel able to fully give herself to a real mating. "I'm sorry, baby."

She shrugged. "It is what it is."

"Did you know that Jesse and Harley aren't true mates? They imprinted."

"No, I didn't know that. Their bond is very strong."

"Imprint bonds can be just as strong as true-mate bonds."

"I know." Mila rolled back her shoulders. "I've accepted my situation. Made my peace with it. I'm ready to move forward."

"That doesn't mean you have to relocate to Russia and enter an arranged mating."

"I don't *have* to enter one, no. I'm *choosing* to see if there could be anything between me and Maksim."

Maksim . . . His wolf despised him already. "You say you've accepted that you won't have your true mate," said Dominic, keeping his voice gentle, "but that's not exactly true if you need to go all the way to Russia to find some peace, is it?"

"It's my cat who hasn't made her peace with it, not me. Every time she sees him and his female together, she grows a little bit more bitter. If she's not around them, maybe she can find contentment with someone else."

"Wait, what do you mean by 'she sees them?' They're local?"

She licked her bottom lip. "They're part of my pride. Adele is actually my cousin. You've met Joel already."

"Shit." That explained the male's behavior earlier, Dominic thought. Joel had developed an odd sort of attachment to her. Nothing remotely close to a mating bond, but something that made the male feel both protective and possessive. That wasn't good for Mila or her cat, and it was little wonder that she wanted to be far away from the pride.

Dominic put his bottle down on the counter. "Come here." He drew her to him, curling both arms around her. She didn't tense in his hold as he'd expected, she went pliant against him. His wolf rubbed up against her, wanting to soothe. "How many know about this?"

"Just Alex and my parents."

He rested his chin on the top of her head. "I can see why you feel the need to get away."

"You're not going to tell me I'm making a mistake and I should hold out for something better?"

"Do I think you could do better than an arranged mating? Yes, I do. But I can't blame you for trying to save your cat's sanity by putting some distance between you and Joel." Dominic also couldn't see her ever committing herself to someone she wasn't sure of, so there was every chance that things wouldn't work out between her and Maksim, but he didn't say that. She didn't need negative comments right then.

Mila pulled back enough to look up at him. "I'd really like to drop this now."

He wanted to know more about Maksim, but Dominic cautioned himself not to push. She'd already told him plenty, and it hadn't been easy for her. He wanted to ease the lines of strain on her face. Wanted her smiling and laughing, not dwelling on shit.

"All right." He brushed her curls away from her face. "I guess we can talk about how hot and desperate you are for me." Her mouth quirked a little, just as he'd hoped.

"Hot and desperate, huh?"

"Yeah, I'm all ears if you want to share. It's never good to hold stuff in."

She shook her head, incredulous.

"Come on, don't be shy. There's no shame in admitting that you find me hard to resist."

"Well, with all that warped charm, how could I not?" she said, her voice dry.

"Exactly. But, hey, it's fine if you don't want to talk. We could play a game instead."

"A game? I'm almost afraid to ask what kind of game your filthy mind has come up with."

"How about . . . *Titanic*?"

"*Titanic?*" she echoed, her brow furrowing.

"Yeah. When I yell 'Iceberg,' you go down." He watched as her smile widened and the lines of strain on her face smoothed out. It gave him a warm, fuzzy feeling to know he could make her tension slip away like that. He tucked her curls behind her ear, thinking how fucking beautiful she was. "Come on, Mila, I promise to return the favor." He dipped his head and pressed a kiss to her neck. "We're friends. Friends make each other come."

She chuckled. "No, they don't."

"Special friends do." He planted a kiss on the other side of her neck and inhaled deeply, filling his lungs with her scent. "Give in to me, Mila," he coaxed, his voice deep and thick with need. "Let me make you feel good."

Fighting the temptation building inside her, Mila squeezed her eyes shut. "Why do you have to push this?" Much to her embarrassment, it was almost a whine. "My rejecting you gave you a challenge, I get it, but—"

"You're not the first person who's turned me down. The difference between you and them? They were playing a game, wanting to have the upper hand so they could lead me around by my dick. But you . . . there aren't any mind games with you. No manipulations. You simply respect yourself far too much to be a faceless fuck to someone. I like that. Respect it. Respect *you*." Breezing his thumb along her cheekbone, he kissed the soft curve of her lush mouth. "You could never be a faceless fuck to me, Mila."

Maybe not, thought Mila, but she'd still never be more than a fuck, would she? "Yeah, well, I'm sure you have plenty of *special friends.* You don't need another one."

"Despite what you might think, I'm not someone who'll fuck anything that moves." But Dominic wasn't offended that she might think it—he'd carefully cultivated that image. "I have as many standards as the next person. I'm not ruled by my cock. In fact, I have more self-control than most. I just don't do commitment. Does that make me a bad person?"

"I never said you were a bad person. And I'm not asking you for commitment—"

"Then stop fighting me." He nibbled her lips with his own, tempting her, teasing her. "Don't you want me inside you, Mila? Don't you want to feel my cock stretching you . . . filling you . . . fucking you?" He grazed her bottom lip with his teeth and then swiped his tongue over the small hurt to soothe the sting. Her body melted slightly into his, and he sensed that she was close to giving in to him, but just not close enough.

He remembered what Taryn had said earlier. Mila knew he was good with words, she wouldn't be swayed by compliments. He needed to give her something he hadn't given the women in his past. He'd done it earlier when he gave her and her parents the truth about his family. He'd give her another truth now.

Dominic caught her face in his hands. "I haven't touched another female since I first saw you on that stage. I haven't wanted to. Haven't found one even remotely tempting. I want you so fucking badly, it's like there's no room for anyone else in my head. I have to know what it's like to be in you."

If Mila hadn't been looking right in his eyes, hadn't seen the pure sincerity glimmering there, she might not have believed him. There was also sheer determination there, and she knew he wasn't going to tip his hat and walk away. But if she did finally give him what he wanted, he might very well walk away afterward. The thrill of the chase would be sated, and then she might not hold any sexual interest for him. Maybe they'd bump into each other from time to time, and maybe he'd even do a little harmless flirting, but that would probably be it. And that thought was sad enough to make her swallow hard.

Continuing to fight him on this was pointless, though, Mila acknowledged. She'd cave at some point. She knew that now. Knew she was weakening. Why not just enjoy one night with him? If there was a repeat of it, great, but if not . . . well, like he'd once said, they'd have fun.

There were many rumors about Dominic's sexual prowess. She'd heard he was well endowed, had excellent recovery time, and was by no means a selfish lover. All points in his favor. And it would mean that she would have some wickedly fun memories to keep her warm when he was gone.

Dominic cursed when she backed up, and he had to fist his hands against the urge to reach for her and yank her to him. He wasn't leaving. Not yet. "Mila—" She whipped off her shirt, revealing very pretty breasts spilling out of a black lacy bra. "Fuck."

"Well, I suppose we could," said Mila, needing it to be clear that he hadn't seduced her into acting against her better judgment. Needing it to be clear that this was *her* decision. Mouth curved, she backed up, intending to lead him to her bedroom. He matched her step for step, following her, eyes locked on hers. She lowered the zipper of her fly, and it was like the sound acted as a trigger. He lunged.

Bunching his hands in her curls, Dominic took complete possession of her mouth. Dominated. Ravished. She tasted of chocolate and the same need that was roaring through him, thickening his cock and testing his control. An instant palpable heat ignited between them and sparked the air like static electricity.

Keeping his grip tight on her hair, Dominic angled her head, sinking his tongue deeper. Eating at her mouth, gorging on her taste. He was fucking ravenous for her. Couldn't think about anything except being balls-deep inside her.

Lifting her, he pressed her against the doorjamb, feeling her nipples stabbing at him through her bra. He punched his hips forward, roughly grinding against her clit, as he consumed that mouth he was absolutely obsessed with. His wolf urged him on, pushing him to take and possess her right there and then.

Legs tight around his waist, Mila sifted his hair through her fingers, raking her nails over his scalp. His kiss was greedy, intoxicating, and a blatant demand for surrender. His tongue licked and tangled with hers; his teeth nipped and grazed but didn't mark. She couldn't drag enough air into her lungs, but she didn't care. Only wanted more.

She was wet and hot and so damn needy. Delicious endorphins flooded her brain and raced through her body. An untamed sexual energy swept her under, dragging her to a place where there was no room for logic or rational thought.

She let her head fall back as he gripped her ass and rocked his thick cock against her clit. Sexual aggression was coming off him in waves, and he kept letting out little snarls that *totally* pushed her buttons. The guttural sounds fired her cat's need.

Mila bit down on his lip. "Fuck me." His mouth latched on to her pulse and sucked. She melted into him, giving whispered directions to her bedroom as he carried her farther into the apartment. The moment he lowered her onto the mattress, she tugged at his shirt. "Off."

He obliged her and, yeah, she was pretty sure she almost came. Solid shoulders, hard chest, washboard abs. Just inches upon inches of honed muscle. And when he shed the rest of his clothes, revealing yet more toned skin, a very defined *V* at his hips, and one hell of an impressive cock, she might have moaned a little in sheer delight.

As he dragged off her jeans and thong, she took a moment to admire the very detailed tattoo of a red Chinese dragon that rested above his heart, ran along his shoulder, and curled around his bicep. "Tell me why you got—"

"Later," he said, clawing off her bra. Dominic let his eyes drift over her, absorbing every line and curve. She was slender and toned with the perkiest breasts and delicately flared hips. Her skin was smooth and sleek . . . fuck, he wanted to bite it. "Beautiful," he rumbled.

Filling his hands with her petal-soft breasts, Dominic leaned over and sucked a nipple into his mouth, loving the texture of her. Her claws raked his back hard enough to sting but not hard enough to break the skin. His wolf growled in dissatisfaction, wanting her mark on his flesh.

Dominic drew her breast deeper into his mouth and let her feel the edge of his teeth. She hissed, but the sound turned into a gasp as he latched on to her other nipple. He lavished it with the same attention—sucking, licking, and lashing it with his tongue.

Arching into him, she grabbed a tuft of his hair. "Dominic. In me. Now."

"Typical cat. Likes instant gratification." He trailed kisses down her body, pausing briefly to explore the intriguing peacock feather tattoo on her side, and then knelt at the foot of the bed. He spread her legs wide and drew the scent of her need deep into his lungs. A growl rattled his wolf's chest. "Fuck, you smell good." Dominic nuzzled her swollen, glistening folds. "It makes me wonder . . ."

She braced herself on her elbows. "What?"

Parting her folds with his thumbs, he blew on her clit. "If you taste just as good." He swiped his tongue through her slit, scooping up all that cream. "Hmm, you do." He clamped his mouth around her pussy.

Mila's eyes fluttered shut. "Oh God," she rasped, fisting the sheets. His incredibly skilled tongue licked, traced, probed, and swirled, exploiting every erogenous zone that he found. Her breaths came quick and fast as the friction built inside her. Hot sparks of need danced over her heated skin, and her pussy ached to be filled.

Hovering on the brink of a powerful orgasm, she bit her lip almost hard enough to draw blood. "I'm gonna come." And the bastard eased off. Her cat's upper lip quivered in annoyance, and Mila hissed through her teeth. *"Dominic."*

Lapping lazily at her pussy, Dominic hummed. "Just hold on for me a little longer." She tasted so fucking good, made the most amazing, smoky, cock-hardening moans. He sipped and licked and savored, stringing her body tighter and tighter without throwing her over the edge. She cursed and squirmed and made a noise that was suspiciously close to a sob. He needed her this way. Needed her mindless and so desperate to come that she couldn't think straight. Couldn't think of anything but him.

He dipped his tongue inside her dripping-wet pussy, seeking more of her cream, and her walls fluttered around his tongue. Yeah, she was close. "That's it, come." He wrapped his lips around her clit, sucked it gently, and rammed two fingers inside her pussy. She came hard and loud, claws slicing into the bedsheet, her pussy clenching his fingers. And Dominic *had* to fucking know how that pussy felt around his cock.

Panting, thighs shaking, Mila sagged into the mattress. The rumors about this guy's sexual expertise clearly were not exaggerated. Awesome.

As his weight settled over her, she opened her eyes and gripped his shoulders. So much leashed power under all that sleek tanned skin, she thought. It was an aphrodisiac to her cat. "You've got some skills, GQ."

His mouth curved into a languid smile. "Glad you think so." Sliding a hand under her ass, he tilted her hips. "Wrap your legs around me, Mila. That's it." He lodged the thick head of his cock in her pussy and heard himself groan. Fuck, she was so hot. So tight. It was a struggle not to slam home in one smooth, aggressive thrust.

Mila bit her lip as, inch by slow inch, he sank his cock inside her. Her pussy burned as it stretched around him, but she didn't care about the pain. Didn't care that she felt so full she could burst. She needed him to *move.*

Dominic growled into her ear. "I'm going to fuck you now, Mila. Going to fuck you so hard, it'll be burned in your memory. I'll always be up here," he added, tapping her temple. "You'll never forget the feel of me. Never." He withdrew in one slow glide, grinding his teeth as her pussy tried sucking him back in. And then he rammed home, snarling at the sharp dig of her claws in the flesh of his back. "Fuck, yeah."

Dominic brutally powered into her. Rough. Deep. Far more territorial than he had a right to be. "And you thought you could stop me from having this pussy." He bit her earlobe. "I can have it any time I want. You'll give it to me whenever I want it. Won't you?"

"Fuck you," hissed Mila, holding on for the ride as he slammed harder, faster. Another thing she'd heard about GQ was that he was dominantly calm in bed, always smoothly in control. Yet, here he was wildly fucking into her body like he couldn't get deep enough. She wondered if any other female had seen him like this.

Mila sucked in a breath as he hooked her legs over his shoulders and slid that thick cock even deeper inside her. Then he was powering into her again, his pace absolutely merciless, his fingertips biting into her thighs so hard she knew they'd leave bruises.

Watching the jaunty bounce of her breasts, a sudden image of coming all over them flashed in Dominic's mind. Fuck, he wanted that. Wanted to see his come sink into her skin. Wanted to mark her with it. Which, of course, he wouldn't do. But now that he'd thought about it, now that the image was in his head, he couldn't shake off the fantasy of it.

Growling, he curled over her and bit her lip. Her pussy was tightening and superheating around his cock, and he knew he wouldn't last much longer. "I'm going to come inside you so fucking hard," he snarled. "Gonna shoot so fucking deep." Knowing her clit would still be sensitive, he found it with his fingers and pinched it just right.

Hot waves of sheer bliss fired through Mila, arching her spine. She let out a choked scream as she imploded, hips bucking, claws digging into his back.

"Fuck." White-hot pleasure tightened his balls, shot through his cock, and whipped up his spine as Dominic came so hard, he felt it in his teeth. He buried his face in her neck as he pumped jet after jet of come deep inside her. Then it was like the strength left them both, and they slumped into the mattress.

Breathing hard and shaking with aftershocks, Mila weakly stroked his back. Damn, she hadn't felt so utterly sated in a very long time. Although he was surprisingly heavy, she didn't try shoving him off. She liked having his weight over her.

As the minutes went by, and they each fought to get their breathing back under control, she idly danced her fingers over his back and traced little scars she found. It was oddly relaxing and . . . wait, his cock was twitching inside her. Thickening. "God, the rumors are true about your recovery time, aren't they?" She felt his mouth curve against her neck.

He swiveled his hips. "I really hope you took my advice and got your rest last night, Mila," he said softly, "because you won't get much of it tonight."

Mila's eyes snapped open when she heard someone creeping around her room—someone who was exceedingly good at not making a sound as they moved, but there was no way of sneaking up on a cat. She didn't panic because, despite it being dark, she could see that the dark figure was Dominic. The digital clock on the nightstand said 3:36 a.m. Ah, it seemed that he wasn't staying. But then, she'd known he wouldn't.

It didn't bother her, especially since she'd known exactly what last night was—sex at its most basic, nothing more. And there had been *plenty* of said basic sex. He'd made her no promises, hadn't bullshitted her to get into bed. But since it would be fun to make him feel awkward about creeping around, she did something guaranteed to get his attention.

Dominic's movements stilled. "Why are you humming *The Pink Panther* theme music?"

"Just thought you might like some appropriate background music while you sneak around my room like a thief," she teased, her voice drowsy with sleep.

He moved to the side of her bed, fully dressed—which was a shame, because one last flash of his body would have been nice. "I have to go," he told her. "Didn't want to wake you."

"I'm a light sleeper." Closing her eyes, she snuggled deeper into the pillow. "Now you get out there and own that walk of shame. Oh, and be careful in case any hit men are hanging around." The bed dipped, and then his hand was brushing the curls away from her face. She didn't look at him. Just lay there as he pressed what was clearly a goodbye kiss to her forehead.

"Sleep well, Mila," he whispered, and then he was gone. And for some inexplicable reason, she got the feeling it was highly unlikely that he'd ever seek her out again. Ignoring the way her stomach twisted at that thought, she squeezed her eyes shut even tighter.

Her cat lay down, sulking. For just a little while, the feline had felt something close to peace. Now that feeling was gone.

CHAPTER NINE

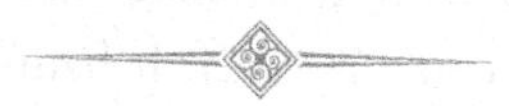

Heading to his Alpha's office, Dominic rolled his shoulders, trying to shake off the tension riding him. It didn't work. Nothing had.

Technically, he should have been relaxed, considering he'd fucked Mila into oblivion the night before. He should have been walking around with the stride of a sexually satisfied male. Instead, he was antsy. Edgy. Like he'd been trapped in a crowded elevator for hours.

He'd finally had her. Finally knew how she tasted, finally knew how it felt to be inside her. Fuck, it had been better than he'd imagined. So much better. But it hadn't cooled his hunger for her. If anything, it had only intensified it. And his wolf wouldn't fucking stop growling at him to track her down.

The second Dominic had thrust inside that deliciously tight pussy, triumph had filled him—not smugness but the sheer male satisfaction that came with finally having that thing you want most. Relief had also coursed through him, relief at being exactly where he'd needed to be for what felt like too long.

There'd also been a greedy possessiveness. It had crawled over him, clawed at his gut, urged him to mark her—something, as a rule, he never did to a woman. And it had taken everything he had not to bite hard into Mila's neck as he exploded inside her.

He'd never needed to fuck someone so hard before, never wanted to see his come sink into a woman's skin, never needed to be permanently etched into a person's memory. The problem was . . . he was pretty sure she was now etched into his.

He hadn't had his usual ironclad control with Mila. Hadn't even dug for it, if he was honest. No, he'd *wanted* to take her that roughly. Wanted it to be a night she remembered.

Another thing he never did was feel awkward if he got caught leaving in the middle of the night. She'd made light of it, hadn't seemed to care. That should have made it easier. It hadn't. Because, for the first time in his life, he truly had felt shamed by it. She deserved better, but he didn't have "better" to give her, so he'd left. What he'd really wanted to do was crawl back in that bed with her.

He hadn't originally had any intention of sticking to a one-night stand, but he wasn't sure it would be a good idea to have a repeat of last night. Not given how many of his rules she'd tempted him to break. Not given that his wolf had become quite possessive of her. It would be bad for the beast to develop an attachment to her, considering she was immigrating to Russia and planning to mate with some bastard called Maksim.

His wolf snarled, and Dominic snapped his teeth. The thought of another male's hands on her made him feel far too dangerous.

Reaching Trey's office, Dominic rapped his knuckles on the door. The Alpha had summoned him by text, saying there was a "delicate matter" that needed to be discussed, so Dominic wasn't surprised to find both his Alphas and Betas, the Head Enforcer, and the other four enforcers inside the room.

Both Alphas were tense as bows, and that raised his wolf's hackles. Something was wrong. The others were exchanging uneasy looks, clearly no wiser than Dominic about why they'd all been summoned.

Sitting on the leather rolling chair behind his desk, Trey gestured for Dominic to close the door behind him. He did so and then stalked farther into the room, his nose twitching at the scents of air freshener, stale coffee, and hot ink from the printer. Except for the whooshing of the ceiling fan, there were only the sounds of birds chirping and trees rustling filtering through the partially open window. The hint of a breeze carried with it the ozone scent of rain.

"What's happened?" asked Dominic.

Trey ceased tapping his pen on a sheet of paper that rested on his desk. "I received a call from Emmet Pierson twenty minutes ago."

Dominic's wolf peeled back his upper lip. "What did he want?"

"Let me guess," said Roni, her face scrunched up in distaste. "Rosemary went whining to him that her visit here came to nothing."

"Yes, she did," said Trey. "But that's not all. Rosemary tried to kill herself last night."

Jaime's mouth fell open. *"What?"*

Just as stunned, Dominic could only stare at his Alpha.

"She swallowed a bunch of pills." Trey rubbed at his nape. "She's in the hospital now. The doctors pumped her stomach. She's alive, but her father says she's not responsive—just sitting there, staring at the walls."

Dominic cursed under his breath. "He blames me, doesn't he?"

Trey nodded. "The day she left here, she went straight to him; told him that you're her true mate and that when she made that same claim to you, you laughed at her and sent her away."

Dominic's wolf bared his teeth. "She's not my true mate."

Trey raised his hands. "I never thought she was."

"I don't think *she* even believes it herself. Not really."

Perched on the edge of the desk, Taryn tilted her head. "Why do you say that?"

"She didn't make that bullshit claim until I told her she was wrong about me wanting to be a perpetual bachelor. I think she just blurted out that we were true mates in the hope that it might make a difference to me." Dominic raked his fingers through his hair. "Fuck."

"That's not all." Trey gripped his pen tightly. "Pierson made a statement to an online anti-shifter paper."

Sighing, Trick leaned against the tall filing cabinet, careful not to knock the photos and drawings that had been attached to it with magnets. "Lay it on us."

Trey lifted the sheet of paper from his desk. "To sum it up, he talked of how his daughter is a 'latent' wolf, said that having shifter blood ruined her life. He basically blames it for her divorce, since he believes she'd have otherwise conceived children with her ex-husband. Then he mentioned you, Dominic. Said shifters talk about how precious our true mates are, but that's nothing but a lie. Said that you mated Rosemary, formed the bond, but then turned her away because her animal never surfaced."

Fisting his hands, Dominic swore viciously. His wolf was pacing madly, lashing out with his claws. "The motherfucking bastard."

Ryan grunted his agreement at that assessment.

"There's more," Trey added, grim. "Pierson said that the rejection ripped out her heart and left her with nothing—that the bond has tied her to you, keeping her a prisoner, and now she's unable to cope with life. He also claimed he went to our pack for help but that we turned him away."

"He told us at the restaurant that he doesn't believe mating bonds are metaphysical things that can't be broken," said Dominic.

"And I think he meant it," said Trey. "I also think he doesn't really believe she's your true mate—he'd have said so if he did at the restaurant. No, this article is not a devastated father coming forward with a heart-wrenching story. He's taking what he *thinks* are lies about our kind and twisting them to make you come across as a conscienceless bastard."

Tao, the Head Enforcer, made a sound of disgust. "I get that Pierson's upset and wants someone to blame, but this is fucking bullshit. It's also the kind of thing that stirs up the anti-shifter extremists.

Granted, they're not as organized or well funded as they used to be, but they're still dangerous."

Tense seconds ticked by as everyone seemed to take a moment to digest everything.

Dominic looked at Trey. "What now?"

The leather chair squeaked as Trey leaned forward. "Now you lie low."

Both Dominic and his wolf bristled. "I'm not hiding."

"No, you're not," said Trey. "But you do need to keep a low profile for a few days. This article has already been shared on other sites and blogs and forums. You can bet your ass that a crowd of anti-shifter extremists will be standing outside our gates within a matter of hours, holding up 'die demons' billboards and making as much of a scene as they can. They'll be chased off, but they'll no doubt come back."

Taryn slid off the desk with a sigh. "He's right, Dominic. They usually get bored within a few days. Until then, it's best you avoid your usual hangouts and don't draw any attention to yourself. It'll blow over fast. These things always do."

"In the meantime, we'll make a statement on the pack blog," said Trey.

Ryan's eyes narrowed. "What kind of statement?"

"A video." Trey clicked his pen on and off as he continued. "We'll tell the truth of the matter, and although it seems a shitty thing to do to someone who just tried to kill herself, we'll mention that it's not something she hasn't tried before."

Roni blinked. "Say that again."

It was Taryn who explained. "Rhett's unearthed a *whole* lot of information on Rosemary Pierson. She has a history of stalking, for one thing."

"Stalking?" echoed Dante, draping an arm around Jaime's shoulders.

"Yep," replied Taryn. "An old boyfriend, her ex-husband, *and* her ex-husband's new girlfriend all got restraining orders against her. She wrote them threatening letters, harassed them on social media, and turned up at their houses and places of work. She's also tried to kill herself twice in the past. Once as a teenager, and once after her divorce."

"I can see now why her father was so desperate to get her what she wanted that he offered me money to mate with her," said Dominic. "He was worried she'd have a relapse of some kind."

Trey nodded. "That was my thought. The ex-husband resembles you a little. I've got to wonder if that's why she fixated on you. There are a lot of shifters out there, but she chose you—one who was highly unlikely to give her a commitment. That made no sense to me. But it could be that she was subconsciously drawn to you because you reminded her of what she lost and desperately wants back."

Marcus scraped a hand over his stubbly jaw. "Do you think Emmet will stop at the article, or do you think he'll make another sly move?"

"I don't know." Trey twisted his mouth. "That may depend on how damaging the article is for us."

"If we move fast, we should be able to minimize any damage," Trick reasoned.

"The extremists will pounce on this, but I don't think we have to worry too much about the public believing Pierson's lies," Tao stated. "*Especially* when they hear about Rosemary's history."

Scrunching the printed article into a ball, Trey tossed it in the wastebasket. "I don't like that we'll be airing her dirty laundry, but we need to show that her unstable behavior started *long* before she ever met Dominic."

Taryn straightened her shoulders. "Then let's get it done."

Sitting at the office desk, Trey, Taryn, and Dominic used the camera on Trey's computer to record a brief but succinct message addressing Pierson's article. They weren't insensitive, didn't directly call Rosemary a liar or claim she was unstable. They just stated the facts, letting them speak for themselves. Before ending the live recording, Taryn passed on her hope that Rosemary recovered soon.

Trey then turned to Dominic. "I know you're thinking that your behavior brought this shit to our door. But you're wrong. Rosemary's and Emmet's behavior did that, not yours."

Dominic pushed to his feet. "I need to let my wolf out. He needs to run." Run off the rage and feel fresh air on his face.

Outside the caves, Dominic shifted into his wolf form. The beast spent hours padding through the woods, chasing small animals, lapping from streams, and traipsing through the shallow river. Tired and much less angry than before, his wolf retreated.

Dominic pulled his clothes back on, still as restless. He had no one else to blame for the situation that he and his pack were currently in. It lay squarely on him, no matter what Trey said.

Did Dominic feel any responsibility for Rosemary's attempted suicide? No, although he did feel shitty for being so harsh with her. The main reason he was so pissed at himself was that he quite simply hadn't seen how unstable she was. She hadn't raised any red flags. Why? Because he hadn't looked below the surface. When it came to women, he never did.

Just as Dante had pointed out, Dominic didn't give people a chance to know him, and he skipped the getting-to-know-the-girl stage. If he hadn't been so fucking closed off and determined not to risk forming ties, he would have seen how troubled Rosemary truly was. His pack wouldn't be dealing with this shit-storm, and maybe she wouldn't be lying on a hospital bed staring at walls.

Fucked. The whole thing was fucked.

Mila was in the middle of unloading the dishwasher when she heard a knock on the front door. Wiping her hands on a small dish towel, she tossed it on the counter and headed into the small hallway. A look through the peephole made her brows lift in surprise and caused her half-asleep cat to snap fully awake.

Opening the door, Mila gave Dominic what she knew was a guarded look. “How did you get in?” Nobody entered the building unless they had the code or were admitted by one of the residents.

Not waiting for an invitation, he stalked into the apartment. “I was about to press the intercom buzzer when Evander came strolling out. He let me in.” Dominic tilted his head. “You look surprised to see me.”

“I doubted I’d see you again unless we were just crossing paths.” She shut the door. “You got what you wanted from me.”

“I didn’t get anywhere near enough of it.” He caught her nape and pulled her close, raw need glittering in his blue eyes. But there was something else there—a barely leashed fury.

Something was wrong, she thought. Very, very wrong. Her cat’s hackles rose. “What happened?”

“Nothing. All is good, Mila.”

She planted a hand on his chest when he would have moved in for a kiss. “Tell me.”

His mouth tightened. “I came here to get away from it, not to talk about it.”

Mila narrowed her eyes. “You don’t get to turn up at my apartment hoping to work out your issues in my bed unless you tell me what’s going on.”

Releasing her, he cursed under his breath. “Like I said, I don’t want to talk about it.”

“Tough,” she bit out, folding her arms across her chest. “I told you that Joel is my true mate. Most of my pride don’t even know that. But I gave you that truth. I trusted you with it. You can return that trust, or you can go. Choose.”

His face softened a little, and his eyes darkened with something that made her stomach do a little flip. “You’re hot when you’re all assertive like this.”

She would *not* be distracted. "Well?" she pushed.

Sighing, he strolled farther into the apartment and sank into her living room sofa. "The father of a human I had a one-night stand with offered me money to mate with her."

Mila blinked, almost rocking back on her heels. "Wow. So what, she wants herself a shifter mate like we're accessories?"

"Turns out she thinks she has an inner wolf." Dominic told her about Rosemary's beliefs and gave her a rundown of the offer that Emmet Pierson had made him. Dominic hadn't wanted to talk about it, but now that the words were tumbling out of him, he felt a little better for it. "Naturally, I said no to his bribe. Rosemary turned up at my territory a few days later. I was clear that I wasn't her true mate, wouldn't be forming any bond with her, and that she had no inner animal."

"All of which she needed to hear."

"Yeah. And that should have been the end of it. But it wasn't; she tried to commit suicide." Dominic still couldn't quite wrap his head around that. "Her father blames me, so he chatted a pile of shit to a journalist who posted an article about it online. Emmet exaggerated the whole thing to make it sound like I had bonded with her and then thrown her away because her animal hadn't surfaced."

"Bastard." Mila settled on an armchair. "I can understand that he's hurting, but he has no damn right to blame you. Sounds to me like she's not in touch with reality. He fed her fantasies by giving them credibility—something he no doubt realizes now. He's pointing the blame at someone else because he can't stand the weight of it."

Dominic nodded, flexing his fingers. "He threatened to cause problems for us the day we met at the restaurant, although he wasn't specific about what those problems would be."

"You feel guilty, don't you?"

"I don't hold myself responsible for what she did, but I can't help feeling bad about how hard I was on her. Maybe I should have just allowed her to have her fantasies about being part shifter so that she could at least live with whatever comfort that brought her."

"I doubt that it would have helped her in the long run."

"If I'd bothered to look beneath the surface, I would have seen that she isn't stable. But I didn't bother. Never do."

Mila waved a dismissive hand. "Plenty of guys sleep with women they don't know. It doesn't make you a shitty person." She cocked her head. "Have you ever been in a relationship?"

A smile softened his mouth. "What, you're wondering if maybe a girl once broke my heart, and I'm determined to avoid feeling that pain again? No. Nothing like that. There are a few reasons why I've avoided relationships. Mostly, I just don't think it's fair to start a relationship with someone unless you can be sure that you'll be what they need."

Mila pursed her lips. "I get it. While coming to terms with the fact that I'd never have my true mate, I stuck to shallow flings because I just wasn't in an emotional place where I had anything to give. I'd have had no right to ask for a commitment from anyone."

"And now you are in a place where you have something to give?"

"I think so." She exhaled a heavy breath. "I'd say we should go sit out on the balcony and relax—it's a real pretty view. But Vinnie's paranoid that there could be a sniper waiting on a rooftop somewhere, pointing a rifle at my apartment."

Dominic frowned, tensing. "Could they shoot through the glass?"

She shook her head. "All the windows and balcony doors in the building are bulletproof. Vinnie's into illegal shit, remember? He wanted to be sure that no one in his pride paid for that."

As something occurred to him, Dominic asked, "There's no way that the person who put the bounty on your head did it to get at Vinnie?"

"It seems more likely to me that they're trying to flush out Alex. Besides, Vinnie has a lot of contacts. If someone in his circle put a hit out on me, he'd have heard about it." Pushing off the chair, Mila added,

"I just need to finish unloading the dishwasher and then I'll be back. Want a beer?"

"Sure." As she passed, Dominic grabbed her hand and smoothly pulled her onto his lap. "Or you could just straddle me like this. Yeah, I prefer that."

Mila probably should have pulled away, but she could almost *feel* his need for touch. Wondered if he even sensed that need himself. She found she couldn't deny him.

They sat in silence as he smoothed his hands up and down her back, doodled patterns here and there, massaged her nape, dragged his fingers down her neck and along the curve of her shoulders. It was as if he was tracing her, memorizing the dips and curves.

All the while, he pressed soft kisses to her face and neck. His cock was rock hard, but he didn't make any moves to seduce her. She got the feeling that he needed comfort more than he needed sex, so she let him have his way. Massaged his chest and shoulders until his muscles were no longer rigid.

Although the anger hadn't quite left him, a growl of contentment rumbled out of his chest, and she had the feeling that it came from his beast. "Your wolf seems to have relaxed."

Dominic raked his teeth down her throat. "He has what he wants now. He's been hounding me all day to come see you. Touch you. Take you."

Drawing back a little, she said, "I got the feeling you were saying a permanent goodbye to me this morning."

"I was," he admitted. "You tempt me to break my own rules, and that's not good. But I was kidding myself when I thought I could stay away from you." And then he closed his mouth over hers and sank his tongue inside. Before long, he had her naked and riding him right there on the sofa. He came like a fucking freight train.

They showered before tumbling into her bed, where he took her again after indulging in a long, thorough taste of her pussy. They fell asleep, but he woke sometime in the night, just as he always did unless he was in his own bed.

Not wanting to sneak out—and knowing she'd probably hear him if he tried—he lightly trailed his fingers down her arm and said softly, "Mila? Mila?"

Her eyes fluttered open. "Hmm?"

"I gotta go."

"'Kay." Her eyelids fell shut. "Leave the money on the nightstand, would ya?"

His mouth quirked. "After the stuff I did to you last night, *you* owe *me* money."

She smiled but flicked her fingers. "Be gone. Some of us like to sleep."

He pressed a kiss to her shoulder and then rose from the bed. Having pulled on his clothes, he said, "I'll call you later."

"You don't have my number." Frowning, she looked up at him. "Do you?"

He just gave her a mysterious smile. "Later." Ignoring his wolf's growl of displeasure and his own desire to get back in that bed, Dominic forced himself to leave.

CHAPTER TEN

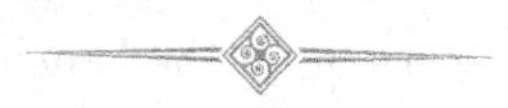

A week. That was all the peace Dominic got before Pierson struck again.

Perched on a smooth rock that was shaded by one of the trees dangling over the river, Dominic watched the kids of the pack play. Tao and his mate, Riley—a raven shifter who was also the pack's Guardian—were supervising the children. Trick and Dante were also there, kicking a ball around with Kye. Tao was carrying Dexter around on his back, while Sienna was trying to catch the leaves that Savannah, who was hanging upside down from a tree branch, was letting flutter to the ground. Lilah was pointing at some ducks that were swimming in the shallows, asking Riley numerous questions about the birds.

It was a tranquil spot on their territory. Shards of sunlight danced off the steady torrent as it splashed over rocks and crashed against a half-built beaver dam. Reeds nodded in the breeze that carried with it the scents of wildflowers, wet earth, and clean water. Wildflowers ran along the gravelly banks, where many algae-stained rocks sat—there was a little turtle resting on the one nearest to Dominic. The moment would have been relaxing if not for the reason his Alphas had called him out here.

Fucking Pierson had struck again. Another online article—this one more vindictive and disparaging. Rhett had discovered it an hour ago, and it had already been shared on multiple online platforms. That news was bad enough. But what his Alphas were now asking of Dominic only increased his anger.

His wolf was currently pacing, agitation in every step. He occasionally lashed out with his claws, showing no signs of calming. He also kept pushing to the surface just enough for Dominic's eyes to flash wolf. The animal wanted the Alphas to see his displeasure.

Taryn and Trey were sitting on the bench opposite him, looking both apologetic and concerned. But there was pure steel in their words. They didn't feel good about their decision, but they weren't going to back down. Dominic had known them both long enough to be sure of that.

Leaning forward, Trey clasped his hands. "You know I'm making sense, Dominic. I was pretty sure that Emmet wasn't done being an asshole—especially since his first article was considered by most to be fiction—so I'm not surprised that he's pulled another stunt. But this follow-up article has me worried, because it's all about *you.* Not him, not the pack, not shifters in general. Hell, Rosemary only got a brief mention here and there. He's utterly focused on you now."

"Yeah, I noticed," said Dominic, his tone flat. The human had gone through a lot of trouble to dig into Dominic's past, clearly searching for dirt. He'd managed to find out that Dominic's mother had left his father and that Lincoln had died shortly afterward. But Pierson's source of information either hadn't known more or hadn't been willing to talk in depth about it, because Pierson seemed unaware that Lincoln had turned rogue and managed to kill a few people before being killed himself.

"It was smart of Pierson to twist the story the way he did, right?" Dominic's smile was bitter. Pierson had falsely claimed that Lincoln had killed himself after Allegra had left him because he'd been unable to deal with the agony of it. "I mean, by saying that the whole 'abandoning a mate' thing runs in my family and that I *knew* it would destroy Rosemary because I'd seen it happen to my father, he made me seem like a cruel motherfucker."

"I'm more concerned about his mention of a nonexistent rumor that you drug women for sex," said Taryn, rubbing her thighs. "Not that I think anyone will believe that shit. Anyone who knows *you* will know you'd *never* do something like that. Also, her mental state couldn't have been a result of a drug you gave her because, hello, she didn't try to kill herself until two weeks after your 'date.' The drug would have been *way* out of her system by then. Plus, she tried to kill herself twice before she had even met you. Still, anti-shifter assholes could pounce on that accusation."

Pierson, the bastard, had not only gone to the trouble of finding out names of the women that Dominic had been seen with over the years, he'd also listed them in his article. He'd made Dominic out to be a womanizer without a conscience who cared only for himself. Although Dominic was no such thing, he'd actually felt a lick of shame when he saw that long list of names, especially since he didn't even remember some of them. He'd have recognized the women's faces, but their names just didn't stick out in his mind.

"It's clear that he's set out to destroy your character," said Trey. "You can handle that, I know. But like I said earlier, it's not fair to expect Mila to have to handle it. And she *would* have to handle it, Dom. Humans snap photos of shifters all the time, and you're a particular favorite among them. If someone snaps a picture of you while you're with Mila, Emmet could turn his attention on *her*. Keeping your distance from her until all of this blows over is for the best."

And therein lay the reason why Dominic's wolf wanted to claw his own Alphas.

"Especially since she's dealing with her own shit right now." Taryn stretched her legs out in front of her. "I'm guessing Emmet thought the first article would make people turn on you, but it didn't. With any luck, this article will be just as ineffective. From the online responses that Rhett has seen so far on various blogs and forums, most people aren't buying Emmet's claims—particularly because the first article contained so many untruths. But Trey's right: this will put you in the spotlight, and that spotlight will shine on whomever you're seen with."

"Also, Rosemary may see these articles and photos," said Trey. "If you're photographed with Mila or any other female, Rosemary could do something else stupid—maybe to them, maybe to you, or maybe to herself."

Dominic flexed his fists. "I won't put my life on pause because of those lying assholes." He hadn't even let his *own* reservations keep him away from Mila, and now Trey wanted Dominic to give the *Piersons* that power? Fuck that.

Dominic had made the decision to enjoy what time he had with Mila before she left for Russia. He'd seen her every day since the first article was released a week ago. Sometimes at the barbershop, sometimes at her apartment, sometimes at the club.

Her parents even had him over for dinner again, which Mila hadn't protested this time around. He liked her family. Liked that they made him feel so welcome. It gave him a sense of belonging that he'd only ever had with his pack.

Dominic had also hinted at her moving to his territory until the bounty was off her head, and that conversation had gone exactly as he'd expected. So he'd had to content himself with keeping a lookout for her. If he heeded Trey's order, he'd no longer be able to do even that.

"I'm not asking you to put your life on pause, I'm just saying it's best for you to keep some distance from Mila until everything cools down."

Dominic narrowed his eyes at the other male. "This isn't you being concerned for Mila. You're thinking that if she gets dragged into this, you could end up making an enemy of Vinnie."

Trey shrugged. "It's something we have to consider, sure, but I'm not worried about Vinnie. My main concern is *you.* And I know that if Mila *were* pulled into this, you'd feel like shit. From what I've heard, she's a smart girl; she'll understand. She might even thank you for it."

Brows snapping together, Dominic snorted. "She's a highly dominant female shifter, Trey. She'll be offended that I'd even *insinuate* that she couldn't deal with any blowback from the articles. I won't get any thanks, because I'll have hurt her pride."

"But she'll get why you did it."

Dominic fisted his hands. "Would you stay away from Taryn, knowing she had a price on her head and could be attacked at any moment?"

"No, but Taryn's my mate. I don't know what Mila is to you. I'm not sure if *you* know what Mila is to you. But if you don't claim rights to someone, you can't act like you have them. So unless you're telling me that you *have* laid some kind of claim on her—even if it's only temporary—you don't have ground here." He fell silent, giving Dominic the chance to voice a claim . . . but he didn't.

"She's surrounded by her pride, Dominic," Taryn reminded him. "You know they'll keep her safe. And I'm sure they'll keep you posted if you ask them to."

Dominic wouldn't need to ask, since he already checked in with Tate daily, asking for updates on Mila's situation. Strangely, the Beta had never told him to butt out of pride business. Really, Dominic had no right to constantly keep tabs on her. She wasn't his. Hell, she wasn't even wearing a temporary mark from him. But he just needed to be certain that she was okay. His wolf needed it. Either Tate was taking pity on him or Mila's parents had dragged the Beta into their little plot.

"And Mila's not so easy to take down, is she?" Taryn added. "That's not the point, I know. I'm just asking you to remember that you're not leaving some naive girl to fend for herself. Mila's tough. She can handle her shit. And she has plenty of people around her who will keep her safe. If I didn't wholeheartedly believe that, I'd fight Trey about asking you to pull back." Taryn sighed. "As for our next course of action—"

"No more videos," Dominic cut in. "We've stated our case, it hasn't changed. There's nothing new to say. Any attention we give to Emmet makes him seem credible."

"I agree," said Taryn. "We can post something simple on our blog that says we hope the public sees his story for what it is—an angry father looking for someone to blame for his daughter's pain."

"If you want," began Trey, "I can call Mila myself and—" The Alpha's brows lifted as Dominic's eyes flashed wolf again and a territorial growl rattled in his chest. "I sensed that your beast didn't like me telling you to stay away from her, but I didn't see the possessiveness until just then. I'll bet that emotion is new to him."

Dominic just grunted.

"Taking that into account, it might be best to put some space between your wolf and Mila," said Trey. "Or he's going to be highly fucking pissed when this thing between you and her ends, and he'll want to challenge the male she's entering into an arranged mating with."

"Do you think it's possible that she could be your true mate?" asked Taryn, her voice soft.

Dominic fisted his hands. "No."

"You should be open to the idea," she advised. "Plenty of people don't sense that they're around their true mate. It can take a while for—"

"She's not mine." The words were like gravel.

"You can't know that for sure."

"I can. I can't tell you why because it's not my secret to share, but I can tell you that I'm absolutely certain I'm not her true mate."

Clearly reading between the lines, Taryn gave a slow nod. "That's a shame. But it doesn't mean you can't still have something with her." Standing, she straightened her tee. "I'll go speak with Rhett and get this blog post done."

"And I'm going to join that football game before Kye gives me another dirty look for not playing." Trey raised his brows at Dominic. "You coming?"

"No." He had a call to make, so when the Alphas walked away, Dominic whipped out his phone and dialed Mila's number.

She picked up after a few rings. "Hey, GQ."

Her smoky voice snaked over both him and his wolf, as comforting as it was arousing. "Hey, what you up to?"

There was a slight hesitation. "No weird dirty line?"

"I'm saving them for when I next see you."

"You don't sound like yourself. What's wrong?"

Fuck, she read him too easily. He sighed. "Pierson had the journalist release a follow-up article, and it's bad." Dominic brought her up to speed.

"I really hope someone stomps on that motherfucker's dick."

Dominic's mouth curved slightly. "One can but hope." He scratched at his nape. "Trey's concern is that this is going to put a spotlight on me, and that whoever shares the spotlight could then be targeted by the Piersons. He thinks it's best if I keep my distance from you until all the trouble dies down. I can't say I like the idea, but I also don't want this fucked-up mess touching you." No response. "Mila?"

"It's understandable," she finally said, her voice a little stiff. "After all, I kept my distance from you when I realized I had a bounty on my head. Oh, wait, no. I trusted that you could take care of yourself, and I respected that you have your own mind."

He cursed. "It's not like that, Mila. I *know* you can protect yourself—I've seen it firsthand. But this guy won't come at you physically; he'll attack your reputation, which may then bleed over onto the barbershop and your family. He'll do his best to dig up your secrets, and then he'll twist what he finds, just like he's done to me. If you read the second article, you'll understand."

A heavy sigh. "Fine. Whatever. I hope for your sake it blows over soon."

Something about her tone put him on edge. "Mila, I'm not using this as an excuse to put space between us, if that's what's going through your head. That's not who I am."

"But it's best to put that space there. I'm leaving the country soon, and it's probably not fair of me to be fooling around with you when I should be thinking about Maksim."

Dominic snapped his teeth. "Fooling around? Is that what you'd call it?" His wolf peeled back his upper lip just enough to bare one fang.

"And what would you call it?" she challenged.

He swore under his breath. He didn't have an answer for her, because he didn't know what the fuck was between them. He'd never had it before. "I'm going to call you every night, Mila. And you'd better fucking pick up."

"Why would I do that?" she asked tartly.

Because his wolf would need to hear her voice. Because Dominic needed to be sure he was in her thoughts. But he didn't say any of that, knowing it would just give credence to her bullshit "we shouldn't be having sex because I should be thinking about that Russian bastard" thing. So instead, Dominic said, "Because if you don't, I'll spank that sweet ass when I finally get my hands on it again." It wasn't a lie.

CHAPTER ELEVEN

She needed a swim, Mila decided a few days later. It was always a good way for her to unwind. Always got rid of the tension from her muscles and allowed her to escape from her thoughts. And since she'd spent the past week and a half always glancing over her shoulder, knowing it would only be a matter of time before another hit man struck, Mila was wound far too tight. So she bagged up her bikini, towel, and other essentials before heading down to the communal pool in the basement.

Halfway down one of the stairwells, she came across none other than Adele. *Shit.* Her inner cat rose to her feet with a hiss. Mila forced a smile. "Adele, hi."

Adele's face brightened. "Hey, I've just come to pay my mom a quick visit. How are you doing, sweetie?" Always so damn nice.

"I'm good."

Adele puffed out a breath. "Knowing you're on a hit list and could have people watching your every move . . . God, your head must be fried."

Well, yeah. "It's definitely not much fun."

"You must be infuriated with Alex for causing trouble and then leaving you to deal with it."

Mila bristled. "I don't think it happened quite like that, but we'll see."

A playful glint entered Adele's eye. "On a much lighter note, I heard you're involved with one of the Phoenix Pack wolves. Ingrid tells me he's quite a dish."

Chest tightening, Mila felt her smile falter. This was really *the last* discussion she wanted to have with this female. "He is." She hadn't seen him since the day before Pierson's second article was released, but Dominic had called her each night and sent her several text messages. Very sexually suggestive text messages, complete with cheesy lines.

"Valentina must *really* like him if she invited him for dinner. *Twice.*"

"Yeah, she does." Mila had expected her mother to be offended on Mila's behalf when she heard Dominic's reason for staying away from her. Instead, her mother had found it "cute" that he'd want to protect Mila. It seemed that GQ could do no wrong in Valentina's eyes.

Adele glanced around, as if checking they were alone. She lowered her voice as she went on. "Joel doesn't like him much. He worries that the wolf is too much like Grant. But I happen to agree with Ingrid—life's all about living. If this Dominic guy can make you happy, even for just a little while, you should grab on to that."

Her cat lashed out with her claws, not liking the sound of Dominic's name in the mouth of this feline who'd stolen her true mate. Mila tried making excuses to leave, but Adele just kept on talking.

"And I hope you'll reconsider immigrating to Russia. We'd miss you. And Joel . . . well, he hasn't made many friends in the pride. Doesn't click with people easily. But he considers you a good friend, and I wouldn't like him to lose one of the very few he's made."

God, Mila's mouth was hurting from the strain of keeping the fake smile in place. "I can understand that. He's very lucky to have you."

"I'm the lucky one." Adele put her hand on Mila's shoulder, and her cat wanted to bite it. "You take care." With that, she headed up the stairs.

Letting out a long breath, Mila continued her descent to the basement. Pacing within her, her cat hissed and spat—she despised Adele almost as much as she despised Joel.

He'd come to the barbershop that morning to have his hair cut. Strangely, it hadn't been as hard for Mila to touch Joel as it usually was, but it had been no less easy for her cat. The only thing that had ever calmed the feline in Joel's presence was having Dominic there. How annoying.

When GQ had called her with the news that Trey wanted him to stay clear of her, Mila had been furious. Some might have said that he was only following the order of his Alpha, but she'd seen the darker side of Dominic and knew there would be no forcing him to do *anything* he didn't want to do.

Affronted, she might not have answered any of his subsequent calls, but she'd lost some of her anger after reading Pierson's second article. It was one thing to hear Dominic give her the gist of it; it was another to read it for herself and see all the lies and hurtful insults spun together.

Both she and her cat remained offended that he'd think she needed protecting from anything, but Mila could see why Dominic would be willing to heed his Alpha in this. Pierson wanted metaphorical blood, and he was slicing out at GQ in whichever ways he could.

Not that she'd have cared if the human turned his attention her way—she could handle a little fart like him, no matter how he came at her—but Dominic would want things to settle down, not escalate. If Dominic were seen with another female, things would *definitely* escalate. So yeah, she'd taken his calls and responded to his texts.

She'd also kept an online-eye on the responses to both of Pierson's articles, relieved to find that most people weren't giving any weight to Pierson's words. Some females, claiming that they "knew" Dominic well, had sworn he would *never* drug a woman. A few of the other commenters claimed to be friends of Rosemary's ex-husband and confirmed that she was indeed pretty disturbed. Whether they were true or not, those particular comments would piss off Emmet—Mila was all for that idea.

As she pushed open the basement door, her cat wrinkled her nose. The strong scent of chlorine permeated the thick, moist air. She was glad to see that the pool was empty. She liked having it all to herself and really wasn't in the mood to listen to laughter and shrieking echoing around her. She wanted to be alone.

The pool was pretty basic. There was a waterslide at the shallow end and a diving board at the other. Near the life jackets was a pile of water toys and kickboards.

She peered through the door to the attached fitness room but couldn't make out if anyone was inside. It was quite popular among the males of the pride, especially Tate, Luke, and the enforcers.

In the changing room, she swapped her clothes for her bikini and scrunched her curls up into a hair tie before stuffing her bag and towel in a locker. Mindful of the slippery tiles, she walked back out to the pool. The water gently rippled and lapped at the edges. Thankfully, it was still empty of people.

Holding her breath, she plunged into the pool. The cool water swallowed her, felt almost welcoming. She swam for the surface and sucked in a mouthful of air, shoving the wet tendrils of hair out of her face. For a few moments, she just floated there, enjoying the feel of the water lapping against her skin.

There was something very peaceful and calming about being in the water. There was no bombardment of sensations or list of things to do. Just her and the water. It enabled her to switch off, which she sorely needed to do right then.

The silky water slid over her skin as she swam length after length. Her tension gradually slipped away, but she didn't stop. She kept going. Pushed herself until her muscles were screaming for rest. Yet, she felt better. More relaxed. Her head no longer felt crowded by thoughts.

Hearing a slight plop of water, she glanced over her shoulder. No one. Not even a shadow under the water. Frowning, she shrugged it off. Ready to get out, she began a gentle swim toward the metal ladder—

Something tightened around her ankle and yanked her under. The shock of it almost stole her breath. She looked down. It was a rope. No, a snake. It was a fucking *snake.* Triangular-shaped head. Wormlike lure on the end of the tail curled around her ankle. Large dark bands surrounding a black, short, robust body.

Death adder. One so huge that it could only be a damn shifter.

Panic clawed at her insides, but she wrestled it down before it could engulf her. Her heart pounding, she kicked her leg wildly and slashed the fucker's long body with her claws. Its hold loosened enough for her to wriggle free of its grip and kick for the surface.

Sucking in huge gulps of air, she bobbed there for just a second. Get out, she told herself. Get. Out. She made a frantic swim for the ladder, knowing she had a better chance of fighting the snake if she were out of the water.

Sharp pain blazed up her leg. The little bastard had bitten her. *Fuck.* Adrenaline racing through her system, she swam faster. Almost there—

The snake snatched her ankle and pulled her under the water again. Raging, she kicked and thrashed and clawed at the creature. Her cat's fury pulsed in her blood, feeding her anger. The feline wanted the freedom to battle the snake herself, but its smaller body had less of a chance against the creature.

Helplessly inhaling the water, Mila kept on fighting. Or tried to. Her muscles were weakening, and she wasn't sure if it was from the venom or the struggle. The chlorinated water stung her nose, pricked at her eyes, and burned her throat.

The snake tried to curl around her chest. *Oh, the fuck no.* She stabbed her claws deep into its body and twisted her hand, making yet more blood stain the water. The snake jerked away, releasing her, and she quickly kicked for the surface again. She gasped for air, spluttering, coughing, and choking.

She clumsily grabbed a metal rung of the ladder. Triumph would have filled her if she didn't feel so heavy and drained, which was no doubt thanks to the venom. Managing to climb a few of the steps and drag herself weakly onto the tiled surface, she lay flat on her stomach, greedily inhaling huge gulps of air. She wouldn't get far, she knew. Wouldn't make it out of there, and her throat was too raw for her to scream for help.

Her frantic daze darted around, searching for a weapon or—

There was a whistle near the kickboards.

Her heart jumped. She could use it to signal for help. Water drizzled down her body onto the tiles as she army-crawled her way to the whistle, conscious that it was her only chance. Snatching it, she put it to her mouth and blew hard. The weak, shaky screech bounced off the walls. She did it again and again, but the sounds got fainter and fainter. No one came.

Something shackled her ankle yet again. A large hand this time. That hand pulled her backward. Her nails scrabbled at the tiles, but it was no use. Panic wrenched the breath out of her as the water swallowed her whole. It gushed into her mouth and shot up her nose yet again.

She didn't get a chance to properly look at the male holding her tight and dragging her deeper and deeper. The water flooded her lungs until it felt like they'd explode.

Again, she wrestled the fear beating at her. But she lost. Could barely move, let alone swim or fight. Yet, little by little, a sense of tranquility crept in, pushing away the panic. Her vision began to darken, and total paralysis finally set in. Just as the darkness dragged her under, the water shook as if something heavy had landed in it.

Lounging on his bed wearing only his jeans, Dominic pinched the bridge of his nose as he spoke into his phone. "Charlene, I said I'm fine, and I'm fine." He'd been undressing, planning to take a shower, when he'd heard his cell ringing. He'd hoped it was Mila. Hearing her voice would have gone a long way to cheering up his broody wolf.

"Well, you don't sound fine," said Charlene. "And *I* sure wouldn't be fine if there were two messed-up articles about *me* floating around."

"How pissed is Lennie?" he asked with a sigh, referring to her mate.

"He didn't like seeing my name on an online list of your past bed-partners, but he likes you well enough that he's more pissed *for* you than *at* you. After all, it's not your fault. Emmet Pierson has made many enemies by posting that list. A lot of the women on it are mated now, and their men will not be *any* happier than Lennie is. Speaking of Lennie . . . he's out with his buddies tonight. I could come see you, cheer you up," she offered.

"I'm good, but thanks. And I don't think your mate would like it much anyway."

She snorted. "He knows you and I are just friends. He won't get jealous."

"No, but he wouldn't be happy if someone took pictures of you coming and going from my territory, considering you were on Pierson's infamous list. The human would twist that information to make it seem like you're cheating on your mate. Lennie wouldn't believe it, but others might."

"Wait, there are people hanging outside your territory?"

"There were earlier. Trick and Marcus keep chasing them off, but they come back."

She made a noise loaded with sympathy. "I'm so sorry this is happening to you. I wish I could do something."

"It'll all die down soon." That was what he kept telling himself.

There was a slight pause. "I expected to see you at the club on Friday, since you seemed determined to wear Mila Devereaux down," she said, her tone neutral. "I guess this means you've given up. It's for the best. You should be looking for a girl you *like*, not another one to enjoy simply for a night. You're getting too old to be chasing skirts."

But he *did* like Mila. In fact, he'd kind of . . . well, he missed her. A little. Sort of. Maybe.

"You sure you don't want some company?" Charlene asked. "You'd be doing me a favor. I'm bored out of my mind here."

Hearing a beeping from his phone that indicated another person was trying to call, he glanced at the screen. Tate's name was flashing there. "Charlene, I have to go."

"Why, what is it?"

"Probably nothing." Hanging up, Dominic then answered Tate's call. "Any news?"

"Don't go postal," said Tate.

Dominic sat upright. "What's happened? Where's Mila?"

"She's fine," Tate assured him. "But there was another attack. Some bastard tried to drown her."

Dominic's wolf sliced out his claws. "They did *what*?" He was already off the bed, grabbing a T-shirt out of his closet.

"In the basement swimming pool. Really, she's okay. But I figured you'd want to know."

"I'll be right there."

Having pulled on his tee and shoes, he left his room, slamming the door behind him. Then, his blood boiling, Dominic stalked through the network of tunnels, heading for the exit. Fuck, he should have convinced her to move to his territory, where he could have kept a close watch over her, where she'd be safer. Moreover, he should never have agreed to keep his distance from her. If he'd been at her side tonight, he might have put a stop to the attack before it started.

Although he was pissed as fuck at Trey for issuing the order to steer clear of her, Dominic was more pissed at himself for heeding it. He could have protested. Could have declared that Mila was *far* more to him than a female who warmed his metaphorical bed—Trey would have respected that. But Dominic hadn't wanted to admit that truth to himself, let alone to others.

He'd told her that he wasn't using Trey's order as an excuse to put physical space between them. He'd thought he meant it. But Dominic realized now that he'd been talking out of his ass. He'd done to her what he did best—he'd pulled back. "I'm such a fucking prick," he muttered under his breath.

Sharply turning a corner, Dominic saw Trey and Dante walking in his direction.

"What's going on?" Trey demanded, obstructing his path. "You look like you want to rip someone's throat out."

He did. "Mila was attacked again." Dominic quickly relayed Tate's news to them. "I need to see her."

"Dom—"

"*Don't* tell me to stay away." Dominic's voice was quiet but laced with something very, very dark. "I need to see her, and that's exactly what I'm gonna do." If that meant disobeying a direct order from his Alpha, so fucking be it.

Trey sighed. "If you're seen with her, you could send more unwanted attention her way."

"Yeah, you've said that already. I listened to you. I kept my distance. I trusted that her pride would take care of her. But she's been *hurt,* and I don't even know how badly."

"The pride has two healers—"

"You're not hearing me, and I don't know why." Dominic took a determined step forward. "I'm going to see her. You don't have to like it, but it's happening."

Exchanging a look with Dante, Trey sighed again. "Then we'll come with you."

"You don't need to—"

"Mila's clearly something to you, so if you really feel you need to see that she's okay with your own two eyes, then fine. But you're not going out alone. We're coming with you."

His jaw clenched, Dominic gave a reluctant nod. "Then let's go."

The three of them headed down the steps of the cliff face and into the concealed parking lot. No one objected to him driving. Dante rode shotgun while Trey sat in the back.

"So," began Dante as they passed through the iron gates, "are you ready to accept the truth yet?"

Dominic flicked him a sideways glance. "What truth?"

"That she's not just a bed-buddy to you," the Beta replied. "I know you, Dom, so I'm pretty sure you've been doing your best to rationalize why she draws you to her. At first, you no doubt blamed it on her rejecting you—and I'm sure that did play some part. But I think what really drew you was that, from day one, she *saw* you."

Dante didn't say "the way your parents never did," but Dominic heard the words.

"Also," the Beta went on, "she expects you to give her more than the facets you choose to show people."

Something else Dominic's parents hadn't bothered to do.

"In case you hadn't noticed, you've been a cranky fucker since Trey told you to keep your distance from her. You haven't spouted a single cheesy line to any of the females. Haven't even left pack territory much, which I'm guessing is because you didn't trust that you wouldn't go to her. Your wolf wanders off during the pack runs, still pissed as hell at Trey. But your wolf isn't the only one who's possessive of her, is he?"

Dominic's grip on the steering wheel flexed. "No."

Dante's tone softened a little as he said, "Stop trying to find a reason *why* you want her so badly. Just accept that you do. Let yourself have her."

"If you're thinking it's not that simple because she's not your true mate and has made plans to enter into an arranged mating, you're wrong," said Trey. "It's only as complicated as you allow it to be."

Dante nodded. "I know you well enough to know you worry you'll be a shit partner, Dominic. But honestly, I don't think that's going to be an issue here. It would be if she were your true mate because, to you, a bond like that can be a trap—you'd have automatically held back from her. But you don't have that worry with Mila. You know she's not your true mate. You know that no mating urge will suddenly strike you and take the decision from you. You know you have a way out if you need one—the same way out that your father desperately needed. Imprinting bonds can be broken without either party turning rogue. But they can also be as strong as true-mate bonds *if* the couple pour everything they are into it."

"I think what Dante is trying to say is, 'For the love of all that's holy, do not walk away from this girl—give it what you've got.'" Trey raised a brow at the Beta. "Is that about right?"

Dante pursed his lips. "Yeah, that sums it up. Well, Dom, what are you going to do?"

Reaching a red light, Dominic eased up on the pedal. "The same thing I'd decided to do before I even hopped into this SUV: I'm going to tell her I've decided that she's mine."

There was a long beat of silence, and then Dante and Trey exchanged a look.

"Our boy's growing up," said Trey.

"About damn time," muttered Dante, but he was smiling.

CHAPTER TWELVE

Mila wasn't *the least* bit impressed to once again have a bunch of infuriated cats in her apartment. What made it even more irritating was that it wasn't just a handful of people this time. No, most of the pride had gathered in her apartment—which was driving her very territorial cat crazy. Especially since two of them were Joel and Adele.

On first arriving, Joel had given Mila a tight hug and then spent a good fifteen minutes trying to convince her to move in with him and Adele for a short while so that she wouldn't be alone. She'd declined of course, which almost led to a shouting match. But one look from Valentina had made him snap his mouth shut. Now he was standing on the other side of the room, seething, while Adele did her best to calm him.

Mila had anticipated his anger. He didn't want her for himself, but some deep-seated part of him couldn't stand the idea of her being unsafe—wanted to protect and watch over her. But since her cat viewed that as an imposition, she kept hissing and spitting at him.

Pulling her attention away from Joel, Mila gave the room a once-over. Her pride mates weren't just pissed; they were shocked. They'd never felt unsafe in the building before. They'd always considered it impenetrable. Well, impenetrable by anyone other than a wolverine—there was no keeping a wolverine out of anywhere they didn't want to be.

Speaking of wolverines . . . So far her mother hadn't said a single word, which was bad. A quiet Valentina was a very dangerous Valentina. She was busying herself making everyone tea and serving them pastries—well, everyone except for Vinnie. She blamed him for the hole in security and had no problems indirectly communicating that. And it wouldn't be long before she was communicating it *directly*.

From what Mila could tell, Vinnie also felt that the blame lay squarely with him. He, Tate, Luke, and the pride's enforcers were currently talking among themselves, discussing various ways the snake shifter could have found his way inside the building.

After questioning the snake, they'd come to Mila's apartment and given her what little information they had on the male. In sum, he was yet another asshole wanting to claim the bounty on her head. Awesome.

As her father tucked a blanket around her legs, Mila frowned. "I'm really okay."

"Well, we're not, so let us fuss over you a little." James sat next to her on the sofa. "Need more tea?"

"No, thanks." Despite the tea and pastries her mother had plied her with, Mila could still taste the chlorine. Could still smell it, even though she'd had a very long shower. Could still remember that moment when the water flooded her lungs and made her chest feel like it would burst.

If it weren't for the pride's healers, her airways would no doubt be burning, and the venom would probably still be affecting her. And if it weren't for Tate's intervention earlier, she'd be dead. Not a happy thought.

Valentina took her empty cup from her. "I called your uncles."

Mila winced. "Mom—"

"They can help, Mila. They have . . . certain skills." As in, they were excellent hunters and knew a thousand ways to kill a man. They also never left bodies to find—mostly because they ate them, teeth, bone, and all.

"They also make a point of poking at Dad and trying to convince you to leave him." She loved her uncles, she truly did. She just preferred they stay away from James.

Valentina jutted out her chin. "Your father can handle my brothers."

"It's Skeletor I can't stand," said James with a lip curl.

Valentina's nostrils flared. "James Devereaux, you *will* cease calling my mother 'Skeletor.'"

"It's just a little nickname," he said, full of innocence. "Nicknames are a demonstration of affection."

Hearing knuckles rapping on the front door, Valentina shot her mate a "we're not done here" glare and then stormed off.

Feeling the beginnings of a headache coming on, Mila closed her eyes and rubbed at her temple. It made her a bitch, really, but she wanted everyone gone. She appreciated their concern and support, she just couldn't deal with having so many people around her right then. And her cat couldn't relax so long as Joel and Adele were in her private space and—

"Ah, Dominic," Valentina greeted. "It is good to see you."

Heart jumping in her chest, Mila snapped her eyes open. Her cat's pacing came to an abrupt halt.

Seconds later, he came striding into the living area, and his eyes instantly sought her out. Then he was making a beeline for her as if they were the only two people there, not bothering to return any of the greetings he received. Her cat regarded him carefully, a little miffed with him for staying away.

Just like the time he'd spoken with the jackal, his dominance and intensity were pulsing around him. His infectious impishness was nowhere to be seen, but it hadn't been replaced by anger or tension or any other emotion. No, he was cool and in control. But that shrewd, ruthless, unforgiving side of him had come to the surface.

He sank straight into the spot that her father—who looked rather pleased by GQ's arrival—voluntarily vacated. Palming her nape, Dominic pressed a light kiss to her mouth. "I came as soon as I heard. How are you feeling?"

She swallowed. There was something . . . different in the way he was looking at her. Something that made her all tingly and wary at the same time. "Okay, thanks to Tate."

"What happened exactly? All Tate told me was that someone managed to get into the building and tried to drown you in the basement pool."

Mila took a deep breath and then told him about the attack. "Tate got there in time to drag the fucker off me. While Luke detained him, Tate gave me CPR. The healers took care of the rest."

"CPR," Dominic echoed, surprised by how steady his voice was. She'd had to have CP-fucking-R. That was how close she'd come to death. That was how close he'd come to losing her before he even had the chance to explore what was between them.

Tightening his grip on her nape, Dominic shot an accusatory look at Vinnie, asking, "How the hell did he even get into the building?"

"Our theory is that he entered in his snake form," replied Vinnie. "They can fit through all kinds of small places. We're working on finding all those cracks so that we can ensure another of his kind can't repeat the move."

Dominic's jaw hardened—because it was too little, too late. He'd trusted that she was safe there. "I'd like to see him. Where is he?"

Vinnie licked his front teeth. "He's . . . indisposed right now. I'm afraid he can't talk." Translation: he was dead.

Trey quickly introduced himself and Dante to Mila before turning to Vinnie. "I'm guessing the snake was a bounty hunter."

"He was," confirmed Vinnie. "His name was Roland Blum. He was a lone shifter."

Trey pursed his lips. "Never heard of him."

"We had a little . . . conversation with him about who sent him." Vinnie looked at Dominic. "It went along the same lines as the conversation you had with the jackal at the club. He saw the bounty on the website and tried to cash in. He had no information that could lead us to whoever put out the hit."

As Vinnie and Trey talked more about the website, Mila turned to Dominic and quietly asked, "Why did Tate call you about the snake attack?"

Dominic moved his hand from her nape to trace the shell of her ear. "Because I told him to contact me if anything happened to you. I call him every day, looking for updates. I also gave him some suggestions for securing the area."

Mila narrowed her eyes. "You've been coordinating with my cousin?"

Dominic shrugged. "I like to be helpful." She opened her mouth—no doubt to insist that her safety was none of his business—so he used his fingers to gently pinch her lips shut. "We can argue about it later. Or would you rather do it with an audience? Because plenty of people are watching us right now." She briefly glanced around, saw that he was right, and gave him a look that said "fine." He released her mouth. "Good girl." He looked up just as her mother appeared and handed him a cup of tea. "How are you doing, Valentina?"

She sniffed. "I am tempted to slash Vinnie's throat for not being aware of the weakness in security."

Dominic didn't doubt that she was serious. He turned to Mila. "What disturbs me is that the snake knew where to find you."

"It was more likely luck on his part," said Mila. "If he got inside through a crack in the foundation of the building, he would have gotten straight into the basement. He probably planned to head to my apartment, but then I walked straight into his grasp. Bastard."

"There should not have been ways in which intruders could enter," clipped Valentina, her voice loud enough to carry.

Vinnie grimaced. "We'll fix any cracks in the building, any uneven doorjambs, and any other gaps we can find to make sure nothing like this happens again."

That wasn't enough for Mila's mother, though. No. She gave the Alpha a ration of verbal shit, and he didn't bother defending himself. That was one thing Mila respected about Vinnie. He owned his mistakes. Didn't make excuses for himself. Still, it wouldn't be long before he lost his patience with Valentina, an eventuality the woman was no doubt counting on. The wolverine was itching for a fight, and that was bad.

Mila looked up at her father. "Dad, I think it's time you got her out of here."

"I was just thinking the same thing." James put a hand on his mate's shoulder. "Mila's tired. How about we all go home and give her some space?" When Valentina started to object, James added, "She'll have Dominic with her, she'll be fine."

A conspiratorial look passed between her parents, and Mila rolled her eyes. They liked the idea of her being alone with Dominic. But since she wanted everyone gone, she didn't complain.

Joel crossed the room. "I can stay with her. Adele and I can keep watch while she gets some rest." He directed a look of challenge right at GQ that made Mila tense.

Dominic gave her thigh a reassuring squeeze and then smoothly got to his feet. "Not necessary," he said to Joel. "I got her." After everyone said their goodbyes to Mila, Dominic herded them to the door, assuring them all that he'd take care of her and call them if they were needed. He also promised to keep Trey and Dante updated on whatever came next.

Joel, the asshole, lingered at the doorway. "It's sweet that you'd come to her rescue," he said sardonically, "but you're not what she needs right now. You're not what she'll ever need, and I for one think that—"

"You don't want to get in my way when it comes to Mila," Dominic warned him. His wolf wanted to rake the face of this male who, if things had been different, would have claimed her for his own. But things weren't different. Joel had made his choice, and that meant Mila was none of his fucking business.

The blonde who Dominic was guessing was Adele tried leading Joel away, but he kept his glare locked on Dominic as he said, "I'm Mila's friend—"

"And if she wanted you to stay, she'd have said so," Dominic pointed out. "Just as she'd have told me to leave if she wanted me gone."

Grinding his teeth, Joel took an aggressive step toward him. "I read those articles about you. Yeah, both seemed to be piles of shit. But that list of names—that long, *long* list . . . I don't want Mila added to that. I don't want her to be just another woman whose name you probably won't even remember a few years down the line. She deserves better than that. Better than *you*."

Dominic couldn't even blame the asshole for thinking Mila was no one to him. Hadn't he in fact forgotten a lot of those women's names? But Mila was different. Since he had no intention of explaining himself to Joel, Dominic lifted a brow and asked, "Are we done here?"

Again, the blonde tried leading Joel away. Again, the asshole resisted. "She's got enough problems right now—as evidenced by the attack on her earlier. She doesn't need to be dealing with your problems as well."

"And what do I need, Joel?"

Wincing, Joel turned to look at Mila, who was standing a few feet away. He cursed, taking a moment to weigh his words. Yeah, telling a dominant female what they did or didn't need wasn't wise. "I just don't like that he's bringing more trouble to your door," Joel said carefully.

"Well, thanks for sharing that," said Mila. "But it's *my* door, Joel, not yours. *I* say who can and can't walk through it—not you or anybody else."

The blonde gave her an apologetic look. "I'm sorry, Mila, he's just a little tense after hearing—"

"You almost died, Mila," Joel clipped. "If Tate hadn't heard that whistle, you'd be dead right now. So fucking forgive me if I'd rather that someone wasn't piling more danger on you." With that, he pivoted on his heel and stormed out.

"Sorry," the blonde repeated, backing out of the apartment.

Closing the door, Dominic turned to Mila. Her face hard, her body rigid, her eyes closed, she just stood there. He slowly crossed to her, eating up her personal space, and skimmed his fingertips down her throat. "Open your eyes, baby."

He'd expected to see torment there. After all, the male who would have been her mate was acting like he had rights to her—rights he'd given up—and just wouldn't back the fuck off and give her the space to truly heal. Because despite what she liked to think, she hadn't truly healed. Not fully. And her cat had a *long* way to go before she'd feel at peace.

What Dominic hadn't expected to see when she lifted those eyelids was her cat staring back at him. There was a warning there. The feline had been badly hurt, and she was letting him know that she'd tolerate no more of it. He wondered if, unlike Mila, the cat had sensed from his body language that he wanted "more," and she wanted him to know that she'd be watching him closely. She wasn't warning him to stay away, though, so he took that as a win.

His wolf strained against Dominic, wanting to get to the cat, wanting to reassure her. But the feline withdrew, and Mila's blue eyes took him in.

"I thought you were supposed to be keeping your distance from me," she said.

He slid his hand up her arm. "Tried it. Didn't like it. Won't be doing it again." He nuzzled her neck, needing a lungful of her scent. It felt like weeks since he'd last been inside her. He wanted to bury his cock deep in her pussy, wanted to taste and touch and take her hard.

But she was strung tighter than a bow. Needed comfort. Needed to forget what a shit evening she'd had so far.

Taking her hand, Dominic led her to the bathroom, where he slowly peeled off her clothes, keeping his touch light and easy.

"I already had a shower," she told him.

"I haven't, and I don't want to take one alone." He shed his own clothes and pulled her into the shower stall. The spray of hot water drummed at their skin and pattered the tiles and frosted-glass door. He soaped her body, working the fruity gel into a creamy lather, filling the humid air with the scent of grapefruit. Neither of them said a word. The only sounds were the drum of the water and the whirring of the fan.

Feeling the stress seep from her muscles, Mila closed her eyes. His cock, hard as a rock, dug into her lower stomach. But he didn't make any moves on her. Aside from the occasional press of his lips to the corners of her mouth or the column of her throat, he didn't even kiss her. His touch was soothing. Reverent. Calming. There was also something . . . claiming about it. Like, in skimming the pads of his fingers over every part of her, he was leaving some sort of mark on her. *His* mark.

But that couldn't be right, she thought. Dominic wouldn't go so far as to lay any kind of claim on her—no matter how temporary. He was just . . . comforting her. Exposing yet another side of himself. A sensitive side that would shelve his own anger and frustrations to concentrate solely on her.

After washing her hair, he rinsed them both off and used a soft towel to pat her skin while she used a smaller one to towel dry her hair as best she could. Only when he'd toweled himself off did he shepherd her into the bedroom.

Holding her close, he skimmed the tips of his fingers along her collarbone. "Feel better?"

Muscles deliciously loose, her cat much more relaxed, Mila nodded. "You're good with those hands in more ways than one."

Mouth curving, he buried his face in her neck and inhaled deeply. "Missed that scent. Missed you. And you missed me, didn't you?"

She swallowed. "Maybe."

He breezed his lips along her jaw. "Give me your throat."

"Fuck, no."

He smiled, having suspected already that she'd never submit so easily. "You need—" She yanked off his towel and fisted his cock tight; the pleasure of it made him hiss out a breath. He loved that boldness in her. Loved that she was unashamed of her sexuality and made her own demands.

Devouring her mouth, he thrust into her grip as she pumped him with that talented little hand. A hand that wouldn't be stroking anyone else like that, he thought with a growl. There was something heady about that. About knowing that no other man could touch her.

Fuck, he was already close to coming, which meant he'd need to remove her hand from his cock before he exploded on her instead of *in* her. While the thought of his come on her skin held great appeal, he needed to be inside her tonight.

Curling his hand around hers, he peeled her skilled fingers away from his cock. "Not ready to come yet." Crowding her with his body, he tipped her back onto the mattress but remained standing. "Stay."

Her mouth thinned. "I'm not a dog."

"No, you're a very pretty kitty. *My* kitty."

His? Mila snorted to herself, sure he didn't mean it. He carefully peeled open her towel, like he was unwrapping a present. She drank him in, mouth drying up at all that hard muscle and restrained power. His gaze drifted over her. Hot. Territorial. No one had ever *dared* look at her that way. And it was more than just a little weird that her cat didn't bristle.

Wary, Mila licked her lips. "Don't be getting possessive, Dominic."

Bending over her, he planted a fist on either side of her head. "It's too late for that warning. And you know it." He sucked a nipple into his mouth.

Inhaling sharply, Mila drove her fingers into his hair. He bit and licked and suckled like a master. That clever mouth ravished her nipples, making them throb with pleasure and pain. She pulled on his hair, trying to drag him onto the bed. Instead, his mouth trailed a blaze of fire down her stomach before he got to his knees at the foot of the bed and clamped his mouth around her pussy.

Mila's eyes fell shut as he licked at her slit. Then he was rolling the tip of his tongue around her clit before expertly pumping it inside her. The friction built and built as she moaned, shook, and bucked. And then she exploded. He didn't stop. He drove her hard and fast toward another orgasm . . . and then he stopped before she could come, the asshole.

Aching to be in her, Dominic stood upright, gripped her thighs, and angled her hips toward his cock. "Nothing better than fucking you while your taste is in my mouth." Forcing the head of his dick past swollen muscles, Dominic slowly sank inside her. "Love watching your pussy stretch for me. There's always that little bit of resistance for just a few seconds, but then I'm in you. And you always take every inch. I wonder how much of my cock your mouth can take."

She gave him an imperious look. "You'll just have to keep wondering."

"Oh, I'll have that mouth, Mila." Dominic slowly and smoothly pulled back until just the head of his cock was inside her pussy, grinding his teeth at how fucking hot and slick she was. Just as slowly and smoothly, he buried himself balls-deep. Dominic groaned. "So fucking tight." Resisting the urge to pound into her, he gave her yet another slow thrust. And another. And another.

Mila tried arching into his thrusts, surprised by his leisurely pace. Dominic was usually aggressive. Forceful. Unrelenting. She wasn't sure she liked the change, because it was a hell of a lot easier to think of it as just sex when it was earthy and raw.

Fisting the sheets, she shoved her hips at him, hinting for him to pick up the pace. He didn't. She teasingly squeezed his cock tight with her inner muscles. Again, he ignored the silent demand, letting out a throaty little snarl that made her pussy contract around him. She did not know what it was about that fucking sound, but it totally did it for her.

Never a quitter, she clamped her pussy down on him again. Still, though, the awkward bastard kept up that agonizingly slow pace.

Digging his fingertips into her thighs, he lifted a brow. "What is it, Mila?"

"Move faster," she ordered. "Harder."

He slowly dragged his cock out of her pussy, leaving only the head inside. "You want it rough?"

"Yes," she bit out.

"Why?" He lazily thrust back inside her. "So you can pretend this is just fucking? It's not, Mila." He shuffled her up the bed as he knelt on the mattress. "You know it's not." Again, he pulled his hips back. "Don't you?"

"Well—"

Sluggishly sinking back into her pussy, Dominic curled over her and flexed his hips, stabbing his cock so deep that her lips parted and agonized pleasure flashed across her face. "Feel how deep I am. I'm going to come while I'm this deep. Gonna make sure every inch of your pussy feels me and knows it's mine."

Mila's heart jumped. "Yours? Look, GQ, you said yourself that no one's made you feel possessive before. That's all this is. The emotion's so new that you don't yet know—"

"No more of us pretending this is just fun," he said, ignoring her. "No more of me leaving in the middle of the night. No more of you talking about going to Russia. We're going to let this thing between us play out. We're going to see where it takes us."

"The arranged mating—"

"Won't happen." He swiveled his hips, wrenching a little gasp out of her. "The only reason the idea of it attracts you is that it's not much different from a business deal. There doesn't have to be feelings involved. He'll take you as you are just so he can have the alliance—you're okay with that because, no matter what you like to think, you don't feel you can give everything you are to someone. Not yet. But the whole fuckup with Joel left you with a void, and you're desperate to fill it."

Mila wished she could argue with that, wished he was wrong, but she was terribly afraid that he wasn't. "What if you're right, and I can't put my all into this? What if *you* can't?"

"Neither of us are going to find it easy to be totally open. Maybe that will make this harder. On the other hand, maybe it will make it easier since we'll both be able to relate to what difficulties the other is having. We'll soon find out. Like I said, we'll see where this takes us."

"And what if it takes us somewhere good?" she asked, her voice cracking. "What if imprinting starts? Are you going to get scared of that? Are you going to run?"

"I'm not afraid of commitment, baby. If this takes us somewhere good, all the better."

"What about your true mate? If I say yes and we later imprint on each other, I'll be robbing you of something special—a life with your true mate."

"The same thing would apply if you mated with that Russian asshole." His wolf bared his teeth at the mere mention of him. "But, baby, I would never see it as you 'robbing' me of anything. I'm making the choice, here and now, to explore this with you. I'd be a fucking fool to walk away from it. I point-blank refuse to. I want to see where this can go. And so do you." He gave her another slow thrust. "Don't overthink this, Mila. There's no need to. Just stay. Fuck Russia, fuck Maksim. Stay with me."

Slipping his thumb between her folds, Dominic rubbed her clit just right as he thrust forward again and latched on to her nipple. The triple assault scattered Mila's thoughts, making it difficult for her to focus. "Shit. Not fair."

"Did you think I'd fight fair?" He lashed her neglected nipple with his tongue. "Stay with me."

Mila swallowed as his hooded eyes stared down at her, glittering with resolve, possession, and a promise of . . . home, maybe? She couldn't really describe it. But it was like he was holding out a metaphorical hand—an invitation and an offer. Her cat took a step toward it. And the part of Mila that had worried she'd never feel that she belonged to anybody after having missed her chance with Joel reached out to Dominic.

She tightened her grip on his hair, hissing. "If you fuck me over, GQ, I will plow your ass with a goddamn plunger—and I'll make you like it."

He chuckled, relief and masculine satisfaction pouring through him and his wolf. "That's my girl. My Mila." Pulling back his hips, he snarled. "Now you're gonna get so fucked . . ." He slammed home, biting hard into her neck, growling as her pussy clamped down on him. *Mine.* Dominic hammered into her, keeping his teeth locked on her flesh, spurred on by every moan and gasp and whispered demand.

Curving her body into his, Mila dug her claws into his nape and shoulder. Every slam of his cock was pure bliss, winding her tighter and tighter. Making her burn hotter and hotter. She was so agonizingly close to coming, she shook with it.

Dominic's balls tightened as her teeth scraped over his neck. He knew she wanted to bite him and leave her own mark. Could sense her fighting it. "Would you want to see me with another woman, Mila?"

"I always do. They flock around you," she hissed, her eyes flashing cat. And he saw the warning there—the feline wouldn't tolerate that shit.

"So make sure they know not to go near what's yours," he said. Sharp teeth dug down hard into the crook of his neck, acting like a whip of lightning to his cock. *"Fuck."* Dominic slammed harder into her pussy, forcing his cock deep, making sure she felt him in her womb. Those teeth didn't release him. No, they were locked tight on his flesh, and that only made it hotter.

His balls drew up, and he felt that telling tingle in the base of his spine. Dominic snapped his hand around her throat, snarling against her mouth. "Come for me, Mila."

It was the damn snarl that somehow did it. Mila's lips parted in a silent scream as white-hot pleasure rippled through her body, sizzled its way up her spine, and shattered her from the inside out.

Dominic swore as her pussy squeezed and contracted around him. Jamming his cock impossibly deep, he came so fucking hard it almost blew the head off his dick, jetting rope after rope of come inside her. *Marking* her.

As the strength left them both, he released her legs, letting them slide to the mattress, but he didn't otherwise move. Just lay over her, his face buried in her neck while her fingers lazily danced over his back. He had to be crushing her with his weight, but she didn't complain.

"Wasn't kidding about the plunger, GQ," she slurred.

His lips curved. "Such a vicious little thing; I like that." He licked over the none-too-subtle bite he'd left on her neck, his smile widening at her little shudder. "I've never marked anyone before."

"Neither have I."

"Good."

"What triggered the whole 'we're gonna see where this can go' thing?"

Bracing himself on his elbows, he breezed his thumbs over her cheekbones. "It was always going to happen—Tate's phone call just sped it up. His first words were, 'Don't go postal.' I got this sick feeling in my gut, and my imagination went haywire. I knew you weren't dead because Tate would have begun the conversation *much* differently. But dozens of other scenarios played out in my head in mere seconds, although it felt a fuck of a lot longer.

"And it hit me that we'd wasted so much time dancing around this thing we have—and we *do* have something here, Mila—rather than just accepting and exploring it. Life's too short for that shit. I'm not wasting any more time. I'm too old to bullshit myself about what I feel and want. And I'm done trying to rationalize it."

Satisfied that this hadn't been some spur-of-the-moment thing that he was likely to regret later, Mila nodded. She could tease him a little, though, right? Glancing at the wall, she blew out a breath. "I guess I'll have to tell my uncles to postpone the arranged mating."

He stiffened. "Postpone?"

"Well, this might not work out. I need to keep my options open and—"

Grabbing her wrists with a growl, he pinned them above her head. "You better be fucking kidding me." But he was smiling because the little witch was laughing. "You're gonna pay for that, Mila."

"What, you gonna spank me, GQ?"

"As a matter of fact . . ." Dominic withdrew his half-hard cock, flipped her over, and brought his hand down hard on her ass. The little witch was still laughing.

CHAPTER THIRTEEN

A god-awful beeping sound woke Dominic. Beside him, Mila reached over to the nightstand and turned off the alarm. He was just about to snuggle up to her when she fluidly slipped out of bed and stood tall, as alert as a fucking marine. He blinked. "Were you already awake?" he asked, his voice thick with sleep.

Pulling on an old flannel shirt, she said, "Nope. I was having a really strange dream that I was playing poker with Wonder Woman."

He flicked a quick glance at the digital clock. Only 7:15 a.m. "Come back to bed, baby."

"Gotta be at work at nine."

"Doesn't mean you can't come lie with me for a minute," he pointed out, but she'd already disappeared into the bathroom. She returned after only a few minutes, looking fresh as a damn daisy. Then . . . it was like she was on fast-forward mode as she moved around the room, brushing her hair, changing into fresh clothes, and dabbing on a minimal amount of makeup without even looking in a mirror—he'd never seen anything like it. Honestly, he was tired just watching her.

Shaking his head, he asked, "How can you go from a deep sleep to wide awake, and then be completely ready in a matter of minutes?"

She shrugged. "Call it a leftover from my childhood. And adolescence."

"A leftover?"

"I lived with two wolverines, GQ. If you didn't get to the breakfast table fast, you didn't get breakfast."

Huh. He hadn't thought of that. As she went to walk past him, he snagged her shirt, yanked her close, and then rolled her onto her back beneath him. "Better." He took her mouth in a long, lazy kiss. "Good morning."

She combed her fingers through his hair. "Good morning. Bet it feels weird waking up in someone else's bed when it's not the middle of the night," she teased.

"I did wake up, remember?" Spooning her, he'd played with her clit until she was dripping wet and then fucked her right there, like that, before they both fell back asleep. He hadn't felt even the smallest pull to leave. "In the past, I always went home because I didn't want to lead anyone on."

She looked at the ceiling. "You know, I've never understood why some guys worry that if they stay the night at a woman's house, she'll think it means something. Honestly, if a guy fell asleep in my bed and didn't leave before morning, I never thought it meant something. I figured he was fucking tired. And since I very much hoped he had worn himself out making sure I had had myself a good time, I didn't see it as a bad thing."

Well, Dominic supposed that was indeed one way to look at it. "I don't know anyone like you."

She sniffed. "I'll take that as a compliment."

"Good. It was meant as one." Nuzzling her, he yawned.

"Go back to sleep if you're still tired."

Drawing back, he brushed his nose over hers. "I want another kiss." She lifted her mouth to his. Smiling, he began to slide down her body. "I didn't say *where* I wanted it."

After making her come with his mouth twice, he fucked her hard into the mattress. Ignoring her bitching about how he should have done it *before* she'd washed and dressed, he slapped her ass and headed into the bathroom. He did his business, brushed his teeth with a spare toothbrush he found in a drawer, then pulled on his clothes.

Checking his phone, he noticed a text message from Taryn asking how Mila was doing. The nosy she-wolf was also poking for information on how Mila had responded to his insistence that she was now his. He rattled off a quick reply, assuring her that all was well, and then went in search of Mila. He found her sitting on the living room sofa, sipping coffee while reading something on her cell phone.

"Coffee's in the pot, if you want me to get you some," she said without looking up.

He dropped a kiss on her head. "I'll get it." When he returned from the kitchen, she was still preoccupied with her cell phone. Mug in hand, he settled on the sofa next to her and nipped the tip of her ear. "What are you reading?"

"The numerous texts I received from my pride mates this morning, asking how I was feeling. Many of them are also fishing for details on whether or not you stayed."

Marveling at how it didn't feel the slightest bit weird or awkward to be waking and spending his morning with Mila, he said, "Taryn, my Alpha female, wanted to know if you were okay and whether you'd accepted that you're mine. The pack is going to want to meet you." He splayed his hand on her thigh. "I want them to meet you."

"I can't tonight. We're invited to my parents' home for dinner."

"Sounds good."

"You say that *now.* But my mother's brothers will be there."

Dominic's eyes widened. "More wolverines? Excellent."

Mila shook her head in disbelief. "Yeah, you definitely have some screws loose."

"Will they be pissed to hear that there'll be no arranged mating?"

"Don't know." She gave him a patronizing smile. "Don't worry, I'll protect you from them."

"Good of you." Tracing the brand on her neck, he asked, "How do you think your pride will feel about this?"

"Probably glad, since it means I won't be moving to Russia. None of them were happy about it. My parents will no doubt be ecstatic that their little plot to get us together worked. They think you're the shit. Honestly, I was surprised they didn't change their minds about you after seeing that long list of names in the online article."

He winced. "Makes me look like a player, doesn't it?"

"You're not a player. You didn't play *anyone*. You just did your best to keep people at bay. One day, when you're ready, you're gonna tell me why." It was a statement, but it held no pressure.

He squeezed her thigh. "Yeah, one day."

"I noticed Charlene was on that list." She sipped her coffee. "That explained a few things."

He frowned. "What things?"

"You know, that she feels she has some sort of . . . well, I wouldn't say *claim* to you, but there's a little possessiveness there."

Dominic shook his head, having never picked up on such a thing. "She's mated."

"Like you once said to me, just because someone is imprinted on another doesn't mean they can't still have lingering feelings for someone they were previously involved with. You were once involved with Charlene." Mila took another drink from her cup. "She has a proprietary note to her voice when she talks about you."

His hackles rising for a reason he couldn't quite explain, Dominic narrowed his eyes. "And she talked to you about me?"

Mila nodded. "A few times."

"Saying what, exactly?"

"The first night you spoke to me at the club, she later warned me in a very friendly way that I wouldn't get a happily-ever-after from you. You know, like she was just looking out for me. The day after she caught us coming out of that little alcove where you'd kissed me, she sent me a text—I'm guessing she got my number from the employee files or something—saying that she'd heard about the jackal attack, hoped I was okay, and that she was very thankful that you had been there to intervene. She then cautioned me to remember that you were a ladies' man, and I shouldn't read anything into your concern for me. Said she believed the only person you'd ever commit to would be your true mate."

Motherfucker. Confused as to why the fox would interfere like that, Dominic shook his head. "Charlene knows I've never been eager to find my true mate. At one time, she was very much the same, which was why I was comfortable having a brief fling with her as opposed to a one-night stand. I knew she wasn't somebody who'd read anything into it."

"Why did you end it?" asked Mila, putting her empty cup on the coffee table.

"I didn't. She did."

"Did you object?"

"No. I had no reason to. There was nothing between us."

Mila couldn't help but wonder if maybe Charlene had *wanted* him to object. Maybe the fox had hoped that by pulling away from him, she'd spur him into pushing for more. "How did you feel about her imprinting on someone else?"

"Happy for her. I thought of her as a friend, nothing more." Setting his cup on the coaster on the coffee table, he added, "She tried discouraging me from pursuing you. When she mentioned over the phone yesterday that I hadn't been to the club, she assumed I'd given up on you, and she seemed pleased by it. Said I was too old to be chasing skirts."

"Maybe she's just looking out for you in her way and wants you to find someone you can settle down with—someone *not* me. People often aren't fond of pallas cats."

"Well, I'm very fond of my cat." Dominic lifted her and sat her on his lap to straddle him, marveling at how she seemed to fit there just right. As she went lax against him, he smoothed his hands up her back. "Very, very fond." He kissed her, licking into her mouth. Feasting and savoring until his head spun with her taste. "I shouldn't have pulled back from you and put distance between us."

"No, you shouldn't have."

"It won't happen again." Dominic didn't miss the spark of doubt in her gaze. "I'm all in this, Mila. I made a commitment to you, and I don't have to tell you that I don't take shit like that lightly. I wouldn't have put that brand on your neck if I wasn't sure that you could trust me to honor it. I can't promise you that I won't fuck up, but I can promise you that I'll give this everything I have. Okay?"

Mila twisted her mouth. "All right. I promise to do the same."

He gave her a lazy smile. "That's my girl." He kissed her again, sipping from her lips, liking the way her heartbeat quickened. The same heartbeat that had briefly come to a halt the previous evening, he remembered. And that thought was enough to take his breath away.

Never again. The next time danger came her way, it would find him in its path. "I've got to be honest, I'm not feeling good about you staying here after what happened in the basement."

She smoothed her hands down his hard chest. "Vinnie and the boys will secure the building."

"It should have already been secure. If I hadn't trusted that you were safe here, I wouldn't have kept my distance. In fact, I would have worked on getting you to stay on my territory for a while."

"Can you honestly tell me that a snake shifter couldn't have found a way onto your territory in much the same way that it did this building? Because you'd be totally lying if you said yes. In any case, I won't be hiding away on your territory or anywhere else. That's not who I am, and it's not who my cat is."

"I respect that you're a highly dominant female, baby—"

"Prove it. Don't try to change me. Don't ask me to go against my nature. I know you want to protect me. But wrapping me up in cotton wool truly wouldn't help the situation. The hit isn't personal to me. It's just a means of flushing out Alex. If I seem too difficult to get to, a price might suddenly appear on my mother's head, or my father's. Then the pride would be scrambling, trying to protect us all at once. Their attention and resources would be divided. Only two things will help—finding Alex and learning the identity of who put out the hit. I'm hoping Nick's hacker-ally can help with the latter."

Dominic fucking hated that he couldn't deny she made sense. Still . . . "I don't want your parents in the line of fire either, but I can't agree that it's better for the threat to remain focused solely on you."

"I'm not asking you to agree with it. In your shoes, I wouldn't like it either. But the pride has a better chance of protecting me if I'm the only one they need to worry about." She put her finger to his mouth when he would have protested. "Let it go. Choose your battles wisely. This isn't one you'll win, and I think you know that already."

He sighed. "I rehearsed this conversation in my head several times. You always gave the same responses you did just then."

She shrugged. "I can only be who I am, Dominic."

Drawing her close, he dabbed a kiss on her mouth. "Then you leave me only one option."

"What does that mean?"

"It means you have a brand-new shadow." He smiled. "Say hi."

"I don't need to be shadowed."

"No, you don't. But it'll make me feel better to have you in my sights. Would you really expect me to do anything else? I'm a highly dominant male wolf, baby. I protect, defend, and stand beside what's mine."

She heard what he didn't say: he respected her level of dominance, and he needed her to accept his in return. And she couldn't exactly dismiss it, could she?

With her elemental understanding of how dominant shifters worked, her cat didn't bristle at his need to be close to her. In fact, the feline approved of it. "You'll get bored."

He frowned. "Being around you is never boring."

"It will be after you've spent hours just sitting around the barbershop, doing nothing."

"Watching over you isn't 'nothing.' Especially when it gives me peace of mind." He scraped a hand over his jaw. "I need another shave anyway. And wouldn't it be nice for you to have me there to distract your pride mates when they come to check on and possibly fuss over you?"

Actually, it would. "What about when they start asking about our marks? Which they will, because they're all nosy as hell."

"I'll just tell them the short version—I charmed, melted, and romanced you."

She snickered. "Romanced. Right."

"Hey, I can be romantic."

"Sure," she said drily, stretching out the word.

"Okay." He straightened his shoulders. "Roses are red, and so are other flowers. Take off your panties, I just need a few hours."

"Oh my God."

He chuckled. "Kidding, kidding, here's a good one. Roses are red, fit for a bride. Get flat on your back, and spread your legs wide."

She stood up, shaking her head. "There's no helping you, there really isn't."

"Yeah, I know." Fisting her shirt, he dragged her back onto his lap. "Not done with that mouth yet."

Later that day, Mila raised her hand to knock on her parents' front door, but then she paused. "Quick warning: My uncles . . . well, they don't *hate* my dad. They just hate that he mated their sister and wouldn't move to Russia. But it means they can be assholes toward him. It's mostly Isaak. He likes to pretend Dad isn't even there. Of course, Dad just thinks it's all pathetic, but it can make dinner conversation awkward."

Dominic palmed Mila's nape. "Baby, Trey's grandmother makes a point of insulting most of the females in our pack at almost every meal—I know all about awkward."

"My uncles might give you a little grief, since they're snobs when it comes to other breeds. They only respect their own kind."

He shrugged. "It makes no difference to me whether they like me or not."

Mila couldn't imagine them *not* liking Dominic—he could win over anyone. He'd hung around the barbershop all day. Theoretically, it should have been annoying to have him constantly watching her and taking up space. It wasn't. Especially since he always supplied everyone with coffees, dealt with any pride mates who came nosing around, and was sure not to get in her way while she worked.

She'd expected him to get restless and start doing dumb shit to entertain himself, but he'd seemed happy enough to just laze around and chat with people. *And* watch her in a way that made her blood heat. He'd also had fun cornering and kissing the life out of her during her breaks.

Turning back to the door, Mila was just about to knock when it flew open.

Valentina smiled. "You are here." She ushered them inside and kissed both their cheeks, making a huge fuss over Dominic. Rolling her eyes at that, Mila turned . . . and found herself swept up in a massive hug.

"Uncle Isaak," she greeted with a smile, patting his back.

Grinning broadly, he held her at arm's length. "My little Milena! So beautiful, just like your mother."

Dominic's brows lifted. "Milena?"

Isaak frowned at him. "It is good, strong Russian name."

Sergei pulled her close, his face soft. "Do not worry about this assassin matter. We will find your brother. Aleksandr will not have gone too far."

"Aleksandr?" echoed Dominic.

Isaak shot him another frown. "It is good, strong Russian—"

"We got it, we got it," James cut in.

Isaak cocked his head. "I hear a squeak, Valentina. Perhaps you have vermin."

Valentina swatted his arm. "You will not play these games with my mate." Turning to Dominic, she said, "These are my brothers—Dimitri, Isaak, and Sergei. Boys, this is Mila's man, Dominic Black."

Dominic nodded at the three male wolverines as they silently assessed him. They looked very much alike—dark, muscled, hair slicked back . . . kind of like the bad guys in *The Matrix*, minus the sunglasses.

With his chest puffed out and mask of sheer arrogance, Isaak seemed to stand out most. Shorter than his brothers, Sergei gave Dominic a somewhat genteel smile to put him at ease, but there was far too much cunning in those amber eyes for anyone to be relaxed around that guy. As for Dimitri . . . he just seemed to broadcast "try me, motherfucker" with his menacing glower and dark aura, even as he hugged Mila so gently. Oddly, though, Dominic got the sense that Sergei was the most dangerous of the three.

Dimitri looked at Mila. "What about Maksim?"

"I'll kill him if he even thinks to come for her," Dominic said in a calm, matter-of-fact tone. "Ripping out his throat won't bother me in the slightest."

After a long moment, Dimitri gave a small shrug. "We will still get alliance without the mating, it is no matter."

Sergei moved closer to Dominic, his nostrils flaring. His nose wrinkled in distaste. "A wolf, Milena?" Letting out a put-out sigh, he gave Dominic another once-over. "At least you are not cat."

James's brows snapped together. "Hello, *Mila's* a cat."

Sergei glared at him. "Our Milena is wolverine."

"No, she's a pallas cat," James stated.

"Her animal has the skin, muscle, and bone of a feline, but it is not the body that is important. Our Milena has soul of a wolverine—we all see it. Therefore, she is wolverine."

"No, she's really not." James raised a hand when Sergei would have argued. "I'm done. Let's sit and eat."

Mila gave her father's hand a supportive squeeze as they headed to the dining table. She sat between him and Dominic while Valentina piled food on plates, filled glasses, and generally fussed over everyone before finally joining them at the table.

Digging into his meal, Dominic silently marveled at how fast and how much the male wolverines ate as he listened to them talk of the many people they'd spoken with about Mila's brother. Alex had been sighted in various places, but he didn't stay anywhere for long and didn't seem to be heading in a particular direction. "How long does Alex usually go roving for?"

"A few months at a time," Mila replied, holding a forkful of pasta to her mouth. "Though he did disappear for a year once."

"A year?" Dominic repeated.

"Wolverines like to roam," said Isaak, his voice deep and gruff. "It is in our nature, our blood, our bones. Only a mate can anchor us."

Dimitri lifted his glass. "Aleksandr roams more than most, though."

Lips thinning in disapproval, Sergei nodded. "The boy needs a father."

James bristled, pausing in slicing into his meat. "He *has* a father."

Isaak glanced around. "I heard another squeak, Valentina."

Giving her brother a light slap on the head, Valentina urged, "Eat your food, Isaak." That only appeared to amuse the male.

Sergei drummed his fingers on the table. "Tell us more about the website your mother mentioned, Milena."

"Dominic knows more about it than I do," she said, but she relayed what information she had. Dominic added a few details in between bites of food.

"How confident is the other wolf that he can crash the anonymity network?" asked Dimitri.

"Very. If Donovan says he can do it, I believe him," said Dominic.

"Once we have the website manager's name, we will deal with him," declared Sergei. "First, we must track Aleksandr. A wolverine can only be found by another wolverine. We will retrace his steps. He will be found, Milena—do not worry."

Isaak nodded. "Then we will kill who put out the hit. All will be fine."

"Except that Mila's cat will probably attack Alex the second she sees him," said James, shooting her a droll look. "I can't count the number of times I saw that feline launch at his face in a fury. She always got him good."

"He always deserved it," Mila asserted.

Dominic's mouth quirked. "You fought a lot with your brother?"

James snorted. "They fought *constantly.* There was no disciplining them over it. If I yelled at her for hurting him, he'd turn on me, saying no one got to shout at his sister. The same thing happened if I yelled at him for hurting her. They stuck together, even as they drove each other insane."

Isaak lifted his chin. "Wolverines always stick together. It is in our nature, our blood, our—"

"Bones, right." James sighed. "I remember the time I went out into the yard to find that Mila had dug a shallow grave. She was also shoveling dirt back into it. It was only when I went over that I saw Alex lying in the grave, out cold and hog-tied with a goose egg on his head. When I asked her what the hell she was doing, she said, 'It's a kindness, Daddy, he's not fit to live.'"

Dominic chuckled. "How old was she?"

It was Valentina who responded, mock frowning at Mila. "Ten."

Sergei nodded, proud. "Even then, she knew to bury evidence of her crime."

"Why did you try to bury him alive?" Dominic asked her.

Her mouth tightened. "He drew satanic symbols on my bedroom floor and threw all my underwear into the front yard."

Dominic frowned. "Why?"

Mila sipped her soda. "Alex never needs a reason to be an ass. He often breaks into my apartment in the middle of the night and raids my fridge."

"He doesn't have his own home?"

"Sure he does, but he's a scavenger of the worst kind."

"He will be angry that he did not get hand in making death adder snake pay," said Valentina.

Mila flexed her fingers. "I fought that motherfucker hard."

"Well, of course you did," said Isaak. "You are an Ivanov."

James sighed. "She's a Devereaux, actually."

Isaak looked at his sister. "There is more squeaking."

Valentina slapped the table. "Isaak Ivanov, you will cease with your games!"

Isaak leaned toward her, scowling. "You could have had good Russian mate! Wolverine. Strong. Powerful. Instead, you chose dumb, psychopathic cat!"

Valentina's eyes flared. "He is not dumb or psychopathic!"

"A man who does not drink vodka must have heads in the freezer and bodies in the walls!"

"I will not do this with you!"

Mila turned to Dominic with a sigh. "Unreal, right?"

Smiling, he draped an arm over the back of her chair. "Is it wrong that I really like your uncles?"

Rubbing her temple, she grabbed her glass. "I had a feeling you'd say something weird like that."

CHAPTER FOURTEEN

"Miss Devereaux?"

Looking up from where she'd been cleaning her station, Mila took in the lean, balding, slickly dressed male walking toward her. His scent reached her first. *Human.* That meant he'd believe that she, too, was human. His smile was open and polite, but her gut told her he was as sneaky as a cockroach in a Michelin-star restaurant. "That's me."

His smile widened, flashing a set of gleaming white veneers. "My name is Emmet Pierson. I'm an attorney."

Well, fuck. This was just what she damn needed. Someone had snapped photos of her and Dominic together when they were walking down the street yesterday, and those photos were uploaded to the internet. Dominic—who was currently at the deli across the street getting them lunch—hadn't been happy about it, concerned that Pierson would see the pictures and then target her in some way. She didn't care that the bastard had approached her; she cared that Dominic would feel responsible.

Picking up on Mila's agitation, her cat sat up straight. Hopefully he didn't start talking smack about Dominic, because the feline wouldn't handle it well. The last thing Mila needed was her eyes flashing cat, giving away that she wasn't human.

Feigning ignorance, Mila echoed, "Attorney? Am I being served papers or something?"

"No, nothing like that," he assured her. "This isn't a legal matter. I was hoping you and I could talk. There's a coffeehouse just across the street."

Like she'd go anywhere with this asshole. "That's not possible, I'm afraid. My next client will be arriving soon. Why don't you tell me what this is about?"

He cast a glance at Evander, who was stacking shelves and looking for all the world like he wasn't paying them a lick of attention, but she knew the male cat would be listening to every word. She also knew he'd leap on the fucker if Pierson proved to be a physical threat. Well, Evander would *try*. Mila would get there first.

"It's regarding my daughter, Rosemary. She is a latent shifter; her inner wolf has been in a deep sleep all her life."

Mila tilted her head. "I didn't realize latent animals slept. I thought they were just unable to surface."

Pierson's smile went a little hard around the edges. "That is only in some instances." He smoothed a hand down his black suit jacket. "Two articles were recently posted online about her devastating circumstances. Have you not read or heard of them?"

"I don't keep up with the news. It's all sad and depressing."

"True enough. I will give you a quick rundown of the situation. Rosemary's husband divorced her when she was unable to conceive a child, so she was already in a fragile emotional state when she came across her true mate. He could have made her so much better. Instead, he made her worse. Rejected her for being unable to shift. She tried to commit suicide." His breath hitched just a little too dramatically. "She's doing better. She started talking again, although she doesn't say much and still spends long periods of time simply staring at the wall."

Struggling to keep her tone even, Mila said, "While I sympathize, I'm not sure how this relates to me."

Pierson took a deep breath and straightened the lapels of his jacket. "It has come to my attention that you are involved with a male shifter from the Phoenix Pack."

"Dominic, yeah."

"He is Rosemary's true mate." He threw out the sentence like it was a bomb, and her cat predictably rumbled a menacing growl, lashing out with her claws. "He didn't just reject her, Miss Devereaux. No, he swept her off her feet and formed a true-mate bond with her. Then he threw her away. Perhaps it was all a game to him, or perhaps he couldn't stand the weakness that she possesses as a latent shifter."

It was becoming harder and harder not to pop this guy right in the face. Silently encouraging her cat to stay hidden, Mila said, "It doesn't make sense that Dominic would ever hold prejudice against latent shifters. His Alpha female was once latent."

"Then it was simply a game for him. He hasn't even visited Rosemary since she tried to kill herself. Hasn't expressed an ounce of remorse and refuses to admit that she's his true mate."

"And you're sure that she is?"

Pierson's eyes hardened. "Rosemary recognized him as hers."

Mila shrugged. "It's not uncommon for people to make that kind of mistake. They can confuse infatuation with—"

"It was no mistake," he clipped, his tone leaving no room for argument. But Mila got the feeling that he very simply *needed* to be right. Needed to have someone to blame other than himself for what had happened to Rosemary.

Lifting her chin, Mila said, "I'm sorry, but I find it difficult to believe that Dominic would ever do the cruel things you're accusing him of. Plus, if his animal was truly mated to another, I doubt it would accept my presence in his life."

Pierson took a step toward her. "I came here to give you a friendly warning. This is not a man—if you could even call him a *man*—that you should want in your life. To him, women are objects. Toys. He has no respect for them. And he'll hurt you just as he's hurt others. If you have any sense, you'll get rid of him."

"I appreciate the warning." Mila tipped her head toward the door, gesturing for him to go.

Nostrils flaring, he said, "Be smart, Miss Devereaux. Don't let this creature ruin your life."

Baring a fang, her cat lashed her tail like a whip. "You're not really concerned for me. There's another reason you want me to separate from him. What is it?" But Mila already knew. Pierson had decided that if his daughter couldn't have Dominic, nobody could. Not just as revenge for Rosemary, but because he didn't want Dominic to be happy. She also had the feeling that Pierson would carry on this hate campaign for *years* if he wasn't somehow stopped.

"There are plenty of reasons why you should cut him from your life. Only one of those pathetic shifter groupies wouldn't see that."

Mila's gaze snapped to the door as it swung open, letting in a stream of traffic noise and the scents of hot bread, meat, and peppers as Dominic stepped inside, deli bag in hand. His blue gaze was hard and intent on Pierson, who went tense as a guitar string the moment he noticed the newcomer.

Sensing her male's anger, Mila's cat became even more agitated. Dominic's body language was casual and relaxed, but he was spilling a dark, ominous energy that almost clotted the air. It was like being in the same space as a jungle animal while it lazed in the grass, watchful and alert—you were acutely aware of the threat they presented and knew that their cool composure could change at any given moment. It was intense enough to make anyone feel like prey, even a female as dominant as Mila.

Settling his focus on her, Dominic prowled toward her, each step slow and predatory. Any anger had been swiftly buried and, God, she seriously envied his ability to be so emotionally unreactive in shitty situations.

"You're back," said Mila with a smile. "Good, I'm starving." Knowing she needed to get him away from the human before he could provoke Dominic into doing something notable for his next bullshit article, she grabbed Dominic's arm, intending to lead him to the break room. Evander would get rid of—

"I guess you are a shifter groupie after all," Pierson sneered at her.

Just like that, Dominic's posture went from deceptively casual to blatantly menacing. Mila closed her eyes. *Shit.*

With an overwhelming drive to protect and defend buzzing through his veins, Dominic placed his body between Mila and Pierson. His wolf's chest rattled with a guttural growl as he stood snarling at the human, the animal's legs quivering with the need to lunge. Dominic could have ignored practically anything the human tossed out, but not an insult to his woman. Never that. "You need to be gone," he said, his tone cool and calm.

The bastard really didn't get how much of a fuckup he'd made. It was one thing for the human to play games with Dominic; it was a whole other thing to involve Mila. Coming to her place of work and *breathing her air* was going too far for Dominic and his wolf.

If Pierson was a shifter, he'd have understood that. He'd have understood just how hard he was pushing by paying a visit to Dominic's woman and letting this shit touch her. Shifters had killed for less.

"It's *you* who doesn't belong here," sniped Pierson, his voice shaky with an apprehension he was striving to hide. "This isn't shifter territory. You've got enough of your own species chasing after you—you don't need to be polluting the lives of humans."

Dominic took an aggressive step toward him but kept his voice low as he said, "Hear me, Pierson. You. Need. To. Go."

"I second that," said Evander, moving closer.

Mila fisted the back of Dominic's shirt. "Don't let him provoke you. He *wants* you to lay your hands on him. He *wants* you to throw him out."

"I know that, baby."

Maybe it was simply Dominic's use of the endearment, maybe it was the way his voice had softened—Dominic wasn't sure. But Pierson's spine snapped straight, his hands balled into fists, and his face turned red and mottled.

"Damn you, you have a mate lying in a fucking hospital bed!" Pierson burst out. "Can you really be so heartless as to—"

"Your daughter knows she's not my true mate," Dominic clipped. "She spun you a tale, and you bought it. You bought it because you *wanted* to."

Pierson's nostrils flared like a bull's. "I have—"

"You wanted there to be something or someone that could stop her mental state from deteriorating," said Dominic. "But by buying into her fantasies, you made them more real *for her*. You see that now. You feel you're partially to blame for her attempt at suicide, but you can't face that, so you're displacing the blame." Mila had pointed that out, and she'd been right.

"All you had to do was mate with her!" Pierson snapped. "That's it!"

Dominic flexed his hands, fighting the urge to grab the bastard by the throat. His wolf wanted to mangle and maim the human. "You're still not hearing me."

Mila smoothed her hand up Dominic's back. "He's hearing you. He just doesn't want to hear you. Like his daughter, he finds life more comfortable if he only believes what he wants to believe."

In one slow stride, Dominic covered the space between him and the human. "You're done here, Pierson. You're going to leave now. You're going to leave, and you're going to stay away. You won't come near Mila again."

"Or what?" challenged Pierson, his eyes flickering with anxiety.

"Or you'll make yourself a lot of enemies." Dominic's pack, a pride of pallas cats, a bunch of wolverines—people whom the human didn't have a hope in hell of taking on. People who would make Pierson pay one way or another, and not necessarily with violence. His life would be worth shit. And since cats were notorious for holding grudges, the pride would make him pay for a *while.*

Pierson jutted out his chin. "I'm sure the public will enjoy hearing how I came here in peace only to be threatened and forcibly thrown out."

"We have CCTV footage," said Evander, looking mildly bored. He whipped his phone out of his pocket. "I also took the liberty of recording the entire conversation. I'd think twice before you make things worse than you already have, if I were you."

Clamping his lips shut, Pierson cast a glare at all three of them. And Dominic saw the warning there—he wasn't done. The human stormed out of the barbershop before anyone could say another word.

"I texted Tate to give him a heads-up about Pierson," said Evander. "He'll follow the asshole to his car and make sure he leaves without any delay."

"You really recorded the conversation?" Mila asked.

Evander nodded. "When he introduced himself as Emmet Pierson, I figured there was a good chance he'd later twist whatever happened here, so I took precautions." With that, Evander turned back to the shelves.

Stroking his hand over Mila's hair, Dominic dropped a kiss on her mouth. His wolf pushed up against her, needing her scent to calm him. "You okay?"

"Yeah." She sighed. "I knew he'd turn up eventually and try to talk to me, 'one human to another.'"

"How's your cat?"

"She'll be calmer when you are."

Dominic brushed his nose against hers. "I wanted to kill the fucker. He had no right to come here. No right to drag you into this. I should have—"

"Don't even start with the 'I should have stayed away from you' shit. It's not your fault. Pierson *chose* to up his level of asshole-ness. Besides, you would have pined without me. A grown man pining is not attractive."

Lips quirking, Dominic echoed, "Pining? I don't pine."

"Hmm."

He curled his hand around her chin. "You sure you're all right?"

"Yep," she said. "Just supremely hungry. Feed me."

He held up the deli bag. "What do I get in return?"

She snatched it out of his hand. "Duh. My stimulating company."

Sitting across from Jesse in the Velvet Lounge that evening, Dominic waited impatiently for Mila to come onstage. The VIP area was much less crowded than the main floor, featuring only a handful of booths and tables. Aside from the two solo drinkers at the small bar, the VIP patrons were talking, laughing, snapping photos, and bobbing their heads to the music. It wasn't so loud that people had to shout into each other's ears to be heard, but it was enough for Dominic to feel the beat of the bass beneath his shoes.

Jesse sighed as one of his pack mates led a skimpily dressed female away from the stage after she tried climbing onto it. "Someone always gives it a shot, without fail."

It made Dominic feel better to know that anyone who attempted to hop up there while Mila was performing would be swiftly dealt with.

Jesse's gaze dropped to the neckline of Dominic's shirt. "You know, if you hadn't tugged your collar aside and given me a look at Mila's brand earlier, I'd find it hard to believe you were wearing one. It's even weirder knowing you marked Mila too. I saw her mark—it's pretty distinctive, not to mention highly visible. Which makes me think that your branding her wasn't just possessiveness; it was a declaration of intent."

"She's mine, she needs to know it. Other people need to know it."

"I'm glad you followed my advice and persevered when she turned you down."

Dominic frowned. "You told me to give up."

"I was using reverse psychology, so technically, I was encouraging you."

Mouth curving, Dominic snorted. "Whatever." Picking up his bottle, he took a long swig, letting the cold beer slide down his throat.

"Do you think you might imprint on each other?"

"Honestly, I'm not a person who thinks too much about what the future holds. I try to enjoy the now." Like he'd told Mila, they'd let this play out and see where it took them.

"Just be aware that imprinting can begin without any prompting from you or Mila. It might take you by surprise."

Dominic tilted his head. "Did it take you and Harley by surprise?"

"Not at all. From the time I was a juvenile, I knew she'd be mine one day. I wasn't ready back then—in fact, I was a fucking mess." Idly spinning a cardboard coaster that was stained by a condensation ring, Jesse sighed. "Even though we had history and a good foundation to build on, imprinting didn't start straightaway. I'd hoped that the claiming bite would be enough to trigger it, but it wasn't."

"You put a claiming mark on her *before* you'd imprinted?"

Jesse winced. "Yeah. It was shitty, I know, since claiming bites don't fade. If we'd parted ways, she'd have had to look at it in the mirror every day for the rest of her life. But I had no intention of letting her go. I'd have done whatever it took to keep her."

"How long did it take for imprinting to begin?"

"A few months, but it's not the same for every couple. Imprinting can happen fast, slow . . . can even take years. The females of my pack believe that for the couple to *fully* imprint, they need to have the building blocks of a lasting relationship—trust, respect, loyalty, acceptance, love—but that the process can start before *all* those emotions come into play. The first sign is when you find you're wearing each other's scent. Then you start to feel small echoes of each other's emotions. But it's so much stronger when the bond fully forms."

The DJ said Mila's name over the loudspeaker, and the crowd immediately started hooting. Dominic's body tightened as, mic in hand, she breezed onto the stage in that catlike way she had. His wolf perked up, no longer brooding that she wasn't close by. She flicked a brief look at Dominic and gave him an enigmatic smile just before she launched into a song.

"Seriously, she's got an amazing voice," said Jesse. "It's just effortless for her. She's also got a strong stage presence."

"And she's all mine." The satisfaction of that went bone deep.

Jesse chuckled. "Never thought I'd see the day when you said those words."

Silence fell as they watched her perform. As usual, Dominic found himself absolutely blown away by her innate talent and those smoky, scratchy vocals that drove him crazy. He wanted nothing more than to drag her off that stage and shove his cock inside her, to drown himself in all that passion, and reassert his claim on her. His wolf was all for that idea.

"Is it true that Mila has already met her predestined mate?"

His eyes snapping back to Jesse, Dominic stilled. "Where did you hear that?"

"Taryn told Shaya, who then told Harley, who then told me. They don't know the details, though. Taryn said you just hinted at it."

He should have remembered that Taryn, being best friends with Shaya, told the woman everything. "Yes, she has. I've met him."

Jesse blinked. "You met him?"

"He joined her pride after he imprinted on one of her cousins." Dominic slid his gaze back to Mila as he continued. "He has a subconscious draw to be close to Mila and protect her, so he hangs around her a little too much."

"Fuck, that's got to be hard on her."

"It is. Her cat *loathes* the fucker."

"Imprinting bonds can fade, though," Jesse pointed out. "That's why they're a double-edged sword. Yeah, it means you have a way out if you need one. But it also means *she* has a way out. If Mila's true mate ever splits from her cousin, he might then sense that Mila's his—the imprinting bond won't be there to block the frequency of the true-mate bond anymore. He could try claiming her."

Like Dominic would let that happen. "Wouldn't make any difference to Mila or her cat. They don't want him. Mila doesn't hate him, but she doesn't pine for him either. He broke something in her cat, and she'll never forgive him for that. Plus, I think she'd feel he'd regard her as second best, since he initially chose Adele—Mila wouldn't do second best."

"So his presence doesn't make you or your wolf feel threatened?"

"No. You'd think it would, wouldn't you? But it doesn't. Maybe it's because Mila's not someone who'd tolerate possessiveness from just anyone. And she admitted she's never marked anyone before." He drained the last of his bottle. "I hate that Joel has rights to her—it doesn't matter that he can't claim them, they're still there—but maybe I don't feel threatened by him because she *chose* me. She didn't leave this mark on me because she felt compelled to do it by the mating urge. She did it because I'm her choice."

"I get what you mean," said Jesse. "It gives you a sense of security. And it's good that you're not letting jealousy be a factor or that you feel like you're somehow competing with him because of what he *could* have been to her. Harley sometimes got hung up on the fact that she's not my other half. And she's not. But she's my center. Mila can be that for you, if you let her."

The Mercury enforcer held up a hand and added, "I'm not saying you *should*, nor am I trying to push you. If you want to take it one day at a time, fine. But that might change, so I'm going to share with you the advice that Nick gave me. He said that if I wanted to imprint on Harley, I'd have to drop all my protective walls and give her all of me, said I'd have to be sure I *could* do that before I demanded anything from her or gave her any promises."

Which couldn't possibly be as simple as it sounded. "Was it hard?"

"Damn right, it was. I didn't think I'd struggle so much to open up to her. I didn't even realize I was still holding a part of myself back until she almost died right in front of me. In the long run, emotionally protecting myself made *her* physically vulnerable."

Pausing, Jesse gave him a searching look. "You're open in a lot of ways, but you're closed off in others. If you ever find yourself wanting to imprint on Mila, you can't give her only the parts you choose to give her. You can't hide behind walls or masks. You have to expose your vulnerabilities, fears, secrets, and personal pain. She'll be someone who knows you inside out, and that's something you have to be comfortable with or an imprinting bond won't form.

"A partial imprint won't be enough for your animal or hers, which means both will eventually withdraw from the relationship. Then you'd be forced to end it whether you wanted to or not. In other words, there's a lot riding on whether you have what it takes to imprint on her."

At that moment, the song came to an end. But, encouraged by the crowd, Mila quickly launched into another. Pride flooded Dominic at how much raw talent she possessed, watching the dancers react so crazily to her. An instrumental break started, and, like last time, Harley stepped forward with her electric violin.

Charlene appeared and placed two fresh bottles of beer on the table. "Here you go, boys." She looked down at Dominic, her brow creased.

"I haven't heard from you since you hung up on me the other day. Everything all right?"

"Fine," he replied, his voice a little curt. He'd originally planned to immediately confront Charlene about her attempts to warn Mila away from him when he got to the club, but she hadn't been there when he arrived. Looking at her now, he decided to play dumb instead, interested in what she'd say and do.

She glanced at the stage, and her lips thinned. "I don't need to ask what's brought you back here. I saw that you were photographed with her recently, so I'm guessing you haven't given up trying to seduce her yet. She's wearing someone's mark, sweetie."

"I know." It clearly hadn't occurred to Charlene that Dominic had been the one to put the mark there. He let his gaze drift back to Mila. It was impossible for him to look away from her for long. He loved watching her, loved knowing he owned that talented creature up there.

"And I see that you're not going to let the mark bother you." Charlene huffed. "Well, she's a fool for turning you down over and over. You don't think she's playing some kind of game, do you? Trying to push you into chasing her, which would give her the upper hand?" There was the slightest note of distaste in her voice as she spoke of Mila, and it made his wolf snarl.

"Mila doesn't play games."

"I agree she doesn't seem like someone who *would.* I just can't see why she'd reject that pretty face of yours."

"When she has people warning her that I won't give her a happily-ever-after, it's no wonder she didn't tumble straight into my arms, is it?"

The fox's eyes flickered.

"Who's been saying that shit to her?" demanded Jesse.

"People with too much time on their hands," said Dominic.

Charlene danced her fingertips over his nape. "To be fair to them, you're not a relationship kind of guy."

Dominic nudged her hand away from his neck, making her brow pucker. Neither he nor his wolf wanted her touching him. "You once said the same thing about yourself, Charlene. Now you're mated. People change."

"Yes, they do," she said, putting his and Jesse's empty bottles on her tray. "I keep telling you that you're too old to be chasing skirts. You should let me set you up with a friend of mine."

"Don't need your help, Charlene."

"You don't need my help to score, no, but you do need help convincing nice girls that you're not a player. Pierson's articles certainly didn't aid your case. Have you had any more trouble from him?"

He cast her a hard look. "That's pack business."

She rolled her eyes. "Fine, don't tell me. At least let me introduce you to my friend."

"Like I said, I don't need your help."

"Yes, but what you want—"

"Is standing right there on that stage."

Oh, that seemed to piss the fox off. "Surely you're not still holding out hope that she'll throw some crumbs your way," Charlene snarked. "I never had you down as a sucker for punishment. Where's your pride?"

A growl rumbled out of him that took her off guard. "Careful."

Jesse's eyes turned cold and flinty. "Charlene, I know you have a job to do. I'm confused as to why you're not doing it."

Cheeks reddening with what was probably a mix of embarrassment and irritation, the fox stalked off.

"What is her problem?" Jesse asked him.

"Don't know, don't care."

"Why didn't you tell her that you're with Mila?"

"Because I don't have to explain myself to her."

"You're pissed at Charlene for something," Jesse sensed. "What did she do?"

"She was the person who warned Mila away from me." Shaking off his anger, Dominic clapped along with everyone else as the song reached its end and both female performers took a bow.

"Did you ever pursue Charlene?" asked Jesse, his gaze speculative.

"Didn't need to," replied Dominic, picking up his fresh beer bottle.

"Okay, I'll put it another way. Have you pursued anyone other than Mila?"

"No."

"Maybe that's Charlene's problem," Jesse mused. "She's happily mated, but her ego will have a problem with seeing you go after Mila when you didn't invest any time or energy in pursuing her. Foxes can be pretty vindictive, and they're highly competitive."

Dominic took a swig of his beer. "I doubt it's that."

"Don't forget, Charlene is known as the female you had the longest fling with. She takes a certain pride in that, especially since so many females set out to tame you and consistently fail. There's a rumor that you won't commit to anyone because Charlene broke your heart when she dumped you and later mated with Lennie. Charlene obviously hasn't disabused anyone of that belief because it remains a rumor. It's something else she'd probably get a kick out of."

"She just offered to set me up with one of her friends."

"And if it worked out, she could—in a roundabout way—take credit for 'taming' you, since she set the whole thing up. On the other hand, she might purposely match you with someone you wouldn't gel with. Who knows?" His eyes snapped to something over Dominic's shoulder, and he smiled. "Ah, here are our girls."

Our girls. Dominic liked the sound of that. Having put down their bottles, both he and Jesse stood as their "girls" hopped up the small set of steps leading to the VIP area. Dominic spared only a brief smile for Harley, who went straight to her mate. His attention was on the feline behind her, whose eyes were as bright as her smile—she always looked drunk on adrenaline after a performance.

Dominic hauled Mila close and kissed her, licking into her mouth, devouring her. Was it weird that he'd missed her? Probably. They hadn't been apart long, but she centered him somehow. He didn't care to overthink it. "Flawless performance, as always. Gotta say, baby, every time I see you up there, all I can think about is fucking you."

"Classy feedback," said Mila, smoothing her hands up his arms.

He chuckled, splaying a possessive hand on the small of her back. "Isn't it, though?" He kissed her again, so fucking greedy for her he almost shook with it. His wolf drank in her scent and touch. "Love your taste." He brushed her hair over her shoulder, baring her neck, and pressed a kiss to the bite there. Yeah, he wanted all the people he could feel watching them to understand it was *his* mark.

Mila's mouth twitched. "I think you made your point to all the gawkers."

Sitting, he pulled her onto his lap. "Just wanted to be sure there'd be no misunderstandings."

Jesse caught his eye and slid his gaze toward the bar. In the reflection of the mirrored wall behind the bar, Dominic could make out the sour look on Charlene's face as she plonked down the tray. She started talking in angry whispers to one of the lone drinkers at the bar, as if she knew him well. Dominic frowned. He recognized the male. Thought maybe he'd seen him at the barber—

"You've caught quite a bit of attention, Dominic," said Harley, her eyes twinkling.

Mila hummed. "I'll bet plenty of tongues are wagging right now."

Dominic nipped Mila's ear. "There's only one tongue I'm interested in. It's a very talented tongue. I know it wants to lick my cock—I don't know why you won't let it. That's just mean."

She shrugged, giving him a look of mock sympathy. "I'm a pallas cat, sweetie. We're all mean."

"What if I give my cock the most thorough wash it's ever had and make sure it's *really* clean?"

"It wouldn't make a difference."

He grinned. "Ah, I see, my baby likes to suck dirty cocks."

Shaking her head at his idiocy, she grabbed his beer. "Like I've said before: hopeless."

"Hey, I'm here to fulfill your every fantasy. If what you want is to suck—" He cut off with a groan as she swirled her tongue around the neck of his bottle. "Ah, that's not fair."

"As my mother would say, 'Fair? What is fair? I not know this word.'"

Jesus, his cock throbbed at her smoky voice speaking in that thick Russian accent. Dominic crushed her to him. "Say that again."

Laughing, she nipped his ear. "I want to dance. You coming?"

"Coming? Later. Hopefully a couple of times."

Rolling her eyes, she slid off his lap. "Always have sex on the brain, don't you?"

"Around you, yeah."

With his front pressed against her back and one arm looped around her, he steered her through the club. As they were nearing the dance floor, Mila picked up a flash of red in her peripheral vision just as someone called out in delight, "Dominic!"

He twisted quickly, keeping Mila in front of him so that she stood between him and the other female, who came to an abrupt halt. "Eden," he greeted simply.

Mila felt her scalp prickle. The brunette didn't even look at her in spite of the fact that he was wrapped around Mila like a freaking victory flag. No, Eden just eyed him like he was candy while smoothing a hand down her red dress. Going by her lustful, nostalgic smile, she knew him biblically. Ugh.

Intellectually, Mila understood why the female wasn't deterred by her presence. It wasn't disrespect on Eden's part; it was that it would simply never occur to her that Dominic thought of Mila as more than tonight's entertainment. Still, she was pissed. Dammit, he was *hers*. Her cat bared a fang, wanting to peel off the bitch's flesh. "How are you?" Eden purred.

"Fine," he said, his tone even. "Have you met my Mila?"

The brunette stilled, and then her brows shot up so high, they almost hit her hairline. "*Your* Mila?" Her gaze dropped to Mila, and her smile faltered. "No, I haven't. Although you do look familiar." Her gaze then cut to where Dominic's fingertip was circling the bite on Mila's neck. Lips parting in shock, Eden blinked at him. "So, wow, I did not see this coming. Like ever." She moved closer, reaching out to touch his shoulder. "I mean—"

"Lower your fucking hand," said Mila, her voice cold as frost. "Hey, I get it. Dominic didn't do commitment before now. It's hard to believe he's suddenly changed. Hard to truly respect that mark on my neck when you're not convinced it has any real meaning. Well, it has meaning to me. And unless you want me to jam a chair leg so far up your skinny ass that you'll be forced to choke on your own shit, you need to back the fuck up . . . *fast*."

Shuffling ever so slightly backward, Eden lowered her hand and swallowed nervously. "I remember you now. You're the one who hurt my pride mate, Randal, a few weeks back at Enigma. You smashed a barstool so hard over his head, you fractured his skull. He's doing okay now, in case you were wondering."

"I wasn't." The male tiger had tried slipping a drug into Mila's drink—he'd had it coming. "You can go now."

Eden looked from Dominic to Mila. "Enjoy your evening." She sashayed away, but Mila's cat didn't relax.

He put his mouth to her ear. "Did you really hit her pride mate over the head with a barstool?"

Her mouth quirked at the mix of pride and humor in his voice. "Twice," she replied.

Chuckling, he patted her ass. "Get moving."

On the dance floor, the mass of bodies bopped, gyrated, and swayed as they laughed, kissed, and hooted. He caught Mila's nape and pulled her flush against him, splaying his free hand on her ass. His cock, hard and full, dug into her stomach, reminding her what it felt like to have him inside her.

She hooked her arms around his neck as they swayed. Writhed. Grinded. His mouth alternated between devouring hers and ravishing her neck. Each nip was like a whip of pleasure to her clit.

He thumbed her nipple as he sucked the hollow beneath her ear. "Are you wet for me?"

"You know I am."

"Shame we're not somewhere like Enigma right now." The nightclub was exclusive to shifters and allowed full sexual contact—even on the dance floor itself. "I could take you in front of everybody, so they'd know who you belonged to."

She slanted her head. "I wouldn't have thought your wolf would like the idea of you making me come in front of other people."

"He wouldn't be too happy about that part, but he likes that others would get the message that you're taken."

She frowned. "I really don't think that your fucking me on the dance floor would seem at all territorial." She doubted he was new at that activity.

"No, but anyone watching would see me bite you." Her pupils swallowed the color in her eyes, and Dominic smiled. "You like that idea."

She just shrugged one shoulder, nonchalant.

"Hmm. Maybe I should bite you right here and now. Just because."

"That's really not—" She hissed as his teeth sank down on her neck. There wasn't just territorialism in that move. There was an assertion of dominance that made her cat buck. His teeth bit harder, as if to hold her still, and he ground his cock against her.

Gasping, Mila pricked his nape with her claws. And as a mix of possessiveness, defiance, and pleasure whipped through her, she involuntarily raked his nape hard enough to draw blood—hard enough to leave a *permanent* mark. *Oh shit.*

As he pulled back to meet her gaze, Mila said, "I am so, so sorry. I didn't mean—"

Snapping his hand on her throat, he took her mouth with a growl. The kiss was hard and hungry and out of control. "Now we leave. I need to be in you."

She licked her lips. "Yeah, now we leave."

CHAPTER FIFTEEN

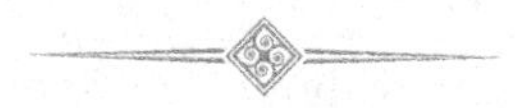

As Dominic drove his SUV up the rocky trail, Mila drank in the scenic views around them. His territory seemed to go on and on—an endless stretch of land that was all majestic trees, steep mountains, and rocky terrain. "This place is *huge*."

"The forest goes on for miles," said Dominic. "Your cat would probably love exploring it."

Oh, the feline definitely would—she was currently enthralled by the vast amount of territory. Mila couldn't imagine what it would be like to have *this* as her backyard. When her pride mates wanted to shift and let their cats play, they either used the rooftop garden of the apartment building or the massive communal yard behind it. The backyard looked neglected to the human eye with its tall grass, thick bushes, nonsensical rockeries, and clusters of mossy trees. But it was a perfect playground for one of Mila's kind.

Pallas cats were highly territorial and didn't like sharing their space. But since her pride mates had been forced to do so since they were kits, they were used to it. Her cat would *love* having this kind of territory to run in.

"See that mountain up ahead?" he asked, pointing. "Look closely."

Squinting, Mila leaned forward a little in her seat. Surprise had her lips parting. "No way. Am I seeing windows and balcony doors?" There were also narrow stairways carved into the face of the mountain. "You live in an actual mountain?"

He nodded, his mouth hitching up. "It has several floors and a huge maze of tunnels that can be hard to navigate at first, but you get used to it."

Fascinated, she twisted in her seat to face him. "How set in the Stone Age is it?"

"If you mean, do we go without electricity and running water, no. The dwelling is as modern as your apartment building."

"Wow."

"I'll take you on a tour, but that will come later. I know your cat doesn't like being in crowded rooms, so I suggested to the pack that we all meet outside. We've just finished building a tree house for the kids at the spot where we sometimes camp for the night, so everyone has gathered there."

Warmed by that, she said, "Thanks. I appreciate it."

"I don't want you or your cat uncomfortable here." Dominic wanted both of them to love it, wanted them to come back again and again—which was why he'd warned his pack to be nice and not run Mila through a gauntlet. Honestly, though, he didn't believe they'd be anything less than welcoming, especially since they were so excited to be finally meeting her.

He drove into the concealed parking lot at the base of the mountain and whipped the SUV into a free space. "Come on. They'll be waiting."

As they walked hand in hand through the expansive forest, Dominic took her down the most scenic route. They crossed the river, meandered through a pretty meadow, and passed a frothy waterfall. He watched her carefully, absorbing every reaction, loving it whenever her face lit up. "So you like it then?"

"Yeah, I like it," Mila replied. Her cat liked it even more. The feline's excitement built as she drank in every scent, every sight, every sound.

Her stomach fluttering, Mila blew out a breath. She wasn't nervous. Aside from the moments before a performance, she was never, ever—

Okay, she was nervous. Not about meeting the pack itself but because she knew it was important to Dominic that they like her. Madisyn and Harley had assured Mila that the Phoenix Pack were good people and that they would like Mila for the simple reason that Dominic mattered to her. Still, that didn't chase her nerves away. And the stomach fluttering intensified when she heard voices and laughter up ahead.

Dominic gave her hand a supportive squeeze. "They'll be nice, just like your pride mates have been nice to me. Well, most of them have."

Mila's head whipped around to face him. "Some of my pride mates gave you shit? Who?"

Her protectiveness made Dominic smile, and he just had to press a quick kiss to her mouth. Though he hated to speak the bastard's name, he explained, "I meant Joel."

"Oh. Well, he doesn't like most people."

Dominic's brows drew together as a thought suddenly occurred to him. "He's very different from me."

"Yeah, he is," Mila agreed. Their biggest difference was that whereas Dominic had an easy way with people and could make friends in an empty room, Joel didn't warm to others easily and didn't consider many people friends.

"Fate pairs us with someone who'll suit our personality. It paired you with someone very different from me."

Something about the way he said that made Mila frown. "And what, you think that means that you and I won't work in the long run?"

"Don't you?"

"No. Adele's very different from me. Sweet, bubbly, and a little oblivious. Yet, she and Joel really do complement each other in many ways."

Dominic's brows shot up. "Never thought of that."

She gave him a patronizing pat on the head. "What have I told you about thinking? You leave that to me."

He brought her hand to his mouth and nipped at her fingers. "Kind of bitchy when you want to be, aren't you?"

"You're only realizing this now?"

The scents of sawdust, tree sap, smoke, and food drifted Mila's way just as they stepped into a clearing. Some people were perched on the fallen trees framing a man-made fire pit. Others lounged on patio chairs or lay on blankets. Plates, cups, and various foods were spread across the nearby picnic table.

A few camping tents had been set up near a small campervan. Mila supposed they were for the adults, who were hardly likely to sleep in the nearby tree house.

It was no typical tree house. It was more like a miniature cabin built on high, thick tree stumps. There was a rope ladder on one side and a spiral wooden staircase on the other. The cabin had a front porch, cute little windows, and a tube slide attached to the center of its base—she was guessing there was a trapdoor that opened onto the slide. Kids were swarming all over it like insects, laughing and squealing.

Digging cans of soda out of the huge cooler near the picnic table, Trey was the first to spot her and Dominic approaching. Even though her cat had met him once before, she went on full alert, eyeing the Alpha carefully, sensing his level of strength, and identifying him as a potential threat.

Built like a freaking tank, Trey headed toward them. He nodded at his enforcer before inclining his head at her. "Good to see you again, Mila. Welcome to Phoenix Pack territory."

And then all the chatter just stopped.

Dominic stifled a smile. It was almost comical the way all the adults turned their heads at once. As they took in the sight of his hand joined with Mila's, they smiled. And he knew that if he hadn't warned them in advance that it wasn't wise to get touchy-feely with a pallas cat, they'd have descended on her as a group. Most of them had pestered him at one point or another to bring her here.

Trey gestured at Taryn. "This is my mate, Taryn."

The Alpha female waved, her smile wide. "Howdy. I was hoping you'd come."

As Trey called for the kids to come down to meet Mila, Makenna spoke. "It's really good to see you, Mila. I'm Makenna. The tower of doom and gloom behind me is my mate, Ryan. Ignore the scowl. It's a permanent thing. Standing next to him is his cousin, Zac. Oh, and that she-demon scrambling over here is my little girl, Sienna."

Mila smiled at the dark-haired girl, who she'd seen plenty of photos of, thanks to Madisyn. "She's Madisyn's goddaughter, right?"

Makenna nodded. "That's right."

"Looking better than you did the last time I saw you, Mila," said Dante. "This is my mate, Jaime, and our boy, Hendrix."

"I'm so psyched to finally meet you," said Jaime, cradling the sleeping baby. She tipped her chin toward the people sitting beside her on the fallen tree. "This is my brother, Gabe, and his mate, Hope."

Sidling over to Dominic, Trey said quietly to him, "We tried to get Allen to come here, knowing Greta would be on her best behavior if he were around, but he's visiting family in Florida."

Dominic let out a quiet curse. Before Mila could ask him if something was wrong, Taryn spoke again.

"Let's get the rest of the introductions out of the way. The boy who's climbing Trey's back is our son, Kye. Over there on the blankets we have Lydia, Cam, Grace, and Rhett." She pointed at the group of people on the lawn chairs. "That's Marcus and Roni, a pair of mated enforcers. Trick, another of our enforcers, is next to them with his mate, Frankie, who is an amazing sculptor. Sitting on the log opposite Jaime is our Head Enforcer, Tao, and his mate, Riley, who is also the pack's Guardian. The boy climbing Tao like a fence post is Dexter, and the little girl with pigtails hanging from the branch above my head is Savannah—they belong to Riley and Tao. The little girl peeking at you from behind Riley's leg is Lilah, she's Grace and Rhett's daughter." Her brow creasing, Taryn gestured at an elderly woman, hesitantly adding, "And this is—"

"I'm Greta, it's a pleasure to meet you." Smiling, the old woman shook Mila's hand, all grace and warmth.

Mila's mouth kicked up into a smile. "Same to you. I'm Mila."

"Such a beautiful name." Greta lightly touched Mila's dark curls. "And such pretty hair."

"Thank you."

"You know something? I've been waiting for my boy to finally meet someone worthy. You took your sweet time," Greta chastised him, her eyes twinkling.

"Oh, you're related?" asked Mila.

"Not by blood, but I think of him as my grandson. He thinks the world of me, just as I do of him." Greta patted his arm. "Now, Dominic, you go find a seat for your Mila, and then get her some food and—Kye, don't climb the camper!" She offered Mila an apologetic look. "Excuse me." Greta walked toward the van and tried to shoo Kye off the hood.

Becoming aware of an unnatural silence, Mila looked to see that everyone was staring at the old woman, their expressions ranging from shock to confusion.

"What just happened?" Taryn asked no one in particular. "Seriously, what was that?"

Frankie looked from Mila to Greta. "What did you do? I mean, she was . . . *pleasant* to you. While sober."

"Greta likes pallas cats, remember," said Dominic.

Makenna's frown smoothed away. "Ah, that's right. That's why she has a soft spot for Madisyn. I totally forgot."

"Can we go back to the tree house now?" Lilah asked her mother, who nodded.

As the kids dashed off, Dominic led Mila toward an empty lawn chair.

"No, she has to sit by me," declared Jaime.

Dominic frowned. "She'll be almost directly across from—"

"By me," Jaime insisted. "I have about an hour to convince her to be my best friend. I can't do that if she's all the way over there, can I? Work with me, Dominic—I'm on a schedule here."

Rolling his eyes, he led Mila to the fallen tree. Gabe and Hope shuffled over, making room for her and Dominic to join them. Instead of sitting, Dominic went to get them some food.

Jaime smiled brightly at Mila. "Hi, I've been *so* eager to meet you. You can imagine we all love Dominic, and due to his obsessive-compulsive dirty-line disorder, we were starting to think he'd grow old alone. You've given us hope." She held a hand up when Mila might have pointed out that it was only early days. "No, even if you and he later part ways, you still bring us hope. You're living proof that someone can cope with his weirdness."

Taryn nodded, her eyes dancing. "I have to tell you, we've all *loved* that you made him work for you."

Grace forked a piece of potato salad. "Things come easy to Dominic, especially with his gift of persuasion. And women have always flocked around him, ready to hop, skip, and jump at his say-so. But it was all shallow. They didn't have any real interest in who he was; they wanted him like you'd want a pretty accessory."

"Or they wanted to be the one who *tamed* him—it would have done something for their egos," Taryn added. "No one really tried to get to know him. No one looked past the surface and saw that more lurked beneath. And no one ever mattered to him before, so we all just want to kiss you."

Lydia nodded. "It's very true. Even Greta does, apparently."

"And let me tell you, having Greta's seal of approval is no small thing," said Frankie.

"She's very possessive of Trey, Dante, Tao, and the enforcers," said Riley, tossing a piece of dry wood into the fire. "Calls them *her boys.* Doesn't like having unmated females around them. Each time one of the guys found his mate, she did her best to chase her off . . . and remains a witch to them to this very day. Except for Roni. She *loves* Roni."

Roni shrugged. "What can I say? I'm immensely lovable."

Dominic sat beside Mila and handed her a loaded plate of food. "Here, baby."

"Thank you." Mila set it on her lap and then grabbed the can of soda he'd held carefully in the crook of his elbow.

Sighing dreamily, Jaime looked at the others. "Aw, he calls her 'baby.'"

Dominic's brow furrowed. "This isn't gonna get weird, is it?"

Dante snorted, carefully taking Hendrix in his arms. "Dude, if my mate's involved, it always gets weird."

Jaime sniffed at him. "So true."

Mila tucked into her food, feeling surprisingly relaxed as opposed to overwhelmed by the number of people there. But then, they made it easy for her to be comfortable when they were so welcoming and genuinely pleased to meet her. Plus, the territory itself was so peaceful that Mila couldn't help but be relaxed. Even with the kids squealing, she could still enjoy the serene sounds of fire crackling, birds chirping, and branches creaking in the breeze.

Once her cat got past the need to watch the pack as if they were potential threats, she began pushing against Mila's skin, wanting out, wanting to explore.

A soda can hissed as Taryn popped it open. "I should probably be up front about this, Mila, and say I'm *so* jealous of you."

Blinking, Mila tilted her head. "Why?"

"Because I really want to be a pallas cat." And the Alpha female sounded amazingly put out that that wasn't the case.

Jaime chuckled. "Taryn's been saying that ever since she saw the video footage of Madisyn kicking the asses of three sows in the restroom at Enigma."

"Speaking of clubs, we were at the Velvet Lounge a couple of weeks ago when you were performing there," said Frankie. "Can I just say, you have a beautiful voice."

Mila smiled. "Thank you."

"On another note," began Tao, roasting marshmallows, "is your father an art thief, Mila? Because you're a total masterpiece."

Chuckling along with the others, Trick said, "I was wondering if your father was an alien, because there's nothing like you on Earth."

Another round of chuckles.

"I was thinking of calling God and telling him I found his missing angel," said Marcus. "Seriously, Mila, is that a ladder in your pants or a stairway to heaven?"

Dominic glared at his laughing pack mates. "I knew you'd all be assholes."

Marcus shrugged a shoulder. "We're just getting some payback."

Mila turned to Dominic with a sigh. "You hit their mates with cheesy lines, don't you? Honestly, GQ, I don't know how you're still breathing."

Dominic smiled. "I save all the lines for you now."

"Lucky me, I guess," Mila muttered. He just laughed.

Standing near the picnic table with Dante and Trey, Dominic drank his beer as he watched Mila help Dexter pile things inside a plastic bucket that was tied to a rope. Kye and Lilah then pulled the rope, hauling the bucket up to the tree house. Dexter was a playful kid but not much for chatting. Right then, though, the cheetah cub was jabbering on and on about something to Mila, who he'd led over there by her pinkie finger the moment she'd finished her food.

Highly protective of Dexter, little Savannah had spent a full five minutes watching Mila with a death glare that spooked most adults. Dominic had tensed when Mila's eyes went cat as she glared right back at Savannah. But that show of strength seemed to have settled the viper, because Savannah was now twined around one of Mila's legs while tugging on Sienna's foot. Yep, the pup also seemed drawn to Mila—Sienna had demanded to be picked up and had been perched on Mila's hip for at least the past half hour.

Someone else might have been annoyed at having kids crowd them like that. Mila wasn't fazed. Nor did she seem overwhelmed having all these people trying to commandeer her time—and they really were trying to. She talked easily with his pack mates, not looking awkward or socially uncomfortable. Maybe that came from dealing with a stream of strangers at the barbershop, day in and day out.

Seeing how well she got along with the females of his pack settled him. It wasn't that she fit in; it was more like she'd slotted into the space as if she'd been there countless times before.

"You know, it's lucky that Pierson didn't notice Mila's mark when he spoke to her the other day," said Trey. "That would have sent him into a full-blown rage—he's convinced a bite means an automatic mating bond."

Taking another swig of his beer, Dominic turned to the Alpha. "She dabs a little concealer over it when she's at work to avoid questions from human clients—but not so much concealer that a shifter with their advanced eyesight wouldn't notice it."

"It doesn't bother you that she covers it?" Dante asked him.

Dominic twisted his mouth. "It does a little, but I get her reasoning. Humans believe she's one of them, and they aren't always nice to people they perceive to be 'shifter groupies.' She doesn't want the barbershop to lose clients or deal with hassle from the kind of religious zealots that turned up outside the Velvet Lounge a few weeks back. Archie conceals his claiming mark while at work for the same reason. Pallas cats like to fly under the radar of humans. So long as other shifters will spot her brand and know she's taken, I can deal with it."

"On the subject of the club, I spoke to Jesse earlier," said Trey. "He mentioned there's something weird going on with Charlene. You never said anything about it. What happened?"

Dominic told him about the fox's warnings to Mila, how Charlene had acted at the club that night, and Jesse's theory about it. "I don't know if he's right, but I know she wasn't happy when she realized I'd marked Mila. She tried hiding it. Smiled as she served us drinks. But she didn't mention the brand."

Dante pursed his lips. "I would have thought Charlene would be happy for you. Maybe she doesn't like pallas cats. But Jesse's theory makes sense too. With any luck, the fox will get over herself quick enough."

"For her sake, I hope she does. Because I can't see Mila or her cat tolerating that kind of shit from Charlene or anyone else." Trey's gaze drifted to where Mila stood. "The kids sure like her. Probably because there's something very . . . calming about her. I can't really explain it."

Understanding, Dominic nodded. "She's very steady . . . genuine. Has her shit together."

Dante pointed at him with his bottle. "You need that in a partner. Need someone more emotionally mature than you. Someone who lets your weird ways roll off her back. Yeah, she suits you well. I can definitely see you two happily imprinted."

Dominic stilled. "Let's not get ahead of ourselves. Mila and I are taking it a day at a time."

Dante snorted. "If you try to tell me that you honestly don't see her in the picture whenever you think of your future, you're only fooling yourself."

Dominic's grip on his bottle tightened. "I like to concentrate on the present."

"Because you had too many bad surprises growing up, so you don't see the point of planning ahead. Allegra . . . she didn't have staying power, Dom. She just didn't. But Mila's different. Stronger."

"I know that."

"Then don't expect her to pick up and leave. Trust that you have it in you to make someone happy. I get that it's easier said than done, especially when your parents told you they had you to fix their relationship and yet they were never happy. But the only people who could have fixed that relationship was them. The weight of that responsibility should *never* have been on you."

"I know all that too," said Dominic, a defensive bite to his tone.

"And yet you've deliberately never taken your hookups further or seriously before now. You've kept them shallow and trivial. That doesn't mean that it's all you're capable of."

"I never said otherwise."

"You didn't have to. I know how your mind works. Think about this." Dante took a step toward him. "I was there the first time you met Mila. She smiled a little as she talked with you, but I could almost feel the sadness in her. The loneliness. It was right there in her eyes." He paused, sliding his gaze to Mila. "It's not there now."

Feeling like he'd taken a punch to the gut, Dominic didn't breathe for a second. The Beta walked away, slapping Dominic's back as he passed.

Dominic looked at his cat, who'd been joined by Roni and Greta. The three were chuckling. Yes, Greta was chuckling. After dumping his bottle in a trash bag, he crossed to the trio.

Finally free of the kids, Mila turned to him, and her face softened. "Hey. Greta's been telling me some stories about you."

Dominic curled an arm around his cat's waist. "Don't believe a word she says." Ignoring Greta's affronted gasp, he stared into Mila's eyes, and he saw that Dante was right. The shadows were gone. She was healing. Still hurting in some ways, but no longer plagued by the emotions that had once stained those pretty eyes. And now he needed to be alone with her. He'd shared her with the pack long enough.

"Come on, I'll take you on that tour I promised you." Unmoved by the protests of his pack mates, who wanted them to stay longer, Dominic guided her through the woods, heading back the way they came. "I like how relaxed and settled your cat feels right now."

"She likes it here."

"How about we let our animals go for a run together before I give you a tour of the caves?"

Mila's eyes brightened. "Yeah, she'd like that."

They both shed their clothes and tucked the pile between thick tree roots. It was a struggle not to stroke and caress Mila's naked form, but he resisted, knowing he'd end up taking her right there if he touched her just once. "Let me shift first. My wolf wants a little attention from you."

"All right." Bones snapped and popped as he shifted. In mere seconds, a powerfully built wolf with salt-and-pepper fur stood before Mila. "Wow, you shift fast." She crouched and petted his dense fur as he shoved his way into her space, rubbing his jaw against hers and licking at her face. Then he was circling and rubbing against her, marking her with his scent. "You're as territorial as Dominic." Answering her cat's need to be free, Mila shifted.

The wolf nuzzled the little cat. Sniffed and rubbed against her. She stood tall, watching him, her eyes narrowed.

The wolf bowed down, sticking his rear in the air and wagging his tail, inviting the cat to play. Claws sheathed, she batted at him with a playful hiss. They tussled. Pounced. Wrestled each other to the ground.

Done playing, they leisurely loped through the woods. Skirted thick trees. Leaped over logs. Chased small animals.

The cat bared a fang when the wolf tried herding her back to their clothes, but her human side insisted it was time to go. With an unhappy growl, the cat followed him . . . but not before first biting into his flank. The wolf didn't even flinch.

Once they'd shifted back to their human forms and dressed, Dominic took Mila into the cave dwelling. She'd expected the tunnels to be dark, but the light-cream sandstone walls kept them surprisingly bright. He showed her around each of the levels, giving her a glimpse of the living area, kitchen, kids' playroom, and the infirmary.

Mila's cat *loved* it. For the feline, the cave dwelling was like the ultimate rockery.

Stopping outside a particular door, Dominic said, "This is my room."

She followed him inside, surprised by the sheer size of it. She'd expected a standard bedroom, but it was more like a luxury hotel suite. It didn't have the impersonal touch of a hotel, though. Not with the charming earthy color scheme, rich oak wood, and little keepsakes scattered around the place.

She skimmed her fingers along the spines of the books that were jammed into one of the small niches in the wall. "This room is awesome. I'm used to having *way* more living space, but this doesn't feel . . . confining. It feels cozy." But maybe that was because it smelled of him.

Dominic crossed to her and drew her close. "I've been wanting to get you alone for hours." He took her mouth in a slow, lazy kiss. "I don't like sharing your attention."

She chuckled. "Brat. I heard you were very good at *sharing*."

Knowing she was referring to the women in his sexual past, he said, "They weren't you." He raked his teeth over her lower lip. "I told you I'd never share you."

She slanted her head to the side as he nipped and licked at her neck. "But last night, you said you were here to fulfill my every fantasy. What if I was curious about a threesome?" She wasn't, but it was fun to tease him. Mila flinched as he bit her pulse *hard*.

"No other man will touch you, Mila." He sucked her pulse into his mouth, soothing the sting.

"Who said it had to be another guy?" Mila quipped. "What if I want a threesome with another female?" She expected him to flash her an impish smirk and say he'd make it happen. Instead he gave a careless shrug, his face serious.

"You'll just have to use your imagination." He tossed her on the bed. "Now, let's get those jeans off. I want a taste of what's mine. Only mine."

CHAPTER SIXTEEN

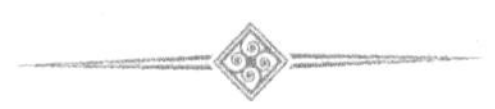

Clenching her hands around the handle of the cart, Mila ground her teeth. "I'm never bringing you grocery shopping with me again."

Dominic's mouth twitched. "You said that last week. And the week before that."

"Well, I mean it this time."

"You said that too."

She hissed. "Do you want me to bitch-slap you? Is that what this is?"

"Already told you, baby, you can slap me around while I'm fucking you. I like it rough and dirty."

Turning away, she shook her head. "Never again are you coming with me." Inhaling deeply, she took in the calming scents of the freshly baked bread and hot doughnuts she'd placed in her cart.

God, the guy was impossible. He insisted on saying embarrassing stuff when people were nearby, like "I'm just not into vaginal fisting" or "I already told you *three* times, I'm not letting you lick my asshole."

He also threw weird shit in the cart when her back was turned. Lubricant. Antidiarrheal medications. Vaginal itch cream. Lice treatment. An *Is My Girlfriend a Lesbian?* self-help book. An "Anal for

Beginners Pack" gag gift. Worse, he hid the damn things so that she often didn't see them until she got to the checkout counter.

Since her pride mates ran and worked at the store—which was on the same street as the barbershop—they understood it was just Dominic messing around. But the shoppers in the line behind her often didn't, so she was the butt of everyone's fucking joke.

Tossing the "Anal for Beginners Pack" onto a shelf, she pointed at his crotch and said, "That monster is not going near my ass. It'll rip me open."

"I'll be gentle."

"And still, it'd be painful."

"Now you're being unreasonable."

She blinked. "Unreasonable?"

"You'll get piercings, tattoos, pluck your eyebrows, and wax not only your legs and armpits but also your pussy . . . but your argument against letting me take your ass is that *'it'd be painful'*?"

She pursed her lips. "That's about right, yeah." With a haughty sniff, she upped her pace as she turned into another aisle.

Coming up behind her, he rested his chin on her shoulder as he curled his arms around her waist. "Fine, I'll behave."

Yeah, she'd heard that before. "No, you won't. And you can stop kissing my neck. It will not soften me up," she lied.

"It already has." Dominic had explored her delectable body enough times to know every little weak spot she possessed, and he had no problems exploiting them. Swirling his tongue over the hollow beneath her ear made her melt into a puddle every time. He nuzzled her with a soft groan. "I wish I could bottle up your scent. I'd spray it on my skin. My clothes. Pillow. Just about everywhere."

She let out an amused snort. "You're so full of it."

"I'm serious." He flicked her earlobe with his tongue. "My wolf wants to roll around in it."

She snickered. "Your wolf is even more possessive than you are."

"He was never possessive before you. Neither was I." Dominic traced the bite on her neck with his fingertip. He often found himself doing that. The sight of it gave him a strange sort of . . . comfort. Each time the mark began to heal and fade, he bit it again. It was one of his favorite things to do.

"You still up for having dinner with my pack tomorrow?" he asked. Since he'd first taken her to his territory two weeks ago, his pack mates had hounded him to bring her for another visit.

"Sure. My cat will want another run on your land, though. Shit, I walked past the bagels."

"I'll get them." Releasing her, he retrieved a pack from the shelf and placed it in the cart.

"We still having pizza tonight?"

"Sure. Who doesn't love pizza? It's my second favorite thing to eat in bed."

Mila almost choked on her own saliva. "You're such an asshole." Especially since he'd said it loud enough for the people passing to overhear him.

He chuckled. "I bring life to grocery shopping. Admit it."

"Life? I guess that's one way to put it." A man brushed past her, and Mila almost flinched at the short sharp prick in her arm. The sensation faded so fast, she wondered if she'd even felt it at all. Maybe it had been static electricity or something, she mused as she watched him walk away. He looked completely innocuous, casually strolling down the aisle with a half-full basket. Still, her hackles rose.

"You okay, baby?" asked Dominic.

She blinked up at him. "Yeah, fine." But the words sounded . . . wrong. The voice just didn't sound like hers. She tried again. "Fine." It was a slur this time. Her vision swam, distorting Dominic's form until it was like looking in a fun house mirror. The fluorescent lights seemed too bright, and the world was spinning around her. Her cat lunged hard, trying to surface. Couldn't.

Mila reached out. Weakly fisted Dominic's shirt. "White male. Blue tee. Black jeans. Dreadlocks. *Get him.*" And darkness fell.

Dominic caught Mila as her legs gave out. *"Fuck."* Panic racing through him, he gave her a little shake even as he held her gently. "Mila? *Mila!*" Hearing the squeak of rubber on tile, he looked to see a male of Mila's description running down the aisle like his ass was on fire. Dominic whipped out his phone and called Tate, who answered fast.

"Yep?"

"Some bastard just drugged Mila." Dominic could smell it on her now. He fired off a quick description of the male. "He'll be coming out of the grocery store any second now. Get the fucker, Tate. Shit, her lips are blue."

"Take Mila to the deli section—one of our healers works there."

Pocketing the phone, Dominic scooped up Mila and ran. Her heartbeat was slowing, faltering, and his own was pounding with fear. His wolf paced, anxious and enraged.

Her eyes wide, a familiar graying woman—Helena, he remembered—dashed out from behind the deli counter. "What's happened?" Her nose wrinkled. "Drugged." She put her hand on Mila's head, and he almost *felt* a surge of power in the air.

The hairs on his arms and nape stood on end, but his focus was on the female in his arms. Soon her heartbeat stabilized, her lips lost their blue tinge, and the color came back to her face. But it didn't chase away his fear. Didn't give him even a hint of relief.

Mila's lids fluttered open, and her big blue eyes stared up at him and the healer. Realization flashed across her face, and she gripped Dominic's arm. "Did you get him?"

"Tate will get him." Dominic wanted that to be enough for him, but his muscles trembled with the need to hunt the motherfucker who'd drugged her himself. His wolf was pushing Dominic to track him down and make him pay.

"I have her, Dominic," Helena told him. "She's fine, just a little groggy. You go help Tate and the others get whoever did this to her. They probably have him by now, of course, but I'm sure you'll only be satisfied when you see that for yourself."

Mila nodded, sitting upright. "I'm fine. Woozy and shaky, but fine. Go."

Dominic pressed a fast kiss to her mouth and then shot the healer a glare. "I'm trusting you with her."

"And I'm trusting you to avenge her," said Helena.

At yet another urging from Mila, he left her with Helena and rushed out of the store. He'd expected to find the male pinned to the ground by a member of the Olympus Pride while other cats gathered around him. Dominic had never fucking suspected he'd find the bastard standing in the middle of the road, holding a long claw to the throat of a crying toddler he'd seemingly plucked off the street.

A sobbing woman was alternating between trying to reassure the child and begging the male to let her little girl go. Vinnie, Tate, Luke, and the Olympus enforcers had formed a loose circle around him.

Mila's attacker yelled something at Vinnie that Dominic couldn't quite make out. Vinnie gave a slow shake of his head. Cursing, the male glanced in every direction. Dominic could imagine what he was thinking. There would be no getting past the cats. No going right or left. Which meant the only place he had to go was . . . up.

Just as that thought crossed Dominic's mind, the male's head tipped back, and his frantic gaze cut to the roof of the nearest store. The pallas cat standing in front of the store narrowed his eyes, as if guessing what the male was about to do, but the toddler was flung at him with such force that the cat staggered backward as he caught the child.

Mila's attacker leaped onto a nearby car, launched himself at the building, and began to climb the gutter pipe. Dominic sprinted across the street and into the alley beside the store. The iron steps of the fire escape clanged as he raced up them two at a time.

As Dominic reached the top of the three-story building, Mila's attacker skidded to a stop on the flat, concrete roof. He might have turned to run the other way, but some of the pallas cats had followed him up the gutter pipe. More pallas cats were dashing up the fire escape that Dominic had used, which meant the bastard was boxed in. And he knew it.

The breeze fanned over Dominic, bringing with it the scents of sweat, panic, sun-warmed concrete, and cheetah. Thirsty for the fucker's blood, his wolf snarled, bracing himself to pounce.

The cheetah glanced around. There was nowhere to hide. Nothing to use as a weapon. And he was once again surrounded. As the cheetah's glance slid to the rear of the building, Dominic knew he was thinking of jumping. *Fuck that.*

With red-hot rage and adrenaline surging through his veins, Dominic flew at the fucker. They collided in a flurry of brutal blows. Punched. Kicked. Dodged. Weaved.

Snarls of anger and grunts of pain rang through the air, joining the shouts of encouragement coming from the onlookers who were egging Dominic on.

Pain rippled through him as the cheetah dealt him a swift, hard blow to the kidney that almost had him doubling over. The guy had a fist like fucking granite. Dominic twisted to block the next punch with his shoulder and then struck the bastard with a solid uppercut. The cheetah's head snapped back as he double-blinked.

Then they collided again.

The cheetah showed no mercy. He slammed that meaty fist into Dominic's temple, dealt him a harsh blow to the solar plexus, kicked his thigh so hard he almost snapped Dominic's femur.

Adrenaline dimming the pain, Dominic fought just as mercilessly, crashing his fist into the cheetah's jaw, slashing out with his claws, and ramming the heel of his palm into the asshole's nose, smiling grimly at the resulting crack.

The cheetah's hand snapped around Dominic's wrist when the wolf swung at him again. Dominic didn't try to pull free. He twisted slightly, slamming his arm against the bastard's throat. The cheetah expelled a pained grunt and then staggered backward.

Even as their breaths came quick and shallow, neither slowed or gave any openings. The battle was fast and chaotic. The cheetah was literally battling for his life; he had to know that even if he defeated Dominic, the pallas cats would immediately pounce unless he got away fast.

His eyes gleaming with pain and anger, the cheetah swung his hips and kicked out, landing a solid strike to Dominic's already swollen knee. *Son of a bitch.* Seething, Dominic slammed his fist into the fucker's collarbone with every bit of strength he had. There was a nauseating snap, and the cheetah's arm sagged.

Taking advantage, Dominic lunged, crashing his body into the other male, who hit the concrete hard. Using his knees, Dominic pinned the cheetah's arms down while he pummeled his face with his fists over and over and over.

Bones cracked. Blood spurted. Rage and pain scented the air.

The cheetah pulled some fancy move, trying to flip Dominic off. It didn't work. The big cat was too weak. Dominic just kept dealing him one ruthless blow after the other. His knuckles burned from clipping his skin on the cheetah's fangs, but Dominic didn't stop. Didn't ease up on this bastard who'd almost taken Mila from him. There was a pounding in his ears so loud, it almost drowned out the gurgle of blood and the sound of flesh slamming into flesh.

"Dominic." The voice was male. Flat. Seemed far away. "Dominic, he's not getting up, man. He's out. You hear me? He's out cold. Mila needs you."

Mila.

His chest heaving, his muscles quivering, his body sore in too many places to count, Dominic pushed his way out of the fog of fury and *really* looked at the male beneath him. The cheetah's face was . . . well, it was a fucking mess. Bloody. Puffy. Almost purple. His nose was broken, his eyes were swelling, and his cheekbone looked fractured. Tate was right. The asshole was out cold.

Standing, Dominic stepped over the cheetah and swept his gaze over the pallas cats. They were all watching him as you would a rabid animal, and he couldn't really blame them.

Vinnie took a slow, nonthreatening step toward him. "We have this, son. Go to Mila."

Flexing his aching fists, Dominic gave a curt nod. "If he has anything helpful to say, I want to hear about it."

"You will," Vinnie told him. "Let Sam heal you before you go."

A male took a cautious step toward him and reached for Dominic's arm, but he didn't touch him. He waited for Dominic's nod before placing his palm on Dominic's forearm. A surge of power crackled through him. Unlike Taryn's energy, it wasn't so much soothing as it was jolting.

Giving the healer a nod of thanks, Dominic rolled back his shoulders. The aches and stings had vanished, leaving only the lethargy that came from an adrenaline crash.

Satisfied, Dominic turned back to the fire escape and descended the ladder. A police car was parked on the road, and two uniformed cops were talking with the human woman whose toddler had been briefly used as a hostage. Some people were snapping photos of her while others were trying to get a good look at what was happening on the roof. From there, they couldn't see shit, which was good.

As he crossed the street, he saw Mila standing just outside the grocery store, surrounded by a small cluster of her pack mates, including her parents, Ingrid, and motherfucking Joel. She shouldered her way through them and went to Dominic. Locking one arm around her, he palmed the back of her head as he pressed a kiss to her hair. He breathed her in, let the scent and feel of her pour into him and steady his wolf.

She pulled back, as if worried she'd hurt him, but he held her tight. "Shit, GQ, you have blood on—"

"I'm fine. Sam healed me. I was just a little banged up. I've had worse."

"Did you get the asshole?" James asked quietly. "We couldn't see what was going on from down here."

"Vinnie and the others have him," replied Dominic. "He's out cold, but not dead."

"He soon will be," Valentina vowed, stroking her daughter's hair.

Dominic flicked a brief glance at the police. "Will I need to give a statement?"

"No," said James. "Those particular cops are part of our pride. They'll put a nice story together. Probably to the effect that the asshole was chased out of the store for shoplifting, and that a bunch of people tried catching him but failed. He was simply too fast, and so he was probably a shifter."

"He was a cheetah. Must be handy having some of your pride mates in the police," Dominic mused.

"It is at times like this," said Ingrid. "How else do you think our species managed to stay under the radar? We have plants in many places."

"Take Mila home, Dominic," Valentina told him. "I will get her groceries and bring them to her."

Eager to get out of there, Dominic hiked Mila up his body and pulled her legs around his waist.

She frowned. "I can walk."

"Don't care." He started for the apartment building, but then Joel slipped into his path. His wolf bared his teeth. "Not now," Dominic gritted out. He didn't even want to know what the male wanted; Dominic needed him gone.

Joel's jaw hardened. "But I think Mila should—"

"Not. Fucking. Now." Dominic shrugged past him and carried her to the building. He didn't put her down until they were in the bathroom of her apartment, where they stripped off their clothes.

Standing under the hot spray, they soaped each other down. Her touch was gentle and soothing as it washed the blood from his skin, but he was soon rock fucking hard. With the adrenaline still in his system and his fear for her safety still fresh, he soon had her pinned against the tiled wall as he powered in and out of her.

No sooner had they dried off, her parents appeared. Valentina fussed over them and put away groceries while James fielded calls from anxious pride members, assuring them that Mila was fine and just needed some rest and privacy. After talking Mila into canceling her upcoming performance at the Velvet Lounge that night, Dominic called Trey, gave him a rundown of what had happened, and promised to keep him updated.

Vinnie, Tate, and Luke later made a brief appearance, checking on Mila and relaying that the cheetah was now very much dead and hadn't known anything more about the bounty than the jackal or snake shifter had. No surprise, really.

Valentina cooked Dominic and Mila a meal and then, wanting to give them time alone, went home with James. And now, as they ate at Mila's small dining table, Dominic couldn't help replaying the earlier incident over and over in his mind. He kept remembering the incapacitating fear he'd felt when Mila had become deadweight in his arms, kept remembering how her lips had turned blue and how her heartbeat had slowed and faltered.

He hadn't felt that kind of fear in . . . well, ever. It was the fear of losing something essential to you. Something you knew you wouldn't be happy without.

And that fucking terrified him.

He'd known he cared for her, known she was important to him. But he hadn't realized that he'd come to *need* her. Hadn't thought she'd dug her way that deep inside him. Oh, he'd figured she might burrow her way there *someday*, but not so damn soon.

Dominic had avoided putting too much thought into what might lie ahead for them, but he had believed everything would move at *his* pace. He figured that if she *did* get past his defenses, he'd be in control of when it happened. He thought she'd only get there if he consciously opened the door wide enough.

He was wrong.

She'd somehow made herself indelible. Wasn't quite *inside* his protective walls, but she had wedged her way through a crack she'd made in them. And now he felt . . . threatened. Which was stupid. But not one single soul had ever made themselves essential to him. Not one. He wasn't sure he liked it. Every self-protective instinct he had was telling him to leave.

Maybe one night apart wouldn't hurt. They were constantly in each other's space, and that wasn't always healthy, was it? It would probably do them both some good for him to—

"You're quiet."

The flatly spoken observation cut into his thoughts, snapping him to the present. She was staring at him, her gaze far too perceptive, too knowing.

Feeling uncomfortable and exposed, Dominic picked up his glass. "It's not good to talk when I have food in my mouth."

"You want to leave, don't you?" The accusation was soft. Empty of resentment or judgment.

Shit. He sipped the wine that Valentina had poured. "Why would you ask that?"

"It wasn't really a question. Your muscles are bunched tight. Like someone coiled to spring . . . *or* to jump up and run."

He arched a brow at the taunt. "I don't have reasons to be tense, considering the day we've had?"

She leaned forward, her eyes narrowed. "I know you. And I know that right now, the thing you want most is to get the fuck out of here. Tell me I'm wrong."

Sighing, he pinched the bridge of his nose. "Baby, there's just a lot of stupid shit going through my head. And no, I don't want to talk about it. I don't need to."

Mila marveled over how someone could be only a few feet away from her yet seem so damn unreachable. Honestly, she might as well have been speaking to him through plate glass. He hadn't just withdrawn, he'd withdrawn from *her.* Had become distant and remote. And his "I don't want to talk about it" was said with such finality that she knew there would be no getting him to share. No, he'd pulled down all the shutters. And she felt . . . alone.

"I imagine you're thinking you should go home to process it all," she said with a mocking edge to her tone. Oh, he'd be making excuses to himself about *why* he wanted to leave; he'd be telling himself it would be good for them. "You're thinking you should spend a night in your own bed for a change, right?" She pursed her lips. "Maybe that's true."

"If you want me to leave, just say so."

"If you want to go, go."

"Jesus, what's crawled up your ass?"

Her chuckle was void of humor. "Oh, I'm not gonna make this easy for you, Dominic. I'm not gonna be provoked into tossing you out of here. If you want to leave, you're going to have to make the choice yourself. But if you do leave, don't come back."

Dominic frowned. "You're saying I can't ever leave this apartment unless I intend to end the relationship?"

"You're going to play stupid now? Really? This is the ditch you want to die in?"

"You just said if I leave, I can't come back."

Her cat rumbled a growl at his derisive tone. Yeah, Mila didn't like it much either, but she also knew the disrespect wasn't real. He just wanted to provoke her.

"Tell me, Dominic, why should I waste my time on someone who could walk out on me after the crap that happened today?" Hell, she'd almost died from whatever drug the cheetah had pumped into her. "I don't know what's put you in self-protective mode, but you're there. I see it. You're giving off 'Don't touch me' vibes, and you shot me down before I could even ask you to share what's bothering you."

He scoffed. "What the fuck is self-protective mode? You're making this out to be bigger than it is. Like I said, I just have dumb shit going through my head. That's all."

"So you're not itching to walk out that door and go home? The idea of staying here with me for the rest of the evening and throughout the night doesn't bother you?"

Dominic ground his teeth. "Why would it?"

Mila shook her head. "Never pegged you for a coward, GQ."

"Says the person who wanted to enter an arranged mating so that she wouldn't have to put her emotions on the line," he sniped.

"I'm not throwing you out of here, Dominic, no matter how personal you get. You want to leave, you leave."

"Yeah, you keep saying that. I'm starting to think you *want* me gone."

Mila slowly stood. "You're right, I don't want you here."

Dominic's stomach bottomed out as hurt rocketed through him. He fisted his hands, ignoring the panic that now clawed at him. He was losing her with every word he spoke. And yet, he couldn't seem to shut the fuck up.

"I don't want you here . . . because I know you don't want to be here." With a calm she didn't feel, Mila cleared the table. She expected him to push up from the table and storm out, but he didn't. He would, though. Any second now he'd leave.

In the kitchen, she rinsed off the dishware and stacked the dishwasher, using the mundane chore to distract her from the anxiety churning in her stomach. When she walked into the living area, it was to find him settled on the sofa watching TV. But he wasn't *truly* settled. He was still tense as a fucking bow. Still raring to walk out whether he wanted to admit it or not. And she wasn't about to sit there and wait for him to do it.

Leaving him to brood, Mila did her laundry and tidied the apartment. By the time she was done, he was still watching TV. Still strung as tight as piano wire. And pointedly ignoring her. Whatever. Her cat took a swipe at him, but her claws were surprisingly sheathed. The feline was worried about him almost as much as she was annoyed with him.

Mila changed into a camisole top and matching shorts, settled in bed with her laptop, and chose a movie to watch. Emotionally drained after the shitty day she'd had, she fell asleep at some point only to jolt awake just as the laptop was beginning to slide off her lap. Cursing, she switched it off and put it on the nightstand.

She could hear the TV in the living room and sensed that Dominic was still in the apartment. That sure surprised her, but she wasn't hopeful that he'd stay. No, he was a million miles away right then. Only he could close that distance, and he didn't seem prepared to do it. Still, though, she wasn't tossing him out, even though her sense of pride told her she should tear a strip off his hide. Nope. He'd have to take that walk himself.

Turning onto her side, she closed her eyes and took a steadying breath. She was just nodding off when the bedroom floorboards creaked. The TV was now off, she realized. Instead of using the bathroom and undressing as he usually did before bed, he sank onto the mattress behind her. He'd come to say goodbye, she thought. Come to admit he wasn't ready for what had grown between them.

Swallowing around the knot of emotion clogging her throat, Mila said nothing. Just waited for him to say some little spiel and leave.

Adjusting the pillow slightly, Dominic sighed. "I was a replacement baby, you know," he said, his voice low. "After my parents lost Tobias and became unhappy in their mating, they had me to 'fix' it. To bring them back together. To give them someone else to love. Only they didn't love me. Not really. You're thinking I'm wrong. That of course they loved me—they were my parents. But it's not always that simple. It should be, but it's not.

"I look uncannily like Tobias, and I think that hurt my parents. Made it almost painful for them to look at me. But at the same time, they loved that they had a living reminder of the son they'd lost. I was always compared to him, and I never came out on top. It disappointed them if I didn't like what he'd liked, or if I wasn't good at what he'd been good at. It was like they could never quite separate me from him in their minds."

Mila squeezed her eyes shut, her chest hurting at the picture he was painting. She wondered if he knew that the loneliness he'd felt back then rang clear in his tone. Her cat leaned into him, wanting to soothe.

"I was never allowed in his room," Dominic went on. "They hadn't boxed up his stuff, they'd left it all exactly as it had been when he died. It was like a shrine to him. My mother would sleep there sometimes. I'd hear her crying, but I learned fast that there was no point in going to her. She didn't want comfort. She clung to the guilt, wore it like a badge.

"She often invited spiritualists to the house, and they'd talk of how Tobias was still close. For as far back as I can remember, she used to tell me that the unexplained noises I heard around the house—any creaks, thuds, scrapes—were my brother's spirit moving around.

"Every year on his birthday, she'd bake a cake for him and light candles, and we all had to sing happy birthday to someone who wasn't even there. I get that they needed to keep his memory alive. I'm glad they were so determined not to forget him. I'm glad he was loved so much, and I'm damn sorry that he died. But I don't like that even though they had me, they never let themselves love me. I don't like that my purpose was to bring them back together, make them happy again. They were never happy. And for a while, I blamed myself for that."

Rolling over to face him, Mila said, "People are responsible for their own happiness. And it sounds to me like your mother didn't want to be happy."

Dominic played his fingers through Mila's curls. "You're right, she didn't. And by leaving, she condemned her mate. She didn't even leave a note. Didn't give any warning. Just packed her stuff and went. My father couldn't handle the distance from her, and so his wolf turned rogue. Mauled two people to death before his Alpha and Beta brought him down. And then there was only me."

No, she thought, there had only been him for a very long time before that. His parents had never made him feel part of a family. It hurt her heart to think he'd spent his childhood suppressing a shitload of anger for the emotionally absent parents who'd had him to replace their perfect child—Dominic had never stood a chance.

He'd never been special to anyone. Never belonged. Never felt fully secure. He'd learned that it was unwise to expect much of people.

It was little wonder he'd cultivated a player image to avoid relationships. Lots of people "performed." Pretended they had it all together, pretended they weren't in debt, pretended their relationships were perfect. Many turned to things like gambling, drugs, or alcohol to numb their pain. But Dominic hadn't tried to numb his pain, he'd hidden it. Hidden it behind a carefree mask. In doing so, he'd isolated himself.

But, really, who could blame him? If she were in his shoes—even if only subconsciously—she'd ask herself what the point was in baring her soul if she felt like she'd never be truly loved for who she was. She'd feel it was better to hold back than to love, trust, and depend on someone.

"Thank you for telling me that," said Mila, knowing it hadn't been easy. He'd had the option of leaving, but he hadn't. He'd stayed. And more importantly, he'd shared.

He pressed a kiss to her forehead. "I wobbled for a minute earlier."

"I know."

"Don't give up on me. I'm not used to . . . I've never needed anyone, Mila. No one has ever mattered to me the way you do." He put her hand over his heart, adding, "I thought I'd be in control of how and when you got in here, but it turns out I'm not. You made your own way into there, and that realization knocked me on my ass, but I'm back up again."

God, he made it impossible to stay angry when he said stuff like that. Now that he'd told her about his upbringing, she understood him better. Understood his earlier need to leave wasn't so much cowardice as him feeling vulnerable and unsure. And fuck if she didn't feel like crying for the lonely little boy he'd once been.

Her parents had always made her feel loved and treasured and safe. He'd never had that. And now that there *was* someone in his life wanting to make him feel all those things, his instinct was to hold her at bay. But he'd pushed past that instinct; he'd stayed. Opened the shutters. Exposed more of himself. Admitted to caring for her, even when he was feeling raw and vulnerable. That took a heap of emotional courage, and it melted every tiny bit of irritation she'd felt. And it would only be fair to return the favor.

"If it helps, Dominic, you're not the only one struggling. You made a few holes in my self-protective walls. Wormed your way inside. I think caring for someone is supposed to be scary. Freaking out is normal. There's so much uncertainty, and questions constantly prick at me. Will it work out in the long run? Will you get bored with just one woman in your life? Will you really be able to offer the commitment you seem to want to give?"

"You really wonder all that?"

"Yes. Caring for you is terrifying. Realizing I don't really have as much authority over my own emotions as I thought I did is just as scary. But feeling so strongly for someone, having them so enmeshed in your life, can also be a very special thing. *If* you let it be. But if you need space—"

"I don't need space." Dominic dragged her on top of him and tucked her hair behind her ear. "I freaked out for a minute, but I do not want space. I couldn't have walked out that front door, baby. Fuck, I doubt I could have even opened it. I'm exactly where I want to be."

Resting her chin on his chest, Mila petted him. "I believe you. But if you *do* at some point feel you need space—"

"I won't, it was just a wobble," he promised her. "I wish I could tell you that I'll never act so fucking stupid again, but it's easy to trip up when you can't see where you're going. That's what this feels like for me. I've never been in a relationship before. I'm in brand-spanking-new territory and doing my best to navigate it. I take most of my cues from you, hoping I don't mess up."

He let out a heavy sigh. "But I hurt you. I'm sorry for that. I'm sorry I acted like a dick. You're the last person I'd ever want to hurt." He caught her face with his hands and brushed his mouth over hers. "Think you can forgive me?"

She drew in a deep breath. "Yeah."

Dominic swallowed. There were no buts, no deliberation, no holding on to her anger for the sake of it, no threats of what would happen if he messed up again. Just a simple acceptance of his apology, trusting that he meant it. And he fucking adored her for that. "You amaze me."

Palming her nape, he gave it a little squeeze. "I swear, baby, this is the only place I want to be. I've never wanted, never *needed*, anything the way I do you. I should have known you'd make yourself this important to me. Should have seen it coming. You're sweet and funny and bitchy and beautiful and so fucking strong. The best thing in my world.

No one will ever be—no one *could* ever be—who you are to me. And I don't have even the slightest intention of ever letting you go."

He took her mouth, sweeping his tongue inside, pouring himself into it, into *her*. He'd meant to go slow, to soothe and comfort and reassure her. But he quickly found himself eating at her mouth.

Possessiveness pounded through him, driving him to take more and more. She fisted his shirt, dragging him closer, giving him what he needed. He feasted, ravished, and dominated, swallowing every smoky, cock-hardening moan. Carnal hunger ravaged his insides and heated his blood.

He needed to touch her. Feel her. Reconnect. Needed to know she still wanted him just as much.

He brushed his nose against hers. "So beautiful. And all mine. Aren't you?"

"Yours."

"Then let me get a good look at what's mine." Bunching the bottom of her top in his hands, he peeled it off, baring her breasts. Before he could catch one of those hard nipples with his mouth, she was sliding down his chest, dragging the tight buds over his skin. Settling between his thighs, she tackled his fly. His heart slammed against his ribs, and his cock practically jumped into her hand. "Mila."

Curling her hand around the base of his cock, she lapped at the head, licking up the pearls of pre-come from the slit. His thigh muscles jumped. Instead of teasing his cock with licks and nips, she swallowed him down.

Fisting her hair, Dominic groaned as the heat of her mouth engulfed him. "Fuck, baby." Keeping her grip firm, she pumped his shaft as she sucked so hard her cheeks hollowed. "That's it, keep those lips wrapped nice and tight around my cock. You don't know how many times I've imagined bunching these curls in my hands while you suck me off."

His control frayed as she kept on pumping and sucking, constantly switching from slow and lazy to fast and hard. Just when he thought she couldn't take him any deeper, she'd swallow a little more. Watching his cock disappear into her hot mouth was a heaven all its own.

Sensations swept him under—her throat contracting around him. Her tongue flicking the spot beneath the crown. Her free hand expertly cupping and rolling his balls. It wasn't long before he felt the telling tingle at the base of his spine.

"I'm close, baby." She purred around him, and Jesus, it vibrated all the way up his dick. Tightening his hold on her hair, Dominic pumped his hips and fucked her mouth. "Swallow it." His balls drew up as wave after wave of pleasure burst through him, and he exploded into her mouth with a growl of her name.

Panting, Dominic shook his head. "Fuck, you're lethal." She sat up, and he flicked a look at her shorts. "Get them off." While she shucked her shorts and thong, he took off his own clothes. Then he grabbed her waist and dragged her up the bed, positioning her glistening pussy above his face. His cock twitched back to life as the heady scent of her need poured into his lungs. "Slick for me already."

One knee on either side of his head, Mila clutched the iron rungs of the headboard as the warm hands palming her ass held her in place. Her cat was a sucker for all that casual strength, loved the way he firmly and boldly held Mila exactly how he wanted her.

Her eyelids fluttered shut as he swiped his tongue through her folds and swirled it around her clit, leaving a trail of fire in his wake. Jesus, that felt good.

He let out one of his little snarls. "I fucking love eating this pussy."

Goose bumps rose on Mila's flesh as he sipped, teased, and drank from her. He was ruthless with that mouth. Used his tongue, teeth, and lips to build the friction inside her until a blinding need lashed at her heated skin.

She might have cupped her aching breasts and thumbed her painfully tight nipples if she'd dared let go of the headboard. It anchored her throughout the storm of sensation he subjected her to. Really, he gave her no reprieve—wrapped his lips around her clit, grazed her folds with his teeth, licked at her slit, dipped his tongue into her soaking-wet pussy. Tremors began to rack her body and—

She sucked in a gasp as he yanked her closer to his mouth, sinking his tongue deeper into her pussy. That ever-so-clever tongue expertly stabbed and swirled and teased. Her thighs quivered, and her pussy fluttered as her release came barreling toward her.

"*Fuck.*" She came hard, her spine arched, her head thrown back, her thighs shaking as an orgasm so powerful it was almost unbearable crashed into her. She rested her forehead on the iron rungs as she tried to catch her breath.

Unable to resist, and seeing no reason why he should, Dominic bit her inner thigh hard enough to leave a mark. His wolf rumbled a pleased growl.

"Was that like a 'Dominic has been here' thing?" she asked, panting.

He grinned. "No, it was a 'this is my pussy' thing." He slid her down the bed, positioning her above his cock. "Ride me, Mila." His dick, once more full and heavy, throbbed in her hand as she grabbed him by the root. "Considering I ate your pussy and you sucked me like a Hoover, we've both had the edge taken off. So . . . who do you think will come first?"

She arched a brow, sweeping the head of his cock between her folds, teasing them both. "Is that a challenge I hear?"

"I reckon I can hold out longer than you."

"I seriously doubt that."

"Yeah?" Dominic grabbed her hip and slammed her down on his cock, stuffing her full. He gritted his teeth as her inferno-hot pussy clamped around him. She was so fucking perfect. So fucking his. And so very, very irritated with him right then, he thought with an inner smile. "I think you'll be the one coming first."

Mila glared at him. "Really?" She squeezed her inner muscles tight around him in retaliation, smiling as he bit out a harsh expletive. "Doubtful."

"I guess we'll soon see who's right." Casually slipping his hands around the iron rungs of the headboard, Dominic said, "Fuck yourself, baby."

He watched as she repeatedly slammed down on his cock, her face flushed, her breasts bouncing. Her pussy was so fucking tight and hot as it greedily sucked him back inside again and again. "Love seeing my dick all shiny with your cream."

She locked her gaze with his, skewering him with a sex-crazed stare that tightened his balls. Punching up his hips to meet her downward thrusts, Dominic filled his hands with her breasts and squeezed them just right. "My cock in your pussy, my brands all over you, my come in your belly. Yeah, I'd say I own you."

"Is that so?"

"It's definitely fucking so."

Mila rode him hard, loving the feel of his long, thick shaft slicing through her. He pinched her nipples, sending red-hot sparks of desperation shooting straight to her clit. Shit, she wouldn't last if he kept that up. Determined that he come first, she raked her nails down his solid chest as she squeezed his dick tight with her inner muscles again, eliciting yet another harsh curse out of him.

He hiked up a brow. "That all you got?"

Leaning forward, Mila smiled. "Of course not." She raked her teeth over his neck and felt his cock pulse inside her. "Want me to mark you again?" It was a whisper. "Do you?" She bit down hard. His dick swelled, throbbed.

Snarling, he fisted her hair and snatched her head back. "Sneaky little cat." Time to up his game, he thought. Gripping her hip with his free hand, he started yanking her down each time he thrust upward, roughly impaling her. Her pussy became impossibly hot and tight, and he knew she was close.

"Come on, baby, come for me." Tightening his hold on her hair, he pulled her to him and sank his teeth into her neck. He kept his teeth locked on her as he pounded harder, faster, deeper. And he felt it happen. Felt her pussy spasm and ripple as her climax—

Her claws slashed his chest, drawing blood, leaving a permanent brand. Like that, his cock fucking detonated, shooting rope after rope of come inside her while her inner muscles rippled around him.

Utterly spent, he lay there with her sprawled over his chest and limp as a noodle. He weakly smoothed a hand up her back. "Told you I'd hold out longer."

"*You* came first," she mumbled.

"No, you did."

A lazy, derisive snort popped out of her. "Full of shit."

"Yes, you are." He flinched as her claw scraped his nipple. "*Maybe* we came at the same time."

"Hmm. Maybe."

CHAPTER SEVENTEEN

On Sundays, Mila often woke to the feel of Dominic's mouth exploring some very interesting places on her body. That particular Sunday morning, she woke to him snuggled into her side as she lay on her stomach, his fingers doodling patterns on her back. There was nothing seductive in his lazy, casual touch. And yet, there was so much greed and possessiveness. Even as the rough pads of his fingers lightly breezed over her, they clearly stated "Mine."

Her cat arched into his touch, purring. She was remarkably cheery. As a rule, the feline didn't do "cheery."

Mila opened her eyes to find his own staring back at her, glinting with masculine contentment and . . . was that worry? She couldn't quite tell. "Morning."

"Morning." He kissed her shoulder, tracing the bumps of her spine. "Did you know that you frown a lot in your sleep?"

She blinked. "Frown?"

"It's almost like your default sleep-expression. My wolf finds it cute." Dominic kissed her shoulder again, his mouth curving into a secret smile.

"You look rather self-satisfied." She narrowed her eyes. "What? Why are you smirking? I feel like I'm missing something."

He danced his tongue over the little cluster of freckles on her shoulder. "You're wearing my scent. And I'm wearing yours. You know what that means." Imprinting had started. Although Dominic worried a little that she might not be enthusiastic about it, he couldn't help feeling just as smug as his wolf.

Now she was no longer just a woman he cared for, she was his mate. It didn't matter to him that they wouldn't be officially considered mates until the imprinting bond formed—he had no intention of letting her go. Any shifter she came across would instantly scent Dominic on her and understand she was taken. When the imprinting progressed, his scent would be permanently embedded in her skin.

Realizing he was right, Mila smiled. "No wonder my cat's in a good mood. How do you feel about it?"

"Smug. Happy. Relieved. I didn't let myself really see how much I wanted this until now. What about you?"

"Happy. Surprised. Annoyed that I didn't sense it straightaway." Her brow creased. "I thought it would make me feel more secure."

"It doesn't?"

She slid her fingers through his hair. "Trying to hold on to you would be like trying to hold on to the wind. All I can do is hope you'll choose to stay."

God, if he could kick his own ass for making her doubt him, he would. Dominic snuggled closer to her. "You don't have to hold on, baby. You have me. I'm not going anywhere."

"You say that now. And I believe you mean it, but—"

"Mila, I don't have to tell you that I've known a lot of women in my time. None of them captured my attention the way you have. None of them made me want more than a bit of fun. I never dreamed about them. Never obsessed over them. Never marked them. Never cared for them. Imprinting is a huge deal for *anyone*, but it's even bigger for someone like me.

"I want this. I want you as my mate. Fuck, if I could get away with it, I'd put a claiming mark on your neck right now even though we're not fully imprinted yet, but I know you won't go for that." He cupped her nape. "Are you hearing me, Mila? There's no danger of me walking away from you. None."

Mila took a deep breath. "Okay."

Relief whooshed through Dominic. Just "okay." Just one word. But there was a wealth of acceptance and faith in it. She trusted his word on this, even though his eventful sexual past might have suggested that he wasn't ready for commitment.

She'd never once thrown his past in his face. Never once judged, condemned, or bitched at him for it—not even when females tried their luck with him right in front of her. It would have been easy for her to take that out on him, to blame him for the hurt she'd felt at the time, but Mila never once had.

She couldn't imagine how much it meant to Dominic that she hadn't given up on him after he'd messed up and hurt her last night. His parents had always found fault in him. Always criticized and lectured him for the slightest infraction. Mila hadn't judged or slammed him. Hadn't tossed him out on his ass, verbally struck back at him, or pushed him away. Instead, she'd left him to either walk out or clean up the mess he'd made. And then, having listened as he'd shared his secrets, she'd demonstrated a level of understanding and compassion—not pity, which he couldn't have taken—that no one else had ever given him.

That was one of the things about Mila that had always made him feel comfortable around her, he realized. She accepted people for who they were—accepted their good points and bad points. Never expected them to be anything else. Never expected perfection. Never expected more of them than what they could give.

Dominic needed that acceptance. Having someone who cared for him exactly as he was . . . he'd never had that before. He wanted to cling tight to it.

"Kiss me," he whispered. She gave him her mouth—no hesitation, no defiance. The kiss was soft, deep, drugging. And he soon had her flat on her back, spreading her legs wide for him. He took her slow and hard, gave her no reprieve. When they were both close to shattering, he snarled, "Mark me again, Mila. On my throat this time, where everyone can see it." The moment her teeth closed around his flesh, he came with a growl of her name.

Her parents popped in to check on Mila just before she and Dominic were about to head to Phoenix Pack territory. Both Valentina and James were delighted to see that the imprinting process had started, and Mila could tell that they intended to take full credit for the fact that she and GQ were together. Yeah, her parents' little plot had certainly paid off.

As all four of them were leaving her apartment, James whipped out his cell to call Ingrid and pass on the news. And seeing how fast her mother was dashing up the stairs to her apartment, Mila just knew that Valentina was intending to call her own mother.

"Ingrid is quite the Chatty Cathy," Mila told Dominic as they descended the stairs. "So it won't be long before the entire pride knows we're partially imprinted."

He squeezed her hand. "Good. The sooner everyone knows, the better."

"How do you think your pack will feel about it?"

He pursed his lips. "That depends."

"On what?"

"On whether they bet it would happen sooner or later. They won't like losing a bet. Still, they'll be happy for us."

Her brow furrowed. "Surely they wouldn't bet on something like that."

"That's just—" Dominic cut off as a familiar unwelcome scent drifted to them. And then, just as they turned to descend the next stairwell, they saw Joel coming toward them. Dominic's wolf stood to his full height, his upper lip curling.

"Hey, Mila, it's good to see that you're—" Joel's nostrils flared, and he came to an abrupt halt, obviously having detected that Mila and Dominic were wearing each other's scents.

Joel looked at Dominic and sighed. "Guess I was wrong in thinking you weren't serious about her." His gaze cut to Mila, and his expression softened. "I'm glad I was wrong. You deserve to be happy."

"Does that mean you'll start being civil toward Dominic now?" Mila asked him.

Joel's mouth curled. "Let's not ask for miracles. I'm assuming this means you're not moving to Russia."

"She's not going anywhere," Dominic cut in. As far as he was concerned, it was only a matter of time before they were fully imprinted on each other.

Joel gave a curt nod. "Good. Well, I can see you're going somewhere, so I'll be off. Take care of her, wolf." Brushing past them, he jogged up the stairs.

Quite frankly shocked that the male cat hadn't voiced any objections, Dominic frowned as he and Mila continued down the stairwell. He waited until Joel was out of earshot before saying, "I didn't expect that."

"He only disapproved of you because he thought you were a user like my ex," explained Mila. "Now that he knows I matter to you, he's okay with it."

Some part of Joel had needed to know that his predestined mate would be cared for. Dominic understood. Still . . . "I expected jealousy."

"He's devoted to Adele. Anything he feels for me is purely platonic. I know it might seem strange that someone could feel nothing romantic for their true mate, but—to put it simply—the love he feels for Adele and the commitment he's made to her pretty much render the bond we might have had invalid." And Mila could finally say that without feeling a hint of hurt over it. Her cat hadn't even hissed at Joel, she suddenly realized.

Dominic gave a slow nod. "I get it." He couldn't imagine that anyone—not even his predestined mate—could ever lessen what he felt for Mila. It was too strong. Too deep. As such, there was no reason why it would be any different for Joel. "But I'm going to be a pain in your ass over this."

"Over what?"

"I can accept that he has no romantic interest in you. But I'm never going to like the little bastard being around you. I'm never going to be okay with you and him hanging out alone or shit like that."

"I wouldn't expect you to." In his shoes, Mila would feel exactly the same way.

"I don't just mean I won't like it, I mean I won't allow it. My wolf would never stand for it either."

Mila and her cat shot him a narrow-eyed look. "Using the word 'allow' was a misstep, GQ. Don't do it again." Reaching the ground floor, she added, "In regard to Joel, I don't intend to spend time with him alone, so just chill."

Dominic opened the front door of the building and gave the area a once-over. Satisfied that no one was lingering around, he pulled Mila toward his SUV. "Just making sure we're on the same page."

She tilted her head. "You don't worry I pine for him, do you?"

He cast her an incredulous look. "Who would ever pine for someone else when they had me?"

"Right," she said, stifling a smile. "Silly question."

"It was. I mean, come on, cocks like mine don't grow on trees, you know."

Sighing, she shook her head. "You are *so* disturbed."

"I resent that."

Glancing up at the sky, she frowned at the frothy gray clouds. "I hope your pack isn't holding a gathering outdoors this time. It's gonna rain for sure."

"I'm not a meteorologist," he began with an impish grin, sliding into the SUV, "but I'd say you can expect a good few inches tonight."

She groaned, clicking on her seat belt. "I should have seen that coming."

"Speaking of coming—"

"Drive, GQ. Just drive."

Laughing, he reversed out of the space. He kept one hand splayed possessively on her thigh throughout most of the drive to his territory. After parking in the concealed lot at the base of the mountain, he led her up the stairs of the cliff face. Fine drops of rain began to fall from the sky, but they managed to make it inside the caves before the light drizzle picked up.

Holding Mila's hand, he tugged her through the tunnels. He found most of the pack in the living area, lounging around talking and watching TV.

Taryn beamed at them. "Hey there, you two. Hope you're hungry, because Grace is cooking up a storm in the kitchen." She crossed to them. "We were going to have a barbecue, but the weather . . . Oh my God."

Trey sidled up to his mate. "What? What is it?" He glanced at Mila and Dominic, his nostrils flaring. "Oh."

Taryn did a little clap. "This is so great!"

"What?" asked Jaime.

"They're imprinting!" the Alpha female practically squealed. She held out her hand. "Now pay up, losers."

Some groaned as they handed cash to the members who were flashing triumphant smirks.

Mila slanted her head. "You really bet on how long it would take for me and Dominic to begin imprinting on each other?"

Counting the bills in his hand, Marcus shrugged. "Me and a few of the others said it would happen by the end of this week."

"I won't say congratulations, because you're not fully imprinted yet, and I don't want to jinx it," said Makenna. Ignoring Ryan's mutterings about jinxes and logic, she went on, "But I'm completely confident that the bond will form soon."

Hand on her heart, her eyes glistening, Greta crossed to them. "I'm so happy for you both." She caught Dominic's face with her hands. "You've done me proud, boy. Very proud. It's about time one of you brought home a female that was worthy," she added, giving the other males the side-eye.

Roni frowned. "I thought you liked me."

"I do, but you were already coming here when Marcus snapped you up," said Greta. "But Dominic . . . he went out there and found himself a worthy female. I couldn't be happier. Wait till I tell Grace." She left the room, smiling in delight.

Burping her son, Jaime stared at the empty doorway. "She hasn't been this psyched up about anything since Kye's birth. Anyway, how are you doing after yesterday's incident, Mila?"

Letting Dominic lead her to the sofa, Mila replied, "Just pissed that I didn't get to kick the cheetah's ass myself."

"I spoke with Vinnie," Trey told Dominic. "He told me you did a fair bit of damage to that bastard."

Carefully taking Hendrix from Jaime, Dominic sank onto the sofa beside Mila. "It was nothing the cheetah didn't deserve," he told his Alpha. Dominic would have gone back and delivered the killing blow if he'd been willing to leave Mila.

"Still no luck finding your brother's location?" Roni asked her.

Gently stroking the side of Hendrix's chubby face, Mila gave the she-wolf a sideways glance as she replied, "No, but my uncles are on it. They'll find him."

Just then, the other children came dashing into the room, closely followed by Riley and Tao.

Sienna waved a newborn baby doll at Mila. "Look! Look!" She roughly dumped the doll onto the coffee table and jammed the bottle of fake formula into the doll's mouth.

Makenna winced. "And that is why we don't let her hold Hendrix."

Dominic watched with a smile as Dexter curled his hand around Mila's fingers and tugged her to the corner of the room, where the boxes of toys were kept. The other kids joined them, showing her the various toys and arguing over who they belonged to.

Sitting at his side, Dante said, "So . . . you're not at all panicking that imprinting has started?"

"Nope. There's nothing to panic about. I want this. I want her as my mate." Dominic put his fist to his heart, smiling. "She's got me, D. I'm gone."

Dante smiled. "Yeah, I know the feeling." He held out his arms. "Hand my boy over."

Instead, Dominic nuzzled Hendrix's head. "I'm not done cuddling him yet."

"Don't be an ass. Give him to me. I only had him for five minutes before Jaime took him, and now *you're* hogging him."

"You're just mad because he likes me better than you."

"Yeah, I'll own that. But I still want my son back."

Chuckling, Dominic handed the baby to Dante.

"Rhett's been keeping track of any mentions of you online, Dom," said Trey, sinking into a plush armchair. "You should know that someone snapped photos of you carrying Mila down the street yesterday. They uploaded them onto a blog dedicated to 'shifter hunks.'"

Marcus gestured at himself. "I'm on there, obviously. They constantly whine that I'm mated, see it as a great loss to the single women out there." He grunted when Roni jammed her elbow into his ribs. "Dammit, woman, did you have to do it *that hard*?"

"No." Roni turned to the TV, dismissing him.

Taryn perched herself on the arm of Trey's chair. "It's likely that Pierson will see those photos of you and Mila."

"Only if he's keeping tabs on Dominic," said Makenna.

Trey rubbed his jaw. "I'd like to say that Pierson will lose interest in you and back down, but I'm not convinced of that."

Dominic shrugged, not caring either way. Nothing could spoil his mood right then. "The other two articles didn't do much damage. I doubt a third will."

"Which is why he might step up his game." Trey's breath hitched as his son literally flung himself at him. "Jesus, Kye."

"Dad, when I'm Alpha of the pack and you're a sad old man with nothing to do—"

"Wait, a sad old man?" Trey asked him.

"It's gonna happen," Kye asserted. "Anyway, after I kick your butt and take over the pack—"

"That's how you're planning to become Alpha? By kicking my butt?"

"You can't take it personally, Dad."

Chuckling, Taryn ruffled her son's hair. Like her own, it was various shades of blond. "Go get your tribe from the corner where they're harassing Mila. Dinner should be ready."

While they were eating at the long kitchen table, Dominic watched his mate interact with the pack. She was used to eating meals alone, with him, or with her parents. Now she was sharing a meal with almost thirty people, most of whom she'd only met once. Yet, she was just as relaxed as when she was alone with him, as if she'd eaten at his territory dozens of times before.

The incessant chatter didn't bother her, nor did the children's persistent attempts to get her attention. And she handled Greta like a pro. The old woman had insisted on sitting beside her. Each time Greta looked about to dish out a bitchy comment to someone, Mila expertly redirected her attention . . . making it the most peaceful meal the pack had shared in a long while.

He loved that Mila was comfortable here and got along with his pack mates so well. It would make the transition from her apartment to his home so much easier. And he fully intended to have her living with him soon.

As the rain had eased off, he and Mila went to his room after dinner, changed into their animal forms, and then padded out of the caves and into the woods. The soil was damp, the grass was slick with rain, and droplets of water kept dripping from the branches above their heads. Neither the wolf nor the cat cared.

They ran. Played. Relaxed. Enjoyed the clean, fresh scent of the rain.

Back in his room, they shifted.

Dominic was about to topple her onto the bed and ravish her when he got a text message from Trey, summoning him to the Alpha's office. Cursing silently, Dominic pulled on his clothes. "Trey wants to talk to me about something. It won't take long, I'll be back soon." Dominic bent and kissed her, then turned to head out. "Don't get dressed," he added before closing the door behind him.

Not a fan of sitting around naked, Mila dug out one of his shirts and slipped it on. Bored, she walked around the room, browsing the shelves and—

Her phone rang. Fishing it out of her purse, she frowned at the screen. Private Number. Tapping the "Answer Call" icon, she greeted, "Hello."

"Hey, Mila, it's Charlene."

Mila silently sighed in annoyance while her cat let out a put-out hiss. She hadn't heard or seen anything of the fox since the night that Dominic marked Mila at the club in front of God and everyone. Charlene had hidden it well, but she'd been a very unhappy bunny.

Dominic had stopped taking the woman's calls, pissed at her persistent interference. Mila had to admit that it was something of a relief—she didn't particularly like the thought of him being friends with a female from his past, but she'd have dealt with it if said female was a *good* friend who was at least a little supportive of his relationship with Mila.

It was tempting to end the call, but her catlike curiosity got the better of her. "Charlene. Hey."

"Are you okay, honey?"

Mila blinked at her gentle tone. "Yeah, fine."

"I saw pictures on the internet this morning of Dominic carrying you down the street. You were so pale, and it looked like he had blood on his hands. There was a brief mention of him being part of a group of people who chased after a shifter. What happened? I tried calling Dominic to ask him about it, but the call went to voice mail. Is he there with you?"

So, wait, the fox had called in the hope of speaking to him through Mila? Was the bitch fucking high? Biting back the urge to order Charlene to cease trying to contact him—which would let Charlene know *exactly* how much this pissed Mila off—she replied, "Not at this moment."

"Oh." There was an awkward pause. "I, um, I wanted to apologize for the things I said. For warning you that Dominic wouldn't give you a happily-ever-after. It appears that I was wrong. I shouldn't have made assumptions. Shouldn't have interfered." She sounded genuinely miserable about it, but Mila wasn't convinced.

It was on the tip of Mila's tongue to ask why Charlene thought she should care either way. "Apology accepted." Ha, such a lie.

Charlene sighed in what seemed to be relief. "Thanks. I hope he'll stop being pissed at me. I don't want to lose him as a friend. We were always close, and we've seen each other through difficult times."

Well, that wasn't the impression that Mila had gotten from Dominic.

"I know I must have seemed like a bitch, but I just didn't think his interest in you would last. You're not his usual type, and he gets bored pretty quickly. It was a damn good idea to play hard to get so that he'd see you as refreshing. Go you!"

An angry flush stained Mila's cheeks. Her cat whipped her tail, baring a fang. "You're implying he's only with me because I *played* him?"

"No, I just mean it was a good approach to have taken. Most girls just throw themselves at him. I'm sorry to say that probably won't change, even though he's marked you. It'll just make them think he's finally ready to settle down, and they'll view you as competition—"

"I can handle it," Mila bit out.

"Handle what?" asked a voice behind her.

Whirling around, Mila saw Dominic staring at her, his shoulders tense.

He prowled toward her. "Who is it?"

"Charlene."

Beyond fucking annoyed that a female from his past had called his mate—especially one who seemed intent on coming between them—Dominic said, "Well, hurry up and finish the call. I have a pussy to eat. In fact . . ." He picked Mila up, tossed her on the bed, and spread her legs.

Mila swallowed as Dominic nuzzled her folds. "Um, Charlene, I have to go."

"Wait, I was hoping to talk to Dominic."

Biting back a moan as he licked at her slit, Mila said, "She wants to talk to you, GQ."

"I'm busy." He grabbed her cell, ended the call, and buried his face in her pussy. It wasn't long before she came hard and loud, thighs squeezing his head.

Collapsing on the bed beside her, Dominic pulled her close and nuzzled her neck. "I love that you smell of me."

Feeling his cock throbbing against her, Mila made a mental note to take care of it once she could feel her legs. "What did Trey want? Pierson hasn't written another article, has he?"

"No. There are photos of me online carrying you down the street. The same person who wrote the articles for Pierson contacted Trey, asking him for comments about the photos, claiming to want our side of the story. Trey blew him off, but he wanted to tell me about it face-to-face."

"Good decision by Trey. The journalist is very anti-shifter, so he probably would have twisted whatever Trey told him. Charlene mentioned the photos just now."

"Did she call to chat more shit to you?"

Mila's cat liked the threat of repercussions in his voice, even though she could take care of the fox herself. "She apologized for interfering before. Said she'd only done it because I'm not your usual type and you get bored easily, but that sounded more like a warning than an effort to excuse her actions."

Jaws grinding, Dominic narrowed his eyes. "She's trying to shake your confidence in me."

Mila nodded. "She said she's worried that she'll lose your friendship. Claims you two were close and have seen each other through rough times."

He frowned. "Well, that's a load of bullshit."

"Yeah, I thought as much. She also praised me for playing hard to get—she thinks that's how I 'won' you. Then she pointed out that girls will continue to throw themselves at you, viewing me as competition—they'll think the mark you left on me indicates that you're ready for a relationship."

Dominic swore. "I'd call her and give her a ration of shit, but I'm getting the feeling that she *wants* me to call her. That she purposely pissed you off to provoke me into talking to her, since I haven't been taking her calls."

"I'm getting the same feeling, although she did seem to enjoy pouring crap down my ear." But if Charlene thought she had a chance of coming between Mila and Dominic, she was dead wrong. And since

Mila didn't want the woman to be a topic of conversation between them, she decided it was time to change the subject. She kissed his throat. "Forget about her. She's not important."

"You're right." Dominic didn't want another female or male in that bed with them. Just him and Mila. "Besides, I have a job for you. It kind of blows, but . . ."

She rolled her eyes, her mouth quirking. "Hopeless."

Brushing his nose against hers, Dominic pulled her flush against him. "Move in with me, Mila." Okay, that had come out of nowhere. He hadn't intended to mention it just yet. But having her in his bed, seeing her so relaxed on his territory, he just couldn't hold back. "I'd move in with you if you asked, but you love it here. Your cat loves it here. Let this be your home."

She bit her lip. "It's a big step."

"You don't have to give up your apartment yet, if that makes you feel better about moving. Think of the pluses. You and your cat will have all this land. It will be even harder for an assassin to get to you. Your brother can't break into your home in the middle of the night."

"Don't count on it. Wolverines go where they want to go—there's no stopping them."

He ignored that. "You'll also have even more space from Adele and Joel. No bumping into them on the stairwell. No Joel knocking on your door to say hey. Your cat will have the room she needs to fully heal."

That was certainly appealing for Mila, but . . . "It's not that simple. If I move here, I'm joining your pack. That means leaving my pride."

Dominic snorted. "You're Vinnie's niece—he'll always consider you an Olympus cat, no matter where you live. Trey will understand that."

"Wouldn't you rather wait until we're fully imprinted?"

"You mean wouldn't I rather wait to be sure we *do* fully imprint," he accused, bristling.

She shrugged. "I don't take things for granted—especially if they're as important to me as you are."

Just like that, his annoyance fizzled away. "We might only be *partially* imprinted, but any level of imprinting is a big deal. It makes you my mate, and I want my mate with me." He gave her a tight squeeze. "Come on, baby, move in with me."

She sighed. "Let me think about it."

"Sure," he said.

Mila's mouth thinned at his easy agreement and lazy smile. "You're confident you'll get what you want, aren't you?"

"Of course." He chuckled when she play-punched his shoulder. "Damn, that hurt. You should make it up to me. Sucking my cock will work."

She rolled her eyes again. "Like a dog with a bone." But she pushed him onto his back and slid down his body.

"I do in fact have a bone*r* and—" He hissed out a breath as she took his cock deep. "Fuck, you're good with that mouth."

CHAPTER EIGHTEEN

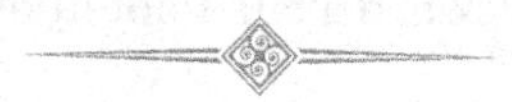

Dominic's eyelids fluttered open as he felt Mila begin to edge off the bed. The room was pitch-black and—

A plastic wrapper crinkled.

Someone was in her apartment, he realized. His wolf shot to full alertness, ready to protect and defend. Silent, Dominic slid out of the bed and went after Mila. Her scent had changed, turned more feral, and he realized she'd shifted. But he couldn't see her. *Shit.*

Adrenaline coursing through him, he crept into the living room and caught a glimpse of a tall, broad-shouldered male coming out of the kitchen with a bag of beef jerky in his hand. The cat launched herself at the intruder so fast she was a blur.

With a loud curse, the male swiftly whipped up his arm to protect his face before she could wrap herself around his head. It didn't deter the cat. She curled around his arm, biting hard and clawing deep. He hissed out a pained breath. "What the fuck, Mila?"

Snarling and growling, she shredded the guy's flesh. The intruder swore, grunted, winced, and ordered her to "let the fuck go." She didn't.

Dominic might have rushed over and intervened, but he'd seen pictures of the other male on the mantel and recognized him as Mila's brother. Figuring the guy deserved a bit of pain, Dominic dragged on his jeans and simply watched as his little cat tore strips out of her sibling's arm. Right then, she was a hissing, spitting, crazed ball of fury.

The only reason his wolf didn't lunge for the surface to join the struggle was that Alex didn't retaliate. The wolverine concentrated on trying to detach her from his arm, prying open her jaws. Each time he managed to loosen her hold, the cat would try wrapping herself around his head. Alex was always ready for the move, though. He'd slam up his arm to block her, at which point she'd go back to shredding the limb. It was easy to see that Alex had a fair amount of experience fighting off the feline.

With a pained oath, Alex held long, curved claws to the cat's flank. "Get off me, you crazy little bitch, or these are gonna cut right through that thick fucking hide of yours." The cat must have dug her fangs deeper instead, because the wolverine grunted in pain. *"Son of a motherfucker."*

With renewed vigor, Alex wrestled with the cat, snatched her by the scruff of her neck, and threw her across the room.

Dominic caught her and held tight. "You must be Alex."

The male tensed, his face hardening. "Who the fuck are you?"

Her ears flat, she let out a wolflike growl that shouldn't have come from a creature so small and cute.

Sensing that she was ready to launch herself at the wolverine again, Dominic kept a firm grip on her and made a shushing sound in her ear. "Dominic Black, an enforcer from the Phoenix Pack," he said as he took stock of his cat. Alex's blood stained her paws and fur, but she was fine. Alex, however, couldn't make the same claim. His arm was covered in ugly-looking welts and deep puncture wounds. "I'm also partially imprinted on Mila, which makes me her mate."

The wolverine took a lurching step forward that had the cat rumbling a dark sound. "Imprinted?"

"Yeah," Dominic bit out. "And since you're the reason she has a goddamn bounty on her head, I have a big fucking problem with you."

Alex's head drew back slightly. "Say that again."

"Your uncles didn't tell you?"

"My uncles?"

"They've been tracking you."

The wolverine shook his head. "I haven't seen them. I came home and . . . shit, there's a bounty on her head? You're sure of that?"

"Yes. You might want to see to that," said Dominic, gesturing to the guy's bleeding arm. As the wolverine disappeared into the kitchen, Dominic petted and nuzzled the little cat. She was stiff in his arms, her sides heaving as she drew in deep, angry breaths. Her green eyes blazed with fury as they locked on Alex when he returned to the room, tracking his every movement, coiled to pounce again.

A small dish towel wrapped around his wounded arm, Alex snatched the bag of beef jerky from the floor. "Imprinted on Mila, huh? We'll get back to that in a minute. First, tell me about the bounty."

"After you left to go roaming, someone who was convinced that you're Mila's roommate came to the apartment building and demanded to see you. She wouldn't tell them where you were, which they weren't pleased about. They said you'd pissed off their boss, and that Mila would regret not cooperating. Their boss must have put the hit out on Mila, thinking it would flush you out."

His brow creased, Alex shook his head. "John Norton was looking for me, that's true. I wired him the money I owed him shortly after I left, so he has no reason to have an issue with me or try to flush me out. He wouldn't give a shit as long as he had his money."

"Then why would he have placed a bounty on her head?"

"I can't see why he would have. It makes no sense." Sinking into the armchair, Alex tore open the bag of beef jerky with his teeth. "It's also not his style. He's the kind of guy who does his own dirty work. For him, it's about maintaining that badass 'I'm-not-to-be-fucked-with' image. Who told you it was him?"

"No one. We can't be sure who it is. We concluded that the person behind the hit was most likely the same person who's looking for you." Settling on the sofa, Dominic petted the cat as he told her brother all about the website, the attempts on Mila's life, and how none of her attackers had had any info on who'd put out the hit.

"Motherfucker." Alex munched on a piece of jerky, his eyes narrowed in thought. "It doesn't fit. It's just not how Norton rolls. And like I said, he has his money, which was all he wanted."

"Well, who could it be then? Mila doesn't have enemies."

"No, she doesn't. But Vinnie does. Maybe one of them put a price on his niece's head to get at him."

That idea had crossed Dominic's mind.

"I need to speak with my parents." Alex whipped out his phone. "I'm gonna find all kinds of texts and voice mails when I switch this on, aren't I?" Sure enough, the cell phone repeatedly beeped as his thumbs tapped the screen. "And this is why I don't like cell phones."

After making a quick call to James, asking him to come to Mila's apartment, Alex hung up and zeroed in on Dominic. "Now, on to the topic of you imprinting on Mila . . . I'd sure as fuck like to know how that happened. When I last spoke to her, she was planning on moving to Russia."

"She just wanted space from Joel, which is understandable."

"So she told you about him." Alex shoved another piece of jerky into his mouth. "How does he feel about the imprinting?"

"He doesn't like or approve of me, but he's glad that she's happy, and he seems to accept that I'm her choice."

Dominic froze as he heard the snick of the front door locks. Then Valentina—who'd clearly broken into the apartment in much the same way her son had—was storming into the living room with her mate in tow.

Alex jumped to his feet as he faced off with his mother. They argued in Russian while James glared at his son, nodding along to whatever Valentina said.

"Can you understand what they're saying, James?" Dominic asked.

Mila's father shook his head. "No, but it's good to present a united front, so I just nod along as if in agreement with Valentina. What did my son have to say for himself anyway?"

Dominic quickly explained what Alex had told him about this Norton guy, adding that the wolverine didn't believe the other male was responsible for putting out the hit. By the time Dominic was finished, both Valentina and Alex had quieted. "Alex thinks it could be one of Vinnie's enemies."

"It's possible," said James, pursing his lips. "He has quite a few of them."

Valentina put her hands on her hips. "I will slit your brother's throat if he is responsible, Alpha or not."

Wincing, James turned to his mate and worked to calm her down.

Dominic nuzzled his cat, who'd relaxed enough to stop glaring at her sibling. "Mila, time to come back. We need you to give us your input."

The cat shot him a truly disgruntled look before hopping off the sofa and leaving the room. When Mila walked in moments later dressed in shorts and a tee, she narrowed her eyes at Alex, who was once again relaxed in the chair and munching jerky.

"Your cat's a vicious bitch," Alex told her, approval coloring every syllable.

Mila snorted at what her cat took as a compliment even as she bared a fang at him. "And yet, you continue to invade her territory. But then, that's what assholes do."

"Easy there, Skindiana Jones—"

"I told you to drop that!"

"—I only just got back, my cupboards are virtually empty." Alex shrugged. "Besides, it's not like you eat anything. Or, at least, you don't *look* like you do. Seriously, you could hula hoop with a Cheerio."

Valentina clapped her hands. "No more of this! You have not seen each other in months, and this is how you behave? Why not greet each other with hugs?"

Mila snickered. "I'd rather remove my spleen with a rusty blade. Well, actually, *his* spleen would be my first choice."

"See, she hates me," said Alex.

"I don't hate you. But if you were slipping off a cliff, I'd go get some popcorn."

Dominic winced as Valentina yelled something in Russian that had both her children snapping their mouths shut. He had the feeling that it had been a threat of some sort.

"Fine," said Mila. "We have a serious matter to discuss anyway." She didn't resist when Dominic curled an arm around her waist and tugged her onto his lap. "How sure are you that this John Norton person didn't order the hit?" she asked her brother.

"I can't be *certain* that it's not him, but I strongly doubt that it is—really, it's not the type of thing he does." Alex's gaze cut to Dominic. "Maybe it's one of *your* enemies."

"There's Pierson," James said to Dominic. "He wants to hurt you. Hurting Mila would hurt you. He might have even just wanted her out of the way to clear the path for his daughter."

Valentina's brows lifted. "It is possible. He is human, but he could have found some way to do it. Or even paid a lone shifter to arrange the hit for him."

"Who's Pierson?" asked Alex.

Dominic gave him a quick rundown of the situation. "It can't be Pierson, though. The first attack on Mila happened before she and I got together."

Alex crumpled up his empty bag of jerky and tossed it in the trash. "When did you first meet the guy?"

"The day after I met Mila, as it happens." Dominic massaged her nape, wanting that last bit of tension to melt from her muscles. "I met him at a restaurant with some of my pack mates, which didn't go so well. Then . . . Shit."

"What?" asked Mila.

Dominic looked at her. "That same day, I drove to the barbershop to see you. He could have had someone follow me."

Mila shrugged. "So? All they would have seen is you getting a haircut."

"And writing my number on your palm. Like your dad said, Pierson could have just wanted you out of the way for his daughter's sake. He's demonstrated that there isn't anything he wouldn't do for her—and I think that's mostly to keep her mental state as stable as possible." Dominic silently swore, berating himself for not already considering it.

"Maybe the daughter did it," James speculated. "If she was so obsessed with you, Dominic, it makes sense that she would have followed you around. She could have followed you to the restaurant that day, hoping to gauge your reaction to the meeting with her father. If she followed you to the barbershop, I doubt she'd have liked seeing you flirt with another female. She believes you're her mate."

Dominic's wolf growled at that. "She *wants* to believe it. That's different." James's theory had some substance, though. Rosemary had claimed to not know that her father would approach the pack, but she'd proven that she was a very good liar. And she wouldn't want to incriminate herself, would she? Playing clueless would have been her best defense.

"Any jealous exes we need to consider?" Alex asked Dominic.

It was Mila who answered. "Well . . . there's Charlene."

Dominic's brows drew together. "She's not an ex. She's just someone I once had a brief fling with." He'd also considered her a friend until recently, but nothing more.

"Yeah," agreed Mila, "but she's done her best to come between us, hasn't she?"

Alex cocked his head. "Who is Charlene exactly?"

"A fox shifter who works as a barmaid at the club where I perform on Friday nights."

Alex flicked his finger from Dominic to Mila as he asked, "So she knows you two are together?"

"Yes. I don't think she has anything to do with this, though," said Mila. "For one thing, she's mated, so even if she *does* have lingering feelings for Dominic, she's hardly likely to act on them. She put some effort into convincing me *not* to get involved with him, sure, but I don't see why she'd want me dead just on the off chance that it could happen. That's real freaking extreme. I mean, what difference would it really make to her?"

"That depends on what her motivation is for trying to keep you apart," said Alex.

"I figure she just has a thing against pallas cats and wants him to be with someone who she thinks is 'better' for him," said Mila.

Dominic rubbed her thigh. "Jesse pointed something out to me that might explain why Charlene is making herself a problem for us. She takes pride in the fact that she's the woman I had the longest fling with and even allows people to believe I haven't committed to anyone because I was heartbroken when she ended things between us." He rolled his eyes. "She knows that's bullshit. Still, as Jesse suggested, her ego could be hurt because I pursued you relentlessly and wouldn't let you brush me off, no matter how hard you tried."

"Foxes are very competitive," Valentina commented. "They can also be sly and vengeful."

"It would explain why she's being a pain in our asses," said Dominic. "But hurt pride isn't motivation enough to want Mila dead."

"People have killed for less," Alex pointed out. "But I'm leaning toward Pierson or his daughter being responsible for the bounty."

Valentina nodded, twirling the ring on her finger. "The daughter has not been thinking clearly for some time."

Dominic rubbed the back of his neck. "I'm not sure Rosemary would even know how to go about something like putting out a hit, though. Plus, I think if she'd seen me flirting with Mila, *she'd* have been more likely to lash out immediately rather than come up with a calculating plot."

Alex pursed his lips. "Then her father is our most likely suspect."

Yeah, Dominic was thinking the same thing. And that meant that the reason his mate had been almost killed *three times* could very simply be that Dominic was in her life. Fuck if that didn't twist his stomach.

As they crossed the street to Ingrid's antique shop later that day, Mila flicked a concerned look at Dominic. As usual, he'd come with her to the barbershop, but he hadn't been his normal self. Oh, he'd put on a happy face. Joked and talked and laughed as she'd worked. But other times he'd sat there with his shoulders slumped, his mouth turned down, his brows drawn, and his gaze inward.

Whenever she was close, he'd reached out and touched her. Stroked her hair, smoothed his hand up her back, kissed her mouth, gave her hip a little squeeze, traced the bite on her neck with his finger. When he wasn't touching her, subconsciously seeking comfort, he was unnaturally still—as if forcing himself not to make any anxious movements.

She didn't need to ask what was weighing on him. It was guilt. He now believed that Pierson was responsible for the hit on her, and so GQ was blaming himself for the danger she was in. Which was quite simply fucking stupid.

Mila wouldn't be surprised if he later announced that they needed to put some space between them, hoping Pierson would then cancel the hit. She'd shoot that shit down fast. The only person she'd let come between them was her or Dominic—no one else. "It might not be Pierson, you know."

Dominic's mouth tightened. "It's likely that it is."

"That's still not a reason for you to be feeling guilty."

He sighed. "Trey was right. I should have listened to him and kept my distance from you until Pierson's little campaign blew over."

Reaching the front door of the antique store, she rested her hand on it. "You're not thinking clearly. Trey gave you that order after Pierson's second article was posted. But the jackal came at me *before* Pierson had even had his *first* article posted, which means the bounty was already on my head well before Trey gave you the order. If Pierson is behind this, you wouldn't have changed anything by obeying Trey."

"Maybe not, but I was selfish. I didn't want to be away from you, so I didn't stay away long." Dominic trailed a fingertip down the side of her face. "I should wish that I'd stayed away from you altogether, but I don't. I can't."

"I'm glad you didn't. You're not responsible for other people's actions. And I'm really not so sure it's Pierson."

Dominic exhaled a heavy breath. "Let's go see what Vinnie has to say." As she pushed open the door and they stepped onto the hardwood floor, a bell jingled above their heads. His wolf wrinkled his nose at the scents of lacquered wood, musty paper, and old cloth.

With one hand splayed on her lower back, Dominic followed her down the narrow aisle, taking in the wood cabinets, hand-carved dressers, grandfather clock, and oil paintings. The smaller items, such as the brooches, vintage hairbrushes, and shaving kits, were either set on display tables or locked in cabinets. He heard voices chatting, hinges creaking, and a dozen clocks ticking out of sync.

Mila came to a sharp stop just as someone rounded the aisle, almost bumping into her, and Dominic could almost hear her internal groan as she found herself face-to-face with Adele.

The blonde gave them a bright smile. "Oh, hi. How are you, Mila?"

"Good," she replied. "You?"

"Great." Blue eyes cut to Dominic. "Hi there. Hope you're taking care of our Mila."

"*My* Mila," he said.

Adele chuckled. "I guess she is—lucky you. Oh, Mila, I heard Alex is back. You must be *so* relieved."

"I am, yeah," said Mila.

"I know it's normal for him to go off alone for months at a time, but when no one could get in touch with him . . . well, I kind of worried something had happened to him." Adele pressed her palm to her heart, blowing out a breath. "Thankfully, that's not the case. And it means Vinnie will now have the answers he needs to get that bounty off your head. It's just a relief all around."

"It is," said Mila, forcing a smile.

"Well, I better get going." Adele patted Mila's arm. "You take care." With one last smile at Dominic, the blonde breezed out of the shop.

His brow creased, he looked at Mila. "She's not like any pallas cat I've ever met."

"You mean because she's sweet?" asked Mila, her mouth quirking.

He pulled her close. "No, you can be very, very sweet." He kissed her, needing a brief taste. "What I mean is that Adele . . . she doesn't seem to have that killer edge, even though she's a dominant female and one of your kind. There's just no fierceness about her."

"Mila!" a voice called out in delight.

They turned just as Ingrid came out from behind the desk and made a beeline for them. She gave first Mila a hug, and then Dominic.

He grinned. "Hey, Mrs. D. You have something on your head. Oh, it's fine, it's just a halo."

Blushing, Ingrid smiled at her granddaughter. "This one's trouble, isn't he? My boys are expecting you. Go right on up."

Dominic followed Mila through a door, down a narrow hallway, and up a curved staircase. The upstairs apartment was small but cozy. It smelled of lavender and citrus cleaner. He could also scent meat and mayonnaise, so it wasn't a surprise to find Vinnie, Tate, and Luke gathered around the kitchen table, munching on sandwiches.

Vinnie urged them to come inside and gestured at the table. Once he and Mila had taken the empty seats, the Alpha said, "I spoke with Alex at length earlier, so I'm up to speed on everything. He came with us to pay John Norton a little visit. Norton claims he has nothing to do with the attempts on your life, Mila. I believe him."

"So this was never about Alex," she said.

Dominic combed his fingers through her hair. "What about your enemies, Vinnie?"

"This isn't someone targeting me through Mila," the Alpha replied. "I have plenty of sources. If someone had put a hit out on Mila to get at me, I'd know about it by now." He picked up his soda can and took a swig. "Alex told me about the conversation you had with him this morning. I never considered Pierson."

"You're not convinced it's him," Dominic sensed.

"Neither am I, as it happens," said Mila. "Pierson's human, so how would he know about that website? If he was going to put a hit out on me, wouldn't he have hired a human?"

Vinnie pointed at her. "That's what has me doubting that he's who we should be looking at."

"I wondered about that too," said Dominic. "But many lone shifters are guns for hire—humans use them more than our kind does. If Pierson spoke to one who didn't want the job, they could have told him about the website."

"Possibly." His plate empty, Tate leaned back in his seat. "We could pick him up. Make him talk."

"Yeah." Luke stretched. "Humans always break easily."

Vinnie grimaced. "I'd rather be sure we have the right person, since we'd have to let him go if it turns out he's innocent."

Mila nodded. "If he mysteriously disappears, Dominic will be the prime suspect."

"Exactly," said Vinnie. "And if it *is* Pierson, well, it's best to let him think we're in the dark. Right now, he's counting on a hit man taking care of the job. If he discovers we know about it, he'll try to get rid of Mila another way. Possibly by involving the extremists. That can get messy. Look what they did to Bracken's family."

Footsteps stomped across the landing and into the kitchen. Dominic watched as a skinny teenage girl with flaming red hair came storming into the room, her mouth tight, her eyes wide with anger.

"Dad, you need to ship that little weasel off to another country—preferably one with lots of sweatshops for kids—or I'm gonna kill him."

Vinnie sighed. "Elle—"

"Look what he did!" The girl held up a sequined top that had long slashes running through it, as if it had been clawed at by an animal.

Vinnie frowned at her bloodstained fingernails. "Why is there blood on you?"

Jutting out her chin, Elle shrugged one shoulder. "He slashed my top, so I slashed his. Not my fault he was wearing it at the time."

A boy of about twelve or thirteen stalked into the room, his shirt torn and bloody. He glowered at the older teen. "Christ, Elle, what is your damage?"

She thrust the top at him. "This! This is damage! You got off lightly, Damian!"

The boy made a dismissive sound. "It doesn't fit you anymore anyway—you've put on more weight."

She gaped. "I lost four pounds this week."

"I *fart* four pounds."

"Well, there's not a lot the Antichrist can't do," she sniped.

His hands fisted. "Stop calling me that! And stop humming *The Omen* theme music through the bedroom wall!"

"Stop calling me Miss Piggy and making whale noises at me!"

"Is it my fault you're the size of one? I think not."

Vinnie sighed. "Elle, Damian, enough." He looked at his son. "Your sister is not fat, so stop with that shit. Elle, your brother is not—"

"The personification of pure evil?" Elle sniffed. "I disagree."

Damian's upper lip curled. *"Drop dead, Jelly Thighs!"*

"Screw you, Beelzebub!"

"Hey, hey, *hey*, enough." Vinnie slashed a hand through the air. "We're done here. Oh, and you'll both be replacing the clothes you slashed."

Mumbling and huffing, Elle and Damian marched out of the room and headed off in separate directions.

Vinnie turned to Dominic. "I gave this advice to Bracken, and now I'm going to give it to you. Either only have one kit with Mila or wait a decade before having a second. Pallas kits don't get along well with siblings of a similar age. Really, given that Mila and Alex are twins, it's a wonder they didn't kill each other as kids."

"We tried," admitted Mila.

"Yeah, so did we," said Tate, gesturing at his brother.

Luke nodded. "Multiple times. I nearly succeeded when I pushed him off the roof, hoping it'd look like suicide. The bastard had put rat poison in my pudding."

Tate shrugged. "Listening to you vomit was better than listening to you breathe."

Mila gave Dominic a mockingly sweet smile. "See what a bright future you have to look forward to?"

Chuckling, Dominic kissed her temple. "Works for me."

CHAPTER NINETEEN

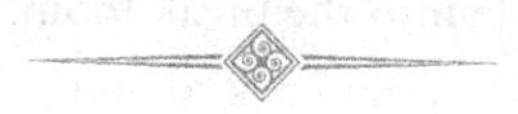

Dipping the string mop into the plastic bucket, Mila yawned. She'd knocked down the freaking tub of shaving cream while tidying her station, and she *totally* blamed Dominic. If he hadn't repeatedly woken her throughout the night with his insatiable cock, she wouldn't be so damn lethargic. She couldn't help but snarl when he came up behind her.

Snaking his arms around her waist, he rested his chin on her shoulder. "Tired, baby?" She could hear the smile in his voice.

"And whose fault is that?" she clipped, wringing the soapy water out of the mop using the bucket's built-in wringer.

"You weren't complaining last night. In fact, you were moaning. Groaning. Whimpering. Almost sobbing at one point."

Mopping up more of the spilled cream, she sniffed haughtily. "I don't sob. Or whimper."

"Oh, you definitely whimper." He nuzzled her neck, inhaling deeply. "And you came very close to sobbing when I spent a good twenty minutes just working your clit with my tongue, refusing to touch you anywhere else."

Fuck if he wasn't right. But she'd never admit it aloud. "Perhaps you lie to comfort yourself—I'm not sure."

He nipped at her neck. "You know I'm not lying, just as you know you're getting turned on just remembering it."

Dammit, she was. "Wrong again."

"Really? Hmm. Then these must be Tic Tacs in your bra, huh?"

A chuckle burst out of her. "Fuck you, GQ."

His shoulders shaking with muffled laughter, he kissed her neck. "I'll get you some coffee." Releasing her, he turned to Archie and Evander. "Anyone else want coffee?" The two male cats called out their orders as Dominic strode into the break room.

Shaking her head, she went back to mopping the floor. She needed to hurry her ass up, since Dean was waiting on the sofa.

She dipped the mop in the bucket again just as the door opened and let in a gust of street noise. She flashed a polite smile at the stocky hyena shifter who was one of Archie's regular clients. "Archie, your three thirty is here," she called out.

The hyena rolled his eyes at her. "Will you never refer to me by my name?"

"When you insist that your name is Hambone, no, I can't call a grown man that."

Dean let out an amused snort. "Yeah, I'm with Mila on that one."

Archie summoned his client over, so Mila quickly warned him, "Careful, the floor's wet." As the hyena sidestepped the wet spot, the door once again swung open. A woman stepped inside and glanced around, seeming unsure, tugging at her black curls restlessly.

"Hi, do you have an appointment?" Mila asked.

The woman's eyes snapped to Mila, momentarily flaring with something dark. "Um, no," she replied. "I just wondered if you could take a look at this for me." She dug her hand into a brown paper bag, seemed to angle the bag toward Mila and—

Thunder rang through the air. A harsh impact slammed into Mila just as red-hot pain exploded in the left side of her chest. She recoiled in shock, her mouth dropping open, her feet slipping on the wet floor. Not thunder, she thought as she fell. Not thunder. *Fuck.*

Gunfire split the air, making Dominic's heart slam against his ribs. He raced out of the break room and into the barbershop . . . just in time to watch Mila lose her footing and awkwardly fall backward. She hissed, and as if weighed down by pain, crumpled onto her back. The scents of blood and gunpowder tainted the air. *Mila's* blood. It seemed to clog his nostrils and churn his stomach, sending his wolf into a blind panic. And for a single moment, Dominic's world stopped.

A vicious, debilitating fear clawed at his insides, raked at his throat, and settled on his tongue, thick and metallic. His wolf froze, rooted to the spot by raw shock.

"Stay back!" ordered the woman near the door, shakily pointing a brown paper bag at Mila while her manic eyes danced from person to person. A bag that had a fucking hole the size of a bullet in it. "Stay back or I'll shoot her again!"

Rosemary. He almost didn't recognize her. She'd dyed her hair black and had it permed into tight curls. She looked a little like Mila. *His* Mila. Who the bitch had fucking *shot*.

Even though Mila had slapped her hand over the wound, blood still bloomed and stained her shirt *right above her heart.* How that heart was still beating, he didn't fucking know. But it wouldn't beat for much longer. No one could come back from such a fatal shot to the chest without medical help. No one.

Mila was conscious, her eyes hard on Rosemary, but her face was creased with pain. Shit, he needed to get to her. Needed to stop the bleeding. Get a healer. *Something.* But he couldn't fucking move while that bitch was still aiming the gun at his mate.

He sensed that Rosemary would shoot her again without hesitation. Would think *nothing* of pumping another bullet into Mila. And then he saw it—exactly what his life would be like without his little cat. Felt the taste of the empty, cold, pointless future that lay ahead of him if he didn't fucking do something.

"Time to go, Dominic," said Rosemary.

The words jolted his wolf out of his shocked state, and the beast let out a mournful howl edged with pure fury. His heart pounding like a drum, Dominic took only a single step forward. "Put the gun down," he told her, marveling at how steady his voice was.

"I saw pictures of you with her," Rosemary spat. "She's in our way. She needs to die."

"And you shot her. No human can survive a wound like that." Luckily, Mila wasn't human, but Rosemary didn't need to know that. "So you don't need the gun now. Put it down."

She licked her lips. "We have to leave. You and me. Now."

She really thought they'd just walk out of there? Every male in the room was ready to pounce on her. Hell, Mila herself would probably give it a try. What's more, Tate, Luke, and the enforcers were outside the door, ready to barge in. But no one would make a move while Rosemary was aiming that gun at Mila. If Dominic could just get her to point it elsewhere . . .

"Look at me, Rosemary," Dominic ordered, because her attention had drifted back to Mila, her eyes filling with hatred. "Look only at me."

Rosemary's brows drew together. "Why are you still over there? I told you, we have to go."

"Go where?"

"Home. We're mates. You don't believe that now, but you will. We just need time."

His eyes darted down to Mila. More blood had stained her tee and was now pooling beneath her. *Fuck.* A chill invaded him all the way to his soul, swept across his skin, and lifted the hairs on his nape and arms. His wolf tugged at the reins, *needing* to get to his mate.

"I'm not real comfortable going anywhere with you while you have a gun in your hand, Rosemary," said Dominic. "Put it down."

The bobcat edged ever so slightly toward her, and Rosemary's gaze snapped to him. *"Get back!"* Finger flexing on the trigger, she glared at Dominic. "If you don't leave with me right now, I'll shoot her again. I swear it!"

His gut in knots, Dominic forced himself not to move. "You trust me to get that close to you without trying to grab the gun?" he asked, hoping she'd point it at him to ensure her own safety. Her eyes narrowed, dancing from him to Mila, and he knew she was weighing whether she should turn the gun on him or not.

Fighting the urge to close her eyes, Mila swallowed hard. She was so cold. Tired. Heavy. She kept her hand on the wound, but it was hard to keep up the pressure when a terrible weakness was pulling her under. The blood just kept pouring out of her, no matter what she did.

Her chest felt like it was on *fire.* As if hot sulfur was bubbling within the wound, and it burned like holy freaking hell. Each rise and fall of her chest sent fresh jolts of pain rippling through her.

Her cat was furious, wanted to surface and pounce on the human with the gun. Mila couldn't have shifted even if she'd wanted to. She was weakening fast, and the need to sleep was pulling at her.

With the little energy she had left, Mila whipped up her leg and kicked at Rosemary's hand, sending the gun flying out of her grip. Stars burst behind Mila's eyes and a blazing, crippling pain seized her chest and rolled over her in waves that made her stomach curdle. She breathed deep, but her vision blurred. Faded. And then the lights went out.

Adrenaline spiked through Dominic as the gun went skidding along the floor. Everyone moved at once.

Dean grabbed the handgun as Rosemary made a dive for it.

Evander tackled Rosemary, taking her to the floor.

The door swung open and a large number of people poured into the barbershop.

Archie and Dominic went straight to Mila, who'd promptly passed out.

Crouching at her side, Dominic's stomach lurched—she was so pale and pasty; sweat beaded her upper lip and forehead. "Baby," he whispered, his voice as shaky as his hands. Cursing, he put pressure on the wound. God, there was so much blood. His wolf paced and raked at the ground, seething, panicked.

"We need a healer in here!" Archie yelled, his face set into a mask of alarm. "At least the bullet went straight through," he said to Dominic. "She wouldn't be lying in a puddle of blood if it hadn't."

Now that he could see the exact location of the wound, Dominic couldn't understand *how the fuck* she was still alive. "How is her heart still beating?" It was weak and irregular, but it was there.

"She has isolated dextrocardia," said Archie. "Her heart is on the right side."

Dominic's eyes fell closed. Something so simple had saved her damn life.

Helena knelt beside them. "You can move your hands, Dominic. I can heal her."

Dominic didn't move an inch. Just watched as Helena laid a hand on Mila's shoulder. As usual, the air went static. He faintly felt a crackle of healing energy work its way through Mila.

"It's all right," Helena told him. "She's fine now. Just weak and tired from blood loss, so she may sleep awhile."

Lifting his hands from the wound, he saw that it had closed. "Thank fuck." Dominic scooped Mila up and held her to him, breathing her in. His eyes stung, and the back of his throat hurt. His wolf pressed against Dominic's skin, nudging her, wanting her to wake.

Her parents rushed over and made a fuss, stroking her face and kissing her hand even though she remained unconscious, but Dominic didn't let Mila go. Couldn't. He needed to feel the reassuring weight of her in his arms or he'd lose his fucking mind.

Hearing a pained cry, he flicked his gaze to the corner of the shop. Luke had detained Rosemary, the fucking bitch, pinning her wrists behind her. She was writhing and spitting insults, but the male held her easily while Tate and the enforcers examined her gun and questioned her.

Dominic tightened his hold on Mila and stood just as her Alpha approached. "I'm getting my mate out of here." He needed her to be someplace safe.

Vinnie nodded. "We can't keep this incident within the shifter community. Humans in the street saw Rosemary in here and heard the gun go off. If we hadn't assured them that we'd already made a 911 call to report a hostage situation, they would have called it in themselves—in reality, of course, we called our pride mates on the police force. People are out there, waiting to snap photos that they might then sell to the press.

"Take her out the rear exit, away from the cameras and nosy-ass spectators. Evander's out there—I sent him to get his car, and I've instructed him to drive you both to her apartment building so you're out of sight and don't need to walk there. To explain that she's healed, we'll downplay her injury a little to the police and say you took her to *your* Alpha so that she could heal Mila."

Dominic shifted Mila ever so slightly in his arms. "Tell your cops they won't be getting a statement out of her. I don't want any more of this fucked-up shit touching her. You tell the little white lie that she's now part of my pack—it'll place her out of the reach of human authorities."

Vinnie gave a slow, satisfied nod. "We can do that."

Her eyes wet, Valentina pressed a kiss to Mila's head. "You keep my girl safe, Dominic. Understood?"

Dominic nodded. "Believe me, Valentina, she's my absolute priority."

After giving Mila's hair one last stroke, James lightly slapped him on the back. "Go, get her out of here."

Shooting one last glare at Rosemary, who was now shrieking his name, Dominic spun on his heel and stalked through the shop, down the length of the narrow hallway, and out the back door.

Evander was pacing near a gleaming black Mercedes. He halted as they approached, his brow creased in concern, and opened the rear passenger door. "Is she all right?"

"Unconscious," Dominic bit out, sliding into the car. Cradling her, he kissed her temple, his eyes falling shut. She'd come far too close to death. Had bled profusely from a bullet wound right in front of him, and he'd been able to do *nothing*. A sense of failure pricked at both him and his anxious wolf, who lay down, resting his chin on his legs.

Evander quickly drove them to Mila's apartment building, but Dominic didn't take her inside. He walked to his SUV, settled her into the passenger seat, and hopped into the driver's side. He needed to know she was safe, needed her to have privacy and peace while she rested. As such, he drove out of the lot and onto the road, heading toward his territory.

Oh, he knew her parents and pride mates wouldn't like it. Understood they'd want to be there when she woke. But he couldn't indulge them in that. Just couldn't. As he'd told Valentina, *Mila* was his priority. He'd do what was best for his mate, not her parents. And Dominic knew Mila wouldn't like it if she woke to find an apartment full of people anyway.

As he drove, he occasionally laid a hand on her thigh or reached out to stroke her hair. She never stirred. Not once. Not even when he finally arrived at his territory and took her out of the SUV to carry her up the stairs of the cliff face.

Walking through the tunnels, he heard chatter and laughter coming from the living area. He didn't head there. He went straight to his room, kicking the door shut behind them. Only then did his wolf lose some of his tension. Dominic's remained.

Not wanting her to wake to the sight and smell of her own blood, Dominic shed their clothes and stepped under the hot spray of the shower. Even the water didn't rouse her—hell, she didn't even so much as pucker her brow. He quickly and carefully soaped her body, washing every flake of dried blood from her skin.

Having patted her dry, he slipped her into one of his shirts and settled her into his bed. He was just about to join her when knuckles rapped hard on the door. A pulse of adrenaline shot into his system, because right then—while his mate was weak and unable to defend herself—any presence felt like a threat.

"Dom? I got a call from Vinnie." *Trey.*

Forcing his fists to relax, Dominic crossed to the door and opened it to find both his Alphas standing there. Stepping into the hall, he pulled the door shut behind him.

"How's Mila?" Taryn asked.

"Sleeping," Dominic replied simply, not in the mood for conversation. He wanted to be with Mila. *Alone.*

Trey looked him up and down. "You good?"

"Yep."

"From what Vinnie said, Mila's family wasn't happy to find her apartment empty, but I think they'll understand why you brought her here."

"Why don't I check on her?" Taryn suggested.

Dominic stilled. "She's fine."

Trey sighed. "I get that your protective instincts are doing the mambo right now, but you know she's not in danger from us. You know that, or you would never have brought her here."

"When she's at full strength, you can see her. Until then, no one comes inside."

Her face soft with sympathy, Taryn looked like she might step forward and hug him. Instead she nodded. "All right. I'll send Grace with food. She doesn't have to come inside. She can leave the tray on the floor out here. Mila will be hungry when she wakes."

Dominic gave a curt nod and returned to his room, locking the door behind him. Maybe it was irrational, but he just didn't trust anyone to be around her while she was so vulnerable. Not a single soul.

Sliding onto the bed, he pulled her flush against him and dragged the covers over them, not wanting her to catch a chill. His wolf snuggled up to her, still anxious. The beast hadn't yet fought his way completely through the raw shock that had gripped him earlier. Hell, Dominic's brain was still scrambling to process what had happened, trying to make some sense of it. One second she'd been fine; the next she was bleeding on the fucking floor.

He caught her hand and pressed a kiss to her wrist, needing to feel her pulse beating against his mouth. "I'm sorry I left you," he said, his voice like gravel. If he hadn't gone to the break room, if he'd stayed with her, he could have pushed her out of harm's way. Could have wrestled the gun from Rosemary's hand before she had the chance to fire.

Intending to be the first thing Mila saw when she opened her eyes, Dominic didn't move from her side as she slept. Not even when Grace knocked to say she'd left a tray of food outside the door. His attention was solely on Mila.

He plucked at her curls, traced her cheekbones and jawline, and dabbed kisses to her face, palm, and wrist. Not a single touch disturbed her sleep. Nor did the ringing and beeping of their cell phones. Was that normal? He didn't know.

Panic tightened his chest and stiffened his muscles until they ached. Helena had told him that Mila would sleep for a while, but he hadn't thought she'd fall into such a deep sleep. The longer she took to wake, the tighter the knot of panic inside him became. It was like there was a large rock lodged in his chest, making it hard for him to take a full breath. His ribs felt too tight, too constricting.

Maybe he should have let Taryn take a quick look at Mila. He could call his Alpha female and ask her to come. She'd—

His heart jumped as Mila's eyelids flickered slightly. Relief swept through him like a tidal wave. "Hey there," he said softly. "Can you open those eyes for me?" Seconds ticked by before her eyelids finally fluttered open and her dazed blue gaze found his. He smiled. "There's my girl. How are you feeling?"

The sleepy glaze cleared from her eyes, and they sharpened as memories no doubt flashed through her mind. She glanced around, and he could almost see her trying to piece together what had happened since she passed out. "Helena healed me?"

"Yes." He kissed her, craving her taste. "I brought you here. Needed to know you were safe."

Sensing he expected judgment for taking her away from her pride, Mila petted his chest. "I get it." In his shoes, she wouldn't have acted differently. Her cat roused, rumbling a growl as Mila felt the echo of the bullet penetrating her chest courtesy of fucking Rosemary. "Where is the little bitch?"

"Your pride mates detained her, but the police probably took her into custody."

"I'll call my parents in a little while and get an update." Mila fell silent as he flicked open the top few buttons of the shirt she was wearing. He carefully danced his fingertips over the little spot on her chest where the bullet had hit her, as if he needed to be mindful of a wound. "It's gone, Dominic. I'm healed." But he still touched her like she was something fragile, like if he wasn't careful, she might suddenly be gone from his arms. "I'm okay."

A breath shuddered out of him. "You almost weren't."

The note of shame in his voice made her snap, "Oh, hell no. You don't get to feel guilty." Her cat would have rolled her eyes if she could have. It was just typical of a dominant male to shoulder the responsibility.

"I *left* you."

"You went to make me coffee."

"If I hadn't, I could have pushed you out of the way and grabbed the gun."

Mila shook her head. "She had it hidden in a paper bag. I highly doubt you would have guessed she was armed."

"But I'd have recognized her."

"You sure? I only saw a picture of her from an online article, but she looked a hell of a lot different today."

"She looked like you," Dominic pointed out.

"Yeah, I noticed." Damn if it wasn't fucked up that the woman had changed her appearance to match Mila's.

"I'd have known her scent. I could have—"

"For all we know, she'd been watching and waiting for you to leave my side before she entered. When she first walked into the barbershop, she didn't home in on me. She glanced around. She could have been checking that you were a fair distance away before she struck."

"And if I hadn't been in the break room—"

She put a finger to his mouth. "Stop. I'm fine."

He swallowed. "I thought you were gonna die right in front of me. I couldn't do shit about it."

"You kept her attention on you. You distracted her. It gave me an opening. I couldn't have caught her off guard and kicked her hand if you hadn't." Mila palmed the back of his head and pulled him closer. He buried his face in her neck and locked his arms tight around her. She sifted his hair through her fingers, soothing him. "Shake off the anxiety, Dominic. I'm okay."

Lifting his head, he kissed her. It was soft. Deep. Reverent. Mila could almost *feel* his need to take her, assuring himself she was alive in the most basic way. She was totally up for that.

Needing more, Mila bit his lip, trying to provoke him into upping the intensity. It didn't work. His hands drifted over her, gentle and oh, so careful as they explored, seduced, and aroused.

Even when he *finally* sank his fingers into her pussy, building the friction inside her, he kept his thrusts slow and easy. Frustrated, Mila clenched his fingers with her inner muscles, hinting for more.

He didn't give it to her.

Mila felt his rock-hard cock throb against her, felt how tightly his muscles were bunched as he fought to hold back. But even when he rolled her onto her back and lined up his cock with her pussy, he kept his control perfectly in check. She didn't like it. Wanted to feel alive, not be handled like she was breakable.

With a surge of strength that surprised them both, Mila shoved him back and got to her knees. "You don't get to treat me like I'm delicate. See me, Dominic. Not the blood, not how weak I was earlier, not flashes of what happened in the barbershop. See me as I am right now. I'm here, I'm fine, and I'm horny as fuck."

"Mila—"

"You don't want soft and slow any more than I do. Take what you do want, Dominic. Fuck me how you really want to fuck me. Remind us both that I'm alive."

His mouth set in a harsh slash, he fisted his hands. "Stay on your knees. Turn around. Grab the headboard."

Well. Mila did as he ordered. Her pulse quickening, her nipples tightening, she waited to see what he'd do.

"Spread your thighs wider. That's it." Pressing his front to her back, Dominic dipped the head of his cock between her plump folds. *So slick.* "Just remember . . . you asked for this, baby." He snapped his hand around her throat and rammed into her, groaning as her hot, soaking-wet pussy squeezed him tight. "Take all of me, Mila." He slammed home again, burying himself balls-deep. *"Fuck."*

Even as her quaking pussy burned in the best way and felt deliciously full, Mila hissed at his blatantly dominant hold. "Let go."

Instead, Dominic flexed his grip on her neck, gritting his teeth as her pussy rippled around him. She liked him holding her this way, she just didn't want to admit it. He caught her earlobe with his teeth and bit. "You told me to fuck you how I really want to. This is what I want. My hand collaring your throat while I take what belongs to me."

His fingers digging into her hip, he fucked her hard. So hard he had to be hurting her, but he couldn't stop, and she didn't ask him to. *"Mine."*

Gripping her shoulder with his teeth, Dominic slid his hand up from her hip to close around her breast, wanting to feel it bounce in his hand as he furiously pounded into his mate. He felt every moan, groan, and whimper all the way to his balls.

Mila wished she could say she wanted him to release his grip on her throat, but there was something heady about feeling all that dominance, strength, and power . . . and knowing he'd never use it to hurt her. With his teeth digging into her shoulder, one hand collaring her neck, another holding her breast in a proprietary grip, and his cock tunneling through her body again and again, she felt utterly possessed.

Mila swallowed as his hand released her breast and slipped down her body. One touch to her clit and she'd go off like a rocket.

He gave her inner thigh a sharp slap. Mila hissed at the sting, but the pain radiated up to her pussy and made it spasm.

"Fuck, you like that."

She gasped as he did it again, but he spanked higher up her inner thigh this time. Again, the burn settled in her core.

As a rush of hot cream bathed his cock, Dominic swore under his breath and pounded harder, faster. Stuffed her full over and over. And he knew he'd never get enough of her. Of this.

His gaze landed on the little spot in the crook of her neck that he'd raked his teeth over more than once. Each time he'd looked at it, he'd thought it a good place for a claiming mark. And now, with his senses swamped by Mila, he had to grind his teeth against the primitive drive to bite down on her neck and claim her permanently as his own.

The urge just kept on taunting him, pushing him, tempting him. Eating at his control. It didn't help that his wolf was pressing him to do that very thing.

When Dominic paused, panting, Mila frowned. "What's wrong?"

Letting his hand slip from her throat, he cupped her hips as he rested his forehead on the back of her own head. "Just give me a sec."

Hearing the strain in those words, Mila clipped, "I don't need you to be in control."

"Yes, you do. Or I'm going to claim you."

Her heart slammed against her ribs. She heard the truth in that statement. Heard how badly he craved to claim her. Felt that same longing to permanently brand him as hers—a longing that was shared by her cat. Mila shrugged. "So do it."

He groaned. "Shit, Mila, don't say that unless you mean it. It'd kill me if you later regretted it."

"I won't. I want this."

"Be sure," he said, his voice unintentionally harsh. "Because there'll be no going back after this. I don't care that imprinting bonds can fade—for me, this will be irrevocable." He dug his fingers into her hips. "You hear me, Mila? If I claim you right now, it's for good. I won't let you go."

"Just fucking bite me."

He sank his teeth down hard, tasted blood, and growled in victory. Ignoring how she tried to buck and squirm on his cock, he held her in place as he sucked and licked at the mark, making sure the permanent brand would never be mistaken for anything but a claiming mark. His wolf rumbled a dark sound that vibrated with pure satisfaction.

Locking one arm tight around her waist, Dominic planted his free hand on the wall above the headboard and licked over the bite. "Mine. Always mine." Then, control obliterated, he was ramming into her again. Possessing her body, asserting his claim on her, taking what was his to take.

As his balls drew up tight, he snarled into her ear, "Come all over my cock, Mila. Let me feel . . . Yeah, that's it, baby." Her head fell back onto his shoulder as she came with a choked groan, quaking and contracting around him. *"Fuck."* He slammed harder, faster, and jammed his cock deep as he exploded inside his mate, his eyes going blind with the pleasure that whipped through his body.

Floating on sheer bliss, Mila slumped, her eyes closed. Only the arm around her waist kept her from collapsing onto the bed. Sated all the way to her soul, she didn't stir as Dominic pulled out of her and tugged her down to the mattress. Then they were lying on their sides, facing each other as he traced the bumps of her spine.

"Look at me, Mila," Dominic softly ordered, needing to stare into her eyes, needing to be sure there was no regret there. When her eyelids fluttered open, all he saw was peace. He drew in a contented breath and pressed a lingering kiss on her mouth. "I don't think my wolf has ever felt so settled."

Her lips curled lazily. "I was just thinking the same thing about my cat."

He gave her a slow, languid smile. "Yeah? Good. Because she's mine too. I want her happy."

Her badass cat *totally* melted when he said stuff like that. "She is."

Skimming his finger over the claiming bite on her neck, he asked, "You sure you're good with this?"

"I'm sure."

"No regrets?"

"None at all." Mila sank her teeth down hard on his neck, sucking, licking, and leaving her own permanent brand.

Cursing, Dominic tangled a hand in her hair. A raw, primal need shuddered through him. His blood thickened, his cock hardened. And for the second time in the space of mere minutes, he lost all control.

CHAPTER TWENTY

Knuckles rapped on the door. "I got a bunch of people at the gate, wanting to see Mila," Trey called out from the tunnel. "No, *demanding* to see her."

Dominic paused in massaging her scalp. After flipping her over and possessing her once more, he'd rolled onto his back and sprawled her over his chest, silently relishing the knowledge that she'd claimed him as her own. They'd been lying there for a while now, relaxing, talking, and enjoying the time alone. Now it was apparently over. "Who?"

"Vinnie, his sons, her parents, and her brother."

Lifting her head, Mila sighed. "Well, at least they showed enough respect not to sneak in."

Dominic's brows pinched together. "You really think they could bypass our security?"

"My mother and Alex could do it, no problem," she said.

"Quick warning," Taryn called out. "They're not happy bunnies right now."

Yeah, Dominic had figured they'd be annoyed with him for not returning Mila to her apartment. "Let them through the gates," he told the Alphas as he and Mila rose from the bed and snatched their clothes from the floor. "Mila and I will meet them at the entrance to the caves."

Mila dragged on her jeans, but since there was blood all over her top, she didn't remove Dominic's shirt. Hearing her cell ring, she fished it out of her jeans pocket. *Joel.* She instantly canceled the call.

"I'm guessing that was Joel by the face you pulled," said Dominic.

"It was," she confirmed. And then her phone was ringing again.

"He's gonna keep calling until he hears your voice and knows for sure that you're fine," said Dominic, beating back the resentment he felt at that. "His instincts will hound him until he does."

She shrugged. "That sounds like his problem, not mine. We both made our choices. Adele's his choice." And neither she nor her cat felt any bitterness about it. "And you're mine."

Fully dressed, Dominic lifted his brow. "If you hadn't known that your true mate was spoken for, would you still have claimed me?"

Mila frowned at the idiotic question. But then, she supposed she'd wonder the same thing in his position. "My claiming you had nothing to do with him or anyone else. I claimed you because, well, I love you. Which is seriously annoying, by the way, because I don't like mushy stuff. If I hadn't known about Joel, I *still* would have loved you. In which case, yes, I still would have claimed you."

His face all soft and warm, he gathered her close. "You love me?" he asked, his voice thick with emotion.

"Yeah. As I said, it's annoying."

He brushed his nose against hers. "Since you don't like mushy stuff, I won't tell you that I love you right back."

Mila's mouth curled, and warmth trickled through her and her cat. "You just did."

"You can pretend I didn't." He took her mouth in a soft, slow, deep kiss that—

Knuckles rapped on the door again. "Um, *hello*," called Taryn. "You guys ready or what?"

Sighing, Dominic reluctantly drew back. "We'll continue this later," he promised Mila. Crossing to the door, he opened it wide to find both his Alphas standing there.

Taryn smiled. "Thanks for finally joining . . ." She trailed off as her eyes dropped to Dominic's claiming mark. Spotting the matching one on Mila's neck, the she-wolf lifted her brows. "*Well.* I have to say, I was not expecting that so soon. I'm doing a happy dance in my head right now."

Trey didn't look so surprised by the claiming marks. "It's about damn time."

"The bond hasn't formed yet," Taryn observed.

"It will." Dominic took possession of Mila's hand and said to her, "Now let's go greet your family."

"Taryn and I will join you," Trey stated. "It's important that Vinnie, as another Alpha, receives an official welcome from the two of us."

Aware of the dynamics, Dominic gave a curt nod and began a brisk walk through the tunnels. "Where's the rest of the pack?"

"Some have gone with Riley and the kids to the playroom," began Trey, keeping pace with him. "Others have retreated to various rooms within the caves. Only Dante and Ryan are in the living area, waiting for us to join them."

Dominic understood why Trey had sent their other pack mates away. If there were more Phoenix members than Olympus members present in the living room, it might look both confrontational and as if Trey didn't trust that he could deal with any problems without additional backup.

"How pissed do you think your family will be with Dominic?" Taryn asked Mila.

Her nose wrinkled. "Not much. My parents adore Dominic, and the others like him a lot too. They just won't be happy that they weren't with me when I woke up."

"Understandable," said Taryn. "If Kye were hurt, and then fell unconscious, I'd want to be one of the first people he saw when he woke."

Finally reaching the entrance to the dwelling, all four of them stood just outside the door. Dominic kept possession of Mila's hand, skimming his thumb over her knuckles. Whoever was manning the security shack must have given the Olympus Pride directions to the dwelling, because Vinnie's vehicle soon came into sight. It followed the rocky trail into the parking lot at the base of the mountain.

Vinnie took the lead as he and the other pride members began to climb the steps of the cliff face, but Valentina pushed past him when they neared the top.

She pulled Mila into her arms and hugged her tight. "You are fine, yes?"

Pulling back to meet her mother's eyes, Mila smiled. "Yeah, I'm fine."

James stroked her hair. "Hey, sweetheart."

As Mila and her parents talked quietly, Trey turned to Vinnie and said, "Welcome to Phoenix Pack territory. You've already met my mate, Taryn."

Vinnie gave her a respectful nod. "Yes, I have. I don't believe you've met Mila's brother—he wasn't present at Madisyn and Bracken's ceremony, or the battle on Mercury Pack territory."

Alex inclined his head respectfully at the Alphas and then slid his hard gaze to Dominic. "Not impressed that you drove off with my sister, wolf."

"Don't care," Dominic said simply, and nor did his beast.

Vinnie twisted his mouth. "I see that you and Mila have officially claimed each other. But I don't sense a bond."

"You will soon enough." Dominic could feel the promise of it—like a low buzz of static electricity in the air.

Valentina turned to him, her hands on her hips. "You did not take Mila to her home. This does not make me happy."

"As I told you at the barbershop, Mila's my priority," said Dominic. "I needed her to be somewhere safe. This is far safer and more secure than her apartment building." And he wouldn't apologize for putting her first, even though he liked Valentina and understood why she was upset.

Valentina's mouth tightened. "I cannot argue that."

"But you want to," James said to her, his lips twitching. Valentina sliced him a look that should have made his balls crawl up into his stomach.

Trey gestured at the door. "Let's go inside so we can talk." He and Taryn led the way as they stalked through the tunnels.

Valentina looked around. "It is an unusual home you have, Dominic."

"My cat loves it," Mila told her just as they reached the living area where Dante and Ryan were each sprawled on an armchair. When both males stood, Mila introduced them to Alex, who made himself comfortable on the reclining end of the sofa like he'd been a regular visitor for years. Yeah, her brother wasn't the type to lean against a wall, on guard. He'd lounge around, casual and composed, fully confident that he could eliminate any threat at a moment's notice. Which he could.

At Taryn's invitation, the others all took a seat. "What happened to Rosemary?"

"She was arrested," said Vinnie. "The police may not charge her for shooting you, Mila. Some will say it's shifter business, since you're Dominic's mate. I told them you are also part of his pack. But others will claim that the human authorities should intervene since Rosemary didn't just shoot you, she held two supposed humans—meaning Archie and Evander—at gunpoint in the barbershop. The cops won't care about the bobcat or the hyena who were also present."

Luke scratched his chin. "Looks like Rosemary got sick of waiting for an assassin to take you out, Mila. She took the matter into her own hands."

Trey exchanged a look with Taryn and then cleared his throat. "I have news. Nick called me ten minutes ago. With the help of other hackers, his contact cracked the anonymity network."

Dominic blinked. "Well, fuck."

"It's run by a polar bear shifter by the name of Dale Forester. I've personally never heard of him." Trey looked at Vinnie, his brow raised in question.

The Olympus Alpha shook his head. "His name doesn't ring any bells."

"He's a lone shifter with more money than sense," said Trey. "Invents security systems for a living, and he's damn good at it. His estate is well protected. Getting to him won't be easy."

"Leave the matter to my brothers," Valentina told Trey. "They need only his address. They will get to this shifter and make him pay. No security system can keep them out."

Taryn glanced at her mate and then nodded at Valentina. "If you think your brothers can reach him, tell them to have at it. I want the bastard to feel the pain he's caused others."

"My brothers will ensure that he does," Valentina assured her.

"Nick's contact collapsed the site, which means there is no longer a price on your head," Trey told Mila. "It wasn't John Norton who put the hit out on you. Nor was it Emmet Pierson or his daughter. Does the name Dean Simmons mean anything to you?"

Mila's brow furrowed. "He's one of my clients. He sometimes brings his nephew, Finley. In fact, Dean was at the barbershop when Rosemary barged in earlier and . . . Wait, you're saying *he* put out the hit?"

Trey simply nodded.

Totally stunned, Mila gaped. Even her cat was taken aback. "But why would he do that? I barely know him, and I've never had any trouble with him." She looked at Dominic. "This doesn't make sense."

Dominic squeezed her hand, anger building inside him. He'd been so close to the fucker responsible for the hit, and he hadn't even known it. "How long has the bobcat been a client of yours?"

She frowned thoughtfully. "Since about a month before the jackal attacked me."

"Am I the only one thinking it's a hell of a coincidence that he was there when Rosemary shot Mila?" asked Dante, to which Ryan grunted in what was probably a "no," but Dominic couldn't be sure.

"Rosemary didn't know him," said Mila. "He tried to sneak up on her, and she warned him off. There was no flash of recognition on her face." Mila shook her head, repeating, "This just doesn't make sense. I never got the impression that he had any beef with me."

"He watches you," Dominic remembered. "Not with lust, though. Not with distaste. But something about you has his attention."

Vinnie rubbed at his jaw. "I only spoke with him briefly earlier. He left the barbershop shortly after you did. Do you have his address, Mila?"

"All his information is in the client database," she told him.

Tate whipped out his phone. "I'll get the address from Archie."

"Good," said Vinnie as his son left the room to make the call. "Then I'll pay the bobcat a visit."

Mila straightened in her seat. "I'll be with you."

Dominic stiffened as everything in him rebelled against the idea of her being anywhere near the bastard who, for some unknown reason, wanted her dead. *Especially* while she wasn't at 100 percent. "Baby, you're still tired from blood loss. You haven't had enough rest to recover."

"I'm fine," she insisted.

"No, you're not. You're pale and shaky. And don't even lie and tell me you're not drained—I can feel it." Her exhaustion brushed at his mind somehow, and he knew it was a result of the imprinting process progressing.

She frowned. "Feel it?"

"You can't feel what I'm feeling right now?"

Mila realized that, yes, she could feel the echo of an emotion that wasn't hers. A soul-deep anxiety. She sighed. "Dominic—"

"You almost died today, Mila." The reminder made his chest tighten and his wolf snarl. "No one can bounce back from something like that in a matter of hours. Rest. Get your strength back."

Mila couldn't deny that she needed that rest, but she also couldn't sit back while others apprehended the person who'd put her life in danger. She lifted her chin. "I'll stay if you stay." Which she was positive he'd *never* agree to do.

His brows snapped together. "Excuse me?"

"If you get a grip on Dean, you won't ask questions. Not while you're in this mood. The only thing on your mind is eradicating the threat to me." She could sense it as clearly as she could sense the tension in the room. "You won't even give him a warning. You'll just kill him. I want answers."

Dominic clenched his jaw, not bothering to refute her accusation. "The 'why' of what he's done doesn't matter."

"It does to me. If you stay, I'll stay. If not, we both go." In which case, she could stop him from killing Dean until she'd at least questioned him. Mila shrugged, leaving the decision up to Dominic, but pretty sure he'd back down. Seconds of uncomfortable silence ticked by, but she met his cold stare boldly.

His nostrils flared. "Fine. I'll stay."

Her head almost jerked back. "Seriously?"

"I know you were counting on me being so determined to get to Dean that I'd backpedal and agree to not fight you on coming along, but your health is more important than my need to rip out his throat." Even though that need pounded through his system, fraying the edges of his control. "Besides, it's best if you keep a low profile for a while."

Mila's spine would have snapped straight if she hadn't been so tired. "It's not in my nature to hide."

"I'm not asking you to hide. I'm asking you to lie low—that's different."

"No, it's not," she clipped. "And you don't get to dismiss my strength."

Dominic ground his teeth, anger blowing through him hot and fast. "A jackal tried to shoot you. A death adder tried to drown you. A cheetah poisoned you while I was standing *right there.* At no point did I ask you to hide, even though I wanted to, because I know exactly how strong you are. I didn't even fight you on your determination to stay in your apartment building.

"I know you're a force to be fucking reckoned with, Mila. And I know it would hurt you if I implied differently, so I shelved my own fears for you. But today, a neurotic bitch shot you in the fucking chest. A human. Easy to take down. But none of us managed it before she could hurt you. None of us. Sometimes, being strong isn't enough."

Mila couldn't argue that, but . . . "There's no longer a price on my head, and Rosemary is no longer a factor, so the danger has passed."

Dominic shook his head. "Pierson's articles and my pack's responses garnered a lot of attention. His daughter just tried to kill you. This is going to turn into a media circus. He's going to lose his shit, and he's going to somehow blame us for Rosemary's actions. Extremists will side with him, deeming you a shifter groupie, and they might try to attack you.

"All kinds of people are going to show up near your building and the barbershop. Reporters, video bloggers, nosy-ass people. It's going to be a security nightmare for your pride. There is no way they can keep a close watch on you during that time."

Vinnie sighed, his expression grim. "He's right, Mila. The street was packed with people when we left. This will be plastered all over the internet. You know from what happened to Bracken's family *exactly* how far the extremists will go. You know how much they love tossing firebombs through the windows of shops, houses, and apartment buildings."

"Don't think of staying here as lying low," Luke said to her. "Think of it as making it hard for any bastards to get near you. Think of it as protecting the pride, even. If the extremists choose to target you, and they believe you're here—"

"They'll bomb Phoenix Pack territory," Mila snapped. "Does that not matter to anyone here?"

"The dwelling is too deep within the land for any bombs to hit it," said Trey. "They might cause damage to the surrounding woods, but that would be all. And we have precautions in place to deal with such events."

James tilted his head as he spoke to Trey. "It won't bother you to have her here, knowing it could bring danger to your territory?"

"She's Dominic's mate—that's all I need to know," said Trey. "And there'll always be a possibility of danger coming our way, because there'll always be extremists. That's the reason why no shifter in their right mind would ever start a war with the fuckers. You can't *kill* prejudice. It'll sadly always exist, which means there will always be people who want to act on it. A war would only lead to pointless deaths, nothing more."

Alex nodded. "The Movement does a good job of handling the extremists anyway. The rates of attacks have lowered dramatically, and the extremists have lost a lot of support from their own kind. With all the PR work that shifter groups have been doing, humans and shifters are coexisting more peacefully than ever before. But, as you said, there'll always be prejudice. Dean's problem with my sister could be that he has something against pallas cats."

"I didn't pick up any prejudice from him," said Mila. "He was just . . . normal."

"The wolf said Dean watched you," Alex pointed out. "That's not exactly normal."

"It doesn't have to mean that he was thinking anything bad," said Mila. "And could you please call Dominic by his name?"

"No."

Just then, Tate strolled back into the room, pocketing his phone. "According to Archie, Dean Simmons is part of the Birch Pride, which isn't more than a mile from here."

Vinnie pushed to his feet. "Then let's go pay him a visit. I won't call his Alpha in advance; we don't want to give Dean a heads-up that we're coming. I'll call you as soon as I get ahold of him, Mila."

Everyone else stood, and Valentina crossed to Mila. Pulling her into yet another hug, Valentina said, "I know it is hard for you to stay behind. But this will go more smoothly if you are not in sight of this male who put a price on your head."

Mila exhaled heavily. "I know, but—"

"Four times, Mila," said James. "In a short space of time, you've almost been killed four times. Take pity on our hearts, and give us a rest from the worry."

When she didn't argue, Valentina nodded in satisfaction and patted Mila's arm. "I will pack some of your things and bring them here." She turned to Trey. "I want whatever information you have on creator of website. My brothers will make him pay—that I promise you."

After accepting hugs from each of her pride mates, Mila followed them to the entrance of the dwelling and waved them off. She stood stiffly in Dominic's arms, leaning against him as he held her tightly from behind.

He nuzzled her neck. "I know you're pissed at me for asking you to stay. I don't even blame you for it. But I can't watch you get hurt again, Mila. I just can't fucking do it."

Thawing at the tortured note to his voice, she turned in his arms with a heavy sigh. "I know. But for someone who wants me to rest, you sure do keep me awake a lot. I'm not complaining, because your cock is rather outstanding when put to good use. I'm just pointing out the hypocrisy here."

His mouth quirked. "This time, I won't make any moves on you. I'll just hold you while you sleep."

"Or you could go do enforcer stuff rather than just lie there with me, bored out of your mind." Not that it would be easy for her to drift off, despite how tired she was. She'd be on edge until Vinnie called her with news on Dean Simmons.

"There's nothing boring about holding my mate. Besides, I like watching you sleep. You make the oddest expressions, kind of like your cat." Linking their fingers, Dominic led her through the tunnels once more. When he was about to make the turn that would lead to his bedroom, a thought occurred to him. "You hungry? We didn't eat the food Grace left for us."

"A sandwich would go down nicely. I'm too tired to handle a big meal."

"A sandwich it is." Switching directions, he took her to the kitchen. Grace, Roni, Marcus, and Trick were gathered at the long table, their eyes locked on Roni's cell phone. And every one of them looked close to cursing a blue streak.

"Tell me that's not Emmet Pierson's voice I'm hearing," Dominic growled.

Roni tapped the screen of her cell, and the sound cut off. "I wish I could. We're just watching footage from the press conference he held outside the police station."

Dominic ground his teeth. "Let me see."

"I'll restart it," said Roni. Dominic and Mila stood behind the others as the she-wolf played the footage from the beginning.

On the screen, cameras flashed and people shouted questions at Pierson. He stood tall, his expression solemn, his eyes cold. "My daughter did not try to kill anyone," he asserted. "Did she hold the people in the barbershop at gunpoint? Yes. But it was only a replica gun. She used it to scare the woman who is trying to steal her mate. Was that a rational move? No. And it goes to show just what mental damage can be caused when a person's mate abandons them. If you want to blame anyone for what happened, blame Dominic Black."

Mila hissed. "Motherfucker."

"People will tell you that Rosemary shot Mila Devereaux," Pierson went on. "If that is true, where is Miss Devereaux's injury? Oh, I'm sure the wolf will claim that his Alpha female healed the human, just as the police were told. But the truth is simple: Miss Devereaux wasn't hurt at all, she was merely taken away so that the shifters could spin a story. Yes, the wolf would have his own true mate locked in a cell just so that he could be free to have fun with his tart. Anyone with any sense can see that truth. I hope all of you have such sense."

Tart? Mila snarled. "God, I think the guy could twist just about anything." Her gaze cut to Dominic. "Not that he's done a good job of it. People aren't likely to buy that your pack would go to that trouble just so you could sleep around. Reporters will want my side of the story now. And if I don't give it, it's as good as saying that his account is true." Dominic had warned her that the media would latch on to it, but she hadn't been so sure.

He smoothed his hand up her arm. "We can post a written statement on the pack's blog, but it won't be a response to this interview. That load of bullshit doesn't deserve the credit of a response. It will just be your account of what happened, but we'll craft it in a way that pokes holes at Pierson's story. We'll also mention Rosemary's history of instability again as a gentle reminder that she's fucking nuts." He guided her to a seat, but she shook her head.

"I've kind of lost my appetite."

"You need to eat. Sit, I'll make the sandwiches."

Grace stood. "I'll make them. You two sit down."

Mila genuinely didn't think she'd be able to eat, but the smells of fresh bread, tuna, and mayonnaise made her stomach rumble. She scarfed it down without really tasting it, her mind elsewhere. Done with her sandwich, she pushed the empty plate aside. Instead of feeling energized by the food, she felt even more tired than before.

She was midway through a yawn when her phone rang. She dug it out of her pocket, and her pulse spiked when she saw that it was Vinnie calling. She answered with, "Tell me you have him."

"Well, I spoke with him," said Vinnie. "But the Dean Simmons I just talked to in his Alpha's office is *not* the bobcat who was at the barbershop earlier."

Her lips parting in surprise, Mila rubbed at her temple. "The guy you just met could still be the person who put out the hit, though, right?"

"He swears he didn't, and I believe him. Plus, he does not have a nephew called Finley. That means the bobcat you know *did* in fact lie to you."

Mila swore and shoved a hand through her hair. Only Dominic's fingers massaging her nape kept her from shooting to her feet and pacing up and down.

"My guess is that he picked a random bobcat and used his identity while at your barbershop," said Vinnie. "Did he ever tell you anything that might hint at who he really is?"

Many of her clients gossiped or talked about their lives, but Dean hadn't been one of them. "No, nothing. We just chatted about general things."

"Hmm. If he notices that the website has collapsed, he'll suspect we're onto him. He'll keep his distance from you."

"That all depends on why he put out the hit." Mila sighed. "I really don't get why he would want me dead, Vinnie. I never picked up even the slightest hint of animosity from him."

"Some people are good at acting."

True enough. Ending the call, Mila looked at Dominic. "Did you hear all that?"

He nodded. "I heard."

"I don't understand any of this." She twisted slightly in her seat to face him better. "You said he watched me. Watched me how?"

"It wasn't ogling. He didn't display any sexual interest in you, so I didn't pay as much attention to it as I should have."

Mila hadn't picked up any sexual attraction either. He'd never flirted with her, but he'd been friendly and polite. "He only ever complimented me once, and that was to say I had a nice voice. He said he saw me perform when he took his girlfriend to the Velvet Lounge."

Dominic's brow furrowed. "You saw him there?"

"No. He just told me about it. But then, it could have been yet another lie, right? I never saw him anywhere but the barb—" Noticing that Dominic had gone stiff as a board and that his eyes were glittering with something very, very dark, Mila asked, "What? What is it?"

"He might have lied to you about having a girlfriend, but he didn't lie about going to the Velvet Lounge. I saw him there. He was alone, sitting at the bar in the VIP section. The only reason I paid him any attention was that he was talking to someone I know well."

Mila narrowed her eyes. "Who?"

A short while later, Dominic was leaning against the security shack when a familiar car drove through the tall gates. She'd gotten here faster than he thought she would. But then, he'd been sure to sound a little lost and forlorn over the phone, not wanting her to suspect the real reason he'd invited her here. He'd told her he needed to talk to someone he could trust, which was true. He hadn't said that *she* was someone he could trust, but he'd known she'd take his comment to mean exactly that.

At his urging, Charlene parked the car in the turnout near the shack and then rushed out of the vehicle, looking somewhat flustered. "Are you okay?"

"I'm good," he replied, hiding the urge to grip her by the throat. Because if his suspicions were true, Charlene had a lot to fucking answer for.

"I heard about the shooting on TV." Her nose wrinkling, she glanced around. "Where is Mila?"

"With her family."

Charlene's shoulders relaxed slightly. "Ah, you let it leak to reporters that she was here so that they wouldn't look for her in the right place. Clever." She edged closer to him, and her brows drew together. "You wear her scent. And her claiming mark." Neither of which seemed to make her happy.

Dominic smoothly stepped back when she would have touched him. No, he couldn't tolerate that right then. "Walk with me."

Charlene blinked. "Sure." As they walked through the fringe of tall, regal trees, she said, "You look so . . . on edge. I don't think I've ever seen you without a smile in your eyes."

"Not much to smile about when I just watched my mate get shot."

"I guess not," she muttered.

"You really don't like Mila much, do you?"

"I don't know her," Charlene answered, evasive. "She seems nice enough, but . . ."

"But what?"

The fox opened and closed her mouth a few times. "I just don't see it going the distance, that's all. I mean, like I've said before, she's not your type."

"That night at the Velvet Lounge when you realized I'd marked her, you had a sour look on your face. Even seemed to rant about it to the guy at the VIP bar. Just who *was* he exactly?"

Tension stiffened her muscles. She lifted her shoulders, nonchalant. "Just some guy. One of our usual patrons."

"You know him. I could tell."

She averted her eyes. "I know him a little, sure."

"Who was he?"

"I doubt it's anyone you know."

"Try me."

She halted, turning to face him. "What's wrong? Why all the questions?"

Dominic took a confrontational step toward her. "Who is he, Charlene?"

She swallowed. "Dominic—"

"Tell me who he is."

"Just a friend of Lennie's."

"His name," Dominic pushed, but she clamped her lips shut. He growled. "If our friendship ever meant anything to you, you'll tell me what I want to know."

She threw up her arms. "Dean Preston. See, you don't know him, do you?"

"Here's what I do know. You've been doing your best to make Mila keep her distance from me, and Dean Preston put a fucking hit out on her. You knew about the hit, didn't you? You knew she was in danger, and you didn't want me in the line of fire, so you tried to drive a wedge between us."

Charlene's eyes flickered. "It's not what—"

"Why didn't you say something?" he demanded, rage curdling through him. "Why? The fucker wants her dead!"

"No, he doesn't. He didn't put out a hit; he just wanted her hurt."

"Is that what he told you? Because if so, he lied."

"No, you're wrong. He has no need to put a hit out on her. He doesn't want her to die."

"Then what *does* he want?"

"He wants his true mate."

Dominic frowned. "What?"

"He found his mate a few months back. Recognized her as his. But she's imprinted on another."

"If she's imprinted on another male, he couldn't possibly know that she's his."

"Dean has visions. He's not a Seer, but he has witch-blood in his family. Long ago, he had a vision of his true mate, and he saw her happy with someone else. He's been determined to find her and prevent that future from happening, but he didn't find her in time. He befriended her, though. He's done his best to get close to her, and he's managed to convince her that she's his true mate. He wants her to leave the guy she imprinted on, but she won't. I can understand that. I love Lennie. I couldn't leave him for someone else."

"What does any of this have to do with Mila?"

"Like I said, Dean befriended his true mate. She trusts him. Confides in him. Told him how hard it is to see her partner fuss over her cousin. Told him how she strongly suspects that the guy she imprinted on is the predestined mate of said cousin."

And then the light bulb went on. Dominic swore. "Adele. Dean's mate is Adele."

"He hates the guy she's with. I think he said the cat's name is Joel. But Dean won't hurt him because it would only hurt *her*."

"And what, Dean put a bounty on Mila's head at Adele's request?"

Charlene gave a fast shake of her head. "No. Nothing like that. As I said, he truly doesn't want Mila dead. He just wants his mate. His theory is that if Mila's in enough danger, it will stir up Joel's protective instincts; it will reach the part of him that acknowledges who she is to him. Dean was excited when he realized that things seemed serious between you and Mila. He hoped it would bring out Joel's possessiveness too."

"Dean wants Joel to realize who Mila is to him. He can't make Adele leave Joel, so he's hoping to make Joel leave Adele." Dominic's jaw hardened. "And you *knew*? You knew he'd put a price on Mila's head?"

Charlene shook her head. "He told me he only ordered for her to be hurt."

"Well, he fucking lied. Probably because he didn't trust that you wouldn't warn her. But regardless of whether he wanted her hurt or dead, you *should* have told her."

Charlene licked her lips nervously. "She's a pallas cat, Dominic. They're tougher than rock. I figured she'd be fine."

Dominic stilled, disbelief smacking him in the face. "You figured she'd be fine? *That's* your defense?"

"I didn't think she'd *ever* come to mean anything to you. I figured you just wanted to test the bedsprings with her."

"That has no bearing on the fact that you should have *told her*."

"I promised Dean I wouldn't! I honestly didn't think anyone would be dumb enough to even *try* to cash in on the contract. I mean, who'd want to fuck with a pallas cat pride? They're *insane*. But after the attacks started, I thought about coming to you. I did. But you would have been angry with me for not saying something sooner."

"I'm still not hearing an excuse that's even close to valid."

Switching from beseeching to defensive in an instant, she jutted out her chin. "Yeah? Well, she almost died today. And it wasn't because of Dean. It was because of *your* ex. You brought that fucked-up shit into Mila's life. So don't get all high and mighty with me about how I could have helped her. *You* could have helped keep her safe by staying away, but you didn't. You just can't keep your dick in your pants. And if she thinks that claiming you will change that, she's a fool. Some people aren't made for commitment—you're one of them."

"Is that what you tell yourself so that your ego isn't hurt by his refusal to commit to you?" asked Mila as she strolled out of the trees, grass rustling beneath her feet.

Charlene whirled to face her, paling. "Mila—"

She put up a hand. "I heard all your excuses, Charlene. Don't need to hear them again. I have only one question for you, and I'd say you owe me the answer. Where do I find Dean Preston?"

"He really doesn't want you—"

"Dead," Mila finished, her voice flat. "Yeah. I heard that. But, see, I don't care."

"There would be no point in me telling you anyway. He has visions; he could have one that warns him you're coming. He'll run."

"We'll take our chances," said Dominic. "Where is he, Charlene?"

The fox's eyes closed, and her expression turned pained. "You'll kill him."

Yeah, he would. "And if you heard someone had put a price on Lennie's head, no matter the reason, what would you do?"

Opening her eyes, Charlene sighed. "I'd break their fucking neck."

"Believe me, Charlene, I'm close to breaking yours. You knew my mate was in danger, and you said *shit* about it. You tried to separate me from her, which would have left her more vulnerable to attack. I'm guessing you did it because you didn't want a stray bullet sinking into me—I don't care, and that's not good enough. Her life is more important to me than mine."

"I didn't know he put out a hit. I swear to God, I didn't!"

"You still should have told her what you *did* know." Dominic paused as several of his pack mates—all of whom looked mighty pissed—stepped out of the trees to circle the three of them. He watched it sink into Charlene's brain that she was surrounded.

"There is only one way you'll walk off this territory alive, and that's if you tell me where I can find that fucker *right now*," Dominic told her. "Bear in mind that you'll tell me one way or another. Dante will get the information out of you. Whether you volunteer that information or need to have it tortured out of you will decide your fate. Choose, and do it fast."

CHAPTER TWENTY-ONE

Charlene made the right choice and confessed all, which unfortunately meant that Mila couldn't kill her. She did, however, deal the fox a blow to the jaw that knocked her clean out for a few minutes. The moment Charlene was kicked off pack territory, Mila called Vinnie and brought him up to speed. Annoyingly, that also meant telling him that Joel was her predestined mate. He hadn't taken that too well, growling, "We'll discuss this after I've paid Dean's Alpha a visit."

It was later on, while she was gathered in Trey's office with Dominic, his Alphas and Betas, Tao, and the other enforcers, that Vinnie called her. She placed him on speakerphone as he relayed the conversation he'd had with Dean's Alpha, Jonah, who claimed he hadn't seen Dean in days. Apparently, Dean also wasn't answering anyone's calls.

"Do you think Jonah bullshitted you to protect his pride mate?" Trey asked, his arms folded, his back against his desk.

"I wouldn't have blamed him if he had, but no," replied Vinnie. "I think Jonah was telling the truth. He agreed to call me if Dean returned, but very few Alphas would put an outsider before their own pride mate, no matter that person's crime."

"I wonder what made Dean cut contact with his pride." Roni poked her inner cheek with her tongue. "I mean, that's not something that anyone would do lightly. Especially if they had family there."

"According to Jonah," began Vinnie, "Dean hasn't had trouble with any of his pride mates, so we can rule that possibility out."

His arm draped over his mate's shoulder, Dominic twisted his mouth. "Maybe Dean did it to protect them."

Mila's brow puckered. "From what?"

Dominic shrugged. "He could be worried we were close to discovering the truth. Maybe he thought that if he made it clear he was acting alone by cutting contact with his pride, they wouldn't suffer any blowback. Especially if he heard from Adele that there were people working on cracking the website."

"It's possible," allowed Taryn, sitting in the leather office chair. "Do you think Adele knows that Dean's responsible for the hit, Mila?"

"My gut says no," Mila replied.

"She told Dean that she suspects you're Joel's mate and that she finds it hard to see how attached he is to you," Taryn reminded her. "If you were dead, she wouldn't have to be hurt by it anymore."

"I know," said Mila, "but she's just not the type of person who would wish anyone dead."

"I agree," Vinnie declared. "In fact, Adele's more likely to be feeling guilty that she's claimed her cousin's predestined mate."

"But not so guilty that she's told Joel the truth or given him up," Trey pointed out.

Mila shrugged. "She loves him." Something that no longer pained her or her cat. "If I met someone who I suspected was Dominic's true mate, I'm not sure I'd be selfless enough to share that suspicion with him. I certainly wouldn't be willing to give him up." If that made Mila a shitty person, so be it.

Dominic kissed her temple. "Just as I wouldn't give you up, no matter what."

"You should have told me about Joel, Mila," Vinnie chastised. "I'm not just your Alpha, I'm your uncle."

Mila sighed. "I didn't tell anyone other than my parents and Alex. My mother constantly pushed me to tell Joel the truth so that he could decide for himself who he wanted. You would have done the same, because you love me and would have hated that I was hurting. Tell me I'm wrong."

Vinnie gave a low, frustrated growl—no doubt annoyed that he couldn't deny it. "It's unfair of you to make that decision for Joel."

"I didn't. *He* made the choice when he claimed Adele, which he knew meant forsaking his predestined mate. And I'm okay with that now. Even my cat is no longer bitter about it. So if we can get back to the point at hand—which is that Dean Preston is Adele's true mate and needs to be found—that would be great."

Tao propped his hip against the wall. "My guess is that Dean's either staying with a friend or at a motel. He'd stay close to Adele, right? He'd want to be close enough to watch over her."

Jaime pursed her lips. "We could check out the motels local to her address. Does she live in your apartment building, Mila?"

"No. She and Joel live in a house that's about a ten-minute drive away from the building."

"You know," began Dominic, doodling little circles on her shoulder with his fingertip, "it strikes me that we don't actually need to search for Dean. Vinnie could talk to Adele, convince her to lure Dean to meet with her, and then we could make a grab for him."

Jaime grimaced. "But if Charlene's warned him that we know his identity, he'll suspect it's a trap. I know she promised she wouldn't tell Dean if we agreed not to inform her Alpha of her part in all this, but foxes are vindictive."

"So is a male whose mate was wronged," said Dominic. "Charlene wronged my mate in a major fucking way; she knows I won't hesitate to report it to her Alpha if she betrays her promise. The guy would be pissed to hear that she made an enemy of us, since her behavior reflects on him. She won't risk being banished."

"I doubt Adele would be willing to help lure Dean out into the open," said Roni. "I mean, she might not want him, but she'll feel some loyalty toward him. Probably more loyalty than toward her own Alpha—that's a primitive instinct she won't be able to ignore."

"It's unlikely that Adele will give him up to me," said Vinnie. "But she might give him up to Mila. I know you don't like the idea of Mila leaving your territory, Dominic, but she's our best chance of getting Adele to talk. Your pack mates can't deal with this—Adele would feel threatened if a bunch of strangers turned up at her home."

His muscles rigid, Dominic growled. Hadn't they just had a fucking conversation about how it was best for Mila to lie low? His nostrils flared. "Why Mila?" he bit out.

"Adele will feel that she owes her something," replied Vinnie. "The guilt of claiming her cousin's true mate has probably been weighing on Adele for a long time. She'll only feel worse when she realizes that Dean put Mila's life in danger."

"She'll be home from work by now, but Joel won't be—that means she can talk openly," said Mila. "If I point out that Dean's been acting behind her back, trying to split her from the man she loves, she'll see that as a betrayal. And if I add that it's only a matter of time before Dean gets desperate enough to talk with Joel and tell him everything, she'll panic. Seeing that Dominic and I have officially claimed each other and that I have no designs on Joel *might* mean she'll see me as an ally."

Marcus shrugged. "It's worth a shot. The worst that can happen is that she refuses to help you and then warns Dean that we have his real identity."

"The worst that can happen is that Mila is attacked again," Dominic argued, a snap to his voice. His wolf was no less tense at the idea of her leaving their territory.

"We'll keep her safe, Dominic," said Trey. "That I promise you. You know none of us would let anything happen to Mila."

"You won't be able to come inside her house with me," she told Trey. "Dominic will, of course. But Adele won't confess her darkest secret in front of strangers."

Trey inclined his head. "Dante, Ryan, and I will wait outside." His gaze slid back to Dominic. "If you want the threat to Mila to be completely gone from her life, this is the fastest way to see it done."

Dominic swore under his breath. "Trey—"

"We'll keep her safe," the Alpha repeated.

Mila intertwined her fingers with Dominic's. "I know you want me here, resting. And I swear to you that I'll do exactly that when we get back. I'll lie low for a while, and I won't even moan about it. Out loud. So the quicker we speak to Adele, the quicker I can go to bed. I want this shit with Dean over with, and so do you. Trey's right, this is the fastest way to make that happen."

They all talked for a few more minutes, and then Mila ended her call with Vinnie and pocketed her phone.

Dominic drew her close and rested his forehead against hers. "It goes against everything in me to take you away from here right now." His stomach sank just thinking about it.

She touched his jaw. "I know, and I appreciate how hard it is for you to push past that." After all, the guy had watched her bleed all over the damn floor of the barbershop. It was little wonder that he wanted to tuck her away somewhere safe. She'd be lying if she claimed that she'd act differently in his position. "But we need to know where Dean is, and Adele's the one person who might have his location. We have to talk to her."

Dominic hissed out a breath. "This whole thing fucking sucks." Especially because he couldn't deny that she made sense.

"Yeah, I'm with you on that one."

As Dante pulled up outside Adele and Joel's house, Mila raised a brow at Dominic. "Ready?"

He gave a curt nod. "If she doesn't spill everything, I'm going to be fucking pissed—just so you know."

"I'm not leaving that house until she tells me what I want to know," said Mila.

Riding shotgun, Trey twisted in his seat. "Ryan will canvass the area just in case Dean is close."

"There's no way to sneak up on a pallas cat," Mila warned.

"Ryan's like a ghost when he tracks," Dominic told her, sliding out of the SUV. "Trust me, if Dean's nearby, Ryan will find him." Hand in hand, they walked up the cobbled pathway toward the townhouse. "You're all right going into the home your predestined mate shares with another female? Can your cat handle it?"

"Handle it? She's surprisingly uninterested. Not because she's forgiven Joel but because she no longer considers him worthy of the energy it took to hate him." Mila rang the bell and blew out a breath. "Let me lead here. I know Adele better than you. We need to go easy at first, okay?"

"Lull her into a false sense of security?"

"We have to slowly lead up to the point and—" Mila cut off as the door swung open.

Adele blinked. "Mila, hi." Her shock was understandable, since Mila had never visited before. Adele's eyes cut to Dominic, and she forced a polite smile. "Hello. Um . . . come in, come in." She stepped aside for them to pass. "How are you doing after the shooting, Mila?"

"I'm good, thanks," Mila told her, her nose wrinkling at the scents of citrus cleaner and freshly cut flowers.

"That's a relief. I would have called you, but your mom told everyone to give you space."

"I figured she would."

Adele rubbed her hands down the sides of her shirt. "If you're here to see Joel—"

"We wanted to speak with you."

"Oh. Okay. Sure. We could—" Her eyes dropped to Mila's neck and then widened with excitement. That excitement bloomed when her gaze snapped to Dominic's neck. "Oh wow! You claimed each other? This is amazing news. Congrats! I mean, I can sense that the bond hasn't formed yet, but I don't doubt that it will. You two suit each other so well."

"Thank you. I agree." Dominic also sensed a large dose of relief mingled with Adele's excitement. If Mila was taken, she'd hardly want Joel.

"Would you guys like some coffee?" Oh, Adele was all grace and courtesy now.

"Coffee would be good," replied Mila. She followed the female down the hall, her footsteps muffled by the lush carpet.

Coats hung neatly on the hooks near the door. Shoes tidily tucked in the nook beneath the stairs. No clutter anywhere to be seen. The large mirror gleamed, possessing not a single smear or fingerprint. Damn, the couple liked their home spotless.

Mila had never believed she'd ever step foot in their home. But seeing the life the couple had made together didn't hurt the way it once would have. In fact, Mila felt a smile curve her mouth as she took in the cute portraits adorning the magnolia walls. Pictures of Adele and Joel laughing, hiking, partying, and dancing at what appeared to be their mating ceremony. Yeah, he was happy.

Mila had never begrudged him that, but she hadn't exactly been happy *for* him. Not until right then. Now that she'd found that same happiness with Dominic, Mila could be truly glad that Joel had it with Adele.

In the kitchen, Adele waved a hand at the table. "Take a seat."

Mila almost hesitated. Seriously, everything was so clean and orderly that it was somewhat off-putting.

"So what brings you here?"

"Actually, I just have some questions about the imprinting process," Mila told her, gingerly perching herself on one of the cushioned dining chairs. "And well, I figured you'd be a good person to ask."

Adele's smile widened. "I'd be more than happy to answer any questions you have. Fire away."

Feeling a little less tense when her mate took the seat beside her, Mila braced an elbow on the table. "How long did it take for you and Joel to fully imprint?"

"A few months, but I heard that it differs from couple to couple."

As Adele made the coffees, Mila asked a few other inane questions. She needed Adele to relax, lower her guard, and open up. That wouldn't happen if she was tense or on the defensive.

The whole time, Dominic kept his hand on Mila's nape, circling the same spot with his thumb over and over. Keeping himself calm, she thought.

While Adele was distracted pouring the coffees, Mila turned to him and whispered, "You okay?"

"I want this over with," said Dominic, his voice equally low. He didn't like being in Joel's house. Didn't like that *Mila* was in Joel's house. His wolf really didn't fucking like that his mate was on the asshole's territory.

Dominic had worried that she'd find it hard to see the life her predestined mate had built with someone else—he'd have understood, would have comforted her even though it would have hurt him to see that this pained her. But she was fine, albeit tired. Likewise, her cat wasn't tense or edgy. And that showed him that neither she nor Mila felt any regrets at the way things had turned out. Dominic had needed to know that.

"Here we go." Adele placed three steaming mugs on the table and then settled on the chair opposite Mila. "Anything else you want to ask?"

Mila cocked her head. "Do you ever feel guilty for choosing Joel over your true mate?"

Her smile dimming, Adele froze with her cup halfway to her mouth. "Guilty? Well, um, I'd like to think that our predestined mates wouldn't begrudge us happiness." Her gaze dropped to the table. "It would be natural for them to be unhappy because we'd chosen another over them, but they could still want *us* to be happy."

Dominic picked up his mug. "Mila stupidly feels guilty that she's 'stolen' someone else's mate. I keep telling her I'm with her because I want to be, but she still feels bad about it."

Adele gave a wry smile. "That's the thing about imprinting. It's special, but it's easy to feel guilty for renouncing your mate or claiming someone else's."

"Yeah." Mila sighed. "But I guess life's too short for torturing yourself."

"Something Rosemary proved today when she shot you in the chest," Dominic rumbled. His throat tightened at the memory. "Thank God for Helena. *And* for Evander, since he tackled Rosemary to the floor after you kicked the gun out of her hand. *And* for Dean, since he dived for the gun."

Adele stiffened. "Dean?"

"He's one of my clients," Mila told her. "A bobcat shifter. It turns out, he's also a friend of one of Dominic's past flings. Charlene told us his story and . . . wow."

"His story?" Adele echoed, swallowing hard.

"He has premonitions, and he once had a vision of his true mate; saw her imprinted on another," said Mila. "He tried to find her before that future could come to pass, but he was too late. Although Dean was able to convince her that she's his true mate, she won't leave the guy she imprinted on. But then, neither would I. It's a shame he can't respect that. Isn't it, Adele? Shame he won't just let you enjoy the happiness you've found with Joel."

Panic flitted across her face. "I don't—"

"He named you to Charlene; he told her about Joel too."

Adele shot to her feet. "I need you both to leave."

"He told her how you suspected that Joel was the predestined mate of your cousin."

Adele paled. "Mila—"

"I already knew."

Her lips parting, Adele stared at her, incredulous. "What?"

"I knew it the second I saw him when you first brought him to meet the pride."

As if the shock of that was too much, Adele plopped back onto the chair. "But . . . you . . . you didn't say anything."

"He loves you; he's happy. I let that be enough for me. *You* never said anything either."

Her eyes falling closed, Adele let out a shaky breath. "I thought about telling him, but it would have destroyed me to watch him walk away." Her eyes opened, glittering with guilt. "I know what I stole from you, but I *need* him. I love him. I can't be without him. He would have chosen you over me."

Mila shook her head. "I don't believe he would have."

Adele snorted. "I see how drawn he is to you. See how he worries about you, how he seeks you out, how easy it is for him to be around you." Her voice cracked. "It kills me, Mila."

Honestly, Mila never thought she'd ever find herself feeling sorry for Adele, but she did. "I know what it's like to love someone who fate gave to another female. I don't know *her*, true—she's just a hypothetical person to me. But I'd be lying if I said I'd have been up front in your position. I wouldn't want to lose Dominic." Mila pinned the other female's gaze. "You hear me? I'm happy, Adele. I don't want Joel. I'm not interested in coming between you. But I can't say the same for Dean."

Her brows squished together. "What do you mean?"

"I mean that he's the person who put the bounty on my head."

"What?" Adele let out a surprised laugh. "No. That's ridiculous. Why would he ever—?"

"He can't talk you into leaving Joel, can he? Dean hoped that my being threatened would somehow stir up Joel's protective instincts and make him see the truth—make him leave you."

Adele vigorously shook her head. "No. No, Dean wouldn't do that. He said he was happy as long as I was happy."

"And I'll bet he meant it. But I'm guessing he thinks *he* can make you happier than anyone else ever could. The name of the person who put the price on my head is Dean Preston."

Adele flinched. "I just can't believe he'd do that. No. *No.* You have to be wrong. He wouldn't risk my cousin's life. He wouldn't do anything that would hurt me."

"Where is he?"

"With his pride, of course."

Mila shook her head. "They haven't seen him in days."

"Call him," Dominic told Adele. "You're in contact with him, so you must have his number. Call him. Arrange to meet him somewhere. You can ask him yourself."

"And you'll be waiting, ready to pounce," Adele accused, her eyes narrowed.

Dominic shrugged. "If he's innocent, we'll have no need to pounce."

Adele rubbed at her temples. "I promised myself I wouldn't meet with him again. It's not fair to Joel. Oh God, I'll need to tell him everything, won't I?"

"That's up to you," said Mila. "You might have a chance at convincing Vinnie to keep a chunk of the story quiet from Joel and the rest of the pride."

Adele swallowed, and the movement looked painful. "He'll leave me. Joel. He'll choose you."

Dominic's nostrils flared. "Mila's not a fucking option for him."

Mila put her hand on Dominic's thigh. "I think you're wrong, Adele. Joel loves you. I'm not saying it won't be a shock, and it might hurt that you haven't been straight with him about a lot of things. But he will understand why you didn't tell him you suspected I was his predestined mate. He's more likely to be upset at you secretly communicating with *your* true mate. So be sure to remind him that although you may have been in contact with Dean, you refused to leave Joel—*he's* your choice."

Dominic leaned forward. "Call Dean."

Adele licked her lips. "I don't have his number. I—"

"He's not going to walk away from you, Adele. Just as Joel's drawn to Mila, Dean is drawn to you. The difference is that Joel doesn't want Mila, but Dean sure as fuck wants you. And since Dean's little plot didn't pay off, how long do you think it will be before he takes Joel out of the equation himself?"

The color left Adele's face in a rush. "Dean wouldn't do that."

"Would you bet Joel's life on that?" Dominic tapped the table. "Call Dean."

"I told you, I don't have his—"

"Call him."

Adele pulled her phone out of her pocket and tapped at the screen with her thumbs. "I don't believe he did this," she said, putting the phone to her ear.

"I hope you're right," said Mila.

After a few moments, Adele's brows snapped together. "He's not answering. He always answers."

"Try calling him again," said Dominic.

She muttered under her breath but did as he asked. "He's still not answering."

Just then, Mila's phone rang. She whipped it out of her pocket. "It's Vinnie." Swiping her thumb across the screen, she answered with, "You have Dean?"

"No, I have news." Vinnie sighed heavily. "Rosemary Pierson tried to hang herself in her cell."

Mila's mouth went slack. *Shit.* Mentally fumbling, she asked, "Is she okay?"

"No," replied Vinnie, grimly. "She's alive, but she's in a coma. And the docs don't expect her to wake up. Her brain went without oxygen for too long."

Mila shoved a hand through her hair, feeling a momentary pang of sympathy for the woman.

"Does Adele know where Dean is?" Vinnie asked.

Mila met the female's eyes. "No, and he's not taking her calls."

"Tell her I expect to see her at the antique store in an hour. She and I are going to have a long talk." The line went dead.

Pocketing her phone, Mila said, "Vinnie wants—"

"To see me in an hour," finished Adele, her expression pained. "I heard."

"So did I." Dominic sighed, giving his mate's neck a gentle squeeze. "I guess we should have expected Rosemary to try something like that. She's never been good at facing reality. Not to sound insensitive, but this will feed that media circus I mentioned earlier."

Mila puffed out a breath. "Her father will now officially want us both dead and buried."

"It will never come to that," Dominic said, his voice low and menacing. "I'll kill him before I let him touch you."

"Not if my cat gets there first."

CHAPTER TWENTY-TWO

Three weeks. It had been three weeks of "lying low" while they waited for the protests outside pack territory to stop and for the media attention to die down. If Emmet Pierson had been feeding it by making statements to reporters, the drama might have dragged on. But he'd been extraordinarily quiet since his daughter's attempted suicide.

Rosemary was still in a coma, and Mila imagined that her father felt partially to blame for it. If his past behavior was anything to go by, Emmet would eventually displace that guilt onto someone else—probably Dominic.

Dean had also lapsed into silence. According to Adele, he still wasn't taking her calls. If he had, she probably would have told him that she'd finally told Joel the truth. Mila only knew this because Joel had told Luke everything while in a drunken stupor at a local bar.

Joel had moved out of the house he shared with Adele, although only temporarily—he needed space to "think." From what Luke said, Joel was mostly upset that Adele had been communicating with her true mate behind his back, just as Mila had anticipated.

Each time Mila's phone rang, Dominic tensed, and she knew he was expecting it to be Joel; expecting the other male to declare that he wanted Mila. While she doubted that would ever happen, Dominic wasn't so sure. He also wasn't so sure that they should be going out tonight, but Mila was done "lying low." He'd tuck her away in his sock drawer if he could. "We all agreed that this is the right move," she reminded him.

Sitting on the bed, he watched her through broody eyes. "Doesn't mean I have to like it."

Crossing to him, Mila straddled his lap and linked her fingers behind his nape. "I know why you're worried, and I get it. But my cat is chomping at the bit. She won't last much longer if I keep her confined here. Don't think I can't sense how edgy and restless your wolf is, Dominic." Her cat was the same. The feline had been seriously moody, lashing out at Mila and just about anyone who came too close. "We're hurting our animals by keeping them here."

"And we could hurt them by leaving."

Mila sighed. It was hard to be annoyed with him when she could feel his tension just as easily as she could feel her own. The strength with which she felt the echoes of his emotions had increased over time, and she *knew* the imprinting bond was close to forming. Could almost taste the promise of it.

"We already had this conversation in Trey's office," she said. "Everyone voted that we continue our lives as normal, starting with me performing at the Velvet Lounge tonight."

"Not everyone. *I* voted that we give it another week. Emmet—"

"I'm well aware that he'll eventually strike one way or another. However, I'm not convinced he'll do it via the extremists."

"I am." Dominic splayed his hands on her back and pulled her closer. "Emmet will blame us for what Rosemary did, and he won't let it go. The extremists are like loaded guns, and Pierson can easily aim them in our direction. He used the media to rile them up before. They haven't acted yet, but they're probably just biding their time—and probably at his order."

"Maybe. But we can't live like this, Dominic." She caught his face with her hands. "Let's stick to what we agreed earlier. We resurface, give him the opportunity to strike in whatever fashion he chooses, and then we deal with him—we end this once and for all."

Dominic clenched his teeth. "Mila—"

"It's unlikely that he'll act tonight. He'll want to lure us into believing he has no intention of coming at us. That way we lower our guards and make things easy for him. But we won't. We'll be ready.

"Besides, humans can't enter the club unless they're mated to a shifter, so there's no way for the extremists to get inside. Which is why I don't think Trey, Taryn, and Dante need to come with us tonight, but I won't fight it. Alex and my parents will be joining us later, remember? I'll be safe at the club."

Dominic blinked. Safe? "You were attacked by a jackal there not so long ago."

"The price is gone from my head, and I don't believe Dean is still a threat. The hit was never about me. It was about Adele and Joel. If the asshole *does* try to enter the club, the doormen will detain him anyway. Harley showed pictures of him to all the staff." Mila gave Dominic a light kiss. "It'll be fine. And you know you like watching me perform while lounging in VIP."

Gripping her hips tightly, Dominic pinned her gaze. "I won't be waiting for you in VIP. I'll be in the greenroom with you, and then I'll wait in the wings while you're onstage so that I can get to you fast if I need to."

Resisting the urge to roll her eyes, she said, "All right, if it'll make you feel better."

"What will make me feel better is getting you back here, in this bed, and pounding my cock into you."

"So romantic."

He just grunted.

A smile crept onto her face. "You're cute when you're surly."

"I'm not surly," he clipped, sounding . . . well, surly. In which case, he lost his ground. With a put-out sigh, Dominic stood. "You ready?"

"I'm ready."

As planned, the Alphas and Dante rode with them to the club. Mila kept her window down the entire time, enjoying the feel of the fresh air on her face, inhaling it like she'd been trapped in a bunker for months.

It hadn't mattered that Phoenix Pack territory was vast and peaceful. Simply *knowing* that she couldn't leave the territory had slowly driven her and her cat crazy. Which was why she'd proposed going to the club tonight. Performing would not only help her relax, it would rid her of that feeling of being suffocated. She never felt freer than when she was performing.

When they finally pulled up outside the club, Mila raised a brow at Dominic. "No one followed us?"

He shook his head. "No." Sliding out of the SUV, he gave the area a once-over but saw nothing shady. Still, his scalp prickled, and he couldn't shake the feeling that something was wrong. It was probably paranoia on his part, given how worried he was for Mila, but the bad feeling remained.

Taryn and Trey walked ahead of them into the club while Dante covered their backs. Dominic could sense that being surrounded by so many defenses was pricking at Mila's pride, just as he sensed her impatience. She no doubt believed they were being overcautious. Still, she was humoring them.

The scents of beer, hair spray, and various breeds of shifter swirled around him. His mouth tightened as he scanned the club. Despite the dim lighting, Dominic could see that the place was packed. Waitresses carefully weaved through the tables, most of which had been claimed. The dance floor was crowded with people dancing, hooting, grinding, and flirting. The bar was lined with patrons, and others stood in clusters here, there, and everywhere.

It was a security nightmare.

Trey sidled up to Dominic. "We'll escort you and Mila to the greenroom, and then we'll hang out in the VIP area where we can best keep an eye on things." The area was on a raised platform, so it would definitely give the wolves a better view of the club.

The Mercury Pack would have the security covered, and Dominic trusted them to be on the ball. But Mila was his mate—the more protection she had, the better. Like Mila, his pack mates didn't think Pierson would act so fast, but Dominic wasn't taking any chances.

Shielding Mila's body with his own, Dominic shouldered his way through the crowds. People called out hellos, seeming surprised to see them. They were especially surprised by the claiming marks that Mila and Dominic wore, so he assumed that they hadn't believed the news that he was mated.

Reaching the greenroom, Trey and Dante did a quick but thorough scan of the space. Satisfied, Dante nodded at Dominic. "It's clear. I'd advise you to lock the door behind us."

Which was exactly what Dominic did, leaving him and Mila alone. He rolled back his shoulders. They were so stiff, they ached.

"Everything will be fine," said Mila, settling on the chair in front of the vanity.

He watched as she swiftly and expertly dabbed on some makeup, her hands constantly in motion. And she was humming. Yes, *humming*. He didn't know how she could be so relaxed. But then, performing was her outlet for stress, he remembered. Being here was probably comforting for her.

Hearing a knock on the door, Dominic felt his body go rigid.

"No enemy is going to politely knock on the door," Mila pointed out gently.

Making a mental note to tell Harley to add a peephole, Dominic opened the door a little. The sight he found sent rage whipping through him. His wolf's ears flattened as a dark, guttural sound rumbled in his chest. "What the fuck?" Dominic burst out.

Joel raised his hands in a gesture of peace. "I just want to talk to Mila."

"Are you *shitting* me right now?" If Dominic had even suspected the guy would show up there, he'd have asked the doormen to keep the asshole out. Joel hadn't done anything wrong, true, but his commitment to Adele was no longer absolute; he might now covet the one thing that Dominic and his wolf couldn't live without. They didn't want Joel anywhere *near* Mila.

"I just want to talk to her for a minute, that's all," said Joel, sounding so fucking reasonable that Dominic wanted to punch him.

"There's nothing you've got to say that she needs to hear."

Joel's jaw set in a hard line. "You do know she can speak for herself, right?"

Dominic's wolf snapped his teeth. "Don't test me."

"I'm not here to stir shit up. I'm here to speak with her. You're her mate, I get it—"

"Then leave."

Joel jutted out his chin. "What I have to say is between me and Mila—"

"There's *nothing* between you and *my mate*," Dominic ground out, his fingers contracting like claws. "There never will be."

"I know. Like I said, I just want to talk to her."

Crossing to Dominic, Mila stood a little behind him and placed her hand on his rigid back. She could feel echoes of his anger and sensed that he felt threatened. No, she thought, he wasn't intimidated by Joel, but he viewed the male as a threat to their relationship. She couldn't have that. Didn't want him ever feeling insecure with her the way he'd felt as a child. "Let him in, Dominic."

"No."

"Let him in." Mila needed to get this done. Not just because Joel would keep hounding her until he got to say his piece—he was stubborn like that—but because she needed Dominic to see that there was nothing between her and Joel. Especially since the imprinting bond would never form if he had any doubts.

"We can give him a few minutes, right?" she said, purposely using the word *we* to show that she viewed herself and Dominic as a unit. The tension didn't leave his spine, but he did relax his hands and back up two steps, allowing Joel to cross the threshold. Mila also backed up, remaining a little behind Dominic.

He jabbed a finger at Joel. "That's enough. You don't move any farther than there."

Joel halted, although his gaze was on Mila. There was no yearning or lust there, only regret and a hint of self-condemnation.

"How did you know I'd be here tonight?" she asked.

"Someone from the pride told me," replied Joel. "They knew I wanted to talk to you."

"Make it quick," Dominic ground out, but Joel didn't glance his way.

His brow furrowing, Joel swallowed. "I didn't sense it, Mila. I really didn't sense that we were true mates. Didn't even suspect it."

"Because Adele is your world—I understand that." Because Dominic was Mila's world.

"But I hurt you," he said, his voice thick. "Didn't mean to. Didn't know I had. My only excuse is that I love her, I always have."

"I don't expect you to feel sorry or guilty for that. I never did." Her cat did, but Mila kept that to herself.

"I still can't believe Adele didn't tell me her suspicions. We always promised there'd never be secrets or lies between us. She betrayed both of us."

"She obviously didn't want to lose you."

"Why didn't *you* tell me? You didn't even hint at it." He didn't seem angered by that, just confused.

Mila shrugged. "There would have been no point. Mostly because Adele might not have been *meant* for you, but she's *it* for you. Just like you're it for her."

He snorted, pain flashing across his face. "If that were true, she wouldn't have been meeting her true mate in secret, would she?"

"She didn't choose him, though," Mila pointed out, marveling over how it didn't feel odd to be pushing her predestined mate toward another female. "Dean tried convincing her to leave you, but she didn't."

"That doesn't mean it was okay that she had coffee with him a few times and that they called each other regularly." Joel shoved a hand through his hair. "She said she was just curious about him, which I guess is understandable. But she's refusing to cut all contact with him, since she doesn't truly believe he put you in danger. She figures that if I can be friends with you, she can at least have indirect contact with her true mate."

Mila suspected that Adele was hoping Joel would offer to sever his friendship with Mila in exchange for Adele's promise to cut contact with Dean.

Joel licked his lips and took a deep breath. "I just want you to know that I never wanted to hurt you. And I'm so, so sorry that I did. I should have seen that you were mine—"

"I'm not yours," Mila said quickly, splaying a hand on Dominic's back when he prepared to protest Joel's words. "I might have been yours, if things had been different. But they're not."

Joel nodded. "Still, I should have seen it. And it must have been hard for you that I could be so close to you yet be blind to it. Which is why I just wanted to say that I do see it now. In your position, I'd want that acknowledgment, if nothing else."

"Thank you for that, but it really doesn't matter now. We both made our choices."

"Whether it means anything to you or not, I'm still sorry. It cuts me deeply to know that by pushing for friendship, I was hurting you all this time."

"Apology accepted."

"And you're happy?" he asked her, sliding a meaningful glance at Dominic.

"I'm happy," said Mila. "I have no regrets about how things have turned out. And if you were honest with yourself, you'd admit that neither do you. You're hurting, but you love Adele. Imprint bonds can be broken, Joel. Don't let that happen."

He swallowed. "I can feel a strain on the imprint bond. Like it could start crumbling any second."

"You don't want that. You're angry with her, but you wouldn't want to be without her."

"It's just hard to—" He cut off, his muscles tensing. And then she heard the snick of a gun.

"Do *not* move," a new voice snarled.

Mila fisted her hands as a burly bearded male came into sight, shaggy-brown hair down to his shoulders. It didn't matter that those eyes were dark blue—she *knew* them. Knew the beard was as fake as the color of the contact lenses and the wig that covered the dark hair she'd trimmed many times. He was also wearing padding to make his figure seem bulkier.

None of that held her attention, though.

She was more concerned with his hands. He wasn't holding a gun. He was holding two, and both were outfitted with silencers. One was pointed at Joel, and the other was trained on Dominic. Mila's claws sliced out, and her seething cat let out a loud guttural hiss that rang in Mila's ears.

"Motherfucker," spat Dominic as a menacing intensity gathered around him like a cloak.

Dean inclined his head. "Yeah, I figured you'd feel that way about me."

"Hello, Dean," said Mila, somehow keeping her voice calm even while panic tightened her muscles and poured down her throat, leaving a sour taste on her tongue. Her heart was pounding with a thick, insidious, all-consuming dread.

She now had a little taste of how Dominic must have felt seeing Rosemary pointing a gun at her. Terrified. Powerless. Enraged.

Unlike Rosemary, Dean's hands were steady as he aimed those guns, and she could see he'd be perfectly comfortable using them. Knew he'd shoot Dominic without blinking, and he'd think nothing of it. *Fuck, fuck, fuck.*

Adrenaline pumped through Mila, feeding her cat's need to act. Lunge. Maim. "You know, Adele doesn't believe you could possibly be the person who put a price on my head, but I think it's safe to say that her faith in you is somewhat misplaced."

A muscle in Dean's cheek ticked. "My original plan was to make a deal with you, you know. I thought the two of us could somehow conspire to separate Adele and Joel. But I quickly sensed that you wouldn't go for that, so I improvised."

"Improvised? You put out a fucking contract on me, Dean."

His jaw hardened. "I need her, Mila. I've needed her since the moment I first saw her in a vision. I spent years looking for her. *Years.* She's mine; she should be with me, *where she belongs.* Not with some goddamn asshole who can't recognize his own true mate even though she's right under his fucking nose."

Stepping farther into the room, Dean sneered at Joel. "Never once asked yourself why you were so drawn to Mila, did you? Adele didn't want to switch back to your pride, you know, Mila. *He* pushed for the transfer, not her. And we all know it's because part of him needs to be near *you.* Even now, when he finally knows the truth, he won't demand to have what's rightfully his."

Dominic snarled, his neck corded, his muscles straining against his skin. "Mila will never be his. She's mine."

Dean frowned at him. "You have a predestined mate somewhere—"

"*Mila* is my mate," Dominic stated, itching to pound his fists into the fucker's face, just as his wolf itched to maul the living shit out of him. "Doesn't matter to me what fate intended. I decide my own fate, and I chose Mila. She'll always be my choice. So you can imagine just how badly I want to slit your fucking throat right now."

"Well, we're about to put your devotion to the test. We'll see how much you really want her after she fucks her true mate right in front of you." Dean smirked at Joel. "You want that, don't you? You might not like that you want her, but you do."

"Not gonna fucking happen," Dominic rumbled.

Joel's nostrils flared. "I love Adele—"

"She's not *yours* to love," snapped Dean. "And you can't deny that you want that female over there who was made especially for you. Yeah, you want her. And now you'll take her right here."

Mila glared at him as a cold anger twisted her insides. The guy had obviously hopped onto the crazy wagon at some point. "You can't be serious."

"Oh, I am," said Dean. "The only reason I didn't kill him long ago is that the abrupt snapping of the imprinting bond could lead to Adele's death. But I heard what he said just now. There's a strain on the bond. It's fragile. If the bond quite simply fades and crumbles to nothing, it won't hit her so hard—she can survive it.

"Now that you both know the truth of who you are to each other, it won't take much to make his bond with Adele fade. The mating urge would then kick in straightaway, and you and Joel will be driven to claim each other. Then Adele will be free of him. Joel, grab that chair and sit in it," Dean instructed. "Good." His eyes snapped back to her. "Now strip, Mila."

"Fuck you," she hissed. Her cat bashed at her, wanting the freedom to attack.

"No, you'll be fucking Joel. And if you don't, I'll fire the gun that I'm pointing at Dominic's head."

Which was no doubt why Dean hadn't *already* shot him, she thought—he knew that threatening Dominic would gain him her cooperation. And while she'd do just about anything for Dominic, she wouldn't do this. It wouldn't keep him alive. Dean didn't plan for anyone other than himself to walk out of this room alive. He just wanted to make sure the imprinting bond between Joel and Adele was severed.

Her only real chance of saving Dominic would be to take her chances and lunge at Dean. He'd have to aim one of his guns at her to defend himself, which would then free either Joel or Dominic to move. Sadly, though, she'd be highly likely to get shot. Again.

"You're wasting time, Mila," said Dean.

Dominic lifted a brow. "You think I'll just stand here while my mate fucks another guy?"

"Well, you can either stand still or be shot in the kneecaps." Dean shrugged. "Either works for me."

"So what, you think Adele will ride off into the sunset with you?" Mila shook her head. "She'll consider this a betrayal."

"No, she'll see that I was right and that all it really took for you and Joel to claim each other was simply having the opportunity," Dean argued. "She'll see it was inevitable and that I saved her pain in the long run."

"No, she'll see that you're fucking twisted—she won't want anything to do with you."

"I'll take that chance. If I don't, I lose her anyway. *Now strip.*"

"Hell fucking no." Her whole body jolted as Dean fired a bullet at Dominic's feet before quickly aiming the gun at his head once more. *"Son of a bitch."* Her cat hissed, spat, and generally lost her mind.

Nostrils flaring, Dominic narrowed his eyes at the little fucker. "I'm going to kill you, you know," he said conversationally.

Dean snickered. "I'm sure you think you—"

Joel sprang to life. With pallas cat speed, he jumped out of his seat and whirled on Dean, slicing at the tendons in the bobcat's arm. A gun dropped to the floor. Fired. But the bullet harmlessly sank into the sofa.

Still, Mila flinched with a curse. She would have made a grab for the fallen weapon if it wasn't somewhere behind Dean. Joel was currently trying to wrestle the second gun from the bobcat, both his hands locked around Dean's wrist.

Dominic whipped out his phone and called Trey. "Need a little help in the greenroom. Alert security. Keep people away." He ended the call without waiting for a response.

Mila bit her lip. "I know it's dumb to get between two dominant shifters when they're fighting, but I feel like we should do *something*."

Intervening in such fights wasn't done in their culture, but Dominic had every intention of doing so at some point. He was happy for Joel to beat the shit out of Dean, but Dominic was set on being the one to kill the bobcat. "Not yet."

Mila shifted from foot to foot, wishing one of the brawling males would somehow kick the fallen weapon her way. Just when Joel seemed close to snatching the second gun from Dean, the bobcat managed to train it at Joel's thigh and attempted to tighten his finger on the trigger. With a snarl, Joel used a surge of strength to shove the gun aside, inadvertently making it point at Dominic.

Her heart in her throat, Mila threw herself at Dominic, knocking him to the floor. The gun fired, and an unbearable heat blazed across her arm. She let out a pained "pissed-the-fuck-off" hiss.

Dominic rolled her beneath him, shielding her. "You okay?"

"Flesh wound," she assured him. Which was true. But it still burned like a bitch.

"I'll kill that piece of shit." The bullet had merely grazed her, to his relief, but it had taken off a good few layers of skin. His head snapped up as his pack mates rushed inside and skidded to a stop, causing Zander, Derren, and Ally to almost crash into them.

"Need a healer over here!" Dominic called out. Mindful of her wound, he carefully pulled Mila to her feet.

She waved Ally off. "I'm fine, it's just a flesh wound. My kind are fast healers, remember?"

"Then think of this as calming Dominic," said Ally, placing her hand on Mila's injured arm.

Taryn squinted. "Is that Dean Preston? I'd ask how the hell he managed to bypass security, but that disguise is damn good. He looks nothing like the pictures I saw of him."

Trey grimaced at the blood Mila was now wiping from her healed arm. "Your brother and parents are gonna be pissed when they get here and find out you were hurt."

Joel slammed Dean's hand against the wall, making the gun clatter to the floor. Joel kicked it aside and then laid into Dean.

Dominic scooped up the weapon as the two male cats tore into each other, snarling and hissing. The fight was ugly. Fists flew. Teeth bit. Claws slashed and stabbed. Dean's wig and fake beard soon toppled to the blood-specked floor.

Joel was faster. Stronger. But Dean was driven by the anger he'd harbored against Joel since his first vision of Adele, and he was venting every ounce of that rage. It was giving him an edge and making him a little crazy—hell, he even tried to tear a chunk off Joel's ear with his teeth. Worse, Dean's padding seemed to be making it hard for Joel to deliver maximum pain.

Zander winced when Dean raked his claws over Joel's crotch. "That bobcat is a vicious fucker, isn't he?"

"He knows that even if he defeats Joel, we'll kill him," said Mila. "Knows he's gonna die tonight. He wants to take Joel down with him."

"The only person who'll die here tonight is Dean," said Dominic. Although Mila was healed, the smell of his mate's blood fed Dominic's anger until it was agonizing for him to hold back and let Joel have his moment with the bobcat. Both males were tiring, and he knew it would only be a matter of—

Joel doubled over with a grunt as Dean's claws stabbed him right in the gut. Eyes wide, the pallas cat staggered backward, heaving in a breath.

Smirking, Dean advanced on his opponent. So Dominic fired at the fucker's ankle. Dean roared in pain, his leg almost crumpling beneath him. Dominic pulled the trigger again. The bullet sank into the bobcat's foot, eliciting another agonizing cry out of him. And then Dean collapsed to the floor.

Clicking on the safety, Dominic tossed the gun aside. Barely holding himself upright, Joel looked as though he still might lunge at the bobcat, but Dominic shook his head and said, "No. He's mine."

Dominic slowly stalked toward Dean, his eyes flashing wolf as his animal reached for the surface. But Dominic suppressed the beast and remained in control.

Flat on his stomach, Dean weakly tried to drag himself toward the other gun.

"Planning to shoot me?" Dominic tutted at him. "That's not very nice." He stilled as a noise drifted to him over the sounds of music thumping.

Healing Joel, Ally frowned. "Was that—? I thought I heard screaming."

Dominic narrowed his eyes. "So did I." He reached out with his senses, and what he heard sent his heart racing. Screaming. Yelling. Gunshots. "What the fuck?"

Mila's eyes widened as she glanced past him. "Dominic—"

He looked down just as Dean's hand closed around the butt of the gun. Bending over, Dominic fisted the fucker's hair and snatched back his head. "I told you I'd kill you." In one merciless swipe, Dominic slit Dean's throat with his claw.

"Outside," said Derren, fisting his hands. "The gunshots are coming from outside. And they're getting louder."

CHAPTER TWENTY-THREE

Leaving Dean's dead body sprawled on the floor, they tore out of the greenroom and down the hall. The music, dancing, and laughter had stopped, and the patrons were all staring at the entrance where two Mercury Pack wolves—Eli and Zander—were pounding their fists on the closed door.

Dominic gripped Mila's arm to keep her from following his Alphas, Dante, and the Mercury Betas through the crowds. Every instinct he had as an enforcer told him to follow his Alphas and find out what the fuck was going on. But he knew he'd never get Mila to wait behind, and he wouldn't allow her to walk into danger.

Eli and Zander stumbled away from the door as a body that looked like one of the doormen came tumbling down the stairs, ablaze and screaming. *Motherfucker.*

Two objects were then tossed inside, both aimed toward the bar. With so many people in the way, Dominic didn't see if the objects hit their target. But in a matter of moments, fire erupted.

His stomach dropped. *Shit.*

Before anyone had a chance to swarm the entrance and attack whoever was out there, the door was slammed shut. His wolf jerked as the fire alarm blared, loud and urgent. Water rained down from the sprinklers. People pounded on the door and threw all their weight against it. Again. And again. And again.

The door didn't budge, let alone open.

Dominic figured that if the door was thick enough to prevent people from breaking into the club, it was also thick enough to prevent them from breaking out. Eli and Zander must have had that same thought, because they gave up on the door and hurried down the stairs to Derren.

The Mercury wolves there all snapped to attention. Orders were shouted. Hand signals were exchanged. But Dominic couldn't understand them. Couldn't do anything but watch as Harley and one of the waitresses rushed over with fire extinguishers.

Rooted to the spot by shock, Mila fisted the back of his tee. "Dominic—" Her eyes followed the flames that rippled across the walls and swept up to the ceiling. Her cat turned as frantic as her heartbeat.

Dominic yanked up the neckline of her tee so that it covered her nose and mouth before doing the same for himself. "It's gonna be fine, baby." Dammit, he had to get her *the fuck* out of there. Even with the fire extinguishers, it was going to be hard to put out a fire in a club filled with goddamn alcohol—especially when that fire sprang to life at the *bar* itself.

The DJ spoke over the mic, urging everyone to follow Harley and Jesse down the hall—Harley would lead some to the side exit, and Jesse would lead the rest to the emergency exit at the rear of the building. The patrons instantly rushed after the pair in a blind panic, unapologetically bashing into each other as they tried shoving their way to the front of the line.

As his pack mates reached Dominic's side, Taryn growled, "Motherfucking extremists! It's gotta be them out there!"

Derren slapped Trey's back. "Call 911 and then get out of here!"

Dante frowned. "You need help—"

"Outside," finished Derren. "There are God knows how many of them waiting outside, and they'll be armed to the goddamn teeth, ready to shoot the shit out of anyone who escapes. The firefighters will come, but not the police—this is a shifter club, so they won't come to anyone's rescue here. Kill the bastards up there so they can't trap us down here! And take Ally with you!" When she went to object, Derren kissed her hard. "A lot of people who try to escape are going to need healing if they get shot! Go! I'll be right behind you!"

Looking tortured, Ally jabbed a finger in her mate's face and yelled, "You make sure you get out of here alive, Hudson! *Alive!*"

Trying to protect Mila from the bodies that were shoving and stumbling, Dominic joined the line that headed toward the exits, knowing his pack mates and Ally would follow.

He agreed with Taryn—the people outside had to be the extremists. And they'd no doubt been sent there by Pierson.

Fire seemed to swirl around the room—charring, melting, warping, and blackening whatever it touched. Smoke hazed and tainted the air. His wolf paced, feeling anxious and powerless because this threat wasn't an enemy he could physically fight.

Dominic lifted his head to see how far he was from the junction that led to the side exit. Not too far. The line had split in two at the junction, and some people were heading for the rear exit. But most, just as he'd suspected, had made the turn that led to the nearby side exit, hoping they'd escape the building faster.

"I called 911 *and* Tao," Trey shouted over the sound of the crackling, spitting flames. "The pack will come."

"What about the rest of the Mercury Pack?" Dominic asked.

"Tao said he'll give them a heads-up just in case Derren hasn't had a chance to call them," replied Trey. "He'll also call Vinnie, so we'll have plenty of backup."

Good, because Dominic was sure they'd need it.

People were hunkering down to avoid the smoke, but it was impossible. It was too thick, too potent. Despite the water coming from the sprinklers and the foam spurting from the extinguishers, the fire continued to hiss and snap as it spread across the club.

Dammit, they should have already been at the damn exit by now. Too slow, he thought. The line was moving too fucking slow. And the fire was moving too fucking fast, fueled by the alcohol.

Dominic had always liked that the club was underground, but not now. If it hadn't been in a goddamn basement, there would have been large windows that they could have smashed their way through to haul themselves out. Instead they were surrounded by brick walls.

The line abruptly stopped moving, and Dominic frowned as he heard banging and cursing and people demanding to know why the doors weren't opening. It wasn't until a deeper panic rippled down the line that he realized the other two exits had also been barricaded shut. They were all trapped down here. *Fuck.*

His wolf raked at Dominic's insides, enraged and eager to get his mate to safety.

"They've *confined* us down here?" Taryn demanded, a little hysterical. "They've actually fucking *locked us in*?"

"It would appear so," said Trey, his voice hard. "Seems that their plan is to burn us alive."

The plan might just work, Mila mused. She hadn't thought it was possible to feel cold while surrounded by fire. But even as the heat seared her skin, causing sweat to trickle along her flesh, she felt icy fingers of dread dance along her spine.

The flames seemed to have a damn mind and will of their own. Almost like they were chasing the people who were trying desperately to get out. Cruelly herding them toward exits through which they had no way of escaping.

Cough after cough racked her system. She wasn't the only one coughing and wheezing. Smoke just kept on thickening the air, burning her nose and throat until they felt raw. God, this was bad. Very, very bad.

Her cat was snarling and lashing out with her claws as everything went to shit around them. Bulbs flickered and shorted out. Glasses and bottles shattered. Tables and chairs creaked. Flames swept up the drapes on the stage. Picture frames clanged to the ground, and the glass inside them splintered.

The line moved forward just a little, but not enough to tell Mila that any of the exits were now open. It was as if people were pushing closer and closer into each other's personal space, determined to escape the heat and the flames. But there was no escape. And she knew the feeling of being confined would drive *everyone's* inner animal insane.

She winced as she felt something wickedly sharp dig into the sole of her shoe. Glass, she thought with a low hiss. Mila would have kicked it aside to spare others the bite of pain, but it was so crowded, she could barely move or—

She jolted as a light fixture up ahead suddenly dropped down, wrenching cries of alarm and pain out of the people in the line, making the tight crowd sway and stagger and jostle each other. If it hadn't been for Dominic's body shielding hers, she might have ended up with crushed feet or something else.

"The damn place is falling apart!" Dante shouted. "What the hell are the people at the exits doing? Surely they can force the doors open!"

Hearing a loud squeal, Mila looked to see a female frantically batting at her sleeve, where little sparks had burrowed. "Shit," Mila muttered, the curse muffled by her tee. "We've gotta do something."

"Yeah, we do." Dominic coughed, tasting ash, phlegm, and fear for his mate. Dammit, he had to get her out of there. "Fuck the line, let's move."

His hand slippery with sweat, he gripped Mila's, finding it just as clammy. Dominic forced his way through the crowd, not caring who he hurt in the process—his mate came first. He kept Mila close, sensing that Ally and his pack mates were close behind them.

Dominic didn't make the turn that led to the side exit—the corridor was too slim and too cramped with people. So ignoring the shifters who swore and snapped at him, he kept on shouldering his way through the other line until he finally reached the rear exit.

The flames hadn't yet gotten this far, but the air was still hazy with smoke. Even so, he could see that Jesse *had* managed to open the door and was standing in the outside ditch. But the wolf was unable to lift the hatch that would enable them all to get out.

Catching sight of Dominic, Jesse said, "The bastards have blocked it somehow, and I'm guessing they've done the same to the side exit, since the lines aren't moving in either direction. The bastards are actually fucking *laughing* up there."

"Laughing?" Dominic echoed. "Those motherfuckers think this is—" He cut off at the sounds of rabid growls, pained grunts, and muffled curses coming from outside.

Moments later, the hatch was yanked open.

Seeing Alex staring down at them, Mila smiled. "About damn time you got here."

CHAPTER TWENTY-FOUR

Moving aside, Alex urged them out, grimacing at the plumes of smoke that rose from the hatch. "I called the pride; they're already on their way."

Coughing, Mila grimaced at the bodies splayed on the ground. Humans, her senses told her. Her brother had dispatched of them quickly and coldly. "Any more extremists?"

Alex nodded. "Some are covering the entrance, and some are sitting in a huge fucking van in the lot. They'll come this way as soon as they realize you all got out. Although everyone's coughing and hacking, they hopefully won't hear you over the sound of the fire roaring and the alarm blaring. Be careful," he added as more people climbed out, their faces stained with soot and tears. "There are snipers on the roof at the front of the building."

"We're on it." A tall male muttered something to his friends, who then promptly shifted, shrugging off their clothes as they flew. *Eagle shifters.*

As Mila and Dominic helped the other patrons out, Ally, Dante, and the Phoenix Alphas apprised the escapees of the situation, urging them not to run off.

"I figure the snipers are there to shoot any firefighters who try to help—it's something they've done in the past," said Mila.

Dominic nodded. "With any luck, the eagles will kill every single one of the fuckers. Can you let people out of the side exit, Alex?"

"It's best not to," replied the wolverine. "Everything that happens in the alley echoes, so the extremists will hear if shifters start filing out of that exit. The humans will then go after them, guns blazing—literally. It'll work better if everyone just comes out the back way."

He had a good point, so they continued to quietly help the other patrons out. Ally took aside any who were burned or otherwise injured, and soon other healers joined her efforts.

A loud cry from high on one of the rooftops made everyone freeze, and a deep voice up there boomed, "They're out!"

"Think there was any chance the extremists on the other side of the building didn't hear that?" asked Taryn.

There was a roar of fury, followed by footsteps thundering down the alleyway.

"Well, that answers my question," said Taryn. "You and Dominic make sure everyone gets out," she told Mila.

Almost as one, Alex, Taryn, Trey, Dante, and most of the escaped patrons shifted. Their animals didn't hesitate to attack the humans who came rushing around the corner, armed to the teeth. Machine guns peppered bullets everywhere. Grenades were slung. The snipers who were still alive picked off the shifters that tried to run or retaliate.

Bodies of shifters toppled to the ground—some changed into their human forms as they did so. That didn't stop the others from charging. There were so many animal noises it sounded like a zoo gone wild. Roars, shrieks, growls, caws, snarls.

A blast of fire split the air, and Mila hissed. A fucking flamethrower. The humans hadn't just brought guns. They had spiked bats, machetes, maces, and belts that were wrapped in barbed wire. Oh, she itched to kick the humans' goddamn asses.

Sirens wailed in the distance, and Mila's head snapped up. *"Finally."* The sirens came closer and closer and closer. Tires screeched to a stop in the lot. That was when she heard more gunfire followed by distant voices crying out in pain.

Ally growled. "Fuck, the snipers are shooting the firefighters!" Her eyes snapped to the hatch as Derren and Eli climbed out. "Where the fuck have you been?" she yelled at her mate.

Coughing, Derren shut the hatch. "That's everyone out."

"Good, because being a spectator sucks," said Mila as she and Dominic stripped, intending to join the fight. The extremists had begun to back up, so a great deal of the battle was now taking place in the alley.

Eli froze. "What's that sound?"

Mila smiled at the familiar roar-growl. "That, my friend, is the sound of a pissed-off wolverine shifter." Her mother. "And she no doubt has my pride with her." They'd attack the extremists from another angle, effectively boxing the humans in. Some of the pride would also hopefully help put the fire out.

Clasping her nape, Dominic kissed her. "Be careful."

"Same to you," said Mila. Then they shifted.

The cat leaped over fallen bodies and sidestepped puddles of blood as she charged into battle. Ears flat, her snarling mate rushed at a human who was swinging a mace. Scrambling up the back of her wolf, the cat lunged at the human. She wrapped her body around his face and sank her teeth and claws into his scalp. Scratched at his flesh. Raked an eyeball. Enjoyed his cries of pain.

The wolf took advantage and barreled into the human. Knocked him onto his back and sliced open his stomach, exposing the man's guts. The cat approved of the bloodthirsty move.

Gunfire cracked the air, and a blazing heat singed the side of her leg. The cat hissed, furious. She went to retaliate, but a bear reared up on its hind legs and slammed its paw at the offending human's head. There was a distinct crack.

Satisfied, the cat turned back to her mate. Adrenaline pumping through them, the wolf and the cat worked as a team as they took down one human after another. They bit, slashed, clawed, and mauled. Ducked, dodged, and weaved away from what came at them.

Soon, the whooshing of the fire hoses joined the animal sounds and human cries. Her pride had to be putting out the fire.

Around them, other shifters attacked the humans—disemboweling, ripping out throats, tearing off limbs, crushing bones, severing spinal cords, clamping jaws around throats to suffocate opponents.

The extremists didn't surrender. Brutal and cunning, they lashed out with their weapons. Even when they abandoned their guns, they kept fighting, sending many shifters tumbling to the ground, defeated and near dead.

The cat's thick hide and fur acted as good protection, but not good enough. She was soon covered in slices, welts, and other injuries. Blood matted her fur. She was tiring. Slowing from loss of blood. Every part of her body seemed to hurt. But she fought on.

Just as she and her mate finished off another human, the cat turned to seek a new target. A wooden bat crashed into her side, its spikes stabbed into her flank, and she was knocked sideways. Red-hot pain assailed her, and the breath left her lungs in a whoosh. Shelving the burn, she righted herself, winded.

The spiked bat hit her again, tearing into her neck. She hissed at the blinding pain. Swayed but didn't fall.

The wolf pitched forward and clamped his jaws around the human's leg. The man lifted his bat, and the feline's heart jolted. She knew he would bring the bat down hard on her mate's head.

The cat sprang. Covered the human's face. Found purchase with teeth and claws. Raked and bit.

The human toppled backward, and the wolf instantly lunged at his mate's attacker. Sunk his teeth into the man's throat and tore it out with a vicious yank.

Lungs burning, heart pounding, the wolf backed away from the corpse and took a moment to glance around. The ground was littered with bodies—some human, some shifter; some dead, some close to death. There were many still standing, and most were shifters.

He noticed his Alpha male and Beta male savagely mauling a human in a wild frenzy. Pallas cats were crawling all over the humans, tearing into them with claws and teeth. A wolverine bit savagely into the shoulder of a fallen screaming human while a margay cat raked at the human's chest. Another wolverine had clamped his jaws around the flamethrower, mangling it with his bone-cracking teeth.

Hearing a whoosh of air, the wolf turned and saw a machete heading for him. He ducked, but it sliced off the tip of his ear. The wolf yelped at the harsh burn of the blade.

The cat readied to leap at her mate's attacker, but a mace slammed into her head, dazing her. She shook her head, cleared the dots from her vision, and sprang with a vicious snarl. The human tried to bat her away, but she was too fast. Went right for his face.

A hand gripped the scruff of her neck as she bit into his scalp. Shaking his head, he desperately tried to pull her away. She dug her claws harder into his face. Refused to let go.

Having delivered the killing bite to his attacker, the wolf turned to his mate. She was clinging to a human who was punching her head. Growling in fury, the wolf crashed into the human. Knocked him flat. Clawed through skin and muscle, scraped bone and—

Something stabbed deep into the wolf's flank. Something sharp and cold. It happened again and again. Yelping, he sliced at the human's stomach, gutting him. The stabbing stopped.

The wolf collapsed, his sides heaving, pain pulsing through him. He tried to pull himself to his feet. Failed. Ribbons of agony rippled through him. The shock of it was so strong, he involuntarily shifted.

Dominic lay there panting, his vision blurring. He slapped a hand to the vicious stab wounds on his side, knew they were deep. Blood was pumping out of them, pooling on the ground beneath him.

Sleep lured him, but he fought it like a bitch. He needed to stay with his cat, who was butting him gently, as if urging him to rise. He weakly stroked her head. "I'm okay."

Surging to the surface, Mila forced her cat to retreat so she could examine Dominic. The blood drained from her face as she saw how bad his wounds were, and a hellish dread wrapped around her chest like a tight band. "Shit, shit, shit."

Her hands trembling, she pressed them over the wounds, helping him put pressure on them. He cursed with a flinch, and Mila winced. "Sorry, sorry, sorry." But she pressed harder, swallowing hard as his warm blood trickled through his fingers and hers. "Ally! Helena! Sam! Taryn! *Someone!*" she yelled over her shoulder.

Mila caught sight of Taryn lying pale and weak against her mate—not dead but drained from healing others. Glancing around, Mila found Ally. The she-wolf was busy healing Tate while Luke gave him CPR. Sam was nowhere to be seen. And Helena, where the fuck was Helena? Mila couldn't see her anywhere. The smoke hazing the air certainly wasn't helping.

Coughing, Mila looked back at her mate. "Someone will come over soon to help you. We just have to wait a minute."

Dominic blinked up at her, his lips parted, his eyes stinging from the smoke. Fuck, his side *hurt*. What hurt more was seeing the fear on her face and feeling it echo through him. No, fear wasn't a strong enough word. It was a soul-deep, all-consuming terror. Cupping her face, he breezed his thumb over her cheekbone. "I'm gonna be okay."

"I know." But Mila didn't know. Not really. He looked far from okay. He was just so pale. Seemed so tired. And an odd sort of glaze was falling over his eyes.

Her cat never fretted about anything, but right then, her heart was beating as frantically as Mila's was. The feline truly feared for him. And it wouldn't take much to send her ape-shit.

Aware of how exposed and vulnerable he was while lying there bleeding profusely, Mila shifted her body over his a little, shielding him as best she could. The move wrenched at her wounds, making her wince. They throbbed and burned, but she ignored them.

There weren't many extremists still on their feet at this point. Those still standing were being tag-teamed by shifters. But her protective instincts pricked at her to guard and defend her mate while he was unable to do the job himself. And he clearly didn't like that she was putting herself at risk, because he snarled. At her.

"Move," Dominic ordered through his teeth.

"No."

He tried to lift himself up, and pain rolled over him in what seemed like never-ending waves that made his stomach churn. He almost gagged. *"Fuck."*

"Stop moving!" she chastised, too anxious to sound gentle right then. Blue eyes swirling with pain fluttered shut, and her heart jumped. "No. Open your eyes, GQ, look at me." He did, but she felt no relief because she could hear how lazy and erratic his heartbeat was becoming.

She glanced over her shoulder again. *"Need a healer over here!"* But Taryn was still out of it, and Ally was now working on her own mate. Sam was healing Luke, who looked in a bad state. And Helena . . . seriously, where the hell was that woman?

Mila turned back to Dominic, whose eyes had drifted shut again. "No, you have to look at me," she ordered, her pulse spiking with panic. "Eyes open, come on." His lids weakly fluttered open, and she touched her mouth to his. "You have to stay with me."

Dominic double-blinked, as if fighting the need to sleep. "Not leaving you."

Hot tears burned Mila's eyes. "No, you're not." But she was terribly afraid that wasn't true. His breathing was so shallow, and his pulse just kept on slowing. Worse, putting pressure on the stab wounds wasn't helping. Each time his chest rose and fell, more blood seeped out.

"Just keep looking at me, GQ, okay? Keep looking at me."

He coughed, and a little blood splattered onto his lips and chin.

The fear encasing her heart swelled and filled her chest to bursting. *Fuck.* "Someone will come. They'll heal you."

She heard an agonized cry of pain—something that came from the gut. And she saw Joel flat on his back with an extremist hovering over him, a jagged blade in his hand. They were close. So close. She could help. And a very small part of her that was purely base instinct urged her to save Joel. But the rest of her rebelled against it, because it would mean moving her hands from Dominic's wounds. She couldn't—wouldn't—do that.

Instead, she called out, "Vinnie! Help Joel!"

Busy gnawing on a fallen human's face, the Alpha cat whirled around and barreled into Joel's attacker. Thank fuck for—

Mila stilled as Dominic went limp beneath her. Her heart slamming against her ribs, she shook him. "Hey, wake up." He didn't. "No, no, no, no." Her chest went so tight with fear, she was surprised she could breathe. "No, GQ, you can't sleep, you have to look at me. Seriously, you *have* to look at me. Right at me." But he just didn't. Worse, his sluggish heartbeat stuttered yet again. *"FUCK!"*

Footsteps rushed her way and a hand landed on her shoulder. Mila knew that scent.

She glared at the healer. "Helena, you'd better do something. If you let him die, I'll slit your damn throat."

"I'll help him, baby, I will," said Helena, unfazed by Mila's threat. "You just keep your hands where they are, because he's in a bad way."

Like Mila didn't already know that. She kept pressure on his wounds, feeling an echo of Helena's healing energy buzz through him. With hope flickering in her stomach, Mila listened as his pulse quickened and his heartbeat steadied. Watched as his many, *many* wounds began to close over. Felt the bleeding beneath her hands come to a stop.

Mila reluctantly moved her shaking hands just as his eyelids opened. She bit back a sob of sheer relief and gave Helena a nod of thanks—it was all she could manage while emotion clogged her throat. The healer gave her a gentle smile, and then a brief spurt of Helena's healing energy jolted through Mila and caused her wounds to knit partially together.

"Too tired to heal you both fully, I'm afraid," Helena apologized before weakly standing. "Have to help the others."

Dominic slowly sat upright, chest squeezing at the unshed tears in his mate's eyes. "Come here, baby." He pulled her onto his lap and held her tight while his wolf strained against Dominic's skin so that he could rub up against her. Greedily sucking in her scent, Dominic kissed her hair. "You okay?"

"Been better," she choked out. Her throat thick, she let out a shuddering breath. "Don't ever put me through that again."

"Right back at ya." Gently rocking her from side to side, Dominic looked around. Although the air was hazy with smoke, he could see that they weren't the only people taking a moment to give or take comfort. Many were cuddling or, like Adele and Joel, were helping to clean each other's wounds. Trey was forcing Taryn to sip water, berating her for overexerting herself. Sadly, there were also some people who were holding limp bodies, their faces creased with grief.

The battle was officially over, and the ground was covered with bodies, bullet shells, weapons, and puddles of blood. Although thick plumes of dark smoke still wafted from the building, it also looked as though the fire was no longer out of control.

"Hey," said Dante as he came toward them, a bunch of clothes in his hands. "Got your stuff. You two all right?"

"Yeah." Dominic took the clothes gratefully. "The rest of the pack?"

Dante's brows lowered as his expression turned grim. "They're fine, but there were a lot of casualties on both sides of the fight. Luckily, none were from the Mercury Pack or Mila's pride. Ryan came about an inch from death, though, so Makenna's gonna give him hell."

Dominic and Mila quickly dressed, wincing as each movement pulled at their barely healed wounds.

"Given how well armed they were," began Dante, "I think the extremists figured that some of us would get out, but not all. They were counting on smoke inhalation to do most of the job for them. If we weren't shifters and tougher than humans, it might have."

Taking in the sight of the charred building, Mila swallowed hard. "Harley must be devastated." The place had been special to Mila, but it had meant so much more to the margay shifter.

"She is," confirmed a new voice as a powerful figure approached. *Nick.* "But we'll fix it up," the Mercury Alpha added, a grim twist to his mouth. "It'll take time, but we won't let the extremists shut us down."

Mila gave him a weak smile. "Still, I'm sorry this happened."

"The extremists did this because they're assholes—you and Dominic were just the excuse."

Lightly squeezing her shoulder, Dominic tugged her closer. "Tell us what you need," he said to Nick.

"There's really nothing for you to do," replied the Alpha. "The fire's almost out. The survivors have been, at the very least, partially healed. And we're not moving the dead bodies. The police will soon be called, because I want them to see exactly how much damage and suffering the extremists caused. Those firefighters were human, which means the police can't and won't ignore this."

Nick's gaze slid to Mila. "I told Vinnie to take your pride and go. Humans don't know your kind exists, and it's best that it stays that way. We'll deal with the police."

Sidling up to Dominic, Luke cleared his throat. "Before I leave . . . I thought you might want to know that there was a guy hiding in a swanky car in the parking lot."

Dominic stilled, and his wolf's ears perked up. "Was there now?"

"Yep. My pride noticed him when we first arrived. I slung him in the back of Dad's van; a few of the pride are keeping watch over him." Luke pursed his lips. "Now, I've never seen Emmet Pierson in person, but I've seen his picture. I'll bet good money that guy in the van is him."

"Really?" Dominic drawled.

"Yeah. I figured, since this shit was all about getting at you and Mila, that you both should have the honor of dealing with him."

Dominic nodded his thanks at Luke. "I got this."

"*We've* got this," corrected Mila.

Since Dominic had no wish to part from her for even a little while, he didn't ask her to remain behind. Instead, with his mate at his side, he stalked down the alley toward the parking lot.

Mila pointed at a navy-blue van. "That's Vinnie's."

Reaching the vehicle, Dominic pulled open the rear double doors. And yes, there was Emmet Pierson. His wolf peeled back his upper lip.

The human was huddled against the wall, trying to keep his distance from the hissing, snarling pallas cats. The felines seemed to be toying with him by pitching forward and swiping out with their claws, ripping his clothes but not drawing blood.

His eyes widened at the sight of Dominic, who fisted Emmet's shirt, dragged him out of the van, and slung him on the ground. The pallas cats hopped out of the vehicle and surrounded them, growling at the human, but they didn't pounce on him.

As he stared down at Emmet in utter contempt, Dominic felt a roiling heat low in his stomach. So many people had died tonight. Even more of them were injured, including Mila. Hell, he'd almost died himself from those goddamn stab wounds. And why? Because that bastard on the ground had sicced the extremists on them to do his dirty work.

Mila cocked her head as she spoke to Dominic. "My guess is he stayed in his car, hoping no one would notice him. And when the tide turned against the extremists, he was too scared to move in case one of the shifters saw him and took his ass down."

Dominic gave a slow nod. "He probably would have tried to drive off at some point if the cats hadn't gotten to him before he had the chance."

Eyes flashing with fear, Pierson still managed to look haughty and indignant. He looked at Mila, taking in all the streaks of dried blood on her face, neck, and arms—it was more than obvious she'd been covered in wounds not so long ago. "Are you really even human?"

She smiled, but it wasn't a pleasant sight. "No, I'm not. Fooled ya, though, didn't I?"

Dominic took an aggressive step toward Emmet. "You sent them here. The extremists. You told them to go after the club."

Bracing himself on his elbows, Pierson edged back a little. "It's a hot spot for shifters—the extremists would have targeted it eventually."

"And thanks to you, they did it sooner rather than later. But it wasn't about the club, was it?" Dominic clipped. "It was about taking my mate from me. You found out she was working here, you suspected she'd come back, and you just bided your time. You made sure the extremists were prepared to make their move when you were ready for them to."

"*Rosemary* is your mate," Emmet bit out. "Deny it all you want, but you know it's true. She's yours, and you abandoned her. And now she's in a fucking *coma*. Did you really think I'd let you go on and live a happy life with another woman? Did you really think I wouldn't do whatever it took to make you suffer as Rosemary suffered? I warned your Alpha that I'd make a bad enemy."

"You also make a stupid one. You shouldn't have come here tonight. If you had any sense, you'd have left this to the extremists. But you just had to be here, didn't you? Had to listen to the cries of pain and howls of mourning, had to watch the bodies fall." *Sick fuck.* He was soon to be a *dead* sick fuck. Dominic sliced out his claws and advanced on him.

Emmet jumped, his eyes widening. "The police—"

"Can't save you from me. No one can." It was ridiculous that he'd think differently.

Emmet edged back fast, still on his elbows. "You'll never get away with—"

"Yes, I will."

A pallas cat bit into Pierson's foot, making him flinch with a sharp cry and—better still—come to a stop.

Swallowing hard, Emmet stared up at Dominic. "You'd really kill an unarmed man?"

"Yes." Bending over, Dominic thrust his claws into Emmet's chest, closing them around his heart. "You tried to take my heart from me, so I guess it's only fitting that I take yours from you." And Dominic yanked it out.

CHAPTER TWENTY-FIVE

Leaning back against Dominic as they settled in the freestanding tub, Mila sighed. Yes, this was what she needed. She mustn't have shifted position much as she slept, because she'd woken stiff with some aches here and there.

The minute they'd returned to pack territory the previous night, they'd showered, washed off all the blood, and collapsed into bed—exhausted from the fight and adrenaline crash. She'd woken the next morning just as Dominic's cock slipped inside her. His thrusts had been slow. Lazy. Gentle. For the first five minutes. Then he'd taken her hard and fast, pounding deep and snarling in her ear.

She hadn't realized that he'd texted Grace, asking her to bring breakfast to their room, until Mila heard the knock on the door. After they'd eaten in bed, he'd ran them a bath. And so there they were.

Mila closed her eyes, enjoying the steam warming her face and his fingers idly skimming up and down her bubble-covered arms. Her cat was completely content to just lie there with her tail curled around her as they snuggled into their mate.

He dabbed a lingering kiss on her temple. "I like you this way."

"What?" she practically purred.

"All soft and warm and relaxed." Tucking his face in the crook of her neck, Dominic inhaled her scent, filling his senses with his little cat. Rumbling a growl of contentment, his wolf brushed up against her.

He'd figured the bath would help her shake off the fear that had still been fresh in her mind—the fear that she'd lose him, that she'd be all alone again. He understood it. Fuck, he'd never rid himself of that image of her covered in wounds. Wounds he'd been unable to address because he'd been bleeding to death on the fucking ground.

Lifting her wrist, he circled her pulse with his thumb, reminding himself that she was safe and well. Thanks to Helena's help and their accelerated healing rate, most of their injuries had healed or were nothing but pink blemishes that would soon fade. He had one or two that might scar, though. And the puncture wounds in Mila's neck were taking a while to disappear—hopefully they would.

According to the text he'd received from Nick, the police were taking the extremist attack very seriously, although that was probably because human firefighters were killed. The police had also been easy to convince—especially with the help of the pallas cat officers—that Pierson had led the attack, so the authorities weren't particularly bothered that his car was there, but the human had mysteriously disappeared. Not after they'd seen just how much damage had been caused and how many unnecessary deaths there had been.

"I want to call Harley and ask how she's doing," said Mila. "But it would be a dumb question, wouldn't it? It might be best to give it a day or so before I call her. What do you think?"

He swirled his tongue over one of the fading puncture wounds on her throat. "I'd say you'd be right to call her in a few days. She'll be blaming herself for what happened, thinking she should have had better security measures in place. She'll put all those deaths on her shoulders. Give Jesse time to put her back together."

Mila sighed. "You know, I wish there was a way to destroy every last one of the extremists, but Trey's right. You can't kill prejudice. The bastards will always exist. We killed some in the battle, but others will spring up to take their place."

He snaked his hand up her stomach and softly palmed her breast, smiling as her nipple tightened and dug into his hand. "As last night proved, wars are just senseless." When she reached back and loosely hooked her arms around his neck, Dominic danced the tips of his fingers along her inner thigh while nuzzling her neck.

She let out a shaky breath. "I won't be able to concentrate if you keep doing that. But I'm not complaining."

Smiling, he nipped the tip of her ear. "Spread your legs a little." She didn't hesitate to give him what he wanted, just let her thighs fall apart. He loved that. Loved that her sex drive matched his. Loved that they both got off on the same things. Loved that her body always responded to him so eagerly. It was as if she were made for him.

But she wasn't, he thought with a frown. She was made for someone else.

Instead of touching her clit as he'd planned, Dominic smoothed his hand down her thigh and said, "I noticed Adele and Joel were huddled together after the battle." His wolf curled his upper lip at the mention of the other male.

Mila's brow furrowed. It was an odd time to have a conversation about the couple, and there were *other things* she'd rather be doing. Like coming. "Hmm. I hope they work things out." And that Dominic would switch his attention back to playing with her body. But he didn't.

"Depends on how she takes the news of Dean's death, I suppose."

"Considering she can no longer deny his part in things, I doubt she'll be grieving much. But so many shifters will be grieving hard tonight. One of them could have been me. I'm still pissed at you for getting stabbed, by the way."

His mouth quirked. Dominic knew she wasn't kidding. "My apologies," he said dryly, which earned him a snort. His smile faded as a memory hit him. "I was pretty dazed when I was lying on the ground, bleeding."

"Don't remind me," she grumbled.

"But I heard Joel cry out. Sensed you were worried for him. What was happening?"

"An extremist was hovering over him with a blade in his hand."

Carefully sitting her upright, Dominic turned her to face him, keeping her legs on either side of his. "But you didn't try to help him." He knew he sounded incredulous. "You stayed with me."

She frowned. "Of course I did. You're my mate."

It was really that simple for her, Dominic marveled. Although he wasn't what fate had intended for her, she didn't view him as a substitute for her true mate. Hadn't chosen him merely because she couldn't have Joel. No, despite that Dominic wasn't predestined to be hers, Mila saw him as her mate. Her claim on him ran soul-deep. What she *could* have had with Joel really didn't matter to her.

Having watched his mother give up on her mate and son because she'd been too deeply mired in her own issues, Dominic had always known he'd have trouble fully trusting his partner to stick around through thick and thin. But Mila had shown that she was no quitter; that she had the kind of staying power his mother had lacked. He'd grown to trust her in a way that he hadn't thought himself capable of. Still, it had been hard for him to feel secure in the knowledge that she was his when she lived in such close proximity to her true mate.

It wasn't that Dominic doubted that she loved or was fully committed to him. She never let him doubt it. But a small part of him—the part he'd hidden behind a mask for years, where no one could hurt, reject, or criticize it—had held back, fearing she wouldn't find him "enough," just as he'd never been enough for his parents. Fearing that he'd been a substitute for Joel, just as he'd once been a substitute for Tobias.

But faced with the choice of having to save Dominic or her predestined mate, she'd chosen Dominic. She'd stayed with him on what was effectively a battlefield and done her best to keep him alive until help came, even if it meant that Joel might die just a few feet away from her. And she didn't regret or feel guilty about it—he would have sensed that. No, she hadn't struggled with her decision whatsoever. And the last little piece inside Dominic that had held back from her for so long took a deep breath and reached for her.

A razor-sharp pain lanced through his head and panged through his chest, disorienting him. He gripped her hips, as if she'd anchor him. And she did. She anchored him in every way a person could. Especially now that the imprinting bond joined them, bright and strong. He closed his eyes, relief and satisfaction spiraling through him. Those same emotions flooded his wolf as their mate became a *part* of them in a way Dominic couldn't describe.

Licking her lips, Mila double-blinked. The abrupt forming of the bond had taken her completely off guard, and now it was warming every cold spot and filling every empty space. Her cat purred and did a long, languid stretch, feeling so much more than just peaceful. She felt whole. And lamely, all Mila had to say was, "Wow."

His mouth curved. "Yeah."

"How did it happen?"

A bone-deep contentment settling over him, Dominic tucked a loose curl behind her ear. "I needed to believe—*fully* believe—that I wasn't second choice for you. I was second choice for my parents, just a replacement for Tobias. And I knew they'd give me up in a heartbeat if it meant having their perfect child back."

Mila glared at him for doubting her. "You're not second choice to me. Never have been."

"I guess my subconscious wasn't so convinced. But it is now." He caught her face with his hands. "Nothing ever has—or ever could—matter to me the way you do. I want everything I can get with you and from you. You're not gonna get a minute's peace, and you're gonna move here."

"Is that so?"

"Yes, and then you'll become my sex slave—something that won't change even when we have pups."

Her lips twitched. "You mean kits."

"I'm good with having both." Sobering, he rested his forehead against hers. "I'll never make you regret choosing me, baby. Not ever."

"I'll never regret it. And I hope you won't regret choosing me either."

"Never," he promised, knowing to his bones that it was true. Knowing she'd always be his "center," just as Jesse had said she could be. Knowing he'd do whatever it took to keep the bond going strong between them.

The funny thing was . . . he'd always thought he'd prefer an imprinting bond to a true-mate bond, because the latter didn't come with a get-out clause. But now that he had this bond with Mila, he detested that it wasn't irrevocable.

Mila tilted her head. "What are you stressing about? I can feel that something's bugging you. The bond doesn't make you feel trapped, does it?" Because she'd worried that would happen.

"No, but I wish it did. I wish it was irreversible."

"You know better than anyone that a true-mate bond doesn't guarantee a lifetime of happiness, Dominic. Only *we* can ensure that. This bond is strong, and it will stay strong. I'll make sure of it, and so will you."

He nodded, taking a deep breath. "I need your mouth, baby." And she gave it to him. The kiss was soft, wet, languid. His blood pooled low, and his cock began to thicken. "I want in you."

Her lips curled. "I can tell." She could feel his dick hardening against her and, thanks to the bond, feel his arousal buzzing through his bloodstream. Her nerve endings sprang to life, and a slow burn began in her pussy. "I've never had sex in a bath before."

"Me neither. I've never let anyone as close to me as I've let you."

"Good. It means there are no skanky asses I have to kick."

Dominic grinned. "My wolf really loves that possessive streak of yours."

Kneeling, she snickered. "So do you."

Yeah, he did. He sucked in a breath as she fisted his cock and brushed it between her folds, flicking her clit with each pass. Then she was sinking down on his cock, slowly impaling herself on him. And it felt like fucking heaven. "Fuck, Mila. I can feel how much you love having me in you."

"Now you'll feel how much I love you coming deep inside me."

Keeping her inner muscles tight around his cock, Mila rode him slow. Teasing him with spiral downward thrusts and little bites to his neck. It wasn't long before he expertly toyed with her clit, forcing her closer to her climax. And then she broke with a silent scream, her pussy squeezing and milking his cock.

She rested against him, panting, feeling totally at peace. Just as her cat did, she thought with a smile.

Knuckles rapped on the bathroom door. "You guys done in there?"

Lifting her head, she frowned at the sound of her brother's voice. "What are you doing here?"

"A better question would be: Why did my pack mates let you into my room?" clipped Dominic. He could understand them letting the wolverine pass the gates and enter the caves, but not enter Dominic's personal slice of territory.

"They didn't," replied Alex.

Mila sighed. "You snuck onto their territory, didn't you?"

"Why are you wasting time asking me stupid questions?" complained Alex.

Dominic sat up straight. "Wait, how the hell did you bypass our security?"

"You ask that like it's hard," said Alex.

Mila gave Dominic a wry smile. "The sad thing is . . . this won't be the last time you find him in our room. You should probably warn Grace that he'll often raid the fridge when he comes here."

"Already did that," Alex told them.

Mila lifted a brow at her mate. "See what I mean?"

"Wolverines go where we want to go—the end," said Alex. "Which brings me neatly to why I'm here. Thought you might want to know that Dale Forester, the asshole who created the website for bounties, is gone for good."

"Told you my uncles would get to him," Mila said to Dominic.

"So he's dead and buried?" asked Dominic.

"There was nothing left to bury. Except some teeth," replied Alex.

Knowing that meant her uncles' inner beasts had pretty much eaten Forester's entire body, Dominic shuddered. "Good to know. Next time you have news, maybe you could just call us instead."

"But that wouldn't annoy Mila or her cat, so there'd be no fun in it," Alex pointed out.

Dominic shook his head. "Whatever. Just go." But when he and Mila walked out of the bathroom a few minutes later, wrapped in fluffy towels, they found Alex lounging in a chair and reading a book. "Unless you want to see your sister naked, you really need to leave now."

Alex lifted a brow. "I've seen her scrawny body before. There's not a lot there to see. But she already knows she's not much to look at."

Mila took a step toward him. "Oh, you little fucker."

He looked at Dominic. "Aren't you put off by all those sharp bones digging into you? Honestly? Not even the protruding shoulder blades? You could play her ribs like a xylophone."

Her cat hissing and flexing her claws, Mila pointed at the door. "*Out*, Alex."

"So you can pretend that if I put a sesame seed on your head you wouldn't look like a pushpin?"

She shifted so fast Dominic didn't get the chance to grab her cat before the feline launched herself at Alex's face.

Dominic sighed. So this would be his life. He could honestly say he was looking forward to it.

EPILOGUE

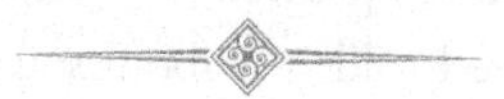

Eight years later

Plucking a fresh beer from the cooler, Dominic blew out a breath. It was approaching evening, but damn, it was hot. The sun beat down on him like a heavy weight, and he had to wonder if he was the only one who'd been thinking that Taryn's idea to have a picnic near the lake wasn't so great. If so, no one had chosen to retreat to the dwelling.

The breeze was light but cool, creaking the branches and bringing with it the scents of warm herbs, sweet flowers, lake water, and the food that was set on the buffet table. Everyone was spread around the clearing. Some stood around in groups, some sat on logs or lawn chairs, others gathered around the various picnic tables.

Mila *had* been sitting with Lydia, Cam, Rhett, and Grace while burping Lydia's baby boy, who had one *hell* of a set of lungs on him. But Mila was now gone, and he couldn't see her anywhere.

He was about to ask Tao if he'd seen her, but Dominic noticed that the Head Enforcer was glaring up at Savannah, who sat in one of the weathered trees that hemmed the clearing. Her brow was furrowed in concentration, and her thumbs were tapping furiously on the screen of her cell phone.

Tao's lips thinned. "You'd better not be texting boys."

Savannah frowned down at him. "Why would I text boys? Boys are dumb."

"Yes, they are. Never forget that."

"I won't—you prove it every day." She swiped out at the little boy who'd climbed up the tree just to pull on her hair. "Ugh, your spawn is being a pain in the butt again, Tao. And I think he's been back in the dirty cave near the river—I can smell it on him."

Sidling up to Tao, Riley planted her hands on her hips and glared at their son. "What have I told you about staying away from the cave? There are bats in there!"

Tao sighed at his mate. "Woman, there are no bats!"

Riley sniffed. "Now you're just lying."

The young cheetah at the base of the tree chuffed in what might have been amusement, sprawled on the grass in his animal form as Lilah idly stroked his back while reading a book.

"Any of you seen Mila?" Dominic asked, but they all shook their heads.

"She might be with Jaime," suggested Riley. "You know how those two can natter on and on for hours."

He spotted Jaime perched on a log, wiping the sticky fingers of her young daughter. Mila wasn't with her, but the Beta female might know where she'd gone. Dominic headed her way, the long grass and wildflowers whispering against his shoes with each step. Sunlight shimmered off the grass stems, just as it did the rippling lake water.

Reaching Jaime and her group, it came as no surprise to see that Dante and Hendrix were arguing. Again.

"Stop calling me Popeye!" Dante rounded on his mate. "Jaime, this is *your* fault."

She just lifted one shoulder. "Can we help it if it's an appropriate nickname?"

Standing beside Hendrix, Jaime's nephew laughed. When Gabe Jr. wasn't hanging in the security shack with his father, he was trailing after Hendrix.

"I'm looking for Mila," said Dominic. "Any of you seen her?" They hadn't. And there was still no sign of her anywhere.

He almost dropped his beer when a little blonde girl nearly crashed into him, singing, *"Cujo."* Sofia squealed and ran off as her father's wolf playfully charged at her. She was as much a born alpha as her parents and older brother. Kye was currently talking with Gabe, Hope, and Taryn near the buffet table as they piled food on paper plates. Kye totally dwarfed his mother now that he was almost as tall as Trey, though not quite so broad. *Yet.* The kid kept having growth spurt after growth spurt.

Dominic took a swig of his beer and then resumed his hunt for his missing mate. Passing Roni, he felt his lips twitch. She was sighing down at her mate and three sons, who were all gathered around a table with chocolate crumbs and bits of sponge cake on their mouths and fingers.

Roni threw up her arms. "Why do you all do this to me?"

The oldest grimaced and popped open a can of soda. "Sorry, Mom."

"We were hungry," complained the youngest, sitting on Marcus's lap.

Her nostrils flared. "*I'm* hungry."

The super-intelligent middle child looked at his mother, somber. "Perhaps you're pregnant again. Statistics say that—"

"Don't throw random facts at me, Keane."

Dominic paused long enough to ask Roni and Marcus if they'd seen Mila, but the enforcers shook their heads. Great.

"Makenna might know," said Marcus, taking a sip of his beer.

True. The females were reasonably close. So avoiding the pine cones that peppered the grass, Dominic stalked to the spot where the she-wolf stood with her little family. Sienna and Ryan were engaged in yet another standoff. The gruff enforcer didn't like that his little girl was growing up, and she didn't like that he treated her like she wasn't.

Hands clenched, she grunted at her father. "*Daaaaad*, I'm not suggesting that I wax my legs or something extreme. I just want a cell phone—most kids my age have one."

"I don't care about most kids." Ryan lifted a hand. "I told you, you can have a cell phone when you're thirteen."

"Which is an unlucky number!"

Ryan clenched his jaw. "There is no such thing as luck."

"There is no such thing as luck," parroted the little boy clinging to his father's back.

Arm wrapped around his recently found mate, Zac laughed. "Are you always going to make fun of your dad?"

"Yep," replied Bastien.

Smiling at their byplay, Dominic tipped his chin at Makenna. "I'm looking for Mila."

Pausing in eating her handful of wild strawberries, Makenna tilted her head. A line appeared between her brows. "Last time I saw her, she was chatting with Frankie."

Well, she wasn't there now, but maybe Frankie could help. Dominic gave Makenna a nod of thanks and crossed to where Frankie was lounging on a lawn chair, rubbing her pregnant belly while her mate massaged her neck. "You look tired," Dominic said to her. But then, she often did these days.

"I swear, it's so hot out here, I could just fall asleep," said Frankie. The rustling leaves on the branch above her head flickered shadows over her face. "It isn't the pregnancy that has me so exhausted all the time; it's this kid. For some reason, he or she is nocturnal. Always kicks and wriggles around through the night, waking me up."

Trick gave her a sympathetic smile. "No rest for the wicked."

Her brows lifted. "So what, serial killers don't sleep?"

"Oh my God. It's just a turn of phrase."

Frankie made a derogative *pfft* sound.

"Either of you seen Mila?" Dominic asked. "I can't find her anywhere. It's like she just disappeared."

Frankie's brows snapped together. "Well, you didn't look very far. She's right behind you."

Dominic pivoted on the spot. Mila was walking out of the trees with Greta. Each was hand in hand with one of the twins. Yeah, twins.

He'd been a mess all the way through Mila's pregnancy. She was just so slender, he hadn't been able to see how she could carry *two babies* at once. Honestly, the pregnancy had been a breeze for her. And she'd gotten through the labor with a calm and steadiness that the pack still marveled over.

The moment Emilia saw him, she beamed. "Daddy!" She rushed over to him on her little legs, her tight curls bouncing everywhere.

He scooped her up and planted a kiss on her cheek. "There's my Em." She wrapped her arms around his neck and nuzzled him. Yeah, his little pallas kit was a proper daddy's girl. "Why do you have dirt on you?"

"It's a boring story."

Everything was a "boring story" when Emilia didn't want to answer a question. He'd wanted to name his daughter Mila or Milena after her mother, but Mila wouldn't go for it. So he'd suggested Emilia, which was close. He suspected that Mila had only said yes because she was a *Game of Thrones* addict and liked the actress who played the queen of dragons.

Unlike his twin sister, Dillon didn't rush over. No, he was a pup who moved at his own pace, no one else's. He was only six, but he already had the ease and swagger of a full-grown wolf shifter. An old soul, Valentina often called him.

"Dad, I don't want a sister anymore," Dillon griped. "Can we swap her for a boy? Or even just a pet?"

"No, we can't. And you love her really."

Dillon curled his upper lip.

"I've been looking for you," Dominic said to his mate.

Mila flicked a look at the twins. "I was looking for them."

"Dillon chased a rabbit into the underbrush and was trying to lure it out," said Greta, flicking a red ladybug from her top. "Emilia offered to help him. Somewhere along the line, they got into a fight and rolled into a ditch."

Dominic groaned. Although Dillon was a pretty easygoing pup and didn't lose his temper often, Emilia knew just how to get under his skin—and the little cat did it a lot, so the kids frequently fought over everything and nothing. They were extremely protective of each other, though.

"Emilia's a loser. I'm going to play with Bastien," declared Dillon. Then he took off.

Emilia's little nose wrinkled. "*He's* the loser."

Dominic tugged on one of her curls. "Neither of you are losers." He set her on her feet. "Now go play." She headed straight to Jaime and Dante's daughter.

Greta put a hand to her chest. "Those kids of yours melt my heart."

"Some would say you don't have one," quipped Riley, passing by.

Greta sucked in a breath, glaring at the raven. "Some would say you're nothing but a hussy."

Riley lifted a taunting brow. "That the best you got, Gretchen?"

"It's Greta."

"I don't care."

Predictably, Greta marched after the raven, delivering insult after insult.

Dominic curled an arm around his mate and drew her close. "Finally, we're alone." The sunlight bounced off her dangly diamond earrings. He'd bought the set for her to wear at their mating ceremony, which had taken place a month after the imprinting bond had formed. The bond had only strengthened over time, and it always seemed to surprise people that he and Mila weren't true mates—they were just that solid.

Even all these years later, he could remember their mating ceremony well. Could remember how gorgeous she'd looked, how happy she'd been, and how they'd gotten very little sleep that night. *And* how most of the males from both his pack and the Mercury Pack had persistently hit on her with cheesy lines.

Dominic pressed a soft kiss to her mouth, dipping his tongue inside just enough to give hers a quick, teasing flick. "You taste good."

"You taste like beer."

"You get drunk on my taste anyway."

She laughed. "I thought it was the other way around."

"It can be both." A shadow drifted over them, and he looked up to see a feathery cloud. "Want more food?"

"Nah, I'm good." She glanced at her wristwatch. "We need to head back inside soon. It's getting late. Frick and Frack need a bath."

His mouth quirked. "You can't call our children Frick and Frack."

"I went halves with you on them; I can call them what I want."

He chuckled. "Anyway, yeah, we'll all be heading back soon. Which is good, because I can't take much more of seeing you in that tank top." The last time she'd worn it, he'd sliced through the thin straps with his claws, tugged down the tank to free her breasts, and then fucked the petal-soft globes until he blew his load all over them.

He hadn't realized she'd sewn the straps until she pulled on the top this morning, giving him a wicked grin that said she knew *exactly* what it did to him to see her wearing it again. Flashes of memories kept flicking through his brain—his cock cushioned between her tits, her nipples hard and dark, her tongue sweeping up the drop of come that landed on her lip.

"Think you can manage not to cut the straps this time?" she asked.

"I can't make any promises." Moving his mouth to her ear, he lowered his voice. "Ever played leapfrog naked?"

"Nope."

"Oh, you've never lived."

"So you want to play a game later, huh?"

"Nah. Really, I just want to have a good, long taste of your plush lips." He sipped at his beer and then tapped her mouth. "And these ones as well, obviously."

Mila rolled her eyes. "That mind of yours is always in the gutter."

Probably always would be. If anyone thought that fatherhood would cure him of his cheesy-line-spouting disorder, they were wrong. He was just careful that the kids didn't overhear. "So do these plans of yours consist of anything other than you going down on me?"

He smiled. "Oh yeah. I'm going to fuck you so hard and deep you can't take it. But I won't stop. I'll keep taking and owning what's mine." And maybe he'd include some anal play. "Seriously, I hope you have pet insurance, baby, because I'm going to destroy this pussy later."

She shook her head. "You really are beyond weird."

"This is not fresh news to you."

"You're right, it's not." Snuggling into him, Mila closed her eyes as the cool breeze slid over her, ruffling her hair and clothes. It was hot as hell, but she wasn't complaining. Despite the heat, it had been a relatively relaxing day. Pressed tightly against her mate as he rocked her from side to side, she listened to the swish of grass, the chirping of birds, and the water burbling. Her cat basked in the serene moment.

As he rubbed his cheek against hers, Mila drew back slightly and scraped her fingers over the stubble on his jaw. "You need a shave."

"You can take care of that for me tomorrow." His mate still worked at the barbershop through the week, just as she still sang at the Velvet Lounge on weekends—it hadn't taken long for the Mercury Pack to fix up the club, adding fresh security measures. And since Emilia was proving to be just as talented a singer as her mother, it wouldn't surprise Dominic if his daughter one day started performing herself.

Even though Mila moved to the pack, Vinnie still considered her part of his pride—and, by extension, Dominic and the twins. Although Dominic had ceased feeling threatened by Joel's presence a long time ago, he was glad that he and Adele had returned to Joel's pride shortly after the battle. They apparently had kids of their own now.

Dominic didn't mind being considered part of Vinnie's pride. The only person in the pride he really had a problem with was Alex. It wasn't that they didn't get along. In fact, he considered the wolverine a good friend. The issue was that Alex still turned up in Dominic and Mila's bedroom whenever he felt like it, and no one had yet worked out how he kept sneaking past their security.

It had been more unnerving the morning Dominic had woken to the sight of her wolverine uncles gathered around the bed shortly after the twins were born.

Isaak had instantly complained, *"You did not give the babes Russian names. Why is this?"*

All in all, though, Dominic liked his in-laws a lot. "Oh, your mom called. She—" Hearing Emilia scream in fury and Dillon let out a battle cry, he turned and saw his children fighting over what seemed to be a pine cone.

Mila sighed in sheer exasperation. "There are several other pine cones all around them."

After breaking up the fight, she declared she was heading back inside with Dominic and the kids. Everyone else decided to do the same, so once everything was packed up, they all returned to the dwelling.

For once, bath time went without incident. Soon enough, she and Dominic were tucking the twins into their beds in the room next door to their own. That *didn't* go without incident, since Emilia threatened to fart in Dillon's face while he slept. And why would she want to do that? "Because," was Emilia's response.

Retreating to the room she shared with Dominic, Mila let out a sigh of relief. The space hadn't changed much when she moved in, since she hadn't brought a lot of stuff with her. But her little touches had made the room less masculine.

Over the years, it had become more *their* space as opposed to a room she'd merely moved into. Knickknacks they'd collected sat on the dresser. Family photos now hung on the walls. Pictures of the twins as babies had been framed and set on the shelves.

She kicked off her shoes. "I'm gonna take a shower. Want to join—" Hands gripped her hips and yanked her back into a hard body. "Well, hello."

Dominic swept her curls aside and kissed her nape. "Unless you want the straps cut again, take the tank off."

Mila's brows lifted. "Not wasting any time getting started, are you?"

"No. I've been thinking about stripping you all day." He swirled his tongue over a freckle on her nape and then blew over it. "Take it off."

Mila shivered at the feel of his cool breath on her neck. "I need a shower."

"You can shower after. Now, arms above your head. Good girl." He bunched the bottom of her tank in his hands and peeled it off, baring all that bitable flesh. He hummed, his lips grazing her cheek. "I like this bra." Black. Silk. Lacy. "But it's gotta go." One-handed, he flicked open the clasp and whipped it off.

"Smooth, GQ."

With a soft chuckle, Dominic swept a hand up her sleek back and knotted his fingers in her hair. "Mouth." She turned her face to his, her lips parted, and he took her mouth. Greedy. Possessive. Almost savage. She sucked on his tongue, and he groaned, deciding she'd be sucking something else later.

Mila reached back and tangled a hand in his hair as he pinched and tweaked her nipples. Her nerve endings sprang to life, and each tug on her nipples sent a spike of pleasure straight to her clit. Yeah, that felt good. As did the hands now squeezing and plumping her breasts.

She melted into him, hissing as he scraped his teeth over her shoulder. He knew every one of her buttons. Knew how to make her crazed with need. Knew how to make her so desperate she begged.

Her cat purred, rubbing against him to mark his skin with her scent. Staking her claim. Warning off other females. Making sure he knew who he belonged to.

Snaking his hands over his mate's delectable skin, Dominic snapped open the fly of her shorts and let them puddle on the floor. The sight of the black lacy thong adorned with little red bows made him swallow hard—it was one of his favorites. Especially because it only took a little tug on those bows to untie them, making the thong fall away. It was like unwrapping a present.

"It's a real good thing I didn't know you were also wearing this little scrap of lace today, or my cock would have been so painfully hard, I doubt I could have walked without limping."

Untying the knots on her thong, he let it drop to the floor and cupped her pussy hard. "Mine." He slipped his finger between her warm folds, rubbing her clit just right. And there was that smoky little moan he loved. "Let's see if we can get you to make that sound again." He caught her clit between two fingers and slid them forward, stroking both sides of the little nub. "Yeah, there it is. Good girl."

He kept on playing with her clit, his eyes drawn to the way her breasts heaved with each ragged pant. His head spun as the heady scent of her need drifted up to him and poured into his lungs. His cock thickened even more. Raging hard, it pushed against his fly and dug into her back.

Dominic dipped his head and grazed her pulse with his teeth. "Shall I let you come before I fuck you?"

"You'd better."

"Hmm. Not sure you deserve it. You knew I'd be rock hard all day if you wore that tank, but you did it anyway. And as we were at the picnic, I couldn't even sneak off somewhere with you and do something about it."

Mila's breath caught as he clamped his mouth over his claiming mark and sucked. "You liked that, though. Delayed gratification is your thing, not mine." She was a cat, after all.

"There's delayed gratification, and there's plain teasing your mate for your own amusement." He slid his hand up to her throat and collared her, brushing his thumb over her pulse. "You made me wait, so why shouldn't I make you wait?"

"Because I'll stab you in the balls if you do."

His lips twitched. "No, I don't think you will," he said, herding her toward the plush chair. "But just in case you're tempted to try it . . ." He bent her over the arm of the chair, smiling at her outraged gasp. "There, that works." Before she could start cursing or complaining, he drove two fingers inside her, grinding his teeth as her tight pussy squeezed them. "So hot. So ready for me." But he wanted her pussy to be dripping with need for him.

Mila's eyes fell shut as her world narrowed down to the two fingers tunneling in and out of her. They sometimes paused to swirl around or trace little circles over her G-spot, but then they'd go back to plunging deep.

Her pussy throbbed and ached for more. Need was roaring through her. Fast. Wicked. Electric. It licked at her skin until her nerve endings were on fire. "Dominic—"

"You need to come, I know." He'd *felt* her arousal build. *Felt* her anticipation prickle at her patience. She was aching for more—he could sense that too. And he loved knowing and feeling what he did to her.

He thrust his fingers faster, harder. Pushed her toward an orgasm he had every intention of denying her. Just when it was about to sweep over her, he withdrew his fingers.

"Son of a *bitch*."

He brought his hand down hard on her ass. "Not nice."

"Ask me if I give a f—" Mila inhaled sharply as the thick head of his cock pushed inside her, stretching her quaking inner walls. Oh God, this was what she needed. His long, thick shaft slowly sank into her, filling her up.

He gripped her shoulders and slammed home, sending the breath whooshing out of her lungs. *Jesus.* And then he was roughly jackhammering into her pussy. Fuck, she was going to be sore later. Not that she cared. Not when it felt so damn good.

She tried pushing back to meet his thrusts, but his lower body pinned hers in place, forcing her to take what he gave. Her moans mixed with his throaty little snarls and the sound of his balls slapping her ass.

Dominic scored his nails down her back, groaning as her inferno-hot pussy greedily clasped and squeezed his cock—just as he'd known it would. Over the years, he'd learned how much pain she liked with her pleasure. Learned what little tricks made her breath hitch and her inner muscles grip him like a vice. She knew some tricks of her own, but she truly didn't need to use them. Honestly, just the succulent scent of her need made him half-crazed for her.

Brutally hammering into her, Dominic traced the bud of her ass with the tip of his finger. "I want this again." He'd taken it many times over the years. Claimed it as his own over and over. And he'd come to learn that she had a quick trigger when it came to anal play. "Don't come until I say you can."

Mila gasped as a wet fingertip circled the bud of her ass and then gently pushed inside. Her claws sliced out, tearing into the upholstery of the chair. He drove his finger deep into her ass over and over. Soon he added a second. Not long later came a third. The whole time, his cock kept on slicing into her pussy, winding her tighter and tighter until every nerve ending felt raw.

God, she was so close. Swept away by the feel of his cock slamming deep, the bite of his claws on her hips, and the feel of his fingers thrusting into her—

His hand came down sharply on her ass. "Come."

Mila's head snapped back as white-hot pleasure fired through her shuddering body, trapping a scream in her throat and making her eyes go blind. He snarled as her pussy clamped down on his thrusting, swelling cock.

While she was caught up in her orgasm, Dominic withdrew his cock and sank the thick head into her ass, groaning at how hot and tight she was. Her body briefly resisted the invasion, but then he smoothly and slowly buried himself balls-deep. *"Fuck."*

"Move, move, move." Because Mila couldn't guarantee she wouldn't come again before he was done. Especially when her pussy still tingled from her orgasm. Gripping her hips, he pumped his cock into her ass. Deep. Fast. Hard enough to feel good but not hard enough to hurt.

Soon, he upped his pace. And it started to happen again. Tension built low in her stomach, hot and wicked. Her thighs shook. Her pussy quaked. Her sensitized skin prickled.

Sensing she was close to coming again, Dominic gentled his thrusts a little. "Tell me. Say it, Mila. Say it and I'll make you come."

She licked her lips. "I love you."

Satisfaction settled over him. "And I love you, baby." He fucked her harder, faster. "More than anything." He shoved two fingers into her pussy and smacked her ass hard. Her orgasm rippled along their bond just as it swept her under. "That's it, Mila, come for me."

Her pleasure spiked down their bond, heightening his own. His orgasm tightened his balls and shot out of his cock. Snarling her name, he slammed deep as he pumped rope after rope of hot come inside her.

All hollowed out, she slumped over the chair, trembling and breathing hard.

Panting, he pressed kisses along the back of her shoulder, gentling her. "Time for that shower." It did his ego some good that she remained half-dazed throughout the short but thorough shower. When they slipped in bed, he pulled her flush against him. "You good?"

"Hmmm." Mila smiled as his hooded eyes glimmered with sheer male satisfaction when they dropped to her claiming mark. The sight of it always put that smug look on his face. His possessiveness of her hadn't eased even one iota over the years. He and his wolf were as territorial now as they were when they first claimed her.

Feeling his cock, hard and insistent, press against her, Mila smiled again. "I wonder if you'll ever lose that quick recovery time." She sure hoped not.

Mouth curving, he rolled her onto her back. "It's a gift." He licked and nipped his way down her body, relishing every moan and lazy sigh. He had a pussy to eat. As he kissed her belly, where his kids had once grown, he said, "I want more."

"Huh?"

"I want more babies with you. But not twins again. I only want you carrying one at a time. Got it?"

She snickered. "I'll see what I can do."

"That's what I like to hear." Positioning himself between her thighs, he used his thumbs to part her folds. "Such a pretty view."

When he just kept on staring, she lifted a brow. "Can you get on with things, please?"

"That would be rude. Your pussy's talking to me."

She frowned. "What?"

"It's saying . . ." Moving her folds as if they were lips, he added, *"Dominic, oh mighty sex god, would you please lick me."*

She laughed. "You are so fucking whacked."

"But you love me."

"Yeah, I love you." And when his mouth sent her tumbling into another climax mere minutes later, she thought she loved him even more.

Settling at her side once again, he pulled her close. "Sleep, Mila."

She would have done exactly that, but then a thought occurred to her. "Shit. Forgot to brush my teeth. I'll be back."

"Could you just do one thing first?" he asked as she stood. "I just need you to get down on your knees and smile like a doughnut. Hey, don't walk off. It was a simple request."

Acknowledgments

As always, I'd like to thank my family first. Not everyone can boast that their husband doesn't bat an eyelid when you talk about the voices in your head. My kids never complain that I'm too deep in the writing cave. They do, however, charge right into my personal space to demand my attention, but I think that shows a gutsy determination.

I'd like to also say a massive thanks to my personal assistant, Melissa Rice, who is absolutely invaluable and makes my release days freaking awesome. She also never tells me I'm weird when I moan that the imaginary people in my head won't do what I want them to do.

A humongous thanks to everyone at Montlake Romance, especially Lauren Plude and Melody Guy. The team's support and guidance has been a driving force for me throughout this series, so thank you to all of you.

Last but absolutely not least, I must thank everyone who has taken a chance on this series—especially those who've been with me from the beginning. Releasing Dominic's story was bittersweet, since it meant reaching the end of the series, but it's not the last we'll see of the characters. They'll have cameos in the upcoming Olympus Pride series, so if you decide to take a chance on it, watch out for those familiar faces. Love you all!

About the Author

Suzanne Wright is the author of *From Rags*; *Shiver*; the Mercury Pack series; the Deep in Your Veins novels; the Dark in You series; and the Phoenix Pack series, which includes, most recently, *Wild Hunger* and *Fierce Obsessions*. She lives in England with her husband, two children (one angel, one demon), and bulldog. When she's not spending time with her family, she's writing, reading, or doing her version of housework—sweeping the house with a look. Visit her online at www.suzannewright.co.uk.

Made in the USA
Monee, IL
24 February 2024